MICHAEL PHILLIPS

FREEDOM MANIFESTO

TRIBULATION CULT BOOK 4:
A NOVEL

FIDELIS
PUBLISHING

Fidelis Publishing ®
Winchester, VA • Nashville, TN
www.fidelispublishing.com

ISBN: 9798993655086
ISBN: (eBook) 9798993655093
Freedom Manifesto
Tribulation Cult Book 4: A Novel

Order at www.faithfultext.com for a significant discount. Email info@fidelispublishing.com to inquire about bulk purchase discounts.

Cover designed by Diana Lawrence
Interior design/typesetting by Lisa Parnell
Edited by Amanda Varian

Manufactured in the United States of America

10 9 8 7 6 5 4 3 2 1

FIDELIS
PUBLISHING

FREEDOM MANIFESTO

TRIBULATION CULT

The Invisible War

Birth of a Remnant

Hidden Jihad

Freedom Manifesto

Contents

Contents

America is the first enemy of Muslims.

—Ayman al-Zawahiri
Published in *As-Sahab*, 2018

☆ ☆ ☆

In time, this so-called democracy will crumble . . .
The only thing that will remain will be Islam.

—New York Imam Siraj Wahhaj
From an address in approximately 2003

PART 1

A SUNDERING

SUMMER 2051

1

Death of a Vision

THE WORLD of evangelical Christianity had not been so excited since Ward Hutchins's proposed announcement of the identity of the antichrist.

That was three years ago.

The election of 2048 was approaching. Hutchins's prophetic articles were being read by tens of millions weekly. Hope ran higher than it had since the final decade of the twentieth century, not only that Christianity was making a comeback against progressivism, but that the rapture and return of the Lord were imminent.

Christians the world over were packing their bags—figuratively of course—for their flight into the clouds!

Ward Hutchins was the standard bearer, the face of Christendom, the exposer of evil, the prophetic voice leading the heavenly train!

Suddenly his voice was silenced. A sniper's bullet the night after the election dashed the hope of millions in one cruel twist of irony. The prophet of God was dead. His former roommate, the man millions assumed might be named in Hutchins's final article, was riding the pinnacle of worldly acclaim as president of the United States.

The balloon of evangelical optimism burst in that moment. It had not recovered since. In need of a heroic figure to step into the gap, to stand tall amid the rubble of defeat, to lift the sword of the Lord, and lead his army forward into the tribulation which was surely at hand, no hero had emerged. What else could the assassination of their prophet signify but that the tribulation had begun!

Still no Elijah, no Moses, no Joshua had stepped forward. Life and the world went on as usual. Hutchins was dead. There was no rapture. The liberal agenda of progressivism rolled on. Hope for spiritual revival, for the approach of the end times, all faded.

2

Birth of a Vision

FIRST WEEK OF JUNE 2051

THE HOPES of Christendom, however, were not dead yet. They needed but a spark to fan the embers again into flame.

Just as suddenly as Ward Hutchins's life had been snuffed out, the evangelical world found a new standard-bearer for the cause of righteousness.

New NBC media darling Mason Templeton broke the story just after the first of June in front of the Presidential Manor.

"I have earlier today been informed by high-placed confidential sources," Templeton began after a brief update on the president's son after his automobile accident, "that a nationwide grassroots campaign is underway with the objective of unseating President Jefferson Rhodes in next year's election behind a Republican duo of Dr. Charles Reyburn and former candidate and senator Harvey Jansen."

Word of his announcement overloaded telephone services and social media within seconds. The revelation had millions of viewers instantly changing channels.

The world of conservatism had been waiting for this!

Dr. Reyburn's book, *Roots: America Reclaims Its Heritage*, published late in the summer of 2048 was a runaway bestseller, briefly shooting Republican challenger Harvey Jansen up in the polls to within striking distance of Senator Jefferson Rhodes in the battle for the presidency, then just three months away. Jansen's ignoble defeat and Ward Hutchins's murder burst the balloon with simultaneous and chilling reminders:

The progressive agenda was ruthless. It would stop at nothing to silence its enemies.

Now suddenly here were Reyburn and Jansen in the news again. Surely a black man like Reyburn would be immune from the same level of hostility Rhodes launched against Jansen in the previous cycle.

"It is unclear at this time which of the two men would occupy the top slot on the ticket," Templeton continued in his bombshell telecast from the south lawn. "Speculation favors Professor Reyburn as the most likely candidate for the presidency. His recent best-selling book has placed him in the national spotlight. Nor are my sources convinced that Senator Jansen would be capable of mounting a serious campaign after his defeat three years ago.

"The film clip we have obtained of a recent meeting in California between the two men, where many supporters were present, is inconclusive, though the purpose of the clandestine meeting at an undisclosed West Coast location was reportedly convened to discuss the election with supporters and potential donors."

As he spoke, the thirty-second, low-resolution video recorded on Lionel Holt's phone from the April event at the Forster and Gordon ranches near Grass Valley played on millions of television screens across the country. None of those present at the gathering of individuals from various small study groups around the country—informally simply calling themselves *Brethren of the Common Life*—had any idea the gathering had been infiltrated by a lackey for President Rhodes's right-hand man Mike Bardolf.

"A week later," Templeton continued, "as will be seen from the next clip, Dr. and Mrs. Reyburn were seen at the Jansen ranch in Laramie, Wyoming. There they spent two days, presumably outlining the preliminary strategy for a campaign that will obviously be an uphill battle against a popular incumbent."

Templeton continued with brief biographies of the two men, footage from the previous campaign, and what was available of the somewhat reclusive Reyburn, including clips from his interview several years earlier with Phil Simons.

Though without the bravado of Ward Hutchins's news-making antichrist predictions, the Simons interview now recirculated through conservative and Christian news outlets like a brush fire. The diverse factions of American traditionalism and Christian evangelicalism were asking if perhaps Reyburn's quiet and confident demeanor was exactly the approach that could take on progressivism . . . and win!

After Templeton's announcement outside the Presidential Manor, it took only days for Reyburn's name to skyrocket in the presidential polls and reignite sales of his book. What people were calling the new *Roots* was quickly back on top of the *New York Times* best-seller list.

Reyburn wasn't exactly what evangelicals would have chosen as an heir apparent to the mantle of Ward Hutchins. A little too soft-spoken and professorial for their tastes. Not enough of the Hal Lindsey aura and prophetic passion in his message.

But he was outspoken about his Christian faith. Better yet, he was famous and had shown himself willing and courageous to take on progressivism without flinching.

If evangelicals were passionate about anything as much as prophecy, it was politics.

The dream constantly resurfaced to place a Christian in the Oval Office and try yet again what had been tried a thousand times in the past and failed—to legislate God's truth with the methods of man and through the governmental systems of the world.

Once again, that doomed hope sprang eternal.

If Dr. Charles Reyburn was no Ward Hutchins, Christians were ready to take what they could get. In his own way, maybe he had something Hutchins did not. He could bring the ideals of his book into the political arena—something Ward Hutchins steadfastly refused to do. As a less polarizing figure, Reyburn might prove a better candidate than Hutchins.

Within a week of the Templeton announcement, church message boards across the country emblazoned the message, *Reyburn for President.* Posters, banners, placards, newsletters, social media posts, and group email messages flooded the country.

3

Press Briefing at Hillsdown

THIRD WEEK OF JUNE 2051

FOLLOWING THE phony campaign literature sent around the country by Mike Bardolf to flush out the secret group and neutralize a potential Reyburn candidacy, Mason Templeton's bombshell announcement resulted in hundreds of excited phone calls and lengthy discussion amongst the expansive network of Brethren of the Common Life groups—more commonly referred to among the believers as BCL.

Mark Forster, Timothy Marshall, and David Gordon—acknowledged though unofficial leaders of the common life network—would have preferred to ignore the uproar and wait for it to die down. The continued media hype and almost daily references to the Templeton report on the nightly newscasts, however, eventually forced their hand.

When one of the announcement letters—purportedly written by Mark Forster, but in fact penned by Mike Bardolf—was leaked to the press and read over the air, they knew an unequivocal response was needed.

Having had more experience with the press than any of the others, Mark and Harvey Jansen offered to take the heat in front of the cameras. It was clear, however, Charles Reyburn was at the center of the firestorm. The media would not be satisfied until hearing from him. After more consultation by phone with the other men, he scheduled a press briefing.

All the networks and local Louisville stations were on hand for the Monday afternoon event set for the third week of June of 2051. It would be held outside the central quad of the Kentucky campus of Hillsdown College.

In front of the press contingent with two dozen of his journalistic colleagues stood Mason Templeton. A huge crowd of students and members of the community spread out behind them. Hundreds of Reyburn for President posters and banners were scattered through what was obviously a partisan gathering of support for Hillsdown's most famous professor.

At the appointed hour, Dr. Reyburn exited Founder's Hall behind him and walked slowly to the bank of microphones.

"I have a brief statement," he began in his characteristically soft voice. "I will take no questions. My statement will speak for itself."

He waited a moment, then continued.

"Where the news originated that was reported by Mr. Templeton—who is with us today I see—that I am, or am considering becoming, a candidate for the presidency, neither I nor any of my friends or former Senator Harvey Jansen have any idea. Let me put the speculation to rest. Neither Senator Jansen nor I are candidates or will become candidates."

Instant shouts from the press corps erupted. A flurry of questions lasted a full minute. Reyburn stood calmly saying nothing. Gradually the hubbub quieted.

Reyburn opened his mouth to speak but was again interrupted. Once more he waited. Silence came a little sooner this time.

"With all due respect, Mr. Templeton," he said, speaking softly, "the report broadcast by you two weeks ago was completely false."

The words were scarcely out of his mouth when yet again a barrage of questions was shouted toward him. Again Reyburn stood calmly waiting. Though it took well over a minute, during which he stood motionless, gradually the noise died away.

Most of the journalists' eyes drifted in Templeton's direction. "My report was based on reliable information, Dr. Reyburn," he said. "Are you calling my informant a liar?"

A few more questions were called out from those surrounding Templeton.

Reyburn stood silent. He continued to wait. He did not reply until it was completely quiet, then resumed in an even softer voice than before.

"That this is more than a mere rumor but a concerted effort to spread a false report," he said, "is clear. Mr. Templeton reported that he was given the information, but he was obviously given false information by someone. Simultaneously letters went out to certain individuals throughout the country announcing a joint Jansen-Reyburn campaign."

Reyburn paused to ensure he would not be interrupted, then continued.

"This too was false," he went on. "There is no campaign. The solicitation for donations did not originate with me or anyone connected with me. My friend Mark Forster, named in these mailings, knows no more about the report than I do. Therefore I am saying the following to the entire country: Please do not send donations or other correspondence to Mr. Forster's address. The mail that has already come has not been opened, nor will future mail be opened. No checks will be cashed. I do not know how to make it any more clear than this—there is no campaign. There will be no campaign website. This is all that needs to be said. There is no campaign and will be none. I call no one a liar. I say only that the report was false."

He stopped and was met by a flurry of shouts and questions. Again, he waited until it died down. He opened his mouth to begin, though immediately several more questions were hurled at him. He closed his mouth, smiled, and again waited. This time he allowed the silence to continue for ten or fifteen seconds.

"Come on, Dr. Reyburn," said Templeton who was not used to being ignored, "don't play games with us."

"As you have not technically asked a question, Mr. Templeton," replied Reyburn, "I will respond only with the observation that either you or your colleagues are deaf or that you are not accustomed to a man meaning what he says. My yes is yes, my no is no. That is all there is to it. I said I would take no questions and I will take no questions. I will not run for president. I will answer no questions about it. This concludes my statement."

He turned, but again Templeton's voice stopped him.

"May I be permitted to ask a question if it has nothing to do with politics?"

Slowly Reyburn turned. A slow smile spread over his lips.

"Very clever, Mr. Templeton!" he said. "You tricked me, and I am willing to take the bait. A cunning ploy. Okay, then—yes, I will take your question."

A few chuckles spread through the press as most of the eyes rested on young Mason Templeton who was adding to his rising prestige by the second.

"I wanted to know what you make of what was reported as unexplained seismic activity last month off the coast of Antarctica."

"I have no opinion," replied Reyburn. "I know nothing more than what I heard on the news. It was said to have been caused by the explosion of a yacht, was it not?"

"That was the report. There are those who doubt it?"

"Thinking it was what . . . underground volcanic activity?"

"That is a possibility . . . or something nuclear," added Templeton in a tone of question.

"That's beyond my pay grade, I'm afraid. Honestly, I've heard nothing, know nothing, and have no opinion."

"Are you concerned about the nuclear problem?"

"Of course. Who isn't now that every Middle Eastern nation has nuclear capability, along with most of the South and Central American nations? Everyone is concerned. The African nations are scurrying to catch up. We live in a dangerous world."

"Do you anticipate an Armageddon event in your lifetime?"

Reyburn did not answer immediately. He drew in a long breath and exhaled slowly. For once the press corps waited patiently.

"You ask big questions, Mr. Templeton," he said, smiling again. "My answer is, I don't know. Tribulation—yes. Armageddon—I don't know."

At last the corps of journalists erupted again as Reyburn turned and walked back toward the building. A great scurrying followed him until he was inside and the doors closed behind him.

4

Activist for Truth

WHERE HE sat watching the interview, Jessup University dropout Dale Birch's brain was on fire. If Dr. Reyburn's book could have such impact, why couldn't he help it along?

He admired the man. But he was too timid about what needed to be done.

This was war. The evils of progressivism had to be attacked forcefully. Too many people were asleep. People had to know what was going on.

Dr. Reyburn had a national platform. He could ignite the conservative revolution.

Yet it appeared he was going to squander this opportunity that had been handed him on a silver platter. This was no time for soft-spoken, do-gooder tactics. It was time to take the gloves off!

Well, I'm not going to sit back and do nothing, thought Dale. It was time for people who cared about this country to stand up and be counted, to take the fight to the streets.

The famous quote hung on the wall of his apartment, *All that is necessary for the forces of evil to triumph in the world is for enough good men to do nothing.* Who cared if Edmund Burke never really said it. The words were no less powerful that their author was unknown.

He didn't intend to be one of those who did nothing. If Dr. Reyburn was squeamish about getting down and dirty in the battle for truth, he wasn't.

He had a few hundred dollars saved up from his job. It didn't pay much, but he was single and he lived in a dump of an apartment. The first thing he would do was buy a cheap scanner-copier that could print booklets.

Dale was at his computer late that same night, writing what he would turn into an eight-page pamphlet.

He'd already thought of what to call it—*A Call to Arms: The evils of progressivism and Islam can be stopped, but it takes enough good people not doing nothing. Pass on the challenge!*

Probably a little too long. But it would grab people's attention.

5

Regrets

EVER SINCE news of the April gathering hit the media, with the reports and mailings and hype about Dr. Reyburn or Harvey Jansen running for president, Heather Marshall had felt terrible.

She knew Lionel was responsible for the video prompting the false speculation. How the media obtained it, she had no idea. But there could be no doubt Lionel had a hand in it and probably also for leaking the addresses of many who had been at the gathering.

How, she couldn't imagine. But who else could it be?

He had been curious, but Heather was suspicious enough to keep on her toes and divulge nothing. Yet somehow word had gotten out. Was Big Brother listening on their phones? David had been warning of the need for caution for years.

If someone was listening, she and Todd were in trouble. They talked on the phone at least every two or three days. What if every word was being recorded!

She wasn't about to get paranoid and conspiratorial quite yet. Besides, now that she and Todd were . . . well, she didn't know what they were. But she *had* to talk to him. She only wished Lionel didn't keep coming up in their conversations.

"Whoever this guy Lionel is," laughed Todd, "I need to talk to him some day!"

"I get furious every time I think of him trying to pry information out of me," replied Heather.

"You're sure that's what he was doing?"

"Why else did he show up at the ranch? No one else would have made the video public."

"What concerns me is how the media got hold of the video. If I didn't know better, I would suspect *me*. I'm sure my past connections, and the fact that I know Mason, has occurred to more than a few people who were there in April."

"Todd, no one would suspect you."

"They don't all know me as well as you do. I'm sure I've crossed a few minds. But if the video came from Lionel, it's obvious he is more involved than mere idle curiosity. Something is going on here."

"Well, it makes me angry! I want to call him and ask him to his face why he did it."

"That would accomplish nothing," said Todd. "We need to wait on God to see what comes of it."

"Listen to you!" laughed Heather. "Now it's you giving *me* spiritual advice. I know you're right."

"Let's stop talking about Lionel. Why don't you come to DC for a visit?"

"What!" exclaimed Heather.

"I'm serious," said Todd.

"Is this an indecent proposal?"

"I would never think of such a thing. I was only thinking that if Mrs. Forster accompanies Mark for his next trip to the capital, you could come with them. It would be nice to see you in my world."

☆ ☆ ☆

A few days later at the Circle F, Heather saw Mark coming up the drive. She walked toward him as he opened the door and stepped out of his pickup.

"Hey, Heather!"

"Hi, Mark," she said, then hesitated. A sheepish look was on her face.

"Something is on your mind," he laughed. "You have mischief written all over you."

"Mischief . . . *me*?"

"You are up to *something*!"

"What would you think," Heather asked, "of my accompanying you to Washington next time you fly out? You're going for your next meeting in a couple weeks, aren't you?"

"That would be great," Mark replied. "Since it may be one of my last trips, Grace and Ginger are going with me. We're treating Ginger to the capital and a visit to New York for her graduation."

"Oh, then I don't want to—"

"Are you kidding. Ginger will love for you to come."

"What about you and Grace?"

"Us too."

"It does sound fun. Thank you. So you're still thinking of resigning your chairmanship of the president's commission?"

Mark nodded. "I have the feeling it's moving in that direction. We'll make a party of it. The condo has two bedrooms. You can stay with Ginger."

"Thank you, that will be fun."

She hesitated timidly.

"I'm going to see Todd," she said. "He invited me for a visit on his turf, he said, since he's been here twice. You probably guessed."

"I had a pretty good idea," smiled Mark.

6

Father and Son

MARK AND Craig Forster were just riding into the ranch after taking some of the cattle up to one of the high pastures. They had been discussing Craig's upcoming final year at Sac State and his plans.

"That reminds me, Dad," said Craig. "I'd forgotten something I wanted to show you that a guy handed me when we were at Ginger's graduation last month."

"Where was I?"

"You and Mom were talking to some of Mom's former colleagues. I was talking to some of the guys in our Bible study group. There was a guy handing out pamphlets. I wanted to ask what you thought about it."

A few minutes later they were seated on two chairs on the front porch. Craig handed his dad the pamphlet. Mark glanced it over and began to chuckle.

"That's quite a title!" he said. "I can't imagine it would go over very well at Sac State. Hardly a place where you want to take on progressivism! I'm surprised he hasn't been arrested for hate speech against Muslims!"

"Yeah, he was getting yelled down pretty good. I thought it might come to blows. He was shoving them in everyone's faces, telling them they had to wake up, that they had to read it, that the government was corrupt—the usual. Not that the stuff about progressivism's not true, but on a secular campus! He was asking for trouble."

"Was there any?"

"Just yelling back and forth. Nothing serious. Most of the pamphlets got tossed on the ground after people took one look at them. The poor guy scrambled around picking them up even as he kept passing them out."

Mark continued to glance over it, turning the eight pages casually until he came to the back cover.

"What . . . wait a minute," he said, reading the name and contact information on the back of the pamphlet. "I know this name."

"Who is it?"

"Dale Birch—I remember Ginger talking about him. She met him at Jessup when she attended a series of Timothy's lectures. He asked her out a time or two, that's why I remember the name."

"Did she go out with him?"

"No, he was a little over the top for her."

"He's definitely over the top!" laughed Craig. "I mean, I agree with most of what he says in here, but I'm not sure yelling at progressives and making them mad and shoving pamphlets in their faces and marching on the state Capitol will accomplish much."

"Does he do that?"

"He was talking about organizing a march, but no one was paying attention."

Mark sighed. "There will always be those who think if they shout loud enough people will be convinced. I'm afraid just the opposite is the case."

"You have to admit, what he says might just as well have been written by you or David. Universal AI surveillance, discriminatory credit policies squeezing Christians out of free markets, China's takeover of the world's technologies, brainwashing drugs in public water systems, planned pandemics, mandatory injections of newborns with the woke gene—"

"That's never been proven."

"I know, Dad. Some of his claims are out there. But most of it isn't that much different than what we discuss in the meetings. The world is pretty far gone. Especially against Christians."

"You're right. Now that you're almost done, do you ever have regrets about attending Sac State?"

"I've thought about that. A few, I suppose. It's not easy being a Christian in an environment where you have to wonder if everyone you meet is gay or trans or some other weird version of brave new world normalcy, and that you'll get in trouble or fail a class for saying something someone doesn't like. On the other hand, the group of Christians Ginger and I are part of, because there are so few of us, share really close bonds. We'll be friends the rest of our lives. I guess I would say, I think it has strengthened my faith, not eroded it."

"Your mom and I see that and couldn't be more proud of you."

"Thanks, Dad."

7

Unexpected Foursome

First Week of July 2051

When the four Californians landed at Obama International two weeks later, eschewing the presidential limousine, Todd was waiting to drive them to the Michelle Obama Housing Complex.

"You'll never guess who I had a chat with yesterday," said Todd as they drove into the city. "The president's son, Bradon Rhodes. He came by my apartment and wanted to talk to me. He's still using a crutch, though the cast is off his leg. He was different. The accident sobered him. He's hoping to see you, Ginger."

"Oh, no!" she exclaimed. "What did I do to deserve this?"

"After his accident, you still have an attitude about him? He was hurt pretty bad."

"You're right—I'm sorry. I shouldn't have said that. First impressions die hard."

"I understand," said Todd. "He told me about meeting you in Seattle. He's embarrassed by the impression he gave. It was actually an extraordinary talk we had. He asked me about why I was involved with you all. He knew more about me than I had any idea. I told him about my spiritual quest, I guess you'd call it. He was very interested, quiet, thoughtful. Just before his accident his grandmother had a serious talk with him about life and priorities and her new spiritual outlook. Somehow he was ready to listen.

"Then the accident . . . it really jolted him. I think he's searching for something . . . life's meaning beyond the political maelstrom, even beyond being famous, watched, photographed. It seems sincere. Some people love the limelight, being in the public eye, being the center of attention. Others gradually see how empty it is. That certainly happened to me. I sense something changing for Bradon too, maybe not unlike what I went through. I think he's genuinely hungry for something without knowing what. He also talked to me about what he overheard in the Presidential Manor and his call to you, Mark."

The others listened with interest.

"The Lord seems to be surrounding our friend the president with unexpected spiritual influences," said Mark thoughtfully. "His mother's long-buried spiritual roots reawakening, Grace and the First Lady forming a friendship, now his son. This is an intriguing development. Though Bradon's frantic call and the accident are worrisome. I've hoped to talk to him again."

"That's another reason he's anxious to see you. But he's been afraid to call or write while recovering in the Manor. He suspects his phone and computer are probably bugged. He's suspicious of his father's right-hand man. He thinks he's the one who was following him that night."

☆ ☆ ☆

A key to a separate apartment for the two girls—an unexpected surprise—was waiting on the table in Mark's now familiar quarters, along with a welcome from the Presidential Manor's personnel coordinator and a message to Mark that the president would like to see him the following morning at 9:30 prior to the scheduled meeting of the Presidential Commission on Religion.

An envelope addressed to Ginger had been slipped under the door of the girls' apartment. Ginger stooped for it, opened the envelope, and read:

Miss Forster,

I hope you will forgive my boldness. I am hoping you will allow me to visit you while you are in Washington. I know I made a terrible impression on you a year ago. Please let me make it up to you. I'm trying to grow and change. In all honesty I don't think you'll hate me too much. But I will not pester you and will leave it up to you. Call me if you would like to get together. If you don't, you won't hear from me again. I will respect your choice. I'm still recovering from my accident, which you probably heard about. But I'm taking a summer school class. I'm finally able to get out of the Manor again, so if I'm in class, leave a message. Thank you at least for considering it.

Bradon Rhodes.

With a curious expression, Ginger handed the note to Heather.

"An interesting development," said Heather, "just as your father said. "It sounds like what Todd said may be true—he is changing."

"What should I do?" asked Ginger.

"He sounds sincere. If it were me, I would give him the benefit of the doubt. But I'm not taking my own advice with Lionel," she added laughing sardonically. "I am finding it very difficult to give *him* the benefit of the doubt! It's all about someone's motives. I don't trust Lionel's motives. Bradon's seem honest."

"I suppose it seems genuine. After everything I'd heard about him, it was hard not to be skeptical at first."

"You know how the news distorts things—even outright lies about people. We know that all too well from Todd's experience. He was part of it. If anyone can see through it, he can, and he thinks Bradon is sincere. People change. I would never have guessed how Todd has changed since before I met him. Now he's a Christian, reading the Bible. He's like a spiritual sponge, soaking up everything he can. Maybe your father's right and God has designs on the Rhodes' family. What if you are part of that?"

"By the way," said Ginger, not so subtly changing the subject, "what *is* going on with you and Todd?"

"When I find out I'll let you know!" laughed Heather.

"Flying all the way across the country to see him—that's pretty serious."

"I don't know about that. But we like each other. We're good friends. He's probably my best friend right now—along with you, of course! Besides, it's a chance to see Washington. I've never been here before."

A knock sounded on the half-open door. Todd poked his head in.

"Are you ready?" he said to Heather, "or would you rather I came back in a bit?"

"No, I'm fine," she said. "Let's go." Turning to Ginger, she added, "Todd's going to show me the city."

"You're welcome to join us," said Todd.

"Are you kidding!" laughed Ginger. "I know you two want to be alone. And I may have a phone call to make."

Todd glanced at her with a look of question.

"I think someone else is hoping for the chance to show her around," said Heather.

"Ah, yes—I know who you mean. I think I can assure you, Ginger, you will find him changed. He's doing his best to ignore the persistent news reports that his accident was caused by his being drunk."

"What did cause it?"

"All he told me is that he was being followed and was trying to get away."

"His note said he was back in school. What is he studying?" asked Ginger.

"Law," replied Todd. "Already planning on law school."

Both girls reacted in surprise.

"I know," nodded Todd. "He's got a long road ahead of him, but he is serious. Last term he was nose to the grindstone. No girlfriends, no frat parties. He's turned into a quiet, motivated, hard-working university student."

Ginger remained plagued the rest of the afternoon by Bradon Rhodes's message. What twenty-three-year-old girl wouldn't jump at the chance to be shown such attention by the president's son? But Ginger's perspective on youthful romance was cautious. She'd seen too many of her church friends who got their twelve-year-old molars early in life hurt by foolish teenage entanglements. She was not interested in frivolous infatuations. Relationships between young men and young women were important proving grounds of character. She took such relationships seriously.

But she couldn't get Heather's words out of her mind, that she might somehow be part of what God wanted to do in Bradon's life. After a few hours sightseeing with her parents and asking their advice, she finally telephoned him that evening.

The result was that Todd and Bradon called together at the housing complex the following morning about the same time a limousine was arriving to pick up Mark for his drive to the Manor. Todd spoke with Bradon and suggested a foursome to make it less awkward for either him or Ginger. With Todd driving and Bradon still wielding one crutch, the two young men would show the girls some of the lesser-known sights of the city, with a sail on the Potomac for lunch.

Watching the four young people leave the complex, and then Mark accompanying his Secret Service escort alone a few minutes later, and surmising that Grace was still in the apartment, a disappointed Mike Bardolf sat for a few minutes in the parking lot thinking dark thoughts. He might wait in hopes she would leave, but he might also waste hours to no avail.

Hopefully they would go out to dinner. He would try again in the evening.

8

Oval Office Showdown

STILL NOT knowing what to make of Bradon Rhodes's frantic call a month earlier and equally concerned about the accident that followed, Mark yet had little idea how widespread were the suspicions, conjectures, and machinations taking place with himself and the BCL group in the center of them. Bradon's warning of danger, however, prepared him for the obvious change in the president's demeanor.

President Jefferson Rhodes wasted no time beating around the bush.

"I want to know about the meeting you held in April," he began abruptly.

"What meeting?" said Mark.

"You know well enough what meeting," rejoined Jeff testily. "The one where Reyburn and Jansen and Court Masters and Todd Stewart and my mother and Linda and all the rest of you were at your ranch scheming and plotting."

Mark listened stunned by the construction Jeff put on it. His words confirmed Bradon's warning as well founded. They had suspected Lionel Holt as the source of the video of Charles and Harvey. In spite of Bradon's call, however, until this moment he had no idea how much about the weekend was known. What could *possibly* be Lionel Holt's connection to the president?

"I, uh . . ." he began hesitantly, "I'm not sure I know what to say, Jeff. It was just a gathering of some Christians for no purpose other than fellowship together."

"All those people with connections to myself and the government—was just coincidence, I suppose?"

"Well, honestly—yes . . . mostly. I was as surprised as anyone when Linda and your mother arrived."

"How did they find out about it?"

"Linda and I've visited a few times since I've been coming to DC. I probably mentioned it."

"You *probably* mentioned it!" repeated Jeff in disdain. "And my mother?"

"That was truly a surprise. She came with Ward Hutchins's mother, which might explain Linda too. Though I'm not sure how your mother heard about the gathering."

"And the others—Jansen, Masters, and Stewart?"

"I'm sorry, Jeff, but that's on you. We met Todd at your event on Bainbridge Island. He hit it off with Heather Marshall who was with us. I believe you were introduced to her. She's been in contact with him ever since. She told him about the gathering, though we had no idea he was coming. His appearance was a surprise too. As for Court Masters . . . let me see. I think he may have written to the Marshalls about one of the books."

"All perfectly innocent?"

"Actually, yes. It was just Christians gathered, as I say, for fellowship."

"Why this particular group of individuals?"

"It mostly originated informally several years ago because of the books of Stirling Marshall's. That's Heather's grandfather. I'm sure you remember me telling you about him when we were in college."

"Yes—Stirling Marshall. I've been hearing about him everywhere I turn these days. What's the big deal with him?"

"We find wisdom in his spiritual writings. That's why we read and discuss his books. Marshall's son Timothy has also written in somewhat the same vein. He is a professor of history in the Sacramento area. He often shares his insights into his father's ideas. It's nothing so mysterious. We're just Christians getting together to learn and talk about ideas."

"Do you know about a document called the Benedict Brief?"

The question took Mark so thoroughly by surprise he was unable to hide his shock. He hesitated.

"I see you do," said Jeff.

"It's got nothing to do with any of this."

"If you've got nothing to hide, why is it so secretive then?"

"There's nothing sinister about it. It's a spiritual paper on the Christian life Stirling Marshall wrote before his death and left with his son—Dr. Timothy Marshall. Timothy has kept it mostly private according to his father's wishes. It's not so much secret but that Timothy's father gave it to him with instructions not to make it public."

"Why?"

"Because most people wouldn't understand it."

"Have you read it?"

Again, Mark hesitated.

"Yes," he answered after a few seconds.

"Then give me a copy. I will be the judge of what people can and cannot understand."

"I'm sorry, Jeff, I can't do that."

"Why?"

"It is not mine to share. It was entrusted to Timothy and one other man."

"Who?"

"A neighbor. I took you to meet him once—a Mr. Gordon."

Jeff took in the information without expression. The pieces were beginning to fit together.

"Well, I would like to read it now to determine if it is a subversive document."

"*Subversive?* Jeff—it's a man's dying spiritual testament of faith passed on to his son. There's nothing subversive about it."

"Nevertheless, I want a copy."

"I am afraid I can't give you one."

"You are refusing your president?"

"If you put it in those terms, yes. I am answerable to a higher authority."

"Then you are pitting yourself against me, Mark. Your refusal confirms my suspicions about Reyburn and the others. You are obviously part of it. Otherwise, why would you be so secretive?"

"I've been as open and up front with you as I can, Jeff. There's nothing to it."

"I don't believe you, Mark. The evidence is all there."

"Surely you heard Dr. Reyburn's press conference. I can tell you categorically there is no campaign or plot or anything else."

"I don't believe him anymore than I do you. Hells bells, Mark, everyone lies about their political aspirations. I insisted I wasn't a candidate too. It's how the game is played."

Mark could not help thinking that Jefferson Rhodes and Charles Reyburn were two very different men. Charles Reyburn would die before telling an intentional lie for his own benefit.

"All I can say is that isn't how Dr. Reyburn plays the game. He plays no games at all. He is one of the most authentic men I know."

"And you are not his campaign manager?"

Mark burst out laughing but quickly stopped. Jeff was not smiling.

"Listen to yourself, Jeff," he said. "Me—a campaign manager!"

"It is no more far-fetched than this conspiracy you're all hatching against me. After all I've tried to do for you, bringing you into my administration—and this is how you repay me, stabbing me in the back!"

"Jeff—please! What can I say to make you believe that—"

"You can't lie to me, Mark!" Jeff shot back angrily. "Playing both sides, pretending to be with me and all the while part of a conspiracy to run Reyburn next year and bring me down. It's treason, Mark!"

Jeff's face was red and he was trembling with rage.

At the word *treason*, a sobering wave of reality finally swept through Mark. His initial reaction to Jeff's wild accusations was disbelief. At last he saw how deep was Jeff's misinterpretation of events. How he could so thoroughly misread it, Mark had no idea. But this was no laughing matter. Bradon's warnings now rang true. He could not help wondering if the accident hadn't been an accident at all. Jeff would never try to harm his son. But if others were involved, it might be more serious than he realized.

Mark was stunned anew to see what his onetime best friend had become. "Jeff, I am so sorry," he said softly. "I am sorrier than I can say that you would think such things of me, that you would think I would lie, that you would think I would be party to subverting the democratic process. None of it is true. I hope you still know me well enough to know I would not lie to you. By being part of your team, I hoped I might contribute to a spiritual awakening in Washington. However, if this is truly what you believe, and if you think I am capable of . . . of . . . I don't even know what to call it, maybe it's best I do not continue on the commission. I've had qualms about it anyway, wondering if I was doing any good for you or the country. I am truly sorry, Jeff. I wish you nothing but God's best. Such will always be my prayer. As it is, and as you have, as you say, lost your trust in me—"

"Say no more, Mark," interrupted the president. "I'll save you the trouble—you're fired. Get out and go home to your cows. As for this little charade—how dare you stand there and pretend not to know what's going on. You can tell Reyburn from me I know his game, and if he continues his attempt to build a grassroots organization and run against me, I will destroy him!"

Mark closed his eyes and his head dropped to his chest. How had it come to this? It was obvious there was no more to say. He rose slowly, a great weight of sorrow on his shoulders.

"I am sorry, Jeff," he said softly, "sorrier than I can say."

He turned and left the Oval Office, Jeff staring after him in white fury.

9

Enlisting the Ally

AFTER JEFFERSON Rhodes calmed down, he left the office, walked down the hall to where the meeting of the Religion Commission was to be held. All the members but Mark were present.

"I am sorry to spring this on you," said the president. "But events have arisen which force me to cancel today's meeting. I have just fired Mark Forster as your chairman. I apologize for the inconvenience. You will all be notified of the time of the next meeting when a replacement has been appointed."

He turned and left as abruptly as he had come, then walked down the hall to Mike Bardolf's office. Annoyed to find his hatchet man absent, he returned to the Oval Office and dashed him a text:

Come see me. Urgent.

Fifteen minutes later Mike walked into the president's private office.

"It's hit the fan, Mike," said Jeff. "Mark denies the whole affair. He's lying through his teeth. They're coming after me—Mark, Jansen, Reyburn, the whole lot of them. If it's a fight they want, that's what they'll get!"

"What do you want me to do?"

"The Religion Commission was a charade anyway. I don't know what I was thinking. But Mark's gone. I'll need a new chairman."

"I think I have just the man, Mr. President."

"We need to move full steam ahead with the rest of the commissions. Begin talking to the proposed chairpersons from the list you gave me. It's also time to institute the protocols of your Manifesto. It's the only way to combat this thing. I want you to get to work immediately embodying its points into a legislative package. I'll begin laying the groundwork with our key congressional allies. I want a draft of a bill in a week or two."

"It will be perceived as radical, Mr. President."

"Couch it in language to make the formerly unthinkable tolerable, then gradually acceptable. We'll implement it in stages. Within a year or two it will all seem normal. I want it passed before the election. That gives us a year."

"I will start on it today."

"These people with Mark and their prophet and Reyburn leading them are a threat to the country. Take them down, Mike. I want these people eliminated as a threat. Destroy this thing!"

It was just what Mike Bardolf had been waiting to hear. His plan had worked to perfection. The president had been so enraged by the Templeton announcement that weeks of pent-up fury at last erupted.

Mike returned to his office, pulled out the document he had begun in Mira Monte and had been working on ever since. It was finally time to restructure it into the format of a bill the president could take to Congress. It would give them sweeping powers to eliminate all who opposed the new order. Along with that, as the president authorized, he would take steps to bring his own commission heads on board. He would also contact his enforcement committee. He would fly out to Mira Monte in a day or two to start gathering his team. He would set up a meeting with Hamad Bahram and arrange for him to take over the Religion Commission and accompany him to California.

But first . . .

He thought a minute. Slowly a smile spread over his face.

He picked up his phone and entered the number.

"Lionel—Mike Bardolf. I've got something I need you to do for me. I need to know when the next meeting of that group of religious kooks is scheduled—your friend Forster and the—"

He paused briefly.

"Right," he laughed. "I know they're no friends of yours. Except the girl—I can tell, you're sweet on her."

Another pause.

"Whatever you say. If you can use her to get the information, no harm done, right? Just find out about the next meeting—when and where. I'll want you there . . ."

He listened a few seconds to Lionel's objections.

"I know," he laughed. "We all have our crosses to bear. Just man up, Lionel. I'll make it worth your while. None of my people will know him on sight. For them to carry out my orders, they'll need you to point him out so they get the right guy."

10

Shocking New Regulations

THOUGH HEARTBROKEN over the breach with Jeff, Mark was actually relieved to have his brief foray into the world of politics behind him. He might never know why he'd felt led to accept Jeff's offer. But he was glad it was over.

Upon their return to California, however, a new crisis awaited them. Almost in panic, the usually calm and steady Pearl West called to ask if he and Grace could come over the following evening for prayer and to offer what counsel they might be able to give.

They arrived at the West's home to find Timothy and Jaylene, Heather, David, and six or eight others of their closest friends, along with Pearl and Dewitt's daughter Diane and husband Rod Statler. The mood was somber.

When everyone was present, Dewitt explained why they asked them to come.

"As some of you know," he began, "the Department of Education has been cracking down on home schoolers for some years now. Mostly it has been a matter of record keeping and paperwork. However, it has gradually become more intrusive, adding requirements for certain curriculums to be taught, and adding testing procedures and documentation to verify these regulations are followed. You know Rod and Diane homeschool our four grandchildren. Up until now compliance has been sufficiently voluntary and based on an unspoken honor system such that they have been able mostly to ignore the more outlandish things they are supposed to teach—that the Constitution is a racist document, gender is a matter of individual choice, and so on. It's nothing new—all that's been part of public education since the 2020s. But homeschoolers have generally continued teaching using traditional and Christian books and materials without serious repercussions. But not long after President Rhodes took office, a new series of regulations was instituted that . . . well, I should let Rod and Diane explain."

The two parents went on to tell of the new curriculum requirements that were far more sweeping than anything they had yet encountered.

"We've had quite a bit of latitude in what we teach," said Diane. "We knew about the new textbooks being used in public schools. As distasteful as they are, we've felt it important to keep up on what's going on in the world. There are books developed by the government especially for homeschooling families, even Christian families, that homeschools are encouraged to use with horribly graphic gay and trans and sexual content that speak of God's wonderful creativity in the diversity of humanity. It's pure pornography!

"It makes me sick even to talk about it . . . pretending that God planned and loves homosexuality, and that freedom of choice, which God also loves, includes choosing whether you want to be a boy or girl and when it is healthy . . . can you believe it—*healthy!*—to begin having sex to lay the foundation for healthy relationships later in life.. It's disgusting—it's nothing but satanic! Of course marriage and the nuclear family isn't part of it. Marriage is never even mentioned, only 'healthy multi-gender relationships,' they call it."

"There's also a US history book," said Rod, "equally heavy on Christian jargon to make it acceptable to Christian homeschoolers with emphasis on the racism of our country's founders, and lauding feminist, black, minority, and gay themes as representing the true bedrock of America's strength, woven throughout with social justice and how white children need to live with white guilt. It's a complete fabrication of a false historical narrative."

"From all I have been able to tell," added Diane, "most Christian schools and many homeschoolers are using these books and just silently going along."

"Then a new directive came from the Secretary of Education a few months ago," said Rod. "They have been monitoring home schools for years. We file annual reports. There's no hiding under the radar like it was in the early years of homeschooling in the last century. They know who we are. This year's new directive said that home schools, charter schools, and Christian schools will now be monitored for compliance with the new regulations. A few weeks later a box arrived with new text books for our older three. Till now we have just ignored the recommended government curriculum. But these books came automatically, with a bill for over a thousand dollars. If we do not pay it, the amount will be deducted from our next income tax filing, with a penalty of another thousand. The government is trying to make home schooling so expensive that parents will have no choice but to send their children to public school."

"The books are horrifying!" said Pearl heatedly. "Some of it is pure pornography—for children! Diagrams . . . ugh—it's disgusting."

"We sent in a check," added Rod. "Now that the IRS is involved in enforcement, we thought it best not to raise any red flags. But a month later *another* box arrived containing paperwork and testing materials. It is very exacting. We have to keep a record of exactly when we teach each unit from the new books and send it in digitally every month, signed by us with a penalty of five thousand dollars if we do not answer truthfully—five thousand dollars for every violation . . . *every* month. On top of that, there are testing materials for each of the children that are very specific. These we are required to send in by mail. Included in the tests are intrusive and horrible questions about gender choice and graphic sexual images which children have to look at and then describe in their own words what is happening."

"It's unimaginable," said Diane. "We could never expose our children to such filth!"

"Yet each student is required to write down that they have read the appropriate chapters in the books," said Rod, "or had them read aloud, that they understand, and that they have seen the pictures and understand them. If we send in fake tests and answer the questions pretending to be the children, that's another hefty fine."

"Government-appointed teachers will begin calling on every homeschool," Diane went on heatedly, "and charter schools and Christian schools. I'm not sure when that will begin. They will use the responses sent in to prioritize the enforcement of the policies. These government teachers will either supervise the teaching of sexual content, or, if deemed unsatisfactory, to teach the material and test for compliance themselves—and in the case of home schools, *without* either parent present."

By now exclamations of shock were spreading through the room.

"We have continued to ignore the notifications," said Rod. "But the notices keep coming, noting that we have not sent in the reports and teaching materials. If we keep it up, we're going to find ourselves at the top of the list."

He paused and shook his head. "It's getting to the point where we either go along or lie or break the law and ignore everything and run the risk of the penalties. We don't know what to do.

"Eventually a notice came stating that we were in non-compliance and demanding that we schedule an appointment with the Sacramento County educational compliance officer at our soonest opportunity. Because of our non-compliance, she will be authorized to enter our home, forcibly if required, and question our children as to whether or not they have been presented the material in the books we were sent. If not, they will be authorized to arrange for age-specific teachers to come in and teach the material themselves and carry out the necessary testing. The penalty for failure to respond may be severe and may include fines, the closing of our school, attachment of my income, even arrest. This, too, we ignored. Then came a second demand, more forceful. Last week came a third, this time threatening."

He took a folded paper from his pocket and passed it around the room. No one spoke for several minutes.

"Who is this educational psychologist who would accompany the compliance officer?" asked Grace.

"That's the worst of it," replied Diane. "They will also send out government-appointed psychologists to non-compliant homeschools to follow up on the visits from the teachers. They will meet in private with every young person from second grade and older to determine if they adequately understand the new gender guidelines. Parents will not be allowed to be present. These psychologists will present each child with the opportunity to change their sex at government expense. Schools and home schools who do not comply will be shut down and their licenses revoked. Children who state their desire to undergo the change will be taken from their homes. After the surgery they will remain at government facilities helping them adjust to the change and learn how to report parents who resist respecting their new gender."

Everyone in the room sat in stunned silence. No one could believe what they had just heard.

"We don't know what to do," said Rod. "Diane's folks suggested we meet for prayer with all of you. We've thought about moving to another state. But it's just as bad everywhere. Even Idaho and Texas are using many of the same books and are regulated by the same federal educational guidelines. We need prayer and counsel."

As he listened, Mark could not help wondering if he had made the right decision about leaving the commission. He had met the Secretary of Education. He'd had no idea what dreadful policies were being instituted. Might he have been in a position to help Rod and Diane? Now he had no means of appealing on their behalf.

If this was the direction the country was going, the problem was far bigger than Rod and Diane. It would impact every Christian family. If taking children out of the public school system could no longer protect them from the LGBTQ agenda, what *could* be done to protect them? Freedom of religion and to raise one's children by the standards of one's spiritual convictions, was being threatened as a fundamental right of America's families.

Mark's thoughts were interrupted by the sound of Timothy's voice.

"There will be many in the country facing the same thing," he said. "We need to pray not only for Rod and Diane, but for Christians and homeschoolers everywhere, in our fellowship and other BCL groups. To what extent can we encourage breaking the law? Suddenly the whole question of civil disobedience becomes very real.

"Can we lie for the sake of our children? Will non-compliance even prevent this horror? If the question is compliance—which is out of the question—versus Rod and Diane being arrested, it seems there are *no* good alternatives. If ever we need the mind and wisdom of Christ, it is now."

11

Parental Counsel

THE NEXT meeting of the BCL was scheduled for the second week of July. Notwithstanding the distance, Todd was not about to miss it, though he did not tell Heather of his plans.

He was not alone in his desire to attend. More than sixty men and women in addition to their local group—which was quickly becoming more than a *local* group, some of the attendees coming from long distances—notified Timothy and Jaylene of their intention to be there. After the gathering in April only three months earlier, and having heard that Mark was no longer on the president's commission, curiosity about developments was high.

With the *Master's Helps Newsletter* becoming a BCL bulletin board of news and information, the interconnected links between an increasing number of smaller groups were expanding exponentially. Most of those coming made plans to stay in motels in Grass Valley or with new friends from April.

Todd flew in two days early. He told neither Heather nor her parents of his plans other than that he would be at the Friday evening and Saturday meetings at David's ranch. Once he was checked in at Roseville's Larkspur Landing, he telephoned Timothy, told him he had arrived, and asked if he could come over to talk to Jaylene and him. Heather did not know he had arrived early, he said. He wanted to keep it that way for now.

Heather's parents had an idea what might be the topic of conversation when Todd arrived after supper that evening. It was not a conversation they'd ever anticipated. For a nationally known personality, Todd was clearly nervous. But he wasted no time getting to the point.

"You probably know what I want to talk about," he began. "Obviously it's Heather. It's no secret that she and I have formed an unexpected yet wonderful friendship. Neither of us could have dreamed where it would lead when we struck up that first conversation on the shores of Puget Sound a year ago. And it's obvious to us both that it's more than a mere friendship."

He paused, drew in a long breath, and let it out slowly.

"Honestly," he continued, "I don't know what I expected when I thought of marriage. I never thought about it much. My career kept me busy and time went by quickly. Then I found myself reevaluating my life and what I was doing in the media at all. Then Bainbridge Island and meeting Heather . . . it was as if she had been sent right then to help me reassess my life and priorities—essentially everything about who I was and what my life meant. I'd never met anyone like her. She wasn't what I would have expected, and I'm sure I'm not what she was expecting either. But here we are, and it's clear we have deep feelings for each other. Actually, I should say I have feelings for her. I can't speak for her.

"So obviously I'm here to lay all that out to you and to get your thoughts. I suppose I'm asking your permission, as her parents, to pursue our relationship more seriously. I'm not quite ready to say I'm asking for her hand in marriage, as they say. I realize she and I still have to grow together. In a way we are still getting to know each other."

He breathed in and out a few times. "I know such things may be out of fashion these days," he went on. "Heather's in her thirties. Most people would consider her independent and no longer answerable to her parents. But I am beginning to realize that being a Christian changes everything. You see things differently. Nothing in the world looks the same. I know how close you all are. If we pursue this I want to have your blessing and for you to be involved in our lives. I love my mom and look forward to your meeting her some day. But she's not a Christian. This is all still so new to me that I need you and Heather, I guess I would say, guiding me along in this new way of life. I am prepared to trust you completely. If you feel it is not best for us to continue as we are, then I will abide by that and return to DC, though I hope we can all continue to be friends."

Todd let out a deep sigh and sat back in his chair.

"There!" he added, laughing lightly, "I've said it!"

"You did indeed!" laughed Timothy. "Good for you, my boy. I'm sure that took courage."

"I've been practicing for a week!" said Todd sheepishly.

"I know I was pretty intimidated the first time I met Jaylene's father. He was a famous geologist. I didn't know what to expect."

"It wasn't so bad, was it?" said Jaylene.

"No, he was entirely gracious. I hope you do not find us intimidating, Todd."

"Not intimidating," smiled Todd. "But the whole thing, you know—it's all new. I've stood before presidents and news cameras, but to talk to a girl's parents you have feelings for, I don't think I've ever been so nervous."

"You have nothing to fear from us, Todd. We are delighted to give you our blessing to pursue your friendship, or whatever it may become, with our daughter. We've obviously been kept in the loop by Heather, so we're not altogether taken by surprise."

He turned to Jaylene.

"I don't have much to add," said Heather's mother. "As Timothy said, Heather has spoken freely to us about you. I think we can all safely assume that the feelings you spoke of are mutual. I do have one question."

She paused and a serious expression came over her face.

"Do you love her, Todd?" she asked after a moment.

Todd did not answer immediately.

"I think I do," he said slowly. "At least, I think I *may* love her. That's a life-changing thing to say about anyone. I think I am learning to love her. Saying you're in love is too important to say casually. So maybe I would say I am learning what it means to say you love someone."

Jaylene smiled.

"Then you absolutely have my blessing," she said. "Had you answered immediately and said, "Oh absolutely I love her," I would have been a little skeptical. Your reply shows wisdom and maturity, Todd. Love is a lifelong process. Though you met, what, a little over a year ago, you've actually spent very little time together. You have to weather some things—misunderstandings and hurt feelings, arguments and differences. You have a lot of growing to do together before you'll know."

"You're right," nodded Todd. "I've been thinking the same thing. Depending on what the two of you think, I've been wondering about moving out here, getting a small apartment and a job. I'm sure I could get hired by one of the local stations here or in the Bay Area or even just a manual labor job. Anything, just to pay the rent. We could see more of each other and, like you say, grow together and see what the future holds. But if you don't think that's a good idea—"

"I think it's a fabulous idea!" said Jaylene. "Heather would be beside herself!"

She glanced toward Timothy.

"I agree," he said. "It seems the logical next step. In fact," he added thoughtfully, "I may know someone in need of . . . I suppose first I should ask how intent are you about working in media?"

"Long term, I don't know," answered Todd. "So much depends on what develops with Heather. She has to remain here—her work, all your work. The family correspondence, I mean. What the three of you do—the group, the letters, the gatherings, your books—I know how important it is. All that has to be a factor in any decisions made. If something should work out between us, I would never take Heather away from that. This is an unusual situation. I would see it as my responsibility to join what *you* are all doing more than Heather joining *my* ambitions and career, so to speak. If we have a future together, it will be here, not in Washington.

"But to answer your question . . . short term—no, I would probably prefer *not* to take a news job right now. I would rather stay out of the public eye and grow as a Christian and with Heather without all the distractions of the media."

"Then I will investigate a possibility I have in mind before I say more. There is one more request I have," Timothy added, "if you don't mind."

"Not at all," replied Todd. "That's why I came to you. I want whatever counsel you can give me."

"Then I would just say, not only are you and Heather still getting to know one another, you are still learning what being a Christian is all about. Heather told us about your time in the Shenandoah hills. It was very moving to hear. But an experience like that, as meaningful as such experiences can be, are but momentary doorways into a lifelong walk with God. Being a Christian is forever. It takes years—five, ten, twenty—to become grounded in what walking with God means. I was in my forties before I began to really understand some things I wish I'd grasped sooner. And I was raised in a Christian home!

"That's why many fall away and lose interest—they're not prepared for the long haul, the lifetime commitment. You are well on your way. You're growing, you're reading, you're studying the Bible. You're involved with good people. All that is important. But it is a lifetime process. I just want you to know what you've signed up for. You need to find good, strong, wise, older men in the faith to mentor and guide you, to be examples to you."

"Would *you* mentor me, Mr. Marshall?" asked Todd sincerely.

Timothy stared back a moment. The simplicity of Todd's question was completely unexpected. In all his years of teaching, never had he heard those words from a hungry young man.

He blinked back sudden moisture filling his eyes.

"What a wonderful thing to ask," he replied in a husky voice. "Of course, it would be my honor, along with the other men of our group. You couldn't do better than to glean from Mark and David and Dewitt."

"You are Heather's father. I most want to learn what *you* have to teach me."

"As I said, I am honored," nodded Timothy. "Meanwhile, until I talk to the man I mentioned, I will give you your first assignment—a book to read."

"You Marshalls have written so prolifically, I don't know that I will ever read everything!" laughed Todd.

"Well, this is not one of ours. It is a story that takes place not far from here about a young man and young woman and what is called "Christopher's Plan." It is a model for preparing for marriage. If you are serious about being mentored, it will explain how we might approach it."

"I will look forward to reading it," said Todd.*

---

* Michael Phillips, *A Home for the Heart* (Bethany House Publishers, 1994).

12

A Talk in the Moonlight

AFTER RETURNING to Larkspur Landing a little before 9:30, Todd telephoned Heather.

"What, you're here!" she exclaimed. "I wasn't expecting you until day after tomorrow!"

"I had some business I needed to take care of before I saw you."

"What kind of business?"

"Private business. Will you be up for a while—could I drive up to see you?"

"Yes! Do you need to ask? I can't wait! I work at the ranch tomorrow. Mark and Grace won't mind if I'm a little late."

"Then I'll head over right now!"

Todd arrived at the home in Dorado Wood some forty minutes later. Heather had been watching from the window and ran out, in the somewhat cumbersome gait that still remained from her childhood rattlesnake bite, to meet him. He was scarcely out of the car when she threw her arms around him.

"My, my!" he laughed, "what's all this?"

"I'm just glad to see you. If you didn't realize it before now, you are rather special in my life."

Todd looked down into her face with a smile. "I think I know that," he said. "And so I probably ought to tell you about my business."

It was a warm evening. Hand in hand they left the house and walked down the deserted street in the combined glow of occasional street lights and a three-quarter moon. It was quiet for several minutes. "I've actually come from your parents' house," said Todd at length. "I wanted to talk to them about us."

Heather felt her hand tremble momentarily in Todd's.

"I thought they should know what I'm thinking," he continued, "and that I should know if they, you know, couldn't stand me and wanted me to stay away from their daughter."

"Todd!" laughed Heather, glad for the release of tension. "You did not!"

"I sort of did. I didn't exactly phrase it like that, but that was the gist of it. I asked if they had any objection to our continuing to see each other."

"Obviously they don't. They love you."

"I still had to talk to them. I told them I cared about you but realized we still had a lot of getting to know each other ahead of us, and that I was serious and wanted to know where God might be taking us. I wanted to know if they were okay with you being with me as we pray about our future. Well . . . that is, you know, if it's okay with *you*!"

When Heather replied, her voice was barely audible.

"You know it is, Todd. You must know how I feel."

"I think I do."

Neither spoke for five or ten minutes. Their hearts were full. Perhaps for the first time, both *knew*, and knew that what they knew was mutual.

They continued to walk and talk softly in the warm moonlight. They did not return to the house until 11:30, talked inside for another hour. Heather was still laying in her bed an hour later, thinking and dreaming things she never expected to think and dream. About the same time, Todd was settling into his room in Roseville.

Heather arrived at the Circle F about ten the following morning, obviously sleepy but with a strange glow about her. She said little to the others. All was explained when Todd drove up around noon in time for lunch. He spent the rest of the day at the ranch trying to make himself useful, though how much work he and Heather got done was doubtful.

Ginger, of course, was full of questions. Heather's answers were cryptic, though she inadvertently dropped the tidbit about Todd talking with Timothy and Jaylene the night before.

Heather's smile said clearly enough there had been a change. It was obvious to everyone that she and Todd had entered a new phase in their relationship. The glances and smiles back and forth between them said more than enough.

That same afternoon Timothy spent with David at the Bar JG—the ranch named for David's great-grandfather, Jackson Gordon. All that remained was to present their proposal to Todd.

Thus, the arrangements were nearly complete by the time cars began arriving at David's ranch for Friday evening's potluck supper of the BCL group, which would be followed by fellowship for most of Saturday.

13

The Ally Chooses Sides

EDITH HOLT kept close taps on everyone in the BCL group. She was familiar with the acronym for Brethren of the Common Life but had no clue what it signified. She did know, however, when every meeting or activity was held.

Her annoyance with the whole thing increased with every new report that came her way. She was constantly seeking to widen her network of informants in Roseville and within the many communities scattered through the surrounding foothills. That none of those involved were submitted to local church leadership was the ostensible objection she and her husband, Stoddard, had to the group. In reality, young Rev. Carmichael, who replaced Mark after his retirement three years earlier was more submitted to the two Holts than they were to him.

Mostly it grated on Edith's pride how those in the group were so satisfied with themselves. Her irritation was exacerbated in that they no longer even tried to keep the group secret. Though she would never admit it, she knew she and Stoddard would be welcomed if they expressed interest in the books they were reading. But she also knew they would not be looked up to and would be treated as newcomers of no higher status than anyone else.

That reality made attendance out of the question. Edith Holt had no interest in being involved in anything where she was not the center of attention.

Stoddard may have been her husband, but she was the devoted mistress of the Ally. She carried out its bidding eagerly. To take down their former pastor Mark Forster for his repeated snubs—and the irrationality of her indignation had risen to the extreme with his appointment to the president's commission—had become the supreme objective of her existence. Where division, disunity, discord, innuendo, and denigrating rumor could be sown, she sowed them with righteous passion.

Edith had seen Mason Templeton's interview and knew from her most trusted informant, her son Lionel, that he was responsible for the video. They also heard about the letters naming Mark as Reyburn's campaign manager. By mid-June she had seen a copy of the letter for herself. When news leaked out two weeks before that Mark had been relieved of his duties on the president's commission, she and Stoddard laughed outright, as they supposed, at Mark's humiliation.

"Serves him right!" said Edith, "getting above himself, inviting all those political people to his ranch, thinking he's going to be *anyone's* campaign manager!"

Smelling blood in the water, she had been waiting for an opportunity to inflict yet more damage to Mark's battered ego. She was on the phone to her son the moment she confirmed the dates of the July BCL meeting, adding the information from her network that a larger than usual number of people seemed likely to be on hand.

"Lionel," she said, "there's another meeting of that group next weekend."

"I am well aware of it, Mother."

"Why didn't you tell me? I had to find out from Gretchen. Are you going?"

"I may be," replied Lionel. "My plans are uncertain."

"What plans?"

"Nothing. It's just that some of the people I work with in Washington may need my help."

"Help with what?"

"I can't say more, Mother. All I can say is there may be fireworks! This may be Forster's last hurrah and the end of that group altogether."

"Really! Lionel, what's going on? You can tell me—I won't breathe a word of it!"

"Let's just say things are heating up."

"Lionel, please—you *have* to tell me. You can't deprive me of seeing the man taken down. If something's going on, I have to know."

Lionel thought a moment.

"I don't suppose there'd be any harm. I'm sure no one will mind. It will be too late by then anyway."

"Too late for what—Lionel!"

"I'll let you know. Just keep the weekend open. I suppose you have a right to enjoy it too. I'll keep you posted."

On the following Friday evening, as David's guests arrived for pot-luck supper, the phone rang in the Holt home. Edith sprang for it.

"Mother, it's Lionel," she heard. "Be at my apartment by nine tomorrow morning."

14

If He Wouldn't, How Can I?

"HEY, TODD!" said Dewitt West as he walked from his car toward David's ranch house and saw Todd stepping off the porch, "you're becoming quite a regular around here."

"I may be a more regular fixture here than you think." rejoined Todd. "Hey, Rod," he added to Dewitt's son-in-law walking up behind him.

"What do you mean, Todd," said Dewitt as they continued toward the house.

"He's going to be David's new ranch hand!" said Heather, bounding toward them. Todd stretched his arm around her as she inched close beside him.

"Is this true?" said Rod. "That's great news."

"This young woman and her parents think maybe I ought to spend a little more time out west. David has obliged by offering me room and board and a little spending money to help out around the ranch. What I'm afraid he doesn't know is I barely know one end of a horse from the other."

"Take it from one who has spent a lifetime around horses," laughed Dewitt, "that is one difference you will be very familiar with soon enough!"

David joined the small group in front of his house. He heard the remnants of the conversation.

"I have been praying for someone to help me out," he said. "I'm too old to take care of this whole place by myself. What you don't know, Todd my boy, you will learn."

"Take it from me again," added Dewitt, "you couldn't have better teachers than David and that lady at your side. She may know horses better than anyone in the foothills. Am I right, David?"

"You are indeed."

"Though that day when she was riding behind me and fell smack on top of a rattlesnake, we could not have known it then."

"The way she tells the story," said Todd, "you saved her life, Dewitt."

"Let's just say a lot of people contributed to it, and that God saved her life because he had important things for her to do."

Heather said nothing but could not help blushing shyly as she stood listening with Todd's arm wrapped around her.

"When do you start, Todd?" asked Rod.

"I'm flying back to DC on Monday," replied Todd "I'll pack up my things, give notice on my apartment, rent a U-Haul, and hopefully be back here and ready to work in two or three weeks."

"And you, Heather?" added Dewitt, glancing down at her.

"What about me?" rejoined Heather.

"What do you think of it all?"

"You need to ask! I can't wait for him to get back!"

They continued to the house as several more cars crawled in line up the drive.

Nearly half of April's attendees would be on hand by the next day. Because of the increased number of those coming from outside the area, most of the local BCL group did not attend the Friday evening potluck. As it was, the forty or so who arrived barely managed to squeeze into David's great room. The Jansens, Masters, and Reyburns were all on hand.

The discussion during the buffet supper and into the evening was spirited. Not surprisingly, conversation mostly centered around the short-lived, though bogus, so-called presidential campaign of Charles Reyburn and Harvey Jansen, both of whom laughed about it with good humor.

Throughout most of the discussion, Mark remained quiet. Not wanting to cast a damper on the evening, at length, however, he felt compelled to tell those who hadn't yet heard about his interview with the president, and the more sinister construction Jeff placed on the events of the previous April's gathering.

"How did they get the video that was on the news?" asked Violet Langdon.

"From a young man in our former church," Mark replied quickly before Heather could assume blame. "He showed up in April. Though he mostly kept in the background, some of you may have noticed him. We wondered what he was doing here, and it later became clear. His parents were flies in the ointment of my pastorate. The whole family has been something of a trial for years. How the video got into the hands of the national media, I admit, concerns me. That so many of you received those letters, too, is worrisome. Not that we're trying to keep our meetings or friendships secret. But with Jeff's suspicions—the president's, I should say—I'm thinking we may need to prepare ourselves for difficult times ahead."

"The homeschooling families in our church all hoped it was true about your running for president, Dr. Reyburn," said Kansan Gerald Stevens, glancing toward Charles. "The regulations and curriculum being imposed upon them are intolerable. Our people don't know what to do."

The room erupted with animated comments from all quarters sharing the same concerns.

"Our people," said Gerald, "are beside themselves. I've seen the mandated books—they're beyond imagining. No serious Christian parent can comply with the regulations. But the threats of government intervention, fines, even arrest, are becoming serious. One of our friends told me that starting next year all home schools will be required to install listening devices in their homes to monitor everything said. Could that actually be true?"

A few eyes drifted in Rod Statler's direction.

"If anything, the situation is worse than you describe," he said softly. "Yes, it is true about listening devices. We just found out that without one, next year we will lose our home school license. We have received the mandated textbooks. What Gerald said is true—beyond imagining. If I were to show you . . ."

He shook his head in despair.

"All I can say is that you wouldn't believe it."

"Are you using the books?" asked Violet.

"Oh, no," answered Rod. "But it's serious enough that we've moved in with Pearl and Dewitt for a while. The Department of Education has our address. We don't want to be there if one of their compliance officers appears at our door."

The room was silent a few seconds.

"This is precisely why many of us hoped one of you would run," now said Martha Powell, glancing toward Harvey Jansen then toward the Reyburns. "Is there any chance you would reconsider?"

The two men looked at one another.

"Speaking for myself," replied Reyburn, "no. Believe me, my heart is aching over what is going on, aching that our national heritage is being ruined. Being in education myself, I feel the dilemma keenly. I don't know what the answer is."

"Why would you not consider running," asked Craig Forster, "knowing you could change these new educational regulations?"

Charles smiled. "A good question, Craig," he said. "You seem to have inherited your father's ability to penetrate straight to the heart of an issue! Let me answer you this way. Let's imagine Jesus sitting here with us—right now, in this room. He *is* here, of course. But what if he were sitting with us in the flesh, alive in his humanity. Could he change these educational directives and guidelines if *he* were president? Imagine we were all imploring *him* to run against President Rhodes. If he said no and you asked him the same question, how would he answer?"

The imagery was so profound that the room was deathly silent. All eyes were focused on Charles Reyburn's dark face.

"I think he would smile," said Charles after a few seconds, "look around at all of us, and say, 'Because it is not my way. It is not my Father's method. My kingdom is not of this world. The world's systems and methods will never bring my Father's kingdom alive in the hearts of men.'"

Charles paused again, then added, "If he would not run for president, as a man who has made it my business to try to follow his example, how can I?"

The room was again silent.

15

Sobering Discussion

"WHAT ARE young parents like Rod and Diane to do, then?" asked Pearl. "These are my grandchildren. What are we all to do?"

"I'm sorry, Pearl," replied Charles. "I don't know."

A somber silence again descended.

"It is almost as if a time is coming," now said Matthew Gardner from Idaho, "when God's remnant will be forced underground."

"Could it really come to that, do you think?" asked Jaylene.

"My grandparents," Matthew replied, "used to talk about two books that had profound impact on Christians back in the Cold War days of the 1960s and 1970s—*God's Smuggler* and *The Hiding Place*. They were about European Christians hiding Jews from the Nazis during World War II, and then later Brother Andrew's exploits smuggling Bibles behind the Iron Curtain when Christianity was outlawed in Russia and the countries controlled by the Soviet Union. The Christian church in half the countries of the globe was an underground church. In spite of progressivism's systematic undermining of Christian values and the nuclear family, we in the West have had it easy during recent generations. Those times may come again."

Where he sat listening intently, David Gordon was revolving many things in his mind. His expression, however, divulged nothing.

"I have no doubt," said DeWitt, "that some form of underground church is probably already forming. In a sense, we are part of it. We are trying, not necessarily to hide or meet in secret but to be circumspect. But what if we *do* one day have to go into hiding?"

"Or hide Christians who are in danger, like the Jews were from the Nazis?" asked Jaylene. "How does that square with obeying the laws of the land?"

"If we are in a tribulation, which seems likely," said her husband, "we may have to make some hard decisions. What do God's people do," Timothy went on, "when it is simply impossible to give honor to the governmental authorities over us—when obedience is not an option, as is certainly the case with these new educational mandates? For years many have gullibly filled their homes with smart devices unconcerned about who is listening. Gerald was speaking of a time, which I believe is coming, when all homes, not only home schoolers, will be required to have surveillance systems installed.

"Until now it's been voluntary. People choose their smart devices thinking they enhance their lives, not realizing they are relinquishing their freedom one step at a time. But a time is coming when they will be mandated. Governmental spying in our homes will be automatic. Light fixtures and appliances will be capable of twenty-four-hour surveillance in every home. AI will become part of building codes.

"It will all be for the public good, of course—to protect children from evil influences. It will not only be how Christians teach their children that will come under scrutiny but *everything* we say and do. *1984* is here. People have gone along with smart devices for decades. I know it sounds conspiratorial, and I am no conspiracy theorist. But the government and high tech are listening to everything. A crackdown on Christians is coming. The attempt to eradicate Christian values from families and schools is one of progressivism's most basic tenets. Neither do I have an answer."

"Timothy is right," Charles began again, "the pressure is intensifying on us at the university level as well. Until recently, not taking public funds was enough to keep us somewhat separate. We have been able to set our own guidelines. But a time is coming when private schools, even universities, will have new mandated governmental curriculum forced upon them or find themselves shut down.

"These moves against home schools are but the vanguard of an attempt to eliminate Christian education from the country. They are going after home schools first because they make an easy target. Home schools are the thin edge of the wedge. It began in the 2020s with attempts to force homeschoolers to teach DEI and woke values. Complete eradication of Christian education is progressivism's ultimate goal. Parents are not so formidable a foe as institutions such as Hillsdown and William Jessup.

"The goal of progressivism is to topple the entire tree of Christianity's influence in our culture. Hillsdown will also become a target and may in time be shut down for non-compliance with the full LGBTQ agenda. There may come a time when AI will be installed in every classroom in the country from kindergarten to graduate seminars. I will be expected to teach outright falsehoods, every word I speak recorded and monitored by AI bots—AI monitoring AI! All this is coming! I could be banned from teaching altogether. These are perilous times for Christians."

"If men like you do not stand up and fight," said Sarah Gardner, "who will? Someone must stand against the ungodliness."

"We must all stand against the ungodliness," rejoined Charles. "But we must stand and fight in God's way, not the world's. What that looks like in every situation, I have no answer. I will stand for truth, as all of us in this room are trying to do. But to mount a presidential campaign I do not perceive to be God's way . . . at least it is not his way for me."

"And you, Senator?" said Rebecca Stevens, turning toward Harvey Jansen.

"I don't know," smiled Harvey sadly. "I fear it would do little good."

"Might you not be able to articulate some of these things," suggested Gerald. "Even if you were defeated again, bringing these losses of freedoms into the public discussion might forestall some of these measures. Most of the country probably has no idea."

"Do you really believe that, Gerald?" said Jaylene. "You may be right. But I am not so optimistic. As far as I can see, church-Christians have been frogs in progressivism's frying pan for two generations. I don't see church people standing up at all. Harvey could run again, and speak all these truths boldly, and most church people wouldn't care. Church Christians elected Clinton and Obama and Biden and now Rhodes. Trump was like the boy with his finger in the dyke. But the flood came anyway. Church people are just as progressive as the rest. The collapse of the family is not on the world, it's on the worldly church. The divorce rate in the church and the admission of women and gays into the pastorate is not the world's fault. It's the church's and that of Christian counselors and pastors who condone it. Maybe I'm wrong. What do the rest of you think? Are the families in your churches standing strong for truth—are the high school and college young people in your churches standing for truth?"

A few comments went around the room. Most were shaking their heads.

"Sad to say," said Lawrence Gibbs, assistant pastor of a large church in Florida, "most of the families in our church are going along, ordering the mandated curriculum and hoping to comply with the regulations just enough to get by, trying to explain things to their children by giving the material a Christian slant. I understand what you say about divorce and remarriage in the church. It's an epidemic. You can't imagine the hostility I've faced for refusing to marry previously divorced couples. People just don't care what the Bible says about such things."

"There's no way to give pornography a Christian slant," said Rod Statler.

"I know," sighed Gibbs. "I have seen the materials. Our state has even added to the federal mandate that home schools video the instruction given, showing the children listening. They are requiring absolute *proof* children are being shown the hideous images of perversion. Many families are so afraid of persecution or arrest that they think they can find ways to go along."

Gibbs paused a moment, shaking his head.

"What I'm about to say has to be qualified," he went on, "as being second or third hand, maybe fourth, for all I know. But I overheard something in the gym where I work out. I was getting dressed and I heard two men talking on the other side of a bank of lockers. If true, it shows how serious they are about enforcing the mandates. It's an exclusive club—some of my congregation bought a membership for me. One of the men, I gathered, was a state senator—obviously a Democrat. He was telling the other man that he was helping write a bill modeled after one that was secretly passed in Sacramento a few months ago. Both states are trying to close every loophole homeschoolers have been using to circumvent the government's educational requirements.

"The California law allows the state Board of Education to work with Child Protection Services to monitor all registered home schools in the state through the home's smart appliances to ascertain whether or not the children are being thoroughly and accurately taught the mandated gender curriculum, and if not, to take punitive action. I don't need to tell you what that means when Child Protection Services gets involved. Now that Florida is nearly as Democrat-controlled as California, there is little doubt such a law is coming to us. This was only days ago. When I get back home I intend to bring the matter before our church leadership and encourage our people to begin disconnecting the smart devices in their homes."

A somber silence descended on the room. If ever they needed a prophet to lead them out of the Egypt of their desolation, thought Mark as he listened, now was that time.

☆ ☆ ☆

The mood the following morning was more upbeat. With the sun shining, the outlook did not seem so dire as cars began pulling into the Bar JG after ten and continued arriving for an hour. By noon some sixty or sixty-five were on hand, with tables and chairs and makeshift benches set out in front of the house spread with leftovers from the previous night, and additions amounting to twice as much as the whole assembly could possibly eat.

"Hey, Rod," said Todd as the Statlers piled out of the West's SUV. Rod came forward with his twelve-year-old son, Seth, and ten-year-old daughter, Hannah.

Todd turned to the youngsters. "How are you, Seth . . . Hannah?"

"Hello, Mr. Stewart," said young Seth respectfully.

"And here's your mother—Hello, Diane . . . Pearl," said Todd, as Pearl and her daughter and seven-year-old Anne and four-year-old Matt walked toward them. "The home schooling's a little difficult these days from what Rod tells us."

"Pretty disrupted at the moment," replied Diane. "He probably told you we've relocated to Mom and Dad's ranch. We're living there now—we hope temporarily. The kids love it, but it takes us out of our routine."

"Well I'm sure your parents enjoy having you. You're safe and secure and among friends for the weekend at least."

"Rod tells me you're going to be living here at the Bar JG. That's fantastic. I'm sure Heather is excited."

"I believe you may be right about that!" laughed Todd. "Here she comes now. You can ask her yourself."

16

The Trap Is Set

SENSING HIGH drama in the wind, Edith Holt tossed and turned all night. She appeared at Lionel's apartment at eight-thirty on Saturday morning. He divulged no details. Whatever was going on, she wasn't about to miss it.

A little after noon two FBI agents arrived.

"Stay back and out of the way, Mom," said Lionel as he went to the door. "These guys are no nonsense. This is a secret operation. They'll wonder why you are here. Don't say anything. I'll fill you in later."

He let the men in. One of them glanced toward Edith with a blank expression.

"It's my mother," said Lionel. "She's okay. We're leaving anyway."

"All right, let's go then, Holt. The team is waiting outside."

With one final glance at Edith, the men left the apartment followed by Lionel.

Edith hurried to the door and opened it a crack.

". . . supposed to pick up the Statlers yesterday . . ." she overheard one of the men say as they walked down the stairs.

". . . no one there . . . place looked deserted . . ."

Ignoring what Lionel said, Edith opened the door and hurried after them.

"I didn't mean to eavesdrop," she said, "but I couldn't help hearing—is it Rod and Diane Statler you're looking for?"

The agent paused, turned back, and stared at Edith with a deadpan expression.

"What do you know about them?" he asked.

"I know them, if that's what you mean," replied Edith. Though never especially intimidated by anyone, she was a little cowed by the man's threatening tone.

"Do you know where they are?" he asked.

"I know they're not at home."

"I know that well enough. Where are they?"

"They went to stay with Diane's parents."

"Why?"

"Something about their children, I think."

"When?"

"Several weeks ago, I don't know exactly."

"Where do the parents live?"

"They have a ranch on the Folsom-Auburn Road."

"What's the address?" said the man, taking out a small notebook.

"That's not where they are now," replied Edith, "if you're trying to find them today."

"Where then?"

"They'll be with a group of people at the Gordon ranch in Grass Valley."

The man glanced at Lionel with a questioning expression.

"That's where we're going, sir," said Lionel.

"Then that will make things easy. Let's go."

They continued down the stairs.

Edith watched from the landing. She saw five black cars in the lot. Lionel and the two men got into one. It pulled out and led the way. The other three vehicles followed.

Before they were out of the lot, Edith was scrambling down the stairs and quickly climbed into her car. She knew well enough where they were headed.

17

When to Disobey

AT THE Bar JG, lunch had concluded a short while earlier. Small groups were walking about visiting and laughing and renewing friendships begun the previous April. Gradually everyone made their way toward David's barn.

In light of the persecutions coming to home schoolers and Christian parents, as well as the rumors about a presidential run, Timothy had asked Court Masters and Charles Reyburn to address the group—Court to speak about precautions he was setting up to protect their communications, and Charles to give his perspective about the role of Christians in politics. Though most had heard his brief remarks the previous evening, Timothy knew there was keen interest in Charles's thoughts. He also planned to read his father's comments specific to politics from his Benedict Brief to stimulate further discussion.

Court took the floor first.

"It's no secret," he began, "that we are being inundated with change faster than we can keep up with. One of the most worrisome areas of change is in communications. Since our fellowship is now worldwide, we depend on other people, the government, and many technologies to communicate with each other. I urge you to be aware that in all likelihood most of us are being monitored. Caution and vigilance are imperative.

"Nothing is safe in the current climate. The *air* itself, quite literally is listening in on our lives. Two of us might walk outside alone and assume we are having a private conversation. All the while every word might be being recorded by a drone we are not even aware of. Listening devices in our homes are also a tremendous problem. Texts and emails, of course, haven't been secure for decades. Telephone calls aren't safe—*everything* is listened to digitally by bots programmed to pick up on anything deemed suspicious or questionable. They are not safe for another reason, simply that our voices can be mimicked by AI. We might not be talking to each other at all!"

A few exclamations circulated among his listeners, though for most this wasn't even news.

"I have been developing what I hope will be a secure communications platform in our new matrix community," he went on. "Anything can be hacked, so I will be constantly monitoring and possibly changing its parameters over time. But for now, let me explain some measures we have begun implementing.

"Most important, except for very urgent matters, sensitive communications should be handwritten and sent as letters the old-fashioned way, in foil-lined envelopes, through the mail. Pay close attention that your letters are not being opened. Continue with email and other electronic communications on normal platforms for innocuous stay-in-touch greetings and news. We want to continue with normal patterns so as not to call attention to ourselves.

"At the same time everyone should set up a secondary private email on EarthMail which is similar to ProtonMail which many of you were familiar with years ago. It is vital you use it only with fellow EarthMail users, otherwise all communications can be infiltrated and monitored. We will be setting up secure usernames and passwords to make it possible for us to communicate via message boards for informal and less sensitive communications. The matrix community I am setting up is built on a self-hosted, air-gapped, and highly encrypted edition of an Element server which will hopefully keep us one step ahead of any governmental agencies trying to break into the system. It should successfully preserve our anonymity. Should a serious hack occur, we will simply pull the plug, disconnect everyone, destroy the servers, and start again. Along with this, we all need to discontinue use of the Cloud and other global electronic storage systems. Shut down your accounts altogether. In as many ways as possible, we need to disengage from the ubiquitous technology that has taken over our world. We cannot do so entirely. But where we can, we must do so.

"I know all this may sound complicated and technological. Some of it is even over my head!" Court added laughing. "But Stella and some of those we work with know all the intricacies. Once these new systems are in place, Stella and I will make a tour to all the BCL groups around the country to help set things up with everyone in person, establishing usernames and passwords, providing new encrypted cell phones, making sure everyone in the matrix community is comfortable and up to speed with what we are doing. We're even talking about using Hyperloop where it is available between some of the major cities.

"Otherwise we'll drive or use high-speed rail since I'm on the federal no-fly list. That may also preclude the train, but we'll have to see. We will also be developing a complex set of code words and jargon for telephone use, both to use for identification to make sure we're not talking to an AI bot—simple words and phrases about the weather or health or work or Scripture with undetectable turns of phrase that only we will know amongst ourselves. We will also develop codes to disguise spiritual forms of communication that could be flagged. We're not trying to develop an unbreakable enigma code. That would probably be impossible. We're only trying to be prudent so no one puts anyone in danger. These codes will obviously have to be delivered in person and constantly adjusted and changed. AI and those who control it are deviously clever. But I am confident that by using the Word of God as a large source of our coding strategies, his Spirit will even be able to blind the AI bots to protect his people."

Court paused. "I think that should cover it as an overview for now," he said. "Stella and I will talk with you individually later to answer your questions and will be visiting many of you, along with other BCL groups, in the coming months. Now I know you are anxious to hear from Charles."

Charles rose and stood before them. "Thank you, Court," he said. "It's mostly over my head too! But I know we all feel safer knowing that you and Stella are watching out for us. What Court has been saying about communications is intrinsically linked to the political realm, though indirectly. In both areas we are called to walk with vigilance in but not of the world."

He went on, recounting briefly what he said the night before, explaining why he personally could not become involved in the following year's election.

"I cannot say I consider it wrong for a Christian to be involved in politics or even run for president," he said. "My friend Harvey has actually done so! I wrestle with the question where spirituality and politics intersect. I have no answer other than that it is an individual matter about which God must lead every man and woman personally. I believe that politics needs good, virtuous men and women of integrity. At the same time I am aware that our Lord lifted not so much as a finger to influence the culture or society or politics of his time. His example weighs heavily for me, which is why my personal convictions preclude *me* from seeking office of any kind. I speak only for myself. How others may be led, I cannot say. If Harvey, for example, should be led differently and should throw his hat into the ring again, he would have my complete support. I honor him as God's man. I would not question his decision."

He paused thoughtfully.

"There is another side to the whole question," he went on, "that in a way is disconnected from how Christianity and politics intermingle. But it is very timely in light of what was discussed last evening and how dedicated parents, educators, and homeschoolers should respond to the evil directions our government is mandating. I am speaking of the question raised by Paul in Romans 13:1–2: *Let every person be subject to the governing authorities.* We must recognize that Paul was speaking to the church of Rome during times of tremendous persecution. Yet the Christians who hid in the catacombs outside Rome did *not* obey this injunction. Paul also told Titus to submit to rulers and authorities. Many of the Christians in the early church, however, defied the authorities. Paul adds that the governing authorities are put in place by God and to resist them is to resist God. I'm not sure I believe that. We cannot necessarily take every word Paul said as infallible. How do we reconcile his words with the reign of Nero, when Christians did their best to avoid persecution? Obviously they did *not* believe Nero was acting as God's authority.

"Peter says we are to be subject to every human institution, yet also said in Acts 5 that his obligation was to obey God not men. Scripturally, there is no clear answer. It is a confusing dilemma. Honestly, I think Paul's injunction about obeying the governing authorities may not always be possible. There again we are faced with the catacomb Christians. Were they resisting God?

"These are difficult questions. If my dear wife were threatened, would I stand by and do nothing? I do *not* believe the progressivism that has hijacked our nation since the Obama years has been instituted by God. If that means disagreeing with Paul's words, you will have to make of that what you will. The evils that may come may be so blatant that we will *have* to disobey the law of the land. As true Christians, it may not be possible to do otherwise. What this will look like, whether the true Church will eventually be an underground Church, I cannot predict more than to say—"

18

RAID

CHARLES'S VOICE was suddenly drowned out by the sound of car engines racing up the drive. They roared toward the house, then skidded to a stop. The racket was so loud that Charles stopped abruptly in mid-sentence.

David and Timothy ran to the open end of the barn. They saw several men jumping out of the three lead cars, dust flying in all directions. Before they had a chance to wonder what it was about, six or eight uniformed police officers piled out, brandishing AR-type rifles and wearing body armor. Three stormed the house, the rest raced toward the barn where their informant told them the meeting would be held.

Seconds later, finding themselves staring at a scene out of a movie, a small SWAT team standing in front with rifles trained on them, half the group stood, the rest sat motionless. No one spoke a word. David, Timothy, and Charles stood to one side like statues. Mark slowly rose and joined them.

Three plainclothes FBI agents walked into the dusky barn on the heels of the armed contingent. They were followed by three police officers and Lionel Holt. A few murmurs of astonishment circulated from those who recognized him.

Lionel stepped to the front, glanced around in the dim light, then strode toward the four men. He walked straight forward and gave Mark Forster an expansive embrace.

"Greetings, Pastor!" he said. "How good to see you again."

"Lionel, what are you—" began Mark.

As Lionel stepped away, two of the officers took hold of Mark rudely and shoved him toward the three agents.

"Good job—well done, Holt," said their leader. "Where's the other one?"

Lionel, who did not recognize David at first, looked about again.

"Ah, there you are . . . hello, Mr. Gordon," said Lionel effusively, slapping David on the shoulder.

The next moment another of the officers was pulling David away with Mark.

"We'll take it from here, Holt," said the agent, then faced the speechless assembly. "I have warrants here," he said, "for the arrest of Mark Forster and David Gordon."

As he spoke, the two men were roughly handcuffed with their hands behind their backs.

Gasps of shock and instant commotion erupted throughout the barn.

"That will be enough!" shouted the agent, "unless any of the rest of you want to join them."

Court Masters now rose. As if by common consent, he and Timothy walked forward.

"Let me see those warrants," said Masters. "There must be some mistake. These men have done—"

"Keep out of it, Masters!" barked the man. "I was told you would be here and was given explicit instructions to arrest you too if you tried anything."

"Can you at least tell me what this is all about?" said Court.

"Conspiracy."

"What! But surely—"

"I told you—stay out of it. My orders are to arrest you along with them if you give me the slightest cause."

Court backed away. Whatever was going on, he could do more good here than in jail.

"Can you at least tell me where you are taking them?"

"County for now. Probably Folsom in a day or two."

"*Folsom*—that's for hardened criminals!"

"Conspiracy is serious business, Masters. These men are considered dangerous."

The agent turned to the uniforms. "Take them away!"

Mark and David were rousted out of the barn to further outrage, while most watched in silent horror. As they were rudely manhandled and shoved into the backseat of one of the SUVs, two large women officers exited the fourth vehicle and came toward the barn.

They walked inside and stepped in front where the FBI agents still stood flanked by three or four uniforms with rifles poised.

"We have another warrant here," said the agent in charge. "Would either Rod or Diane Statler identify themselves."

Slowly Rod stood where he sat beside Dewitt West. At his side, trembling and white, Diane also rose to her feet.

"I have orders here signed by the Secretary of Education in the nation's capital. You have been deemed in non-compliance with mandated homeschooling regulations. This order authorizes us to remove from your care the three oldest children known as Seth, Hannah, and Anne Statler."

As he spoke the two women came forward, pushed their way through the chairs, and took hold of the three children seated next to Diane, yanked them to their feet, and pulled them out of the row of chairs and toward the front of the barn.

Seth and Hannah looked back toward their parents with wide eyes of terror. Young Anne screamed and tried to pull away. A whack from one of the women agents nearly sent her to the ground. Diane cried out, but within seconds the women and three children were out of sight.

The barn erupted in exclamations of disbelief.

"They will be placed in the custody of a group facility in Sacramento," said the agent, speaking above the crying and outbursts filling the barn. "Your bank account has been attached, Mr. Statler, until all outstanding fines and penalties are paid."

The agents turned and left the barn in an uproar, half the women weeping and Diane Statler shrieking hysterically. Hearing the din behind him, the lead agent stopped and turned back into the barn.

"Everyone stay where you are!" he yelled. "My orders are to arrest anyone who causes trouble. That includes you, Mr. and Mrs. Statler. You brought this on yourselves by ignoring numerous notifications. If you lose your children, you have only yourselves to blame. I advise you to get control of yourselves."

He turned and followed the women outside and toward the cars. All three of the children were crying as they were pulled rudely away. Last to exit the barn were the armed SWAT officers. As the two cars pulled away bearing the two prisoners and three children, they finally turned and walked back to the remaining vehicles, which followed away from the ranch along the entry drive.

None noticed the nondescript Chevrolet parked near the gate. Edith Holt had been watching through the pair of binoculars she always kept on hand, her eyes wide at what she could make out of the proceedings. Even she was shocked yet still felt a surge of gleeful adrenalin as she saw the two handcuffed men shoved into one of the cars.

The moment the five SUVs were out of sight, she started her engine, spun around on the gravel drive, and sped after them. She intended to miss none of this!

Edith Holt's information network was highly efficient and wasted no time. By nightfall everyone at Foothill Gospel Ministries knew that their former pastor and the strange old heretic David Gordon had been arrested.

The average American will never understand . . . therefore, the thing to do is to destroy the idea of America . . . We have to dismantle this idea of American exceptionalism . . . we live in an evil country.

—Sachin Peddada

"People's Conference for Palestine," 2025
(Held in the United States, the speech brought rousing cheers from his American audience.)

PART 2

ROOTS FIND GOOD SOIL

SUMMER–FALL 2051

19

Inquiries

THE JULY weekend was obviously over, or at least had changed dramatically. The Gordon ranch was in an uproar of outrage, shock, and disbelief.

Diane Statler was beside herself. She could do nothing but alternately weep and rant. Young Matt never left Rod's arms for fear of also being taken. Most of the others gradually managed to calm down enough to come together and plan what should be done.

Pearl took Diane into the house. Timothy, Charles, Court, Jaylene, Harvey, Heather, Grace, Todd, Dewitt, Ginger, and Craig took seats together to discuss a strategy. The rest gathered around to listen and contribute ideas as appropriate.

"It would appear, Todd," said Timothy, "that your apprenticeship at the Bar JG has begun sooner than we anticipated. With David gone, you will have to see to things here. Heather, you should plan on being here the rest of today and tomorrow until we see how this thing plays out. You'll need to give Todd a crash course about the needs of the horses and . . . well, about everything!"

"I can help too," said Dewitt. "Pearl and Rod can handle things at our place."

"You may have your hands full with family matters," said Jaylene.

"Between us all, we'll get done what needs to get done," rejoined Dewitt. "Two of our three ranches are now without their heads."

"Don't worry about us," said Grace. "Robert will be incensed when he hears what happened. But he can handle the livestock."

Eyes again went in Timothy's direction.

"We need to call everyone else," he said, glancing around. "We need to let others know what happened so they can pray. But also to warn other homeschool families. We have no idea what this signifies or if this portends a nationwide crackdown. I'm not sure what measures we should suggest. For now all we can tell people is that they need to be prepared for the worst."

He glanced at the other men.

"I think I'll leave the rest of you for now," said Court, rising. "I'm going to make some calls and see what I can find out. It's obvious I'm not going to have much clout. But I still have contacts and am on decent terms with Director Parva. Or thought I was."

As Court left the barn he was already punching numbers into his phone.

"I think I'll follow suit," said Harvey Jansen. "My time in DC may have been brief, but I've got some good friends in the Senate."

"What about Governor Foxe?" added his wife behind him.

"Right, why don't you call him, Harriet, while I try to get through to some of my former colleagues."

"I'll call Linda Trent," put in Grace who was doing her best to remain calm. "I don't think any of us are going to get through to Jeff," she added a little irritably. "It wouldn't surprise me if he's behind this."

"What about the First Lady, Mom?" said Ginger.

"Great idea. I'll call her too. She'll take my call. Nothing like a little wifely pressure!"

"Should I try some of my old contacts at NBC, Mr. Marshall?" asked Todd.

"It can't hurt," replied Timothy. "The more hue and cry we raise, the better."

As Timothy was talking, an unexpected idea popped into Ginger's head. Did she dare? Yet this was her father and David and Rod and Diane's children. She would do *anything* to help them!

She rose as Timothy and Todd were talking and crept out of the barn as unobtrusively as possible.

"If the network won't listen," Todd was saying, "the station I've been working for in DC will. I'll call them after I try NBC. We'll set up a makeshift studio and I'll do a live report. My station would love an exclusive. They've been pestering me to get back on the air. I won't tell them I'm about to give notice and move to California!"

Todd left the barn to start making calls.

Gradually the others split into small groups, praying and talking. Heather went into the house and printed out multiple copies of the BCL contacts list from around the country, now numbering over three hundred. She returned and set to work with the remaining men and women organizing a telephone campaign for those who were not otherwise occupied. Prayer chains and cells were soon making calls throughout the country. By the end of the day a prayer network numbering more than ten thousand was activated.

Court Masters returned to the barn after fifteen minutes.

"I'm afraid I've been blackballed," he said. "Whoever's behind this must know I'm involved. A directive was sent out last week instructing no one to talk to me or take my calls. Fortunately, I still have a friend or two who ignored it. I'll drive down to the FBI office in Sacramento. I still know my way around. I'll see if I can at least see where they're taking them. Do you have a lawyer, Grace?" he asked.

"We've never needed one. There's Brent Ray at the church, but he's a crony of Stoddard Holt's—the father of the young man who took the video and identified Mark and David to the FBI a few minutes ago."

"Surely Stoddard knew nothing about this," said Jaylene. "I think he has a few scruples, though I'm not sure about Edith."

"I'll call Brent," said Timothy. "He and I are on good terms. If nothing else, he could recommend someone from his firm. But I think he'll jump in. Lawyers love this kind of thing."

Court was soon on his way into the valley. Half an hour later Todd was setting up an impromptu film studio and experimenting with dozens of the mobile phones on hand to see which would produce adequate video quality. He planned on filming an interview while the incident was still fresh. If NBC wasn't interested, he would send it straight to WJXV in the nation's capital.

As Court's car sped along the drive, Ginger Forster was walking along the path leading through the pasture away from David's barn. It took her some time to get through.

"Hi, Bradon," she said. "It's Ginger . . . Ginger Forster—"

The eager voice of the president's son interrupted before she could say anything further.

"No," she managed to say finally, "I'm in California. I called because I have a favor to ask. The FBI just arrested my dad, and—"

Her voice broke off as she began to cry.

20

Absentee Journalist Makes News

COURT TELEPHONED Timothy two hours later with news that Mark and David were being held separately without bail at the Sacramento county jail pending arraignment. Brent Ray agreed to represent them but thus far had been denied access to the prisoners.

For the first time in almost three years, a little after five o'clock, Todd Stewart found himself standing in front of a bank of cameras and lights—lamps from David's house and several dozen cell phones, one of which was mounted on a makeshift tripod whose signal was being sent live back to station WJXV in Washington. The moment Todd called, they set plans in motion to broadcast live at 8:00 p.m. He would again be seen by hundreds of thousands, if not millions, nationwide if the advance notice sent out by WJXV was picked up by as many stations as they anticipated. It promised to be the biggest scoop in the tiny station's brief fifteen-year history.

"This is Todd Stewart reporting live from the California foothills," Todd began, "with an astonishing story, still unfolding at this hour, of an abrogation of civil rights and due process more reminiscent of third world dictatorships than the United States of America. As I witnessed firsthand just hours ago, an armed tactical squad of FBI agents and local SWAT police . . ."

Where he was watching, Mike Bardolf smiled to himself.

This will put the fear of God into the zealots, he said to himself.

He had already heard from the president, who was equally delighted. *Mark will learn not to toy with me!* Rhodes exclaimed exuberantly on the phone.

This is only the beginning, Bardolf thought as he began to revolve in his mind what to do next. Of course he couldn't keep them in jail. But the purpose would be served.

He wasn't sure what to think of it all. Whether there was a conspiracy or not, allowing the narrative to develop organically—feeding the eager young Templeton enough to ensure it did—would sow enough doubt to lay the groundwork for whatever additional moves he might make. The names involved certainly indicated *something* going on involving high-up people from diverse spheres of influence. He would add to Templeton's narrative that one of the group's leaders, Mark Forster, recent appointee of President Rhodes to head his Religion Commission, had apparently been using his position to infiltrate the administration at the highest levels.

He would follow this in a few days with a report that the group was thought to be stockpiling weapons. The fact that Forster was now a rancher would ideally brand him as a classic redneck. That one of those attending was from Idaho, that hotbed of militia groups, would confirm the rumors all the more.

If they could just lay their hands on the secret Brief and *prove* the conspiracy.

Bardolf was a sufficient student of humanity to realize that for the president it wasn't primarily a matter of religion. He doubted Rhodes *really* believed his friend was involved in a conspiracy. But with political types, you could never tell. To advance their agendas, most zealots professed some kind of religion. These days you couldn't tell about religious types. Even the most mild-mannered sometimes turned out to be closet wackos.

Between Mark Forster and Jefferson Rhodes, it was more personal than politics or religion. It went back to their youth and college days. He still wasn't sure why the one-time friendship became so acrimonious. The Seattle-born son of Joe Biden's friend Harrison Rhodes probably always felt superior to the cowpoke son of a dirt-under-the-fingernails rancher. No doubt that sense of superiority deepened over the years by Rhodes's increasing political success.

He had become the most powerful person in the world, while his friend was now a disgraced minister. Yet when they were together, superior as he felt, Mike could read anger in Rhodes at the mere sight of Forster's calm demeanor, knowing his friend cared nothing for power or prestige. Rhodes's success meant little to him. That Forster did not recognize the president's supremacy was most grating of all—his irritating self-assurance.

Forster's quiet, self-confident countenance infuriated the president. It was as if Jefferson Rhodes was still trying to prove himself. But only prove his superiority to himself. His friend didn't care.

Bardolf smiled. The obvious animosity between them gave him power over the president he would continue to use to his advantage.

21

Good News and Bad

THOUGH HEATHER and Todd spent only three days at the Bar JG together before David's release, they were three of the happiest days of their lives. Working side by side, Heather explaining everything about ranch life—horses, cows, feeding, watering, mucking out, and all the other daily and weekly chores, where everything was kept in the barn and other outbuildings, what all the equipment was used for, how to saddle a horse and drive the tractor, with a dozen maintenance concerns and a variety of other duties intrinsic to ranch life that were second nature to Heather but all new to Todd. They talked constantly as they worked and went on several rides as Todd's confidence in the saddle gradually improved. Having no idea how long David and Mark would be incarcerated, Todd cancelled his return flight to DC.

By the end of their first full day, the Sunday following the arrests, they were exhausted from the emotional strain of the previous day's events mixed with the joy of working and being together. In the year they had known one another, they had never been together so continuously. No longer merely visiting but working side by side with a purpose enriched the time all the more. It was more *real* than the occasional artificial environment of a date or a drive or a sail on Puget Sound or the Potomac.

Knowing what the poor Statlers and Wests were going through—not to mention Grace, Ginger, and Craig—they felt almost guilty for enjoying themselves. Heather did not return to the Circle F Sunday night until after ten. She immediately felt a pang when she saw Grace, obviously not far from tears. No word had yet come from Court or Ray about Mark and David.

On Monday morning the two drove into Grass Valley. With Heather's assistance and much fun and laughter, they outfitted Todd with attire and a new pair of boots suitable for a ranch hand.

Despite the threats, Mark and David were not transferred to Folsom prison and were released on Tuesday. They never saw Brent Ray. Both were charged with conspiracy against the US government, were arraigned privately on Tuesday morning, and on orders from the nation's capital, Palladium member in good standing Judge Rakin Elgar, who took his direction from the second in command at the Presidential Manor, sentenced them to five years' probation and ordered their release.

Court and Stella Masters postponed their flights home, staying on at the Circle F as Grace's guests. Persona non grata or not, Court haunted Sacramento's FBI headquarters most of Sunday and Monday. Following the arraignment on Tuesday morning, he was informed that the two prisoners would be released from the county jail in two hours. Court and Stella, Timothy and Jaylene, and Grace and Ginger and Craig were all waiting for them. They were none the worse for wear. Both were upbeat and almost jovial to have their brief ordeal behind them.

In spite of the rejoicing that immediately circulated throughout the BCL network, everyone realized something had changed. Those associated with the Forsters and Marshalls were now in the crosshairs and must walk carefully. The uncertainty over the fate of the three Statler children remained in doubt and cast a pall overshadowing Mark's and David's release. Rod and Diane were told nothing, had no idea where their children were, and were beside themselves with worry.

They were contacted on Tuesday and visited by a child services officer on Wednesday, at their home not the West ranch. Not knowing Edith Holt had already divulged it, they hoped to keep the ranch unknown to child services. They were told because of their non-compliance with mandated educational regulations, their children would remain at a group home where their well-being and education would be thoroughly evaluated before a decision about their future was made.

"Can you tell us where they are . . . may we see them?" asked Diane.

"That will not be possible as long as you are on the list of unfit parents," answered the woman without expression.

"Do the children's wishes have any bearing on what is done?" asked Rod.

"Not in cases of religious and cult brainwashing, which our records indicate is the situation in this instance."

"Will we be evaluated to see if we *are* fit parents?"

"You have not followed the educational guidelines. That in itself renders you unfit. Time will tell if your youngest will be withdrawn as well."

She divulged nothing more, leaving Diane more disconsolate than ever.

"How could this happen?" she wailed. "How could something we were trying to do for their good turn out so wrong! All those years we prayed for protection . . . how can this be . . . where are those prayers!"

Rod merely closed his eyes and shook his head. He had no answer. All he could think was that he had failed as a father, failed to protect his family. After their faithful years of prayer, how it could come to this was a bitter confusion. The quandary plunged deep into the practical meaning of the sovereignty of God and the essence of prayer. Both despondent parents suddenly found themselves questioning the reality of both.

For days Rod hardly spoke. He walked about with young Matt shadowing him or sat staring into space, a broken man. The guilt and despondency was beyond anything he ever faced.

He could not help Diane, because he could not help himself.

22

Road Trip

BUT THE life of the Christian, the "common life" of faith into which thousands were invisibly being drawn, is a life that ebbs and flows. The purpose for its alternating peaks and valleys is not always visible. Suffering and rejoicing are intrinsic to the life of growth.

In the midst of the great darkness of Rod's and Diane's lives and similar concerns suddenly facing homeschool families across the country, Heather and Todd embarked on a new and exciting phase of their lives together.

Todd shared with Heather all he had talked about with her parents. He had well begun in the book about Christopher's Plan. Though the "m" word did not come up, they had become comfortable speaking of the future as a *shared* future.

They were in no hurry, content to let things develop slowly, allowing Todd's new faith to deepen and expand as he read and studied, and as he and Heather spoke of increasingly deep spiritual things. In addition to the corpus of "Marshall books," Heather supplemented Todd's reading from her own library with books by Schaeffer, Drummond, Kelly, Lewis, the three Commands titles, and of course Thomas Kempis. Todd's hunger was so great he read until nearly midnight every evening, making notes and underlining his own copies of the books.

After David's release and return to the Bar JG, Heather continued to spend several hours a day at the ranch, then gradually resumed her former schedule at the Circle F and in Dorado Hills. She would prefer to spend every waking minute with Todd, but she reminded herself that life had its practicalities.

Todd enjoyed working alongside David *almost* as much as with Heather. He quickly realized why everyone spoke of him with such reverence and respect. He had never met men like David Gordon, Timothy Marshall, Court Masters, Mark Forster, and Charles Reyburn. All three of the local trio were mentors in the new life to which Todd had committed himself. How privileged he felt to work ten to twelve hours a day beside a man of such stature and wisdom as David Gordon.

Soon after David was home, Todd made arrangements to fly back to the East Coast, give notice and move out of his apartment, then return to California where his future awaited him.

The Christian-owned station WJXV hoped his spontaneous on-camera report from David's barn—viewed by a record-breaking audience for the small station and subsequently aired by two national networks—would lead to regular appearances by Todd in front of the camera. The news that he was moving to California came as a blow. They wished him well, however, and promised to air any special broadcasts he might want to film in the future.

He was surprised by the call he received the day of his return to Washington, DC.

"Todd, hello—it's Bradon Rhodes. Ginger told me you were moving out to California."

"I am," replied Todd. "I flew into the city yesterday to wrap things up here and move out of my place. When did you talk to Ginger?"

"A week ago. She called to tell me about her father's arrest and asked if I would talk to my father."

"Did you?"

"Yes, but he was irritated and wanted to know what business it was of mine."

"You don't carry much weight in the Oval Office, I take it?"

"That's putting it mildly," laughed Bradon. "I can't really blame my dad. I haven't exactly been a shining light that has reflected well on him. I'm trying to change that, especially after overhearing him and Mr. Bardolf and trying to warn Mr. Forster, then the accident and everything.

My dad is skeptical about me—I think he considers me a spy. But the reason I called was to see if you needed help moving. I'm only taking one class and mostly boning up on my reading for next term. I've got plenty of time."

"That would be great," said Todd. "Though I'm not planning to take my furniture and big stuff. I'm not quite sure what to do with it. First I've got to box up my office and books and all the personal things I want to take."

"Will you put the rest in storage?"

"I haven't figured that out—I don't know if there's much point. I'm not planning to return."

"If I can help out I'd be glad to. I could sell your things if you like, if you don't get everything dealt with before you go."

"Thanks, I appreciate that."

The relationship between the twenty-four-year-old son of the president and thirty-eight-year-old former NBC star had begun with a few brief exchanges over the previous months, gradually developing into a genuine friendship as together they packed up Todd's apartment, attending to details for his move, cancelling subscriptions and services, renting the trailer and loading it up. With a month after his thirty-day notice before the apartment had to be emptied, Bradon offered to take care of the remaining furniture, sell what he could, and arrange for one of the Goodwill services to pick up the rest. He would also see to the final cleaning once everything was gone.

Todd was appreciative and a little amazed, more convinced than ever that young Rhodes had indeed made significant changes in his life direction. He was delighted to be able to hit the road several weeks sooner than he anticipated.

The day before his departure, a curious almost embarrassed expression came over Bradon's face.

"Would you . . . uh, maybe like some company for the drive?" he asked.

Todd stared back at him.

"You mean . . . what—you want to come with me?"

"If you don't mind. I mean, unless you want to make the drive alone. I don't have class again for a week. Even if I miss one I can make it up."

"That would be great!" exclaimed Todd. "I thought about asking you if you wanted to join me for a road trip. I'd love to have you along!"

"It would be fun, thanks. I'll take care of everything in your apartment when I get back."

"Have you talked to Ginger about it?" asked Todd.

"No," replied Bradon. "But if she doesn't want to see me, I'll hop on a plane back. I'm still trying to make up for the horrible first impression I made," he added laughing. "I don't think she hates me anymore. I guess that's progress."

Todd laughed. "I know she doesn't hate you. We had a good time last month when she and Heather were here."

The following morning, the two young men left Washington about 6:00, drove straight west, taking turns behind the wheel, and pulled into Indianapolis in time for supper where they spent the night. The second day took them to Iowa, and the third to Laramie, Wyoming, where Todd had arranged to spend a day with Harvey and Harriet Jansen. He told them a friend was accompanying him. They assured him his friend would be welcome. He hadn't mentioned his friend's name, though he prepared Bradon for the encounter.

"Shouldn't I stay in a motel or something?" he said. "They won't want me under their roof after what my father did to Mr. Jansen."

"Believe me, you will be most welcome."

"Have you told them I'm coming?"

"I told them I had a friend with me. I didn't tell them your name."

"It's bound to be awkward. I wouldn't blame them for throwing me out."

"You just wait. The people I have become associated with in the last year aren't like any you've ever met. You may be pleasantly surprised."

Notwithstanding Todd's assurances, Bradon was nervous as they drove into the Jansen ranch between five and six after their third long day on the road. Harvey and Harriet were expecting them. They had been sitting on the porch for the past forty-five minutes watching the road, while Harriet went back and forth from the kitchen checking two pies and her pot of beef stew.

They were off the porch and hurrying toward the car almost before the two young men opened the doors.

"Todd!" said Harriet, embracing Todd affectionately. "It is good to see you!"

"And you, Harriet. Hello, Harvey," said Todd, shaking Harvey's hand as the former senator and candidate approached behind his wife.

"Welcome, my dear friend!"

"And . . ." said Todd, glancing to his right where Bradon was sheepishly inching toward them from the other side of the car, "may I introduce you to my friend, Bradon Rhodes."

A look of astonishment spread over Harvey's face as he stared at Bradon in disbelief.

"Not—you don't mean *the* Bradon Rhodes!" he said slowly. "You're not . . . are you the president's son?"

"The very same," smiled Todd.

"Oh, my goodness!" exclaimed Harvey, walking hurriedly around the car with his hand outstretched and a great smile on his face. "Mr. Rhodes! I cannot believe my eyes. It is a great honor to meet you. What a privilege to have you with us—welcome, welcome!"

Bradon had scarcely recovered from Harvey's vigorous handshake when Harriet approached and threw her arms around him.

"I am delighted to meet you, Bradon!" she said stepping back. "May I call you Bradon?"

"Uh, yes . . . sure."

"Then I second my husband's welcome. This is indeed a privilege."

Taken completely by surprise at the outpouring of hospitality, Bradon walked in a daze with the other three toward the house.

The next several hours did nothing to dissuade his astonishment at the reception he had received. He had only come along for the ride. Todd and Mr. Jansen were national figures, far more famous than the president's ne'er-do-well son. Yet the Jansens treated him as a guest of honor.

Scarcely had they finished Harriet's sumptuous supper before friends she had called began arriving to share her renowned apple and peach pies, every one eager to "meet the president's son."

The evening passed in a blur. Never had Bradon experienced anything like it. Accustomed either to being the black sheep of the family, or being overshadowed by his grandfather's and father's reputations, suddenly he found himself surrounded by people who seemed to value *him*—though he couldn't imagine why—who wanted to know what he thought about things, about life in a famous family, and what were his perspectives on the changes in the culture.

As the evening progressed and the conversation gradually moved toward deeper spiritual topics, he hardly understood a fraction of what they were talking about—Christlikeness and the commands and someone named Paul and the prodigal son and another man called Benedict and the kingdom of the world and the Ally—he hadn't a clue what it was all about. But there was no doubt about the warmth he felt among these people, whom he didn't know any better than they knew him.

Strange as it was to say, he felt *loved.* What an extraordinary thing!

He lay in bed when the evening was over, staring up at the ceiling, overwhelmed, still in a stupor of warm and pleasant bewilderment. Strange as it was to say, he felt more at home in this bed and in this room and in this house in faraway Laramie, Wyoming, than he had ever felt at the Presidential Manor. His father would call this the sticks. But he felt *good* here!

Todd and Bradon spent two days with the Jansens. Midway through the afternoon of the second day, Bradon, who had never been on the back of a horse in his life, was wearing a cowboy hat and an old pair of Harvey's boots, and was riding down out of the hills beyond the Jansen ranch alongside Todd, Harvey, and Harriet at the completion of a two-hour ride broken at the halfway point by lunch beside Laramie Falls.

What kind of a time warp have I entered! thought Bradon.

He glanced over at Harvey with pistol and holster strapped to his side—in case of rattlers or wolves he'd said.

This was the man his father had ridiculed. Bradon now realized Harvey Jansen was one of the most honorable men he had ever met.

23

A Rhodes Returns to California's Foothills

BRADON'S EXPRESSION as they pulled out of Laramie the following morning was one of mingled disbelief and incomprehensibility. He did not know what to make of it all. No one in his family's circle of friends or life in the spotlight could have prepared him for this.

After warm handshakes and hugs and assurances from both Jansens that he was welcome any time, and that they hoped he would consider the Jansen ranch a second home, he hardly spoke for half the day.

"An amazing man," Bradon said about noon after a long stretch of silence. "He would have made a good president."

Todd did not reply. Neither did he feel talkative. He had absorbed enough from the loan of Heather's copy of Thomas Kempis to know that silence must be allowed to do its work without a multitude of words diluting the power of the still, small voice.

After crossing the salt flats and a night in Elko, Nevada, their final day of four hundred miles was their shortest. They pulled into the Bar JG about 4:30. David and Heather were waiting for them.

Though David and Bradon had never met, and though hearing about him during the trip, Bradon displayed no nervousness when meeting the host for his visit to California. After his brief encounters with Mark and Grace in Washington, his blossoming friendship with Todd, and the remarkable reception he had received at the Jansen ranch, he was getting used to the fact, as Todd described it, that his new circle of friends were unlike anything he had come to expect from his father's political crowd.

Nor did David change that impression.

"I am delighted to meet you, Bradon!" he said, shaking his hand with a vise grip belying his eighty years. "Come with me, my boy," he added with a wink. "Let's give these two lovebirds a few minutes to themselves! I'll show you where you'll be bunking."

David, who stood an inch or two taller than the president's son, led him toward the ranch house, one arm slung around his shoulder as if they had been friends for years. Heather and Todd wandered off hand in hand, joining them in the house fifteen minutes later. David and his guest were already chatting freely.

As hard as she tried not to show it, Heather knew Ginger was excited about Bradon's visit. Aware of the potential awkwardness, she had arranged for David and the two young men to have dinner at the Circle F that evening.

After Todd and Bradon were settled in, they drove over to the Forster ranch about 5:30, Todd riding with Heather, Bradon in David's pickup.

Everyone was eager to see Todd again. Greetings were enthusiastic, especially from Craig who was outside as they drove up.

"Craig," said Todd, "meet Bradon Rhodes—son of our president."

"Hey, Craig," said Bradon, shaking Craig's hand. "Todd tells me you're a vintage Mustang enthusiast. I've got an old '65 back in DC."

"Wow, that must be worth a fortune!"

"It might be if it was in pristine shape!" laughed Bradon. "It runs, but that's about all it's got going for it. I should say it *did* run, before I rolled it. It's in the shop now. It's definitely seen better days."

"It wasn't totaled in the accident?"

"It's salvageable. I've got a guy fixing it. The engine and drive train are okay but a lot of body work. But Mustang parts are easy to find."

"What color is it?" asked Craig.

"Green."

"Not grabber green!"

"No, those weren't made till '69. They were kind of weird-looking anyway. Mine's the dark highland green—same as Steve McQueen's in *Bullitt*. It's my favorite of the Mustang greens."

"Sweet—I'd love to see it!"

"I'm going to have him overhaul the engine too. Once it's fixed and repainted it will be even better than before. You come to DC and I'll put you behind the wheel."

Hearing the greetings, the others walked out of the house. Ginger crept alongside her brother. Bradon glanced toward her and smiled.

"Hi," she said sheepishly.

"Ginger! Hi yourself!" said Bradon. Before he knew what he had done, he found himself stepping back after giving her a hug.

"Sorry!" he laughed. "I am just glad to see you."

Ginger's face turned bright red. She was rescued by her parents.

"Bradon," said Mark, coming forward and shaking his hand. "It is good to see you again. Welcome to California, and to our ranch."

"Thank you. Mr. Forster," said Bradon.

"You've abandoned your crutch, I see. How's the leg?"

"Nearly back to normal. I feel it now and then, but the doctor's given me a clean bill of health."

"Hello, Mrs. Forster," he said, smiling and shaking Grace's hand.

"None of that *Mister* and *Mrs.* formality here, Bradon," said Mark. "This is ranch country—we put on no airs. Come with me a minute. I want to introduce you to the real Mr. and Mrs. Forster."

He led Bradon to his folks who were chatting with Heather and Todd.

"Mom, Dad," said Mark, "I want you to meet Jeff's son Bradon. Bradon, these are my parents, the *real* Mr. and Mrs. Forster, Robert and Laura. This is their ranch. They're just letting me pretend it's mine. They knew your dad when he was younger than you."

"Good to see you, young Rhodes," said Robert. "Mark's right, your dad was here with us a couple of times. What were you boys then, Mark, fourteen . . . fifteen?"

"Something like that, Dad!" laughed Mark.

"We even got your dad on a horse. But then he had to go and get famous and become president! Anyway, it's good to have a second-generation Rhodes back in the foothills."

"Thank you, sir—uh, *Mr.* Forster," he added with a grin toward Mark. "Todd and I actually did a little riding in Wyoming on our way here."

"Good for you! Wyoming—now that's *real* ranch country!"

Having recovered her embarrassment, Ginger was standing a few feet away listening. Bradon made a graceful departure and walked toward her.

"Hi again," he said with a smile. "I promise, no more hugs!"

Ginger smiled. "That's okay. It took me by surprise, that's all."

"Me too!" Bradon laughed.

"Did you . . . uh, have a good trip out?"

"Yeah. I saw a lot of the country I'd never seen before. We spent two days in Wyoming."

"With the Jansens—Heather told me. They're really nice people."

"You know them?"

"They've been here a time or two."

"Really, what for?"

"They sometimes come to our Christian group."

"Oh . . . right. I should have figured. They were amazing. After, you know, my dad and the last election, they treated me like I was their own son. By all rights they should have despised me. They were unbelievable. No hard feelings at all. They taught me to ride. Todd and I had a great time."

"You and I will have to take the horses out," said Ginger. "Is your leg able to ride?"

"I rode a little in Wyoming. I'm still a bit sore."

"I can't wait to show you around. We have so many great places to ride."

"Don't get too carried away!" laughed Bradon. "I'm a complete novice!"

"We'll take our first ride with Heather. She's our expert horsewoman. She'll have you as comfortable in the saddle of a live mustang as behind the wheel of your old green Mustang in no time."

"What do you know about my Mustang?"

"I was listening!"

24

A Ride to Rustler's Butte

TWO DAYS later, Bradon Rhodes was scheduled to fly out of Sacramento on the following morning. He would like to have stayed on indefinitely. He now saw, or perhaps *felt*, what it was here that drew Todd. It wasn't simply being out of Washington or even being in the country or on a ranch.

It was the *people*!

These people were *different*. It was as if they were from another world. It wasn't just Ginger. It was *all* of them.

But he had things to do, making the final arrangements for Todd's apartment among them, as well as catching up on his summer school class and getting ready for school in the fall. Most of all, he was the president's son. He couldn't fly under the radar indefinitely. He'd been lucky to have three days in California without the paparazzi showing up. He didn't dare stay longer, especially knowing that Ginger's father was being watched. When he and Todd left DC, he told no one of his plans. But if his father found out where he'd been, he would hit the roof.

He probably knew already! thought Bradon.

For the sake of Ginger's family and the rest of these new friends, he couldn't risk staying longer. Though it would be a culture shock leaving this peaceful setting and returning to the eye of the storm.

He lived at the very heart of it—in the Presidential Manor!

After being here he wasn't sure he wanted to be at the eye of that storm any longer. Maybe he should move out and try living his own life. His sister, Melissa, a senior at Georgetown, had managed to do so.

Knowing it was his last day in California, Ginger planned a long ride and picnic on Rustlers Butte.

"It's everyone's favorite ride," she said.

"It sounds intimidating!" laughed Bradon. "Do you think I can do it? I'm still only a few days from my first ride at Harvey and Harriet's."

"We'll take it slow—of course you can do it."

They set out about eleven, across the pasture into the woodland, Ginger leading the way along the well-worn trail Heather always used for beginning riders. After about an hour, she led onto a narrower path that began to climb more steeply.

"We've got a bit of a climb up to the summit," she called back over her shoulder. "If you're uncomfortable, we can walk the horses. Just holler."

Bradon gripped the reins and saddle horn for dear life on the steepest parts but was determined to see it through. When they finally crested onto the plateau of the summit, he let out a long sigh of relief.

"That was a stretch for a city boy like me!" he said. "I wasn't sure I could make it."

"For your first week in the saddle," rejoined Ginger, "I would say congratulations are definitely in order!"

"I don't know how deserved they are. But coming from you, I'll take it."

"What do you mean, coming from me?"

"I don't know, just that you're an experienced expert."

"I'm nothing compared to Heather."

"Well, you're years ahead of me, and—"

He stopped.

"And what!" laughed Ginger as she reined in and they dismounted.

"Nothing."

"No way. You were about to say something."

"Only that you're years ahead of me in more ways than just on the back of a horse."

"What are you talking about? You're older than me. I'm twenty-three—didn't you tell my dad when you were talking you were twenty-four?"

"Yeah, but I didn't mean like that. I just mean that you've got life figured out, I guess I would say. You know who you are, what you believe. Your parents are your best friends. I envy you. I've got nothing figured out—especially now."

"What do you mean, especially now?" asked Ginger as she unpacked lunch from the saddle bags.

"Being here, you know, with you and your folks and Mr. Gordon and Todd and the Marshalls—it's opened my eyes to a different way of looking at things. It's *so* different. Opened isn't even accurate because I don't really understand everything. My eyes are *beginning* to open would be more like it. Driving out with Todd was amazing. He told me about his journey . . . his spiritual journey. A remarkable thing—he was so involved in politics! He was a famous guy. He's walked away from it all to clean manure out of stalls and mend fences and dig ditches. And he loves it!"

He paused thoughtfully.

"I'd never thought about God or anything like that in my life," he went on after a moment. "Not that my grandmother didn't occasionally try!" he added chuckling. "Then talking to you that day a year ago on Bainbridge Island—it was like getting jabbed with a red-hot poker."

"I'm sorry," said Ginger. "I didn't mean to do *that*. Was I too blunt?"

"Blunt, yes. But not *too* blunt. It was what I needed to hear. You nailed me. You didn't even know me, yet you were honest enough not to be impressed by who I was, honest enough to speak the truth to me. I tried to laugh it off. I tried for weeks. But I couldn't dislodge your words from my brain—*Don't you care what kind of person you are, what kind of person you are becoming?* The truth was, I *didn't* care. I had never even thought that I was *becoming* anything. I just took life as it came. Then you zeroed right into the heart of who I was. It wasn't a pretty sight.

"Which reminds me—I need to apologize for some of the things I said that day. I am mortified at my behavior. I was arrogant, dismissive, rude, and crude. I am so sorry. I suppose all that came back to me during the months when I couldn't stop thinking about our conversation. You were exactly right. I was on my way to becoming an immature, selfish—I don't even know what . . . a jerk, I guess."

"Well, I'm glad God used it to begin the growth process," said Ginger. "If I was too blunt, I'm sorry too. I can be that way sometimes."

"I'm glad you were. I needed somebody to splash cold water in my face. But when you say the growth process, is that what you mean by becoming the kind of person you want to be?"

"I suppose so," nodded Ginger. "The first step is knowing what kind of person you *want* to be, then growing toward it."

"That sure describes Todd. He has become a different person. So is there hope for someone like me?"

"Are you kidding! Of course. Todd was ten years older than you are before God began to wake him up. You're years ahead of him!" she added laughing.

"You're just trying to make me feel good."

"I'm sure Todd would tell you the same thing. You and I are young, Bradon. We've got our whole lives ahead of us. Some people don't wake up to life's realities until their forties or fifties, or even later. You're beginning to ask life's important questions at twenty-four."

It grew silent for a few minutes as they slowly ate their sandwiches and corn chips.

"My dad ran up here when he was young," said Ginger reflectively. "He was a track star in high school and college. Set records and everything."

"Really."

"He brought Craig and me on rides here on our birthdays every year along the same trail you and I took."

She thought a second or two. "I wonder if he and your dad ever came up here together. I know they rode when your father visited the ranch."

"I don't know," said Bradon slowly. "My dad never talks about when he was young. Why did they grow so apart, your dad and my dad, when they were best friends?"

"I don't know. My dad grieves over it, I can tell. He loves your dad. My mom knew your dad back in college too. She thinks your dad was behind my dad's arrest."

"I could hardly imagine that," said Bradon slowly. "But when I asked him about it, he got pretty upset. Sometimes I wonder who he is—who *he's* become," he added. "I suppose he's become, like you said before, exactly what he *wanted* to become."

He paused thoughtfully, even a little sadly.

"I'm not sure anything would surprise me," he said after a few seconds. "My mom talked to him about the arrest too. That made him even angrier. Sometimes I don't know what's with my dad. I'm sorry I wasn't of much help when you called."

"Maybe you were. He and David were released."

"*David* . . . Mr. Gordon?"

Ginger nodded. "He was arrested with my dad."

"I didn't realize that. I can't imagine why."

"He's sort of the spiritual head, I guess you would say, along with Heather's parents, of the group we're part of."

"Oh, of course—that my dad is so suspicious of, I heard him and Bardolf talking about. It's so ridiculous. What would be going on? After being here I see firsthand how absurd my dad's suspicions are."

Again it was silent. Realizing it was his last day in California, Bradon drank in the tranquility of the mountain setting as if savoring a memory he was not sure he would experience again.

"What you said before," he said at length, "about God using our conversation in Seattle to begin waking me up or whatever it was you said. Does he really do that? I mean how does that work—it was you talking, not God?"

"How else can God speak but through people," replied Ginger, "and through our thoughts? What you said about not being able to get that conversation out of your mind—that was him too. He was reminding you of it, speaking to you by reminding you of what you and I talked about."

"That's a pretty radical idea—God speaking to *me*!"

Ginger did not reply. What Bradon had said was enough. She let his own words sink in.

"There's another thing I've wanted to tell you about that day in Seattle," Bradon said after a minute. "All that stuff about me being a wild party guy—it really wasn't true. I know you'd heard that. You said something about it that day. It pained me when I remembered. I didn't want you thinking that way about me. I mean, my first years in college I suppose I wasn't very serious as a student. But I wasn't a drinker. I had no girlfriend. I dated some, but nothing serious. The president's playboy son was all fiction."

"Why did people think that?" asked Ginger.

"I think it originated from a picture some reporter took my freshman year. I'd gone to a movie with some others, both girls and guys. It wasn't even a date. When we came out, we were laughing and talking and the photographer caught a terrible expression on my face and one of the girls was looking at me—I think I'd just cracked a joke or something. It was completely innocent. But then it was printed in the paper the next day with the caption, 'Senator's Son the Life of the Party,' and it went on from there. It served their purpose to make more of it than there was. Before I knew it, I had a playboy reputation. I'm embarrassed to say I went along with it. I thought it was cool. I suppose it gave me a certain status. I can't believe I'm saying that. How stupid could I be? I'm mortified for you to have heard those things about me."

"I wouldn't worry about it too much. I think of you as you are now. None of that matters. You have grown beyond it."

"All through high school and college when other guys were doing some not very nice things, something my grandmother said to me when I was eleven never left me. 'Bradon,' she said, 'never allow yourself to do anything you would be embarrassed for me to see you doing. If you remember that, it will help you to be a virtuous young man and will prepare you one day for marriage. Remain pure, Bradon, because I will be watching, and God will be watching.' I hardly knew what to think of it. I never thought of myself as any different from anyone else. I wasn't particularly virtuous, like she said, though something inside me kept me from wanting to drink or swear or . . . well, you know the worse things. I knew it was wrong. I never forgot what my grandmother said. I knew she prayed for me too."

"There, you see. God was speaking to you through your grandmother too. I've met her, did you know that?"

"No—really? When?"

"Last April when some people were here."

"The gathering my dad got so upset about."

"She's known my dad for years. Now that you've told me that story, I can see that God has had his sights on you a long time, Bradon Rhodes. God wants you for a son."

Bradon took in the words, though he hardly grasped their full import.

After another fifteen minutes, they headed back down the mountain the way they had come.

"I did tell you, didn't I," said Bradon, "that I'm planning to stop off for a couple days in Laramie on the way home?"

"Yes—to see the Jansens again. They were here last April too."

"Yeah, that's one of the things that upset my dad so much. He's convinced they're out to get him."

"The Jansens met your grandmother too. But I'm not sure why you're going to see them again."

Bradon laughed. "Neither am I! I guess I just want to know them better. They have no children of their own. I felt like they were treating *me* as a son."

"I didn't realize they had no children."

"They invited me, and, well . . . I felt loved when I was there is the only way to say it. I know my folks love me and all that. But growing up in the whirlwind of the capital, with my dad's endless meetings and elections, and now living in the Presidential Manor . . . I hardly saw my dad growing up. We lived in a fishbowl. Being with the Jansens, just sitting around in a quiet atmosphere talking, or not talking . . . it felt like home. I felt more comfortable than I ever am in Washington. Harvey and Harriet are *nice* people."

The next morning, after leaving David and stopping by the Circle F for goodbyes to everyone there, Todd drove Bradon into the valley and to the airport for his flight to Laramie.

25

A Tense Summer

THE ARRESTS, news reports, and conspiracy rumors gradually faded from the twenty-four-hour news cycle. The country at large soon forgot them, assuming that whatever nonsense the far-right Christian group had been up to, it hadn't been that serious. Most never knew whether or not the two men were released from jail, and didn't much care.

Tensions ran high for Christians through the summer of 2051. The evangelical segment of Christendom, even among its progressive wing, could hardly keep from noticing the ramped up anti-Christian rhetoric, and a vague sense of disquiet. If a former well-known pastor and friend of Ward Hutchins could be arrested, what did that signal about the church's future?

Churches were already being taxed—their tax-exempt status ancient history. What might be next? Were more restrictions inevitable?

The concerns were far greater among congregations with homeschooling families and churches operating private or charter schools. They had all been receiving the new education mandates. Suddenly the debate about what to do became very personal.

Word of the abduction, as some called it, or more kindly, the *removal* of the Statler children from their homes, spread through the homeschool community like a brushfire before a high wind. Parents were afraid. The discussions were far-reaching and daily about how far they might go in complying with the required curriculum and testing, while protecting their children from the worst of it.

That no more children had been "removed" was an encouraging sign. At least no one knew of others. But the fear spread that what had happened to the Statlers was only the beginning.

Threatening notices continued to families and schools that failed to send in the required documentation. Personal visits followed. It appeared to most that they *must* go along or potentially lose their children. Better, they reasoned, *they* teach about homosexuality and gender choice and white racism than that progressives and obviously biased gay instructors teach them.

Worst of all was having to explain pornographic images to their children as the lesser evil alongside the horrifying possibility of a lesbian or gay official doing so, all the while encouraging children to experiment with what they saw in the pictures, and to resist their parents' old-fashioned and restrictive Christian ideas. The greatest fear was that their children would be encouraged to demand sex change operations, to which by law, after reaching the age of eleven, they were entitled even against parental opposition.

The debate raged within Christian circles how to meet the crisis. Future generations of children were at stake.

Complicating matters were the unwitting informants, some with innocent motives, others not so much, whose loose tongues came within hearing of this or that individual who knew someone who knew someone else, as gradually more potential "troublemakers" were added to governmental watch lists.

Every church had an Edith Holt, and a cadre of allies ever seeking to ingratiate themselves with the powerful. Their ilk would sooner side with officialdom for the crumbs of importance it gave them than be caught dead associating with the likes of one like Mark Forster or David Gordon.

Most churches had men and women of high virtue, spiritual character, and wisdom just like they had their Edith Holts. But the David Gordons were more difficult to identify, saying little, calling no attention to themselves, seeking neither leadership nor the spotlight. They mostly remained out of the vortex of church "affairs" whose tone was set by the Ally.

Thus the Ally spread its net to ensnare go-along believers in Christendom's worldly churches. The Edith Holts of those congregations, however, had never heard of either the Ally or the remnant, and would scoff if they were explained to them.

26

Apprenticeship Begins

STRANGE AS it seemed, the departure of Bradon Rhodes from the intertwining life of the Gordon and Forster ranches left a vacuum none of them anticipated. His bright, curious, hungry, and surprisingly humble demeanor was a stimulus not only to Ginger but also to Todd, David, Heather, and everyone in the Forster and Marshall families. Whether or not it could accurately be said that he was spiritually searching, he was definitely on a road of growth leading in that direction.

Their ever-expanding common life fellowship was moving unexpectedly straight toward the heart of the Jefferson Rhodes family!

But as Bradon Rhodes was moving closer to that life, it was obvious that Diane Statler was sinking. She never recovered from the effects of having her three older children ripped out of her heart, as to her it seemed they had been. After their return following a month in the government-run educational facility, life in the Statler home could never return to normal. The children were scarred, somber, confused, questioning, fearful, and damaged.

Nightmares were a nightly occurrence. They had been changed forever.

Meanwhile, Todd had never enjoyed life so much. He completed the book about Christopher's Plan while in DC and was eager to embark on his apprenticeship in earnest, mentored and spiritually shepherded by Heather's father and mother as well as the other two men God had brought into his life.

Working together, he and David grew closer than most thirty-eight-year-olds would imagine they could feel toward a man more than twice their age. He read every book suggested by Heather or her parents and studied the Bible according to the reading plan Timothy set up for him. Throughout most days he and David discussed the Christlike life, Christian ideas, even doctrine. The influences of the men and women surrounding him fed into Todd's blossoming soul the expansive principles of an outlook on life and the world unimaginable a few years before.

He spent most Saturday afternoons with Timothy and Jaylene. They shared family principles of authority and family structure that were completely foreign to him. Yet all he was learning fit together like an intricate puzzle of truth—every piece occupying its perfect place in the whole.

Never had Todd felt so invigorated and alive. Though he recognized himself a babe in the faith, his developing friendship with Craig Forster, a mature young college man, was like that between an older and younger brother. They had *fun* together, went to old car shows around the Sacramento area, jogged and cycled on the American River Trail, and often worked side by side at one or the other of the neighboring ranches throughout the summer prior to Craig's senior year at Sac State. Their conversations were not so deep as Todd's with David. But Craig's character rubbed off, rounding out the picture deepening within Todd—though he did not know it as such—of what the true Church was.

Not growing up in an institutional church, Todd remained unaware how radically different the perspectives of his new friends actually were from most of organized Christendom. He assumed that all Christians and churches shared a similar outlook. He would learn in time what a radically distinct microcosm of the eternal Church he had stumbled into—rather, been *led* to—when wandering away from the crowd on Bainbridge Island.

His journey was one all true Christians must eventually engage in, or else wither into lifelessness in their pews. It was the quest to discover the eternal Temple, for the building of which they were being fashioned into living stones.

Gradually the Marshall outlook, as some called it, penetrated into every corner of Todd's being by spiritual osmosis, and changed every facet of his life.

27

The Freedom Bill

DURING THE summer of Todd's apprenticeship with David, events on the national stage were escalating. While Todd grew strong and tan in the California sun, Mike Bardolf was busy.

His twelve proposed presidential commissions took shape and began functioning according to the guidelines he had established. Hamad Bahram was now chairman of the Religion Commission. Mike's Committee for Enforcement was expanded to every state and all major US cities.

Among Bardolf's more ruthless proteges whom he put in charge of this enforcement committee was a relatively young man of thirty-five, Bruno Volker, with the FBI for twelve years, son of a Palladium member, and, if anything, more merciless than he was himself. If Mike had been capable of fear, he might even have been a little afraid of Bruno. As it was, his only fear was not being in control. Thus far, young Volker did not threaten that.

He gave Volker orders to spare no effort to locate the so-called Benedict Brief, and to use whatever means of intimidation were necessary to get that information from the leaders of the cell groups associated with the Marshall-Forster organization. All his efforts thus far had been in vain. No one had heard of it. Even Volker, a man as suspicious as Mike Bardolf, was convinced they were telling the truth.

Meanwhile, Mike completed converting his Freedom Manifesto into the new presidential bill which they dubbed the "Freedom Bill." He presented it to the president, then, with but a few minor changes,

Rhodes invited new Speaker Ross Black and Senate Majority Leader Nawar Aswad and his dozen most trusted allies in both congressional chambers to the Oval Office to present the bill. The president stressed its importance in light of the ongoing conspiracy threat originating out of its California nucleus. Meanwhile, that threat continued to be investigated by the FBI.

The sweeping proposals of the bill against conservative and Christian groups and churches raised a few eyebrows even among these highly progressive congressional leaders. But Rhodes emphasized that the danger was present and real.

In the end they all agreed to get it through their respective chambers virtually intact. After the removal of the Bill of Rights from the Constitution during the administration of President Samara, none saw constitutional roadblocks to its passage.

It would probably be best, however, noted Ms. Aswad, that the specifics of the bill be kept out of the news and shielded from the American people.

28

Private Meeting in Laramie

August 2051

IN AUGUST Todd received a totally unexpected telephone call. It was from Bradon Rhodes.

"Todd, it's Bradon. Everything's wrapped up with your apartment. I've got your deposit and I'll send it to you."

"Keep it—you earned it."

"No way, man!" laughed Bradon. "It's your money, not mine."

The line went quiet as Bradon grew serious. "That's not the main reason I called," he resumed after a few seconds. "I have what might be a crazy request. I've been thinking about a lot of things—stuff you've said, things Ginger told me. I'm starting school in a few weeks. After that my life's going to get pretty hectic with all the demands of pre-law. I was wondering, if you could get away. What would you think about meeting me at the Jansen ranch? I'd like to talk to you."

"Sure," replied Todd. "But why don't you come out here? Everyone would love to see you."

"I need to do this without Ginger knowing," Bradon replied. "The things I want to talk to you about . . . she can't think she's the reason. I mean, in a way she is. She's the one who got me thinking in the first place. But you know what I mean, I can't have her thinking I'm doing it, you know, to impress her or something."

"Fair enough. I get that. Why at the Jansens?"

"I'm comfortable there. I need to be away from distractions, either in Washington or California. And it's nice not to be watched every minute."

"And your father—what does he think about you becoming so friendly with his onetime political rival?"

"He doesn't know. I wouldn't dare tell him. He doesn't know about any of it—my visit there, the Jansens."

"Does he know I'm living in California?"

"I don't know. Probably. He's watching what's going on with the group. I've picked up hints that he and Bardolf are still convinced the group is political and that Mark and the others are planning something against him. Luckily, I've managed to drop out of the news since abandoning my playboy image. My mom and dad are too busy being the president and First Lady to keep track of everything I do. So far they haven't associated me with the rest of you. I'm sure Bardolf knows, but for some reason he hasn't told my dad. That's exactly how I want to keep it. When I fly I use my mom's maiden name, Bradon Nelson. So it's halfway legit. Your pal Masters got me a driver's license as Bradon Nelson, so no one pays much attention. So far I've been lucky."

"Your dad's bound to find out eventually."

"I'll cross that bridge then."

"Well, to answer your question, I'd be happy to come to Laramie. I suppose I could use my apartment deposit for that. Let me know when and I'll be there. It will be good to see Harvey and Harriet again."

☆ ☆ ☆

A week later Bradon arrived in Laramie a day and a half before Todd drove into the ranch in his rental car from the Cheyenne airport an hour away. He was almost shocked, though delighted, to see how comfortable Bradon was with the Jansens. He was reminded of his own developing friendship with the three California men. Unlike him, Bradon had grown up with a father. But often a young man needs additional mentoring beyond what a father is able to provide. It seemed that Harvey Jansen, as unlikely as it could have been foreseen, was filling that role in the life of the son of the president.

Harriet was obviously beside herself to have a young man to cook for and make a fuss over. She poured out all her latent maternal instincts on their young guest. Though the Jansens had worked with young people all their lives as teachers, having Bradon in their home was especially meaningful to them.

"I'm afraid we only have the one guest room, Todd," she said apologetically. "We're now calling it Bradon's room. It's large and has two beds. I hope you won't mind sharing."

"Of course not. We city boys are learning the ranch life, aren't we, Bradon," laughed Todd. "Being bunk mates is part of it, right—the Jansen bunkhouse!"

The rest of the day was spent chatting informally, walking about the ranch, and a drive through Laramie with Harvey and Harriet as their guides. The tour included a stop at the school where both taught and was the scene of the heroics that made Harvey famous.

"I am so happy to be back in the classroom after my brief stint in politics," he said. "With respect to your father, Bradon, it's not a world I was comfortable in or one, in my opinion, that cultivates personal character and Christlikeness."

The word hung in the air a moment, then Bradon smiled.

"I'm still not used to the way you people talk," he said. "I've never even heard half the words you use. Like *Christlikeness*—what a thing to say? What a thing to aspire to? Yet you talk as if it were the most natural thing in the world."

"As it is, Bradon, my boy," rejoined Harvey. "There was a book a great Chinese Christian wrote about a century ago called *The Normal Christian Life*. Unfortunately, there's not much in the book about Christlikeness. However, the title may be the most important part of the book. Some of us who get together occasionally at Mark's or David's in California call our experience together the *common* life. Growing into Christlikeness is meant to be the common, normal, everyday life that Jesus's disciples are supposed to live."

Again Bradon laughed. "There it is again," he said. "Disciples! Who talks like that, as if anyone can be a disciple, not just those twelve men in the first century."

"Anyone can. *Everyone* ought to be. Discipleship in Christ is the only goal in life that matters."

They drove the rest of the way back to the ranch in silence.

A dinner feast from Harriet's hand, capped off by pie and ice cream, left the two young men bursting physically and spiritually from the outpouring of friendly hospitality.

29

A Late Talk

"I SEE YOU brought some good reading with you," said Todd when they were alone in their room later that evening, nodding toward three books on the nightstand beside Bradon's bed.

"Ginger sent them," replied Bradon. "She and I've been writing a lot. I'm working my way through them, but it's heavy going. The ideas are so new."

"It was the same for me. I read Heather's mother's book *Discovering Einstein in Genesis* and her dad's more recent book *The Essentials of Living Christian Discipleship.* After that it was her grandfather's books. I felt overwhelmed at first."

"Tell me about it!"

"It's a lot to take in. It's a whole new outlook on life."

"That's why I wanted to talk to you. I mean, I love Harvey and Harriet—they're really good to me. Obviously, I'm pretty fond of Ginger too. Despite what my father did to David and Mark, her whole family has welcomed me, like everyone in California. But you're different."

"How so?"

"They've all been Christians, as far as I know, most of their lives, or for a long time at least. Yesterday Harvey and Harriet explained a lot of things. It was great—really helpful. But you're new at it. You came from the same background as me—politics, Washington, the liberal world, public school where everything you're taught comes out of the progressive playbook. We grew up probably thinking similarly—you know, like everyone else does in that world. I never even knew people like the Forsters and Marshalls existed! Yet when you met these people and encountered these new ways of thinking, you know, like I said earlier—Christlikeness and being disciples and all that—you figured out what it meant. Or I assume you did. You seem comfortable with it now."

"I'm still learning," said Todd. "It took me a while. But yes, I'm comfortable with it. I see that it represents truth—a truth the modern world doesn't want anyone to know about. Now that I see it clearly, I'm hungry to learn and grow and absorb as much as I can. I'll never go back. Who wouldn't rather have the truth than all the nonsense the world *pretends* is true?"

"But you *did* figure it out. That's what I want to know—I want to know *how* you made sense of it all."

Todd nodded thoughtfully.

"A tall order," he said. "I read a lot, like you're doing. I asked a million questions. Heather was patient with me. I began learning how to pray. That was weird and a little frightening at first. It was a long, slow, learning and growing process. But I was hungry. I *wanted* to understand. I *wanted* my life to mean more. So I didn't resist the new ideas. I took them in and tried to be objective and asked myself if they made sense."

They continued to talk, Bradon full of questions, until well past midnight.

30

Two Young Men of Virtue

THE NEXT day, the three men spent about the ranch—Harriet coming and going between her kitchen and their outdoor activities—with two rides on horseback, much talk, and a deepening camaraderie between the two young men and the wise, soft-spoken teacher, former senator, and presidential candidate. Harvey's second love behind Harriet was teaching God's truth and Christian character to growing young people. He could not have enjoyed the day more.

That evening the conversation between the four continued to stretch the two young men's minds. Harvey and Harriet shared their own personal stories, which neither Todd nor Bradon had heard before, as well as many insights and principles about Christian marriage and God's intended role in which for husbands and wives to function together. Everything dovetailed with what Todd was learning from Heather's parents.

Much of it sounded archaic and strange in Bradon's ears. But they insisted they were timeless biblical principles that applied as much to relationships between men and women in 2051 as they did in 1951 or 1851 or even AD 51.

"The modern world might think them ridiculous," said Harriet. "But the fragmented state of the family, and the divorce and infidelity rate, makes it clear the feminist model doesn't work."

It was equally obvious to the two young men that Harriet Jansen, like Grace Forster and Jaylene Marshall, was a contented and fulfilled woman, with a career and an affirming husband, both of whom believed in the scriptural roles of men and women, functioning in balance, harmony, and mutual respect. Bradon clearly saw the difference in their marriage and that of his parents.

Bradon and Todd went for a long walk the following morning prior to Todd's drive back to Cheyenne preparatory for a 4:00 return flight to Sacramento that evening.

It was quiet for several minutes as they left the ranch house. Inside, Harriet and Harvey watched them retreat into the distance.

"A couple of fine young men," said Harriet quietly. "What might God be doing with them?"

"We may be looking at the next generation of leaders in the BCL movement," mused Harvey. "Three years ago during the campaign, who could have expected Jefferson Rhodes's son to become like a son to *us*? God always has more up his sleeve than we can imagine."

Harriet laughed. "You do have a way of putting things, Harvey! But you are right."

☆ ☆ ☆

"I, uh . . ." Bradon began as he and Todd continued slowly away from the house, "I think I want to be a Christian, though I'm still not entirely sure I even know what that means. But I want to be a better person, a growing person, you know—the kind of person someone like Ginger can be proud of and maybe even look up to someday. Or who you can be proud of . . . that I can be proud of myself."

A smile came over Bradon's face. "I guess the most important thing," he added, "is to become a person *God* can be proud of."

"That's kind of an amazing idea," said Todd. "I've never thought of that. But you're right."

"So what do I do, Todd? I'm still intimidated by words like *disciple* and *Christlikeness* and some of the other things. What makes someone a disciple or just a Christian at all? How does someone like me who doesn't know anything—how do you start? What do you do?"

It was quiet a long while as they walked along. Finally, Todd drew in a deep breath.

"Why are you asking me?" he said in a serious tone. "Wouldn't you rather ask Harvey or Mark or David—someone who's more an expert than me? I'm only about a year ahead of you!" he added, laughing. "I'm still a spiritual novice."

"That's exactly why I'm asking you," rejoined Bradon. "I don't want an expert. I've learned a lot from Harvey and Harriet, don't get me wrong. I love them like second parents." He paused and chuckled. "Harriet said that from now on their guest room will be my room. My poor dad would have a fit if he knew where I was. But what I am asking now, I need to hear it from you. What did *you* do?"

Again it was quiet. Todd was thinking hard. Bradon's question was completely unexpected.

"I guess the first thing I would say," he began at length, "is that if you want to be a person Ginger and God and you can be proud of, is to start being that person. *Be* a person you can be proud of. Be good, kind, considerate, unselfish. I think that's where it begins. From what I can see you are already doing that. I should say, *trying* to do that because that's all anyone can do—*try* to live in Christlike ways. We may not always do it very well—I don't feel I do—but in the trying, God takes up the slack. That's how Heather explained it to me. Every step you take with one foot, it's like he strengthens the muscles in the other leg to take the next step. I just made that up," he added laughing. "I'm not sure if that's a good analogy!"

"Why do you say I'm already doing it when I don't even claim to be a Christian?" asked Bradon.

"You're trying to be better, aren't you? Trying to grow."

"Yeah, I think so."

"That's where it starts. In my experience, being a Christian doesn't happen all at once. Maybe for some people it does. But it wasn't that way for me. It was a progressive thing. I grew, I learned, I tried to pay attention to how I thought and behaved. Gradually the ideas and perspectives of what being a Christian meant got into me. I absorbed them and tried to understand them and make sense of them. Remember, I'm no authority, that's for sure! I don't know if that's how it's supposed to happen, but that's how it was for me. I see that same progression in you.

You've changed a lot since the first time we met, Bradon. That's what I mean. You ask how to start—you've already started. You started when you decided you *wanted* to change, *wanted* to become better."

"Ginger's always talking about becoming," nodded Bradon.

"You *are* becoming, as I hope I am. Another thing Heather's taught me is to ask for God's help—help to grow, help to be good and kind and unselfish, help to understand who he is and what he wants."

"By asking for God's help . . . you mean pray?"

"That's what I mean. It's a little strange at first. But it gets easier."

"Who should I pray to—God or Jesus?"

"It doesn't matter. Both . . . or either one. Jesus is God. And God is our Father. The words and the way you pray don't matter. They're listening to your heart, not the words. I would say to pray and tell God you want to be his son, you want his Spirit to live inside you, you want to live as Jesus's follower. Praying was eerie for me at first. I was all alone in the woods and I felt God all around me. But I tried to do it—just talk to him. I told him I wanted him to live in me and I wanted to be his son, and I wanted to grow. I asked him to help me. You don't hear about those kinds of things in the world these days. Most people would think I'm crazy if they heard me talking like this. But that day changed my life."

"Did you pray out loud?" asked Bradon.

Todd thought a moment. "You know . . . I can't remember. It was so vivid, it was *like* I did but I don't actually know."

He told Bradon more about his day in the Shenandoah mountains. Heather's essence of Christianity letter came into it as he shared about the events leading up to that day.

"I'd love to read it," said Bradon.

"It was enormously helpful in putting the ideas of Christianity into perspective. I'll ask her to send you a copy."

"It really does sound like that day changed your life."

"Looking back, I realize I was on the road already for a long time. Yet when I drove out to Shenandoah, I probably wouldn't have called myself a Christian. On my drive back to DC, I knew something had changed. I was ready to say, 'I *am* a Christian. I have decided to follow Jesus and do my best to live by his example and by what he told his disciples to do.'"

"That's an amazing thing," said Bradon. "I've never heard a story like that in my life. That's obviously why you gave up everything and are happy now being a ranch foreman rather than a media star."

Todd laughed. "I suppose you're right!" he said. "But I don't feel I've given up anything. I've discovered life! Another thing I'm learning is that God has plans. Who could have known your grandmother sending your dad to camp where he met Mr. Forster would come full circle like this, with you and me—two of the most unlikely guys!—talking about Christianity?"

"It's uncanny, though you're right!" laughed Bradon.

"I think it's because we're both hungry for more in life," rejoined Todd. "A hungry heart wanting to grow and *become* is something God treasures. That's another new thing I'm trying to get my head around—that God *loves* me and is pleased that I want to know him. Imagine—God *pleased* with me because I want to know him!"

"That's an amazing idea."

"You will look back, just as I do, and realize that God has been drawing you all this time, maybe even from before you first saw Ginger. He uses *all* our life's circumstances to draw us. If we are listening and responding to his quiet voice in our hearts, good things happen along the road to *becoming* even before we realize it."

"You sound like a preacher, Todd!"

Todd roared with laughter. "Sorry—I guess I got a little carried away. I'm just trying to tell you how it was for me."

"It's good to hear it from someone who's been in my shoes. It's a lot to take in."

"Like I said, I'm only about a year ahead of you."

"Then you're a fast learner," said Bradon. "You sound like you've been a Christian for years. So give it to me in twenty-five words."

Todd laughed. "I said that same thing to Heather and she wrote me a five-page letter!"

"I'd love for you to write me one! Give me your elevator version."

"Okay, I'll give it a shot," said Todd. "You asked what you should do—in a nutshell I would say, keep reading, try to begin praying, ask God to lead and guide you in what you should do. Ask for God's Spirit to dwell in you and reveal himself to you and help you be a disciple of Jesus.

Maybe *ask* isn't the right word. *Invite* him to be in you and dwell in you. Then do what you sense him telling you. That's one thing they're always telling me. It's a constant theme—that you learn and understand more from *doing* what Jesus said than by reading or studying or anything else. Learning is good but then you have to *practice* the truths as you learn them. Obedience, they call it. *Obedience is the opener of eyes* is a phrase they love to quote.

"Others would probably explain it differently," Todd added. "Lots of people explain Christianity by talking about sin and the importance of repentance and asking God for forgiveness and how Jesus's death makes life with God possible. That *is* important, of course. Certainly, there's a lot more to Christianity than what I've just said. Sin and forgiveness and the meaning of Jesus's death are pivotal. And you'll learn about all that. But Heather didn't throw everything at me all at once. Christianity isn't a one-size-fits-all deal. It's completely individual. She sensed what I personally needed to hear for where my life's pilgrimage was. She allowed me to learn what it all meant at my own pace."

When Bradon Rhodes boarded his plane back to DC the following day, he was still looking in from the outside, still wondering how one like Todd Stewart could call himself by such an old-fashioned word as "disciple." Yet everything they talked about was working on him.

Somewhere over Indiana and Ohio, the thought struck him, *If Todd can do this, why can't I? What is there to be afraid of?*

Todd's words returned to his memory, *Just tell him you want to be his son.*

Gradually his thoughts became a conversation between himself and the One he began to think of, not as dwelling somewhere in the distant cosmos but as living within his own heart.

For the next hour, he found himself blinking back tears, unbidden yet welcome. His cleansing thoughts and prayers continued. When he stepped off the plane, if someone approached and asked, "Are you a Christian?" he would have answered, "Yes—I think I am. At least I am learning to become one. And I intend to ask God to help me and teach me more every day about what it means to say, *I am a Christian.*"

It's not Islamophobia to notice that Muslims want to import values into the West that seek to destabilize our civilization. It's cultural suicide to stay silent.

—Charlie Kirk, June 2025

☆ ☆ ☆

It is a duty incumbent on every Muslim to struggle towards the aim of making every people Muslim and the whole world Islamic, so that the banner of Islam can flutter over the earth.

—Hasan al-Banna

From *Jihad*, a collection of writings begun in 1928

PART 3

HIDDEN JIHAD UNMASKED

FALL 2051

31

Facing Imperative Questions

TIMOTHY MARSHALL had been praying for guidance for several months.

What was brewing in his brain since Mark's first meeting with President Rhodes's ill-fated Religion Commission—though in truth it began long before—remained nebulous and undefined. Timothy had not mentioned it to a soul, not even Jaylene. Mark's casual description of the makeup of his commission—he judged three or four to be Muslims and his description of one Hamad Bahram whom Mark met at the Presidential Manor and now replaced him as head of the commission—combined to trigger far-reaching and foreboding thoughts in the heart of Stirling Marshall's son.

Was it time to sound a new warning twenty years after his father's private yet no less influential Benedict Brief?

He could not escape the conviction that coincident with the decline of Christ's church in America, Islam was on the march, with the unmistakable goal, not merely of replacing Christianity as the majority religion of America but of gradually taking over the direction, perhaps even the government of the United States.

For decades China had been considered the gravest threat to American sovereignty. Timothy wasn't so sure. A potentially greater threat, he was convinced, both to America and Christianity, was Islam.

If Islam ever conquered China from within, that would be checkmate. With China's global infrastructure, its technology, financial, and military dominance, and its worldwide stranglehold on manufacturing, business, banking, and space exploration now that NASA no longer existed and Space X had been sold to China, an Islamic-Far-East axis would rule the world in a way Hitler could never have dreamed of.

Men and women were not led globally or corporately in life's most important things. They were individually led through single steps of obedience . . . daily, moment-by-moment. Obedience did not address five years in the future. Obedience lived in the eternal *Now* of the present.

If this was an inner prompting from God, if the Holy Spirit was indeed stirring in his heart, what else could he do but what was being shown him in this *now* in which he lived? The *future* was in God's hands. The *now* was in his.

A sense was stirring within him that it was time for him to speak perhaps a new truth for a new time, to address the insidious infiltration of Islam into the bloodstream of America.

Whether it would be his lasting professional legacy or swan song, he could neither foretell nor cared. What was formulating in his mind was a series of lectures and discussions held at the university for course credit, though also open to the public. Knowing the controversial nature of the idea, he went first to the president of Jessup with his proposal.

"In principle, I like it," said university president Travers. "You're certain to face public opposition if there is an anti-Muslim slant. Though you'll be accused of going liberal by fundamentalist Christians if you're *too* open-minded."

"I know!" laughed Timothy. "In this cultural climate, you can't win. I hope to avoid both extremes, if possible, by structuring the course to look objectively at the foundations, claims, and histories of both, and letting the facts speak for themselves."

"A worthy goal," nodded Travers. "But as you say, in the current climate, that may be idealism speaking."

"I'm aware of that. It could be, too, that by the end of the series I will feel it appropriate to speak somewhat more pointedly. By then I will hopefully be in a position to assess how far to go in asking some of the difficult questions that the facts of Islam's history make impossible to avoid."

"If the discussions get heated, which seems inevitable, it's hard to predict what the result could be. The mere fact that you are a professor at a Christian university would be enough to cause a backlash from the Muslim community."

"In one sense, maybe we shouldn't try to avoid it. They will criticize anything I say. Yet surely there are some intellectually honest and open-minded Muslims out there. I think I am capable of presenting the facts objectively in such a way to leave people to discover the truth for themselves."

"You are the most objective historian I know, Timothy," rejoined Travers. "I have no doubt about your qualification as the right man for this course. I believe it is time for it. Christians have stood by too long silently allowing Islam to take over the brains of more and more Americans. This needs to be done. You have my full support. Just walk carefully. I don't want car bombs on campus or death threats against you."

Timothy nodded, but Travers's words were sobering.

Weeks later, Timothy's course was announced for the following fall term.

32

A Bold Syllabus

SEPTEMBER 2051

IN ANTICIPATION of a modest turnout, Timothy's course, *Christianity and Islam: A comparative spiritual and historical case study*, was scheduled for one of Jessup's smaller lecture halls. Registered students would receive credit for the course after completing two papers and a final exam. The course was unusual in being open to the public for the lectures. Registrations from the community during the final few days proved so unexpectedly high that it was moved to the largest lecture facility on campus.

Timothy walked into a full hall of more than three hundred, including some twenty-five from the local BCL group. The attendees were about equally split between Jessup students and community members, and ranged throughout the spectrum of ages, genders, and ethnicities.

"Tonight's turnout," Timothy began, "is all the evidence we need that interest in Islam in America is higher than it has ever been, especially among Christians. I say that assuming that many, perhaps most of you here are Christians since this course is being offered at a Christian university. Whether interest in Christianity is equally high among Muslims, only those Muslims among us can say. We need to discuss the two religions with an objectivity that will allow a cross-pollination of diverse ideas to provide the fertile soil in which truth can grow.

"These are highly charged times. Objectivity will be difficult. It is no secret that I am a Christian. We all stand somewhere on the spectrum of ideas. We have points of view. There is no such thing as complete neutrality on anything. But that should not keep us from being capable of objectivity beyond the scope of our personal perspectives. Our intent is not persuasion or proselytizing but *knowledge*, accurate not biased *information*, and ultimately *truth*."

Timothy paused to allow his introductory remarks to sink in.

"Neither is it a secret that September 11, 2001, changed the world," he resumed. "At first there was a regrettable backlash against Muslims in this country. Except for isolated incidents, however, the reprisals were short-lived. Most intelligent men and women were able to make the distinction between responsible American Muslim individuals and the terrorist fringe.

"Here at the outset we encounter our first objectivity challenge. Muslims might quarrel with what I just said by insisting that anti-Muslim reprisals were not short-lived, that the bias has continued, and that America has become a virulent anti-Muslim nation. That objection, however, is simply untrue historically. I do not say that as a Christian but as a student of recent history over the past half century. You Muslims among us have to be open-minded enough to recognize that fact without clinging to an Islamophobia narrative.

"In actual fact, just the reverse has been true. Over the years since 9/11, we have witnessed a remarkable *pro*-Muslim surge in the United States, curiously paralleling a like increase in *anti*-Christian sentiment. Muslims today are accorded freedoms to practice their religion publicly and are provided special places to do so, while those same privileges and freedoms are denied Christians. Again, these trends are undeniable facts. Islam is enjoying great popularity and remains growing in the United States while Christianity is in decline. A statue of Mohammed stands prominently in the Capitol rotunda, while all Christian symbols and Ten Commandments plaques and sculptures were banned from schools and governmental buildings decades ago.

"A recent study revealed an astonishing result—approximately 70 percent of Americans have a positive view of Islam, while 85 percent have a *negative* view of Christianity.

"These statistics reveal that whatever anti-Muslim bias may have sprung up immediately after 9/11 dissipated very quickly. We are now living in a country where, in fact, Christians are facing a far greater *anti-Christian* bias than whatever pockets of *anti-Muslim* bias may remain. That is the reality. Minor anti-Muslim sentiment may continue on the fringes, but anti-Christian bias has become endemic throughout our society.

"These trends reflect global patterns everywhere. For the first two hundred years of our nation's history America was considered a so-called 'Christian' nation and for the past half century, according to most historians and scholars, a 'post-Christian' nation. It is likely a hundred years from now the United States will be known as a 'Muslim' nation.

"During these years of change, however, there has been a notable lack of objective scholarship and discussion about the core principles, and thus the veracity, of Christianity and Islam. I hope this seminar will help correct that deficiency. It would be wonderful and for the entire country's benefit if this could begin a wider discussion and bring greater understanding to everyone no matter what his or her individual beliefs."

Timothy paused, focused his thoughts for a moment, and went on.

"Most, it seems, hold their personal views and base their beliefs on what they have been taught. Those teachings on both sides are thoroughly infused with personal opinion, prejudice and bias, traditions, grievances either toward Christianity or Islam. Important in the perspectives of many are also the historic failings and corruptions and atrocities committed in the name of either Islam or Christianity but which are in fact not *true* representations of either. These are all singularly poor foundations upon which to hold any set of beliefs.

"I hope together we can objectively move beyond bias, beyond the indoctrination we have received, beyond the traditions we have grown up in, beyond the persistent red herrings of the Crusades and 9/11, and seek truth where it is to be found.

"We will do our utmost to remain objective, judging no one, and avoiding the tendency to relapse into subjective biases. If and when opinionated argumentation breaks out, I will stop the discussion."

Timothy's pause this time was lengthy.

"All right, then, let us dive in," he began after ten or twelve seconds. "You have all read the course synopsis and brief outline. For those of you in the community who have not had a chance to read all the materials, let me read my overview."

He turned to the lectern in front of him and began reading from his notes.

"We will explore the roots, claims, purposes, historic strengths and weakness, and successes and failures of Christianity and Islam. We will evaluate them by the lives and teachings of their founders, by their texts, and by the historic practices of their followers. We will pay close attention to each of their stated ultimate goals and objectives for individuals and corporately in the world.

"The aims and purposes of Islam and Christianity as religious movements and as defined by their founders will be all-important in our quest for truth. They will establish the purposes of Islam and Christianity as emerging from their core teachings. We will prosecute our quest based on these foundational tenets, teachings, and purposes, not necessarily on the aims and purposes as interpreted by later followers who may, in both cases, not be in harmony with the basic teachings of their founders. While looking at the practices of their followers through history, those practices will be secondary to the founders' teachings in establishing the veracity of the two religions as viable, practical, and self-consistent belief systems.

"With that overview, our seven lectures to be held weekly, as outlined in the syllabus, will focus on:

"One, the *founders*—Jesus and Mohammed, their lives and teachings in brief.

"Two, the *texts*—a summarization of the overview teachings of the four Gospels of the New Testament and the Koran.

"Three, the *purposes* of Islam and Christianity—as defined by their founders and texts.

"Four, the *histories*. This is where our discussion could get controversial, trying to objectively evaluate where the followers of both religions have fulfilled yet also diverged from those foundational objectives. This will require an honest assessment of many historic corruptions of their founders' ideals and teachings.

"Five and six, *doctrine, opinion, and truth*. What role doctrine and indoctrination have played and still play in the transmission of the teachings of Islam and Christianity. The higher query will be the difficult but imperative quest to lay practical hold of a reliable basis for evaluating truth *beyond* doctrine. How are we to assess the fundamental question of *truth*: Which is the *truer* religion? Or can *both* be true in an absolute sense?

"And finally, lecture seven will focus on *truth and lifestyle*—how Islam and Christianity are lived practically and consistently in the day-to-day. What does such practicality have to say about how one chooses and places faith in a belief system he or she comes to believe represents *truth*?"

A long silence followed.

33

The Founders—Jesus and Mohammed

"I RECOGNIZE THAT this has been a lengthy introduction," Timothy went on. "I felt it important for you to know exactly where we are going together. From this foundation, then, let us begin with the two founders—Jesus and Mohammed.

"As most of you know, Jesus lived from approximately 6 or 4 BC to between AD 30 and 33. He was probably a few years older than thirty-three, as tradition has it, at the time of his death. By tradition, Mohammed was born in Mecca in approximately AD 570 and lived to the age of sixty-two. He died in 632. Probably no men's teachings in history have been so widely quoted and embraced and corrupted and used for ends contrary to their purposes as the teachings of Jesus and Mohammed.

"For as complicated as his followers have made Christianity over the years, the teachings of Jesus are relatively straightforward. They mostly concern practical conduct, behavior, thought patterns, and attitudes, with an undergirding spiritual orientation regulated by how we see ourselves in relation to God, and more fundamentally how we view God. His teaching contrasts notably with that of Mohammed in being almost entirely disconnected from temporal society, governments, and nations. It is entirely an *individual* religion. Many throughout history, of course, have tried to interpret Christianity in societal and governmental terms, but in so doing they have almost entirely misunderstood the fundamental message Jesus brought to the world.

"In terms of conduct, behavior, and thought patterns, Christianity reduces at its most basic to being good, loving, kind, unselfish, and forgiving. In terms of how we relate ourselves to God, Christianity is founded in the belief that God is good, loving, kind, and forgiving which is why we are supposed to be also. Christianity is based on the premise that God is the Father of all creation and mankind in particular. This Fatherhood thus defines how we are to relate ourselves to him—as children . . . as the sons and daughters of a good, kind, loving, and forgiving Father.

"That in a nutshell is Christianity as Jesus taught it. Certainly, there is more to it. But at the most rudimentary level Jesus taught that we are a human family, that we have a good Father, that we are to live as his good children, and that we have an elder brother, Jesus, to show and teach us how.

"Jesus teaches us *how* through the remarkably untheological commands and instructions he gave in the four Gospels. This said, of course, no one will deny that in the midst of the relative simplicity of most of his instructions—pray for your enemies, turn the other cheek, don't swear, do good to those who mistreat you, don't judge, forgive, care for the poor, and so on—some of his enigmatic statements also contain great mystery.

"What does he mean when he calls himself the Son of Man? Was his mysterious answer to the high priest prior to his crucifixion an open claim to be the Son of God? What does *Son of God* even mean? This intriguing blend of practicality with mystery throughout the four accounts of his life has made Jesus the most studied yet most inscrutable man ever to walk the face of the earth. When one adds to that the theology and doctrine taught in the rest of the New Testament about sin, forgiveness, and the meaning of Christ's death in making redemption and reconciliation with God possible, along with the astonishing claim that he rose from the dead, the simplicity of the Gospels becomes more complicated yet.

"Mohammed's teaching, by contrast, is more difficult to lay hold of. The mystery is certainly there but not the practicality. Though he lived half a millennium later, his life is more shrouded in mystery than that of Jesus. That may be accounted for by the fact that a worldwide religion based on Mohammed's life and teaching did not spring up immediately. He had followers, of course. But his following did not explode as did Christianity. Thus there were few contemporary and reliable accounts of his life and teachings. Those early accounts are sketchy, as are the origins of the *Koran*. Traditions and legends abound, but *facts* are less numerous than is the case with Christianity.

"When Jesus either walked out of the grave alive after being dead for two days, or was *claimed* to have risen from the dead—depending on one's view of the resurrection—Christianity exploded throughout the western world. Within twenty years it was being spread in Rome, in the heart of the Empire. Immediately oral traditions from eyewitnesses were confirmed by many who saw Jesus and heard him preach. Written accounts soon followed. Christianity exploded so fast that the volume of historic data is enormous and was nearly contemporaneous with Jesus's life and the lives of his closest friends and followers.

"There is no parallel with this factual historicity in Islam. Little about Mohammed's actual life is linked by indisputable historical factuality to reliable eyewitness accounts. There are numerous stories but few *facts*. Many of the legends surrounding his life do not paint the picture of an admirable man.

"This raises the obvious question: How did such a worldwide religion grow out of the life and teachings of a man who was by all accounts not a saint? It is very curious. Jesus *was* a saint, a good man, a kind and gentle man. He was the sort of man good people aspire to follow and emulate. Mohammed was, in many ways, just the opposite—a tribal warrior, a man of war, not a man of kindness and peace.

"Nevertheless, these are the two men, rooted in their individual histories, whose lives and teachings gave rise to the world's two great religions, Islam and Christianity."

Timothy went on to summarize in more detail what was known about the biographies of the two men, spending ten or fifteen minutes on each, comparing and contrasting as appropriate.

He then opened the floor for questions and discussion. Though spirited, the tone set by Timothy prevailed. The lack of argumentation was notable.

34

The Enemy's List

SEPTEMBER–OCTOBER, 2051

THE MORE perilous the times for true Christians, the more active is the Ally. Also active during these months of anxiety in the body of Christ was Mike Bardolf's secret Committee of Enforcement drawn from his devoted band of agents who would obey him without question and keep their mouths shut.

Mike Bardolf had given Bruno Volker the assignment of expanding his investigations to everyone associated with the California group cells, including anyone who had attended so much as a single meeting, as well as every relative, friend, or church contact. He wanted to have the means at his disposal to exert maximum pressure on the entire organization if need be. He assigned Volker a staff of six to carry out the research and legwork, and an ample travel budget to personally visit all the known major cell groups and conduct in-person interviews.

Inquiries began in earnest in late July. Probing questionnaires were sent out, followed by personal visits and interviews whose tone was menacing and intrusive, then interviews with fellow church members, pastors and friends, all the lines of questioning designed to gain maximum personal information. They soon learned how to identify the Edith Holts of most congregations, from whom they unearthed treasure troves of personal gossip, the usefulness of which did not necessarily require that it be true.

The inquiries and investigations into the high-profile individuals who attended the gathering in April yielded nothing incriminating other than that they all, in different ways, had somehow become involved with the Christian group with strange views.

Using metadata of telephone conversations, by late fall the Bardolf committee had built a map of connections linking two hundred fifty Bible studies or home fellowship groups, even if but through a single individual, to the Forsters or Marshalls. They knew every group's leaders and regular members, knew everything about their families, their professional lives, their marital difficulties, possible affairs or scandals, and what churches they were affiliated with.

They amassed a file of over five thousand names, growing daily thanks to an expanding corps of unwitting informants in those churches eager to pass on every tidbit of anyone else's business that came into their hearing. There was truly only one more effective means of information gathering than the gossip pipeline of Christendom. Bruno Volker and his lieutenants took full advantage of that pipeline as the valuable resource it was.

That single *more* effective means emerged from the myriad smart devices owned and used almost 24-7 by every American from age three to a hundred and three. With no idea that their every word was heard and recorded by the vast network of artificial intelligence data banks and that the bulk of their most private activities were also *seen*, most were eager to race out to buy every new deviously intrusive technological device to hit the market. Every person in the country was thus easy to spy on.

Every name on Bruno's List of *Potential and Suspected Right Wing Zealots* associated with the California group, known privately to the Enforcement Committee as the "Enemy's List," were also placed on the FBI's watch list along with known international terrorists and drug lords. The AI surveillance was programmed to send out alerts at any words or phrases that might indicate potential anti-government leanings.

Heading that list were the names Timothy Marshall, Jaylene Marshall, Mark Forster, Grace Forster, David Gordon, Heather Marshall, Court Masters, Stella Masters, Todd Stewart, Alfred Nason, Harvey Jansen, Harriett Jansen, Charles Reyburn, Regina Reyburn, "the Prophet"—with the asterisk added: *Identity unconfirmed, possibly Gordon*—Eloise Hutchins, Deidra Hutchins, Matthew Gardner, Sarah Gardner, Geoffrey

Powell, Martha Powell, Trevor Langdon, Violet Langdon, Gerald Stevens, Rebecca Stevens, Derrick Hanson, and Paula Hanson.

Linda Trent and the president's mother, Sandra Rhodes, were an anomaly. Both were too high profile to actually include on the list. But Mike Bardolf and Bruno Volker were aware of their connections, and were watching.

There were no more arrests. But tensions ran high among the brothers and sisters of the common life who knew they were being surveilled. Throughout the country there was much wrestling in prayer and discussion about how to respond to the questionnaires and interviews.

Growing frustrated after some months, they uncovered no actionable intelligence against anyone in the group. A conversation he had with the president began to replay itself more prominently in Mike Bardolf's brain. Rhodes had commented how Linda Trent had once been sweet on Mark Forster.

He called Volker in.

"See if there's any hanky-panky in Trent's marriage," he told him. "If we could tie her to an affair with Forster during his trips to Washington, away from the little wife, that kind of rumor never hurts. It didn't gain much traction when I tried it with Hutchins, but maybe it would this time. We've got the picture of them embracing from April. See what else you can find out."

A week later Volker paid a chilly visit to Justice Linda Trent. He did just as Mike had instructed—he probed, and none too delicately. His piercing questions about the meeting and those who were part of it nettled Linda. When he zeroed in on possible romantic connections between herself and Mark Forster, she hit the roof.

Even Bruno Volker was not about to go too far with a Supreme Court Justice, and left without further incident.

Linda was on the phone to the Presidential Manor the moment the door closed behind him. After identifying herself, she was put through to the president's private office.

"Jeff, you tell your FBI goons to lay off me!" she said heatedly.

"Linda, Linda—calm down. What are you talking about?"

"I just had a visit from a Neanderthal by the name of Bruno Volker."

"Never heard of him."

"Well *somebody* set him onto me. I don't know who is behind this nonsense about Mark and me. But you were up in arms about a conspiracy. Who could have hinted at something about Mark and me *but* you. There is nothing to it and you know that better than anyone. If anything I was in love with you once, not Mark—though I feel like a fool for not seeing that he was ten times the man you will ever be. So lay off, Jeff—lay off me, lay off Mark and Grace! I can still make life difficult for you."

She slammed down the phone, her face red and breathing stertorously, leaving Jeff chuckling in his office, then breaking out in laughter.

This was delicious! he thought. Arresting Mark had been worth it just for this. Linda was just as big a fool as the rest of them!

As the day wore on, however, her statement about Mark ground deeper into Jeff's subconscious, exacerbating all the more bitterly what was slowly developing into an irrational hatred for his one-time best friend.

Meanwhile, among the unexpected discoveries yielded by the names being constantly filtered, cross-checked, and investigated by the Bardolf committee with a complex series of computer algorithms, were eleven congressmen and women, six senators, nine federal judges, and sixteen high-placed FBI agents affiliated with the group. There were even rumors of a California-linked cell group meeting secretly somewhere on Capitol Hill, whose attendees spanned party lines, and included men and women from all three branches of the government. Court Masters, Alfred Nason, and Linda Trent were suspected as being involved, probably the ringleaders.

For now Mike Bardolf kept his suspicions to himself. He didn't want to inform the president until he knew more, and until he decided how to use the information to his best advantage. What Rhodes didn't know wouldn't hurt either of them.

The committee's investigations continued. Its Enemy's List grew daily.

35

Assessing Historic Objectivity

CONSIDERABLE BUZZ spread through the Jessup campus in the days following the first lecture about Islam and Christianity by semi-retired professor of history Dr. Timothy Marshall.

The faction of students of a more evangelical bent was critical of Dr. Marshall's approach, never referring to Jesus as Lord, questioning what "Son of God" meant, not mentioning the virgin birth or miracles, the cross, the atonement, ransom for sin, and raising the question whether the resurrection was real.

Those familiar with Timothy's general approach to history knew that such was by design. In order to present Christianity so that non-Christians, especially Muslims, would be open and receptive, he had to stand as a neutral observer relying on the historical facts, not personal religious belief, to ferret out truth.

Timothy, meanwhile, remained unaware that even his attempt at objectivity was stirring up debate. In his second talk, he planned to get into the nuts and bolts of the two religions as revealed by their originating texts.

The challenge would not only be to present the *positive* teachings of both religions but to maintain objectivity in realistically examining the *negative* teachings of Mohammed which had no counterpart in Christianity.

The fact that Mohammed did not write the Koran himself made it a text—though more recent than the Gospels—whose veracity and historicity was more difficult to assess. How could it be *proven* that Gabriel spoke to Mohammed as claimed but that he wrote down none of it and later others did write it down, though they had heard nothing themselves. Legends abounded but facts were almost nonexistent. This ambiguity and supposedly supernatural origin of the Koran was fundamental to the question of inspiration.

That query applied to both texts: Were they indeed *revelations of truth from God*, or mere *ideas and doctrines of men* who wrote them down later?

Did the texts and teachings and biographical facts truly originate from Jesus and Mohammed or not?

The near contemporaneousness of the four Christian texts with Jesus's life and that two, perhaps even three of the gospelists were eyewitnesses to his life and heard the teachings firsthand, established its texts, though older, more reliably in history. Even for one who might quibble about the inspiration of the Gospels, the texts and their authorships were provably historical. That did not in itself make the content of the Gospels reliable—perhaps the four men were writing fiction. But the historicity remained undeniable.

It was true that some of the Koran purportedly came from eyewitnesses to Mohammed's life and teachings. But the claim was based on later tradition. No authors' names were known, no dates of writing, no historical facts to attest to when the writings appeared in the historical record, nor which were their own ideas and which were the words of the angel Gabriel.

That was the difficulty with Islam's origins—no one really *knew* who wrote the Koran. All that could be said was that the elements of the Koran gradually *emerged*, and were later copied and collected in the centuries following Mohammed's life. How and when and by whom would probably always remain unknown.

These historical factors could not necessarily validate or disprove *revelation* as from God. They were nevertheless facts that Timothy knew his presentation on the texts had to address.

Two days before his second lecture, one of his graduate students came to him with the news he had become aware of that a small contingent of Muslim students were to be on hand from Sacramento State.

More than ever Timothy would have to walk a delicate tightrope in his presentation. He must present the undeniable difficulties in the authenticity of the Koran in a way that maintained a spirit of objectivity.

He needed to remain objective for the Christians in attendance as well. Formulas and rote teachings were death to the quest for truth, for both Christians *and* Muslims. He approached his courses at the university from a foundation of open-minded academic investigation. He especially had to do so now in this all-important query, setting the example that if Christians expected Muslims to listen to *their* perspectives, they must be mature enough to listen to alternate worldviews with courtesy, respect, and open-mindedness.

Spiritual truth had to be approached as a scientist did in his laboratory of investigation—starting not with preformed conclusions but with reality.

36

The Texts

"WHAT I would like to do this evening," Timothy began his second lecture, "is simply list some of the prevalent teachings of Islam and Christianity derived from the four Gospels and the Koran.

"This may seem a simplistic approach. The religious mind usually gravitates to analysis, doctrine, and the intellectualization of ideas. Islam and Christianity are guilty of this lethal tendency. Most of you will be victims of teachings based on theological analysis and the universal love of asking *how-many-angels-can-dance-on-the-head-of-a-pin*.

"We *love* theoretical analysis! But that is *not* usually the best way to arrive at truth. If truth is our goal, we have to seek it, not theologically but *practically*. The theology may follow, but in my opinion it is not foundational.

"It is my conviction that only in using the straightforward instructions reported by the texts as taught by Jesus and Mohammed can we get clear insights into what Christianity and Islam truly are. Their practical, straightforward, how-to-live-life instructions, not the theologies that have been built upon them. In other words—*practicality*, not analysis or intellectualization or doctrine.

"We have to overlook for the moment whether Christians and Muslims, historically and today, actually *live* by these precepts. Of course they don't. Of course *we* don't."

Timothy paused.

"Of course *I* don't," he added slowly. "*None* of us live our spiritual beliefs and convictions consistently. Christians and Muslims are all in that boat together. We don't live by the ideals of our respective religions. That's what a religion is—an *ideal*, how we aspire to live, how in our human imperfection we hope and pray to grow more capable of living. Our imperfection, and hopefully our growth toward an ideal we fall short of, is built into what a religion is.

"To criticize either Islam or Christianity because throughout history their adherents have done terrible things is no way to arrive at truth.

"We're trying to get to the essence of what Christianity and Islam *are*—the ideals their followers are *supposed* to live by even though they don't do so perfectly. The injunctions, precepts, commands, priorities, principles, and purposes set forth in their founding texts will help us discover the *essence* of Christianity and the *essence* of Islam. Whether some Christian or Muslim you know, or whether Christians or Muslims in history, have *not* lived by those ideals, has little to with the veracity of the teachings. You have to look beyond the hypocrisy of some Christian you know or the hypocrisy of some Muslim you know, and ask: 'What do the founding texts tell me of the *truth* of Christianity or the *truth* of Islam?'

"If the teachings, or ideals are contrary to truth, then that would invalidate those teachings as representing truth. Such a religion could not be called a 'true' religion. It may still have devoted followers, but those followers could not be said to be following *truth*. A so-called religion or belief system, for example, teaching its followers to lie could not be considered a belief system of *truth*. This, too, the founding texts should reveal—whether the teachings of Christianity and Islam point toward goodness and truth and are therefore religions of truth. They both *claim* to be religions of truth. Our job is to see what the texts tell us."

Timothy paused again, allowing his words to sink in before resuming.

"So let's get into it," he said. "The four New Testament Gospels were all likely written in the final third of the first century—the first some thirty years after Jesus's death by John Mark, who was a young boy during Jesus's ministry and probably knew Jesus and heard him teach. The second and fourth were written by Jesus's disciples Matthew and John and the third by a Greek physician, Luke, who was a later convert to Christianity. The Koran was purportedly delivered orally to

Mohammed by the angel Gabriel in stages between 610 and the year of his death in 632.

"As they are more straightforward, we will start with the texts upon which Christianity is based. The first Gospel to appear in the New Testament, though written after that of Mark, came from Jesus's disciple Matthew, and is the best place to begin.

"Matthew sets the tone immediately for the teachings of Jesus, which Mark called the *gospel*—a word which means *good news*. In the so-called Sermon on the Mount which begins in Matthew's chapter 5, Jesus lays a number of very specific injunctions upon his followers. Most of them are so down-to-earth and practical they were revolutionary when Jesus's audience first heard them. They would be equally revolutionary in our day if they were actually lived by Christians. We immediately see why I earlier emphasized practicality rather than theological analysis. It would be difficult not to see the practicality of these injunctions from the mouth of Jesus. And as Mohammed said he revered Jesus, it would seem that Muslims would be equally committed to following these same priorities.

"Though they are added to and amplified through the rest of the four Gospels, I believe we can say that the essence of Christianity is summed up right here. So let us look at the bare bones of Christianity, through the lens of the Sermon on the Mount.

"I will read slowly to give us time to absorb these down-to-earth instructions. Let us imagine we are listening to them from the mouth of Jesus and hearing them for the first time. I believe that between the lines we can hear Jesus saying:

"'These instructions are the defining qualities of thought and behavior for everyone who desires to be my follower. Years from now many who claim to speak for me will urge you to follow this or that doctrine *about* me. They will teach you theologies about me because it is easier to teach theories than to do what I say. If they are not teaching you these things I tell you today, do not listen to them. They will not be speaking for me. My *true* followers will do *these* things. In *these* ways they will set themselves apart from the rest of the world as my followers by the way they love, the way they think, the way they behave, the way they treat others, by the goodness that is developing within them, by their obedience to these principles, and by the way they are growing into God's sons and daughters.'"

A long pause followed Timothy's imagery. The hall was eerily quiet. Slowly he began reading from the sheet in front of him, pausing between each succinct statement from Matthew.

Rejoice when you are insulted, reviled, persecuted, and spoken evil of.
Be the world's salt and light.
Do not break even the least of God's commandments.
Be more righteous than the Scribes and Pharisees.
Call no one a fool.
Be reconciled with your brother before offering gifts to God.
Men, do not look at a woman with lust.
Do not divorce except for promiscuity.
Do not marry a divorcee.
Swear no oaths.
Let your yes be yes and your no be no.
Do not resist an evil person.
If you are struck on one cheek, offer the other also.
If you are sued for your coat, give your shirt also.
Give when asked.
Do not refuse one who wants to borrow from you.
Love your enemies.
Pray for those who persecute you.
Be sons of your Father in heaven.
Do not love and greet only your friends.
Beware of pretending to be righteous to be noticed.
Give to the poor in secret.
Do not pray to be heard by others.
Pray in secret.
When you pray do not repeat rote phrases.
Forgive men their sins.
When you fast, do not look gloomy to be noticed.
Do not store up treasures on earth, but in heaven.
Keep your heart single-minded.

Do not try to serve both God and Mammon.
Do not worry about life, what you will eat, drink, or wear.
Seek first God's kingdom and his righteousness.
Do not worry about tomorrow.
Do not judge.
Take the beam out of your eye before looking at the speck in your brother's.
In everything, treat others as you want them to treat you.
Beware of false prophets.
Hear and do my words.

Another lengthy pause followed.

"These are just the tip of the iceberg," said Timothy. "If we were trying to be exhaustive, we would look at all four Gospels and the list might be ten times as long. But the Sermon on the Mount is useful to encapsulate Jesus's teaching. Most of what we would find in the remainder of the Gospels emphasizes the same code of thought, behavior, conduct, attitude, and life-orientation.

"What many Christians do not realize is the Koran teaches many similar principles. If the words are indeed Mohammed's—or were spoken by Gabriel to Mohammed—some of them point in the same directions. They are not usually spoken so succinctly as those of Jesus. There are relatively few straightforward commands and instructions in the Koran, at least nothing like what is found in the New Testament. Most of its principles come in the form of observations or lengthy teachings. I have rephrased some of these I will now read to you into the form of command to make them easier to compare with what we have just heard from Jesus. Many Christians will be amazed to find in the Koran such principles as:

Make peace in a quarrel.
Speak fairly.
Be moderate in your bearing.
Do justice.
Do not turn away from men in scorn.
Do not conceal truth with falsehood.

Avoid shameful deeds.
Avoid vain talk.
Do not spread scandal.
Walk in humility.
Do not slander or ridicule.
Do not defame.
Do not slander a chaste woman.
Do not envy what others have.
Keep pure in body, mind, and heart.
Be good and kind to your parents.
Do good to your neighbors.
Be kind to those in need.
Keep your promises.
Help one another with acts of righteousness.
Practice the same right conduct you expect of others.
Never be hypocritical.
Do justice to everyone.
Judge justly.
Show charitable kindness.
Protect chastity.
Consider the accused innocent until proved guilty.
Fulfill your promises and obligations.

"The significant difference between these two lists, however," Timothy concluded, "is that Jesus's injunctions are to be lived toward *all* men. In the list I read a moment ago, Jesus was speaking universally to all mankind. In general, however, this list from the Koran applies mostly *to* Muslims in behavior toward *fellow* Muslims. Behavior toward non-Muslims is regulated by different standards entirely. This is a distinction that does not exist in Christianity."

37

Between the Lines

TIMOTHY SET aside the sheet from which he had been reading and looked up for a moment as some shuffling spread through the hall.

"Well and good," he said. "This has been brief. But I think these comparisons tell us quite a bit. From what we have just heard from their texts, both religions can indeed be viewed as claiming to be religions of peace and harmony between men and women, respect and unselfishness, being a man or woman of integrity, and so on. There is evidence in both texts to support those claims. They both have versions of the golden rule. Both speak of goodness and kindness.

"But is this the whole story? The fact that Jesus's injunctions are universal, while those of the Koran are only Muslim toward Muslim, is a huge distinction. We also notice an apparent absence in the Koran of commands toward love and forgiveness. In both thought and behavior, the New Testament speaks of love and forgiveness on every page. They are intrinsic to the very essence of Christianity. These attitudes, and the practices and behavior that follow from them, are glaringly missing from the Koran.

"I simply state this as an observer. It indicates nothing about truth, only that love and forgiveness, intrinsic to Christianity, do not seem intrinsic to Islam. Love, the cornerstone of the Christian message, isn't mentioned much in the Koran. It's an important distinction we should keep our eye on.

"The tone and emphasis of the two texts, too, is much different. As I mentioned, Jesus's words are universal, as applying to *all* mankind—believers, Jews, atheists, rich, poor, Christians—everyone. Of course Christians are *especially* commanded to love one another but not in an exclusivist sense. But Jesus's use of the term 'brother' is clearly intended to mean not only a fellow Christian but also a *brother of humanity.*

"The Koran's injunctions address believing Mohammed-followers, or *Muslims.* This underlying exclusivity is much different than the universality apparent in the Gospels.

"It is safe to say, and I speak not as a partisan but as a historian looking at the texts, that the four Gospels are inclusive and *universal* documents, whereas the Koran is an *exclusivist* document. Make of it what you will, that is simply what the texts tell us.

"An example can be seen in the first injunction I read from the Koran. Whereas I rephrased it as, 'Make peace in a quarrel,' the full passage reads quite differently. The emphasis is mine:

"'If two parties *among the believers* fall into a quarrel, make peace between them; but if one of them transgresses beyond bounds against the other, then *you should fight* against the party that transgresses *until the other party complies* with commands of Allah. But if the other party complies, make peace between them with justice, and be fair.'

"Though peace, justice, and fairness are involved, they come into it only when the opposition relents. Otherwise the Koran commands fighting against one's opponents in the quarrel. There is a much different underlying tone here that is completely opposite to what Jesus teaches. Though Mohammed purportedly revered Jesus's teaching, the Koran often flagrantly opposes what Jesus taught. Again, I pass no value judgment. I only point it out as an observer of these differences in the texts. It also raises the question, if Mohammed revered Jesus as a prophet of God and then God gave him the Koran, how is it the two teachings are in conflict at so many points?

"This distinctive tone and emphasis is apparent everywhere between the lines. What we observe in the Koran is that the same considerations enjoined toward believers—Muslims—such as kindness, respect, humility, righteousness, etc. are *not* required toward non-Muslims. Love and forgiveness don't come into it even with fellow Muslims. Love and forgiveness, so intrinsic to the equation of Christianity, play almost no role in Islam. The more one examines the two texts, the greater this divergence becomes.

"Jesus says, 'Love, forgive, make peace, show kindness—unconditionally toward everyone.'

"The Koran says, 'Only make peace after you have subdued your opponent. Until then fight against them until they comply.'

"As another example, *justice* in the New Testament is generally viewed through the lens of Jesus's words, 'Judge not lest you be judged, for by the same measure by which you judge will you yourself be judged.' In other words, justice is measured as a function of mercy, the golden rule, kindness, and ultimately forgiveness.

"Justice in Islam is altogether different. Justice in Islam is not rooted in forgiveness, as in Christianity, but is founded on the principle of meting out *punishment* to those who deserve it. Between the lines of the injunctions, 'Justice must be done to everyone . . . give full measure and weight in justice . . . protect chastity . . . the accused are to be considered innocent unless proved guilty . . . fulfill all obligations,' it is not difficult to connect the dots to the honor killing—'full measure and weight'—required by Islam in order to *protect chastity* against an adulterous woman or a young woman who marries an infidel.

"Forgiveness is not intrinsic to Islam's equation of justice. Compare this with Jesus's forgiveness-justice toward the woman caught in adultery—*Neither do I condemn you. Go and sin no more.*

"Reading between the lines, then, some of the parallel injunctions I read earlier from the two texts are not as similar as they first appear. We see this harshly strident tone embedded throughout the Koran against non-Muslims and also against disobedient or unfaithful Muslims.

"An important aspect in how each of us evaluates these discrepancies is deciding what we *want* in a religion to which we devote our allegiance. Do we *want* a religion of exclusivity requiring love, kindness, and peace only toward those within that religion, and strife and opposition toward those outside it? Judging from the worldwide following enjoyed by Islam, we must conclude that billions do indeed desire an exclusivist religion.

"On the other hand, do we desire to dedicate ourselves to a universal religion teaching love, goodness, kindness, and forgiveness toward all, however incomplete those ideals may be lived by its adherents? Judging by the worldwide decline of Christianity, it would seem those ideals are desired by fewer men and women with every passing year. We see the same exclusivity of response in political progressivism.

"What this state of affairs may have to say about mankind's future is a question I do not have insight or wisdom to guess. If the greater part of the world desires an exclusivist religion of subduing all who do not agree with its tenets, it strikes me as of concern for the world's future. What will be the ultimate resolution when the conflict reaches a tipping point of who believes correctly and who does not?

"This question opens the Pandora's box of Islam's dark side. Please hear me clearly. I am not talking about 9/11 or terrorism any more than I am talking about the Crusades. Both religions have ample dark sides as practiced by their adherents. That is an important topic we will have to discuss later.

"For the moment, however, we are looking at the texts themselves and the teachings of Jesus and Mohammed. We cannot judge the veracity of either Islam or Christianity on the basis of the failings of their followers. We have to base our conclusions on originating principles.

"Where do we put Islam's dark teachings alongside those of Jesus? Granted, one can find a dark strain in Jesus's words too. He speaks of the fires of hell, about being cast into the sea with a great millstone around the neck, and climaxes the book of Matthew, which began with the Sermon on the Mount, by saying that those who are unkind to those in need will be sent away to eternal punishment.

"It is primarily upon this verse in the twenty-fifth chapter of Matthew that an entire theology of hell has been built which, if one takes the extreme Calvinist view of the elect and the non-elect, is as ghastly and exclusivist as Islam. Those are sobering words. But they are few and far between in the Gospels.

"So while we cannot ignore that the charge of exclusivity can be justifiably leveled against Christianity too, neither can we make more of it than we should. We cannot give this single verse from Matthew 25 a preponderance of importance outweighing hundreds of passages teaching exactly the opposite. Over 500 verses in the New Testament speak of love. We have to read the New Testament with common sense.

Any objective reader can easily recognize Jesus's general teaching to be of love, kindness, and forgiveness.

"The Koran, as I've said, scarcely mentions love—either Allah's love or love for mankind. The tone is completely different. The stark and hostile 'justice' to be exacted against non-Muslims is chilling and terrifying. Nor is it a one-off single verse that gives rise to this perspective. The justice of punishment toward non-Muslims is endemic throughout the entire Koran.

"Did Allah actually *say* to Mohammed to behead infidels? If so, that paints a very troubling image of the God Muslims worship.

"There is another huge difference. Even if an eternally punishing hell is a true aspect of Christian theology, in such a view it is *God* who carries out the divine retribution against so-called sinners in the *next* life. Here and now, in this life, Christians are to love and forgive and leave vengeance to God. How much better that God carry out the justice than to command men and women to treat their brothers and sisters of humanity with such barbarity.

"In Islam, on the other hand, the retribution against infidels is commanded of Muslims in *this* life. It is this difference which makes Islam sobering as a worldview. If everyday Muslims worldwide actually took all the texts of the Koran seriously, the world would be a very frightening place.

"A reputable source cites over 120 verses in the Koran promoting fighting and the killing of non-Muslims. Not the remotest parallel exists in Christianity. A few passages will illustrate the stark contrast with the Sermon on the Mount."

Again Timothy began reading from the paper in front of him.

Muslims must not take infidels as friends.
Muster all weapons to terrorize infidels.
Kill infidels wherever you find them.
Maim and crucify infidels if they criticize Islam.
Terrorize and behead those who believe in scriptures other than the Koran.
Do not seek peace with infidels but behead them when you capture them.

"I set these passages before you as an observer. As I say, you have to draw your own conclusions."

Timothy paused and drew in a deep breath.

"And I think that is where I shall leave it for this evening," he said. "I will now try to respond to your questions."

Instantly no fewer than thirty hands shot into the air, accompanied by half as many questions shouted throughout the hall.

38

The Pamphlet

ON THE Tuesday following his second lecture, Timothy was in his office at Jessup working on research for the third session. Not only did he want to avail himself of his books and the university library, he felt he could be more in tune with the campus "vibe" by doing his preparation on campus. He also wanted to assess the mood and thoughts and reactions of students, and thus made himself visible, doing much of his reading out in the campus quad. Everyone on campus knew him. The exchanges through the afternoon were stimulating in many directions, though he made little progress on his next lecture.

About 4:30, as he was thinking about calling it a day, a young man approached he vaguely recognized but couldn't place. He came forward with a confident, almost presumptuous, air.

"Dr. Marshall," he said, "it is good to see you again."

Timothy rose and shook the young man's hand.

"I do recognize you," he said, laughing lightly, "but I'm afraid . . . "

"Dale Birch," said the young man. "I took your course on the American Revolution several years ago."

"Yes, of course . . . Dale, I do remember. Nice to see you again too."

"I've been hearing about your Islam lectures. There's a buzz about them going around at Sac State."

"You're attending Sac now?"

"Not exactly, but I spend a lot of time there. I wanted to ask you if you would give me five or ten minutes to speak at your next lecture?"

"Oh . . . hmm, I, uh . . . I'd have to give that some serious thought," replied Timothy slowly. "Why do you ask—I mean, what would you want to say?"

"To warn people of the Islamic threat. I know you're trying to approach it academically, but people need to be warned. War is coming. It's not going to be pretty. I've written a pamphlet. If you'll read it, I know you'll see how important it is we get the word out."

He reached into the satchel in his hand, pulled out a thin, stapled pamphlet and handed it to Timothy.

"I'm sure it will help you with your lectures too," he added.

"Okay . . . well, thank you, Dale. I appreciate it. I will certainly look it over."

"I want you to *read* it, Dr. Marshall, not just look it over," young Birch rejoined with an imperative tone. "You need to know what's going on too. They are planning war, Dr. Marshall."

"Who is, Dale?"

"The Muslims. They're all in on it. It's a secret jihad. We have to be prepared."

"Fair enough, Dale," nodded Timothy. "I can tell that you've put a great deal of work into this. So I *will* read it. I will make that commitment to you."

"And you'll give me five or ten minutes this Friday?"

"It's a college course, Dale. It's not an open podium. But let me read your pamphlet. How can I contact you?"

"My phone number's there, on the last page."

With a nod, though without a smile, Dale Birch turned and walked away, leaving Timothy full of many thoughts, wondering for the first time if the lectures were a good idea. What might he be stirring up?

His work on his lecture was definitely over for the day. He told Jaylene about the encounter over supper.

"I know the name," she said. "I never had him in class, but he was the kind of young man who made his presence felt. You had him, didn't you?"

"I did," nodded Timothy. "He was a handful, I'll say that—forever interrupting, opinions and axes to grind about everything."

"Wasn't he expelled eventually?"

"I'm not exactly sure. Now that you mention it, there was some talk, then I never saw him around again."

"I remember hearing something about John Birch being his great-great-grandfather, and he was trying to resurrect the old John Birch Society from the 1950s."

"It wouldn't surprise me."

"You're not seriously thinking of letting him address the lecture group?"

"I couldn't do so even if I wanted to. It's an accredited course and he's not even a student. But I have to read his pamphlet, I owe him that much. I told him I would."

An hour later Timothy eased back in his favorite chair, pulled out the pamphlet, and eyed the title again with mixed emotions: *A Call to Arms: The evils of progressivism and Islam can be stopped, but it takes enough good people not doing nothing. Pass on the challenge!*

Taking on the liberal culture and Islam together—the fellow was asking for trouble. Somewhat reluctantly, Timothy began to read.

It was only sixteen pages, full letter size folded in half, obviously done on a copy machine, low-tech and not without a few errors. He completed it in about an hour. The deep breath she heard beside her told Jaylene that he had finished the assignment he set for himself.

"Well?" she said quizzically.

"As expected," sighed Timothy. "Typical far-right conspiracies, government spying, plans for military takeover, mind-altering drugs in the water, progressive brainwashing, rigged elections, world government control over food production, planned pandemic targeting certain racial and social groups to weed out those antithetical to progressivism's agenda, massive social engineering reaching into every facet of life, covert assassinations on Christians and conservatives, secret societies and government commissions—it's all here, from the Bilderberg Group to the Illuminati to the Knights Templar to the more recent Davos Cartel."

"The conspiracy buffs have been talking about all those things for decades," Jaylene observed. "They just change with the times."

"And remarkably many of their seemingly far-out ideas materialize. Remember the 9/11 theories, the Trump Russia collusion scam, the stolen elections of 2000, 2016, and 2020, the January 6 treason hoax, and the all-time favorite, the JFK assassination. Now the ACH assassination joins these golden oldies from the past! Dale has loaded a few pages with everything but the kitchen sink. He lists these as among the secret Alliance's stated objectives."

"What Alliance?" asked Jaylene.

"Some secret group he says is behind it all, with plans to marginalize, ridicule, and shame whites and Christians in media, academia, and religious institutions; to demonize then erase white Western history from textbooks; to promote recreational drug use to lower initiative and increase government dependency; to promote addictive video-games, and other mind-numbing activities to reduce initiative; to promote race mixing in relationships, and promiscuity to reduce white identity and cohesiveness; to expand drug-based medicine over health-based to increase dependence on governmental health systems; to require a broad base of vaccinations to carry out the social engineering mandate of progressivism through drugs; to regulate water systems with chemicals to control birth rates, thought patterns, and other desired outcomes considered for the common good that will gradually create an unthinking society to be socially engineered at will."

"Like you said, the conspiratorial kitchen sink!"

"His villains are Karl Marx and Saul Alinsky and nearly all the presidents of the twenty-first century except Trump. His theory is that all these groups have secretly come together and are planning a simultaneous takeover of all major world governments, which would then be merged into a single new World Order. Christian leaders would be systematically eliminated, by cleverly disguised assassinations, until, having no leaders or spokesmen, Christianity would die out altogether. He claims to have learned about a secret document called the New World Manifesto which spells out this group's aims. He claims it originated in our own government. How, he doesn't say. It's like most of these kinds of things—long on outrageous claims, short on evidence."

"Yet not *completely* ridiculous," said Jaylene, "probably with enough fragments of truth to make it believable to the gullible."

"That's just it," nodded Timothy. "We know the progressives have been using these tactics for years, going all the way back to Viktor

Domokos. He claims Domokos started and funded an organization more secretive than all the rest which is pulling the strings. He calls it the Fifty-Four Alliance, though he says that's not its real name, which he doesn't yet know. It's all so cloak and dagger it's hard to take seriously."

Timothy began to chuckle.

"One of the most fascinating of his weird theories is the contention that this secret group has been using artificial intelligence, going all the way back to the 2020s, to manufacture lifelike human robots that look, sound, and behave, with mannerism and voice inflections, everything, exactly like all the major world leaders. Within months of a new leader coming to power, they have his or her robot ready. When the moment of takeover comes, they will quietly eliminate the heads of state and replace them with their AI counterparts. They will be able to control them completely, what they say and do, smoothing the way for the New Order, then gradually replacing the robots with their own people.

"He says he has evidence that former President Samara, as Domokos's granddaughter, was part of it. In order to try it out on the public, her AI replacement was secretly smuggled into the Oval Office. While President Samara was in hiding, the robot 'president' took her place for a full two weeks, making public appearances, speeches, even meeting with congressional leaders and foreign dignitaries."

"I think I remember that!" said Jaylene. "There was a brief time when a few people who met with her thought she—or *it*, if there is any truth to the story!—seemed somehow *off*, not quite herself. There was talk about a medical condition. But then it all blew over. Could Dale Birch be onto something?"

"Who knows!" laughed Timothy. "That's the thing about conspiracy theorists—often truth is mingled into their claims and they are later vindicated as having not been as wacko as people thought. With the way AI has taken over technology and business, nothing would surprise me. What if all of Congress and the Supreme Court is made up of progressive robots simply doing as their handlers have programmed them to do and the whole country is being run by this secret Fifty-Four Alliance, whatever it might be. But do you want to know Dale's craziest allegation?"

"I can't wait!" laughed Jaylene.

"He is a great C. S. Lewis fan. He says that Lewis was a prophet but not for the reason people think but for his ability to see far into the future in *That Hideous Strength.* Dale claims, exactly as in Lewis's book, that the head and brain of Viktor Domokos is still alive, and being kept viable, fully conscious, capable of advanced thought far beyond any other human being, and is the mind and brain and demonic power behind the secret Alliance, directing its activities, setting its agenda, and in all ways extending his grand vision into the future. There is some secret compound in California where he is kept. Real-life seances take place when the leaders are in the presence of *the Head.* Yet they are not seances at all, because he is still alive! They literally talk to him and receive his instructions."

"Now that I do *not* believe!" said Jaylene, emphatically though this time without laughing. "That is beyond creepy! There is no way Dale could possibly know such things, even if they were true—which they can't possibly be."

"I'm sure you're right."

"What I don't understand is how he can be attacking progressivism and Islam both. They are opposites. Islam may not be a religion of peace, but in its hatred of many of the pillars of progressivism, Christians and Muslims perceive many things through the same lens. His title implies that Islam and progressivism are linked."

"Not really," rejoined Timothy. "For all his wacko ideas, our conspiratorial friend Mr. Birch may have stumbled onto a truth with enormous implications for Christians."

"Which is?" asked Jaylene.

"That for Christians the ideological war, and what may be a real war in the not-too-distant future, will be fought on two fronts. Though in many ways they are opposite, they are both the enemies of Christian truth—progressivism and Islam. He does not speak in terms of biblical prophecy, but between the lines it is not hard to read tribulationism into his diatribes. There is just enough sense to it, in the middle of the nonsense, that in the right hands, this crazy little pamphlet could ignite a firestorm."

"You really think so?"

"I do. I think it is a dangerous document. Not because it is inflammatory like *Mein Kampf*, but because it contains just enough truth to be dangerous. Dale Birch is no madman like Hitler. He actually has a fairly shrewd sense of the history of Islam's jihad and its threat to Western civilization. He is an intelligent young man who is unfortunately a hothead. I'm more than a little concerned where this may lead."

"He's been passing these out for a while, hasn't he, and nothing has come of it."

"The first I heard of it was at Ginger's graduation in June. That was about three months ago. That's not long. All it would take is for it to get into the right hands—or the wrong hands, I should say—and who can tell what the repercussions might be."

On Wednesday evening, Timothy made the call he knew would probably not be well received.

"Hello, Dale," he said, "it's Dr. Marshall. I called to say that I read your pamphlet in its entirety. You've put a huge amount of research into it. I found much in it fascinating and illuminating. I learned some things I did not know. Your historical outline of the idea of jihad in Islam, I felt, was probably the strongest aspect of your presentation. I would like to talk to you further about it. As to your request to address my next lecture at the university, as I told you, that is simply not possible. The university would not allow it. But I am sincere in hoping we could get together informally in the future."

The phone was silent for a few seconds.

"But, Dr. Marshall," said Dale at length, the agitation evident in his voice, "don't you see the danger? Don't you see that we have to fight fire with fire."

"Jesus said we are to fight fire with love."

"He said he didn't come to bring peace but a sword. Now is the time for Christians to pick up that sword."

"That is not what Jesus meant. I think you know that, Dale."

"All I know is that the world is in trouble, that Islam and progressivism are taking it over. Which of those two will win in the end, I don't know. Christianity is the only hope. We have to stand and fight against both those evils or one or the other of them is going to rule the world before long."

"I agree, Dale. But we have to fight that two-pronged war in Christ's way, neither in Saul Alinsky's way nor in Mohammed's way. We are Christ's army, not a worldly army."

Again the line went silent. When Dale spoke again, his voice was firm and steely.

"Thank you for reading my pamphlet, Dr. Marshall. It was more than I expected. Good bye."

39

A Pop Quiz on Objectives

IT HARDLY needed Dale Birch's pamphlet to inflame the atmosphere surrounding Timothy's third lecture. As Timothy, Jaylene, Heather, and Todd walked across the Jessup campus, seeing Dale passing out his sixteen-page screed in front of the new Christian Humanities building was an unwelcome surprise.

"Excuse me," Timothy said to the others. "You go ahead—I'll meet you inside."

Dale was intrusively shoving pamphlets in front of everyone approaching the building and attempting to engage them in conversation. He glanced up to see Timothy walking toward him.

"Hello, Dale," said Timothy. "I see you decided to take matters into your own hands."

"You wouldn't give me the chance to do it your way. So I had to do what I had to do."

"I don't suppose, as a favor to me, you would stop handing out your pamphlets? It's bound to disrupt the lecture, which I would be happy for you to attend."

"It's a free country, Dr. Marshall. I have the right of free speech."

"Of course. I was just hoping you would do so as a courtesy to me."

"Why should I? You're just sugar-coating the truth. People need to wake up. Your lectures aren't helping."

"I didn't realize you'd been in attendance."

"I haven't been. I know your type. You try to play both sides, offend nobody. This is war, Dr. Marshall. We've got to get in people's faces or this country is finished.—Hey, take this. You need to read it!" he said loudly, hurrying off toward several students wearing traditional Muslim robes.

Timothy watched sadly as they paused. A tall, bearded older Muslim man accompanying his young proteges stepped forward. Within seconds a heated argument was in progress that looked potentially alarming.

Thinking it best not to get involved, Timothy turned and made his way inside the building. There his wife, daughter, and Todd were waiting for him. Mark and Grace had just joined them. The six continued into the lecture hall.

Even before taking his place at the podium fifteen minutes later, Timothy sensed a different atmosphere in the hall. The crowd was larger and the room filled with an electricity of anticipation and uncertainty. Low conversations were everywhere. The presence of a significant number in Muslim garb changed the chemistry of expectation. Were they here to learn and absorb what he had to say, or to argue and counter his attempts at objectivity?

As he stood waiting for the hubbub to subside, he could not help a sense of disquiet.

Keep me calm and focused, Lord, he breathed silently. *Speak your words to every heart, not my own words. Settle my spirit. Help me reflect your invisible presence to all those who hear my voice.*

Timothy drew in a deep breath and began. "Good evening," he said. "It seems we have a larger group than before. Welcome to you newcomers—it is great to have you.

"Tonight we will focus on the purposes, overarching objectives, and ultimate *aims and goals*, of Islam and Christianity as set forth by their founders, and as specified and articulated in their texts—the Gospels and the Koran.

"Assessing these goals and purposes accurately may be more difficult than what we have faced until now. Next week's topic will be a comparison of the *histories* of the two religions. That will surely be controversial. As we all recognize, those histories do not tell a pleasant story, nor do they reflect well on the followers of either religion. What we are trying to do, however, is get to the roots and foundations of the religions without being sidetracked by the atrocities committed in the *name* of Islam or Christianity. Those red herrings will get us nowhere. We are trying to discover the *truth* inherent in the teachings and in the examples of their founders, while not being distracted by the hypocrisies of those who fly the Muslim or Christian banner but do so falsely.

"That difficulty faces us tonight. How can we assess the purposes and ultimate goals without being influenced by men's *interpretations* of those purposes? Even if we rely on the teachings of the founders and the texts, it gets ambiguous and subject to individual interpretation.

"For example, if I were to hit you Jessup students registered for this course with a surprise pop quiz tonight—and invite you members of the community and others to join them—I can only imagine how diverse the answers might be!

"Here is the first question on my pop quiz—*What is the primary, most important, overriding single purpose of Christianity?*

"How many answers would I get?"

Timothy paused to let his question sink in. A few hands went up, but he ignored them, not anxious to turn the evening into a free-for-all of opinions.

"I'll add a few more questions," he went on after a moment.

"Question two—*What is God's primary, most important, overriding single individual purpose within the hearts and lives of Jesus's followers?*

"Question three—*What is God's primary purpose within mankind as a whole?*

"Question four—*What is the primary purpose of the Christian church?*

"Question five—*What is God's primary purpose for his universe in eternity?*"

Timothy smiled and waited. This time no hands went up.

"These questions make you stop and think!" he said. "Come to think of it, maybe I've just settled on the first half of our final exam!"

Light laughter spread through the hall.

"These would have to be essay questions because every one is highly subject to individual interpretation. Even if I made it a requirement that all answers were based on the four Gospels, the answers and interpretations would be all over the map. Even if I limited the scope to just Matthew 5, 6, and 7, they would still be all over the map. These are thought-provoking, deep, serious questions probing to the heart of what, individually and corporately, Christians believe *the essence of Christianity*—its single purpose—actually is."

Again Timothy paused.

"Notice I said a minute ago," he resumed, "that these questions could comprise the first half of the final exam. The second half asks those same questions of Islam. You Muslims in attendance have to be just as seriously minded about the purposes and goals of Islam. If you were in my course, I would expect Muslims to be able to answer the above questions about the purposes of Christianity, just as I would expect Christians to be able to give cogent, accurate, well-thought-out answers to the questions:

"Question one—*What is the primary, most important, overriding single purpose of Islam?*

"Question two—*What is Allah's primary, most important, overriding single individual purpose within the hearts and lives of Mohammed's followers?*

"Question three—*What is Allah's primary purpose within mankind as a whole?*

"Question four—*What is the primary purpose of the Islamic worldwide Ummah?*

"Question five—*What is Allah's primary purpose for his universe in eternity?*"

After another brief pause, Timothy smiled again and went on. "I've raised these questions for a very important reason. My purpose is to force you to think, not only about your *own* beliefs but also about the foundations of Christianity and Islam in their wider contexts. Nearly every one of you Christians will have ready answers and proof-texts, and could write out a full-page essay on every one of those *first* five questions. Probably many of them would be scripturally sound. But on the second five relating to Islam, my guess is that you would be clueless, and probably get failing marks."

Again laughter and nods and comments spread among his listeners.

"You might have opinions. Most of them would probably be wrong. You Muslims would likely be in the same boat, well able to give accurate answers well-grounded in the teachings of the Koran for the second five questions but sadly lacking in your understanding of the first five. You know how it is when a teacher distributes test papers throughout the room and everyone has to grade someone else's paper. Imagine you Muslims grading the Christians' papers, and you Christians grading those of the Muslims! That would be very interesting. All of you would probably get C's—A's on half the questions, and F's on the other half!"

40

Foundational Perspectives

"THAT'S OUR problem," Timothy went on. "And that's the world's problem. That's why I developed this series of lectures—to enable us to answer—intelligently, objectively, and accurately—*all ten questions.* If we are going to coexist, relate to one another on the ground of our common humanity, we do not have to agree but we have to *understand* each other better than most generally do. Maybe you do not feel that is important. I do. We have to know the goals and purposes of Islam *and* Christianity to understand the world we're living in.

"That said, I do not intend to launch into a thorough theological treatise on each of these ten questions. Thousands of books have been written on every one. I raise them to point out the difficulty. But now I would like to return to my first premise, and try to isolate what I believe represent some of the highest and overall purposes of Christianity and Islam.

"Many Christians would say that salvation is the highest purpose of Christianity—trusting and accepting Jesus as one's Savior on the basis of his death for the sins of the world, thereby entering into relationship with him that will continue in heaven for eternity. There is much truth in that perspective, but I would reduce Christianity to a more basic truth:

"God, as creator of the universe, desires that all his created children grow into his good and loving and obedient sons and daughters.

"That in a nutshell is this one man's definition of the purpose of Christianity. Salvation emerges out of *this* foundational truth. This purpose is achieved in the lives of individual Christians as they follow the teachings of Jesus, whom Christians believe is God's Son, and model their lives after his. Thus, salvation is drawn up into it. As a result, God's people are intended to grow by degrees and by their adherence and obedience to those teachings, into what Christians term *Christlikeness*. It is a slow and imperfect process. Most Christians don't exhibit Christlikeness very well. That is the ideal, but it is a slow time coming.

"Please hear me very carefully. It is more than obvious that this is *not* the life-goal of most of those who call themselves Christians. I am not talking about *individual Christians* but about what Christianity as a religion and lifestyle is supposed to teach.

"All the ideas and doctrines of Christianity, including salvation in all the myriad ways Christians define it, and including all the churches and denominations that exist in the name of Christianity, are *supposed* to contribute to that overarching purpose—that God is engaged in the long slow process of fashioning good and loving 'Christlike' sons and daughters. Whether they do or not is another matter. That is the ideal, the goal, the objective. But no one needs to tell us that most churches don't contribute toward that goal very well.

"Now Islam shares much with Christianity in its outlook. But that central idea of personal growth and *transformation* to reflect the character of its founder, is not something Muslims are focused on. For all his teachings, Mohammed is not a man the majority of Muslims aspire to emulate in their daily lives and character. 'Mohammed-likeness' is not a commonly used term in Islam.

"*Make me like Jesus* is a prayer some Christians pray. Maybe Muslims pray *Make me like Mohammed*, but I've not heard that. Neither is salvation an intrinsic component of Islam, in the sense in which Christians understand it, as grounded in Jesus's death and resurrection from the dead. Obviously, there is no death for sin in Islam, nor is Mohammed claimed to be God's Son who rose from the dead. So at their foundations, the two religions are very distinct.

"The basic trilogy of truths upon which Islam is founded, if I may term it such, are *belief, good deeds*, and *prayer*. Goodness, love, growth, and personal transformation—all endemic to Christianity—are no doubt important to many Muslims individually. But they do not represent cornerstones of Islam as a whole. Belief in and obedience to the teachings, however, are equally imperative in both. Though this is a simplistic representation, the so-called Five Pillars of Islam are:

"The Profession of Faith, or *shahada*—simply stated, *There is no god but God, and Mohammed is the Messenger of God.* Also included is the belief the Koran is Islam's holy book of divine revelations. One becomes a Muslim by reciting the *shahada* with conviction.

"The second pillar is prayer, or *salat.* Muslims must pray facing Mecca, Mohammed's birthplace, five times a day: dawn, noon, mid-afternoon, sunset, and after dark. This prayer includes a recitation of the opening chapter of the Koran.

"Number three—alms, or *zakat.* Islamic law, requires Muslims to donate a portion of their income to fellow Muslims in need. Blessings are considered a result of charity.

"Then fasting, or *sawm.* During the daylight hours of Ramadan, the ninth month of the Islamic calendar, all healthy adult Muslims are required to abstain from food and drink.

"And finally, the fifth pillar is pilgrimage, or *hajj.* Every Muslim whose health and finances permit must make at least one visit to the holy city of Mecca in their lifetime, to the Haram Mosque which it is believed was built by Abraham. Muslims from around the world gather in Mecca on the eighth and twelfth days of the final month of the Islamic calendar.

"In addition to these five so-called pillars, much in Islamic teaching exhorts Muslims to live virtuous lives, and to extend Islamic belief through education, preaching, and writing—with clear parallels to Christianity—but also includes the obligation to defend Islam against aggression. This takes the discussion in a new direction."

Timothy paused and drew in a deep breath.

"All right, well and good—no major controversies so far. The belief systems, though different, contain many parallels and aspects in common. However, let's now talk about the elephant in the room. When trying to isolate the goals, purposes, and ultimate objectives of

Christianity and Islam, the elephant cannot be ignored. The elephant is intrinsic to both religions. That elephant is *jihad*—holy war."

Rustling and murmuring spread through the hall.

"The word is obviously supercharged with implications. But let's be clear, though the term *jihad* is singularly Islamic, the words 'holy war' exist in Christianity too. Jihad signifies *struggle*, though it has become synonymous with *holy war*. One of the most famous Christian books of all time is *The Holy War* by John Bunyan, author of *The Pilgrim's Progress*. Those who know no better might criticize Christianity as jihadist too, not realizing that Bunyan's book had nothing to do with world conquest. That said, however, it is still true that at the heart of both religions is an imperative concerning the proselytizing of the world.

"It is a difficult conundrum to address simply on the basis of the texts. Much of Islam's jihad imperative comes from sources over the past 1,500 years other than the Koran and its accompanying document the Hadith. Alongside its troubling passages about killing and beheading infidels, the Koran also warns against aggression. We read in 2:190, 'And fight in the way of God with those who fight you, but aggress not: God loves not the aggressors.' Obviously, this is not a principle that Mohammed's followers have always obeyed. However, 9/11 was defended by many Muslims around the world as precipitated by *US aggression*. Thus, even terrorism has been defended on the basis of this passage. Jihad is often referred to as 'the sixth pillar of Islam.'

"This, however, is a discussion best left for later. For now we simply must recognize the intriguing truth that Jesus's followers have been commanded to take their belief in Jesus—he literally says 'make disciples of all nations'—to the whole world even more directly than is the case in Islam. What is called Jesus's Great Commission commands that his teachings be taken to *all* the world and that disciples be made of *all* nations.

"Is this tantamount to jihad in Christianity? There is clearly a big difference between 9/11 and the selfless missionary work of countless Christians throughout history. But the Crusades objection is always appealing for the skeptic to bring into the discussion, leaving Christians and Muslims at an impasse.

"Circling back to the questions with which we began—the purposes and goals and ultimate objectives of the two religions, we can accurately say that the objective of worldwide influence, even conversion, is shared by both religions. The methodologies advocated by their founders and in their texts, however, are diametric opposites. Can a religion, *any* religion, be considered a true representation of *any* supreme Creator, when it advocates killing as Mohammed does?

"Christians and Muslims will no doubt answer that question differently. I only pose it, as all the questions I am raising, as a historian trying to look at the evidence."

It was good Timothy's lecture was winding down. He concluded after another ten or fifteen minutes. Within seconds the room burst into comments, a few shouts, and dozens of raised hands.

A rowdy discussion followed. Timothy did his best to moderate the vigorous exchanges and keep them from getting out of control before he brought the evening to a close.

Just as he managed to restore order for his closing remarks, a movement at the rear of the hall drew Timothy's eye. One of his listeners rose and made for the exit.

It was Lionel Holt.

41

Surprise Packet from California

IF THE overnight package had been sent to his residence, it wouldn't have appeared until Monday. But the Presidential Manor never slept. For all its incompetence, the post office knew to dispatch all mail by special courier immediately. Mike Bardolf received a call from the Manor operator shortly after its arrival and was on his way minutes later.

Seeing the California postmark, whatever were his expectations resulted in a sigh. The kid had nearly outlived his usefulness and was becoming more trouble than he was worth. But if he'd seen the need to send it overnight, it was worth a look.

He went upstairs to his office, tore open the stiff envelope, glanced over the enclosed pamphlet, then read the letter.

Mr. Bardolf,

I don't know if this is important or not, but I thought you should see it and know what is going on here. I've been watching the Marshalls and Forsters, but not much has happened since the raid on their meeting in July. That sure put them in their place. You should have seen them!

You probably knew Todd Stewart has joined their group. He's working at old man Gordon's ranch of all things.

A little over two weeks ago, Dr. Marshall, that's the father of the girl whose house we broke into to get you those addresses, started a series of lectures about Islam and Christianity. I heard about it but wasn't all that interested. I decided to go last night, and what should I see but that most of their group was there. I'm wondering if these lectures might be how they're trying to get recruits for their plans. This Marshall is usually the quiet one of the group's leaders. But his talks are stirring things up around here. I thought you should know in case they're expanding and trying to start cells on the campuses.

At last night's lecture, the guy who wrote this pamphlet was passing them out. I talked to him a little and he knows Marshall and others in the group. I couldn't find out if he was part of the group itself, but he seemed to be there with Marshall's blessing. There's a lot of pretty far-out stuff in it. After I read it I knew you needed to see it. This might give you what you need to go after the group.

If there's anything else you want me to do, let me know.

Sincerely,
Lionel Holt.

Bardolf tossed the letter aside and glanced over the cover of the pamphlet. An amused grin spread over his mouth at the title. He'd seen enough of this kind of thing, the homemade manifesto of some young kook. He eased back in his chair and began to read. By the third page he was not only sitting up straight, he was reading carefully. The guy had uncannily anticipated his own Freedom Manifesto, though he couldn't possibly have seen it. If he didn't know better he'd think the guy had bugged his office! Mingled as it was with conspiracy nonsense, it was dangerous. If it went public, it could kibosh the Freedom Bill!

Just as he began to grow worried, he reached the passage about Viktor Domokos's head being kept alive. He chuckled as he read. No one would take *this* seriously! What did he have to worry about. *Although*, he thought, *pretty clever idea, young Birch! I wish I'd thought of it fifteen years ago!*

His earlier concerns relaxing, he continued to read. Suddenly his eyes shot open.

Fifty-Four Alliance!

Caramba! How could he possibly have stumbled on the phrase? It wasn't an exact reference to Palladium—but too close for comfort.

He read through the rest of the pamphlet at lightning speed, his active mind absorbing every detail. This fellow was either a prophetic genius or else he had inside information. Some of this stuff could have originated nowhere but here in the Presidential Manor. Could there be a leak, a mole?

He sat back and thought a moment.

Forster! He'd had access within the Presidential Manor for a year!

Who else! Young Holt had proven himself yet again. This crazy pamphlet obviously led straight to the Forster-Marshall conspiracy!

What was their game plan now? And where did this Birch fit in? Still no mention of the Benedict angle? If Birch somehow knew about the Alliance, why no mention of the Benedict thing?

He wasn't sure what to make of Birch's allegation of hidden links with a jihadist element and the president's progressive agenda. That was a stretch. Birch was on the attack in every direction at once. Most of this was the raving of a lunatic.

None of that mattered. Palladium's secrecy was suddenly on the line. That was the most imperative reason he had to be dealt with. He could handle the Forster-Marshall group. But this harangue had to be squelched before it got out. Whatever he knew . . . however he had come by his information . . . Dale Birch had to be silenced.

He thought a moment, then picked up his phone.

"Bruno—Mike here. I've got something that needs to be handled."

He and Bruno Volker chatted for a minute or two as he explained.

". . . I want no details, just do what you have to do . . . into his apartment . . . right—imperative you recover and destroy all copies of the thing . . ."

He nodded as he listened for several seconds.

"Of course, yes . . . goes without saying . . . computer, backups, hard drives . . . right, contact lists, personal data—*everything*. I not only want him silenced and this pamphlet of his snuffed out as if it never existed, I need to know how he came by his information. We have to know everything about him. Report back to me personally."

42

Pistachio

THE UNDERCURRENTS and increasing controversy stirred up behind the scenes by Timothy's Christianity and Islam course didn't change the day-to-day routine at either the Bar JG or Circle F ranches. Livestock still needed to be fed, stalls and pens cleaned, and fences kept in good repair. Cattle, horses, chickens, the few sheep and goats Bob Forster kept, and his two pigs, all went about their business unconcerned with the great stirrings of world events.

That neither ranch had dairy cows kept their respective alarm clocks from having to go off at 5:00 every morning. But Todd and David were up with their coffee and Bibles well before seven, as were Mark and Grace, and Bob and Laura a few miles away—Bob not with a Bible in his lap, though Mark and David, his lifelong friend, continued to gently lead him deeper in his faith.

At eighty, though David still enjoyed an occasional ride into the foothills, he recognized that his most important priority at this season of his life was to pass on the principles of discipleship to the young man God had brought into his life. Nor could he have been given a more eager and willing protégé. He marveled at the rapid deepening of Todd's maturity and understanding of the principles of life with God. Along with Timothy and Jaylene, the former media star was steeped 24-7 in depth of character, humility, virtue, selflessness, and command-obedience. How could his new faith not flourish in the good soil of Christlikeness in preparation for the season when God would raise him up, like his mentors, unto thirty, sixty, and hundredfold fruitfulness in its due season.

Late one morning Heather appeared unexpectedly at the ranch.

"This is a surprise," said Todd walking toward her from the barn as she climbed out of her car.

Hearing her drive up, David emerged from the house.

"David and I have plans for you today," said Heather, smiling mischievously. She glanced toward David. "Are we still on?"

"The trailer's hitched to the pickup," he said. "I'll bring it around."

Three or four minutes later they were piled in and rumbling along the gravel driveway.

"I take it from the empty trailer we're picking up a horse," said Todd. "Is it a rescue situation or an injury project requiring your special gifts?"

"Not exactly," Heather replied with a smile. "Though my assistance may be required."

"You're being cryptic!"

"You are going to attend your first horse auction, my boy," said David. "You're in for a treat."

"I didn't think you were still in the market," said Todd.

"Only for one horse. A very special horse will be joining the Bar JG after today."

"You've already made arrangements?"

"Not yet. We have to pick out just the right animal for what we need, don't we, Heather?"

Todd glanced back and forth at the two, still perplexed. Neither said a word until they arrived at the auction yard near Grass Valley. Ranchers from throughout the foothills were walking about and scrutinizing some hundred or more animals in several corrals separated by age, type, size, and pedigree.

Todd looked about with fascination as they parked and got out. David led the way to a paddock holding some fifteen three-to-four-year-old mares and geldings.

"I think we'll find what we want here," he said as they stood at the railing looking them over. "See any that strike your fancy, Todd?"

"I know nothing about buying horses."

"Then it's time you learned. You have to find an animal you sense a connection with. It's a subtle exchange between man and beast you learn how to read. Those ethereal connections are impossible to predict or even quantify. It's something you feel."

"Why me?"

"Because you're going to pick out a horse that will be yours."

"Mine!"

"You have to find the animal you feel a bond with. We're here to buy your first horse. You will train it and ride it and develop a friendship that will become a big part of your life."

"You're kidding!"

"It's time you had a horse of your own. Heather and I will leave you to spend some time with them and look them over, observing, watching. The horses will be observing you too. One or another of them will feel a connection with you too. That's how it works. It's a mutual process. The chemistry has to be right."

"But I'm no expert."

"You will know. Don't worry, Heather will help when the time comes. She'll know if you've made a wise choice."

David and Heather walked away leaving Todd standing at the rail gazing over the group of young horses. From some distance away, Heather watched while David ambled off to talk to some of the other ranchers whom he had known for years.

Some of the horses remained calm and still, others moved about, two or three seemed skittish, some looked toward where Todd stood watching him, others took no notice. Several gradually sauntered in his direction.

As they inched closer he calmly stroked their noses and spoke softly as they came and went, drawing close then turning away, just as Heather had taught him. Heather gave him ten or twelve minutes to himself, then returned.

"Climb over," she said. "You can get into the corral, walk about. See what you think. They've been sizing you up too. It's time to get up close and personal. That tan mare who's been watching is definitely curious. But she was content to hang back and let the others make the first move. Now you need to walk about among them, mix and let them hear your voice and smell you, see which ones welcome your touch and which shy away."

"Obviously, some of them are too small for me. I did notice the tan one too," nodded Todd. "Neither aggressive nor too shy. I like that. I can tell she's watching."

"For your height you will need a good-sized mount. She's fairly big for her age—I'm guessing she's about three-and-a-half. That's the right age to begin serious training. Someone your size shouldn't ride any animal under four. Even then, we'll need to take it slow."

"I thought you started breaking horses to ride by one or two so they get used to you when they're young."

"*Accustomed* to you, yes . . . *riding*, no. A horse's spine doesn't fully develop until around age six. Rushing it can do long-term damage."

"So I won't be riding any of these for a while?"

"It's a gradual process. If the horse is good sized and mature and with the right temperament, we can start at four—but gently and gradually. Go ahead, climb over."

Todd climbed up the rails, hoisted his large frame up and over the top, then jumped to the ground. As accustomed as he had grown to the animals at the ranch, horses were unpredictable. A few pangs of anxiety surged through him to see fifteen-hundred-pound unfamiliar horses coming his way like before. Almost as if waiting for the others to size him up and observing their reactions, slowly the tan mare moved toward him and gently nudged his shoulder from behind. Todd turned and stroked her head and nose.

"Walk about a little," said Heather. "See what she does."

Todd slowly moved away from the fence. The mare followed.

A few minutes later he returned to where Heather still stood. Still following him, the mare now approached Heather, nickering softly through her fleshy nose as if in greeting.

"She obviously approves of you," said Todd.

Heather said nothing, looking her over carefully, then began whispering quietly as the mare stretched her long neck over the top railing and leaned down toward Heather's face.

In spite of her diminutive size, Heather stepped up on the lowest rail, then scampered up, over, down to the ground as easily as Todd had, then walked slowly away. Now the mare followed her.

"I'd say her connection is with you not me!" laughed Todd. "I should know by now that *all* horses have a connection with you!"

Heather continued slowly through the corral, pausing occasionally to speak quietly and stroke the mare's nose and neck and back. Todd watched, marveling again as he had so many times when they visited other ranches for Heather to assess troubled animals, at the preternatural bond that seemed to develop almost instantly with every animal she encountered.

She returned a few minutes later, the mare still following.

"What's the verdict?" asked Todd.

"It's your decision," replied Heather with a smile.

"If she likes you, that's good enough for me," said Todd. "She obviously does."

"You're right—she has to feel a connection with us both since we will both be training and riding her."

She climbed back out and over the fence. "Spend a little more time with her," she said. "Walk about, stroke her, let her get used to your touch, your voice, your smell. See if she keeps following you and nickers and nuzzles you. Those are good signs."

Heather watched another few minutes, then, seemingly satisfied with what she saw, went in search of David.

When the two returned to the corral, Todd was standing just inside leaning on the top rail, the mare at his side.

"It's all arranged," said David. "Heather said this was your horse. She saw and felt the connection immediately."

"So what now?" asked Todd. "Do we bid on her or what? When's the auction?"

"I've spoken with the owner," said David. "I made him an offer and he was fine with it. The horse is yours, Todd. Let's get her loaded into the trailer."

"Thank you, David. Can you deduct it a little at a time from my pay?"

David laughed. "No need, Todd! This is a ranch business expense."

"Wow, I don't know what to say."

"You will earn her!" laughed David again. "And she will earn her keep."

"I can't wait to ride her. Can we take her out when we get back?"

"Not so fast! It will take some time before we're at that point."

"Oh, right—Heather told me. I forgot. Not until she's at least four. How old is she, do we know?"

"The owner's going to send over her papers. She's three years ten months—never been ridden. She'll also need a name."

Todd glanced back at where his new horse was still standing beside him.

"It may sound funny, but the first time she walked up and I noticed that oblong white splotch on her forehead, it reminded me of the shape of a pistachio nut. Could I call her that?"

"You can call her anything you like."

"That's a great name!" said Heather.

"Then I guess *Pistachio* it is!" said Todd.

The next half hour was spent getting the newly christened Pistachio into the trailer and making final arrangements with her former owner. Once they were on the road back to the ranch, Todd was full of enthusiastic questions.

"Is it really true, what her owner said, that she's never been ridden?" he asked.

"Like I told you," replied Heather, "she's still young."

"Who's going to break her when the time comes?"

"You are!" laughed David. "But if you're envisioning what you've seen on Westerns—the bucking bronco with whip and spurs, breaking a horse by breaking its spirit—all that went out years ago."

"So it's not just getting on and trying to hang on as long as you can?"

"That's Hollywood, and a lot of that went on too. But we don't even talk about *breaking* a horse. It's all about *training*, not breaking—building trust and camaraderie. You've seen Heather do it dozens of times. If you go slow and build trust, by the time they're ready to be ridden it's only a short phase when they might buck a little."

"What will we actually *do* until then?" asked Todd. "Will she just graze in the pasture until you think she's ready?"

"Oh, no," replied Heather. "We start tomorrow, mostly teaching her to trust you like David said, building the bond, deepening the connection. The trusting relationship is the foundation to everything. Your job will be the most important, spending time with her, grooming her, talking and simply being in her presence, always calm, quiet, and gentle. Some people call it liberty training—not using tack at all but working to develop respect and building intuitive communication.

"Then we'll start with a blanket, eventually a saddle. Everything in stages. Horses need to assimilate what they're learning. We'll let her get used to the feel of a saddle and bridle. Then we'll lean on her back, put a foot in one of the stirrups. After she's used to us putting the saddle on and keeping it on most of the day, then taking it off and repeating that every day, maybe in six or seven months when she's four-and-a-half, we'll see if she will allow me to sit on her back. I'm light enough for her to handle by then. If she resists, we'll wait a week and try again. Eventually she will accept it and I'll take some short rides with you leading on foot beside her talking to her and reassuring her."

"It seems complicated."

"Not really. You just have to do everything in the right order without rushing it. I'll show you how to teach her foundational skills, basic instructions—starting, stopping, and turning using gentle pressure combined with voice commands. We'll introduce the tack gradually—headgear first . . . halter reins and bit. The bit is uncomfortable in a horse's mouth at first. It takes a while to get used to. But the bridle is essential for teaching commands. The blanket and saddle and stirrups all come later. Once you're able to lead her with reins and halter, you'll take walks with her, solidifying verbal and other cues. All that's preparatory for riding. The whole process can take a year or more."

"There's more to it than I realized. I suppose I've just been watching you all this time and taking it for granted."

Heather laughed. "I've been doing this for over twenty years. I had to learn too. I'll show you everything you need to know. You'll be a pro in no time."

Later that afternoon Todd's newly named mare Pistachio was getting accustomed to her new surroundings. Todd had spent nearly every minute with her since arriving back at the Bar JG, talking to her, feeding her, brushing her down.

Knowing that horses were drawn to her, Heather kept her distance for the rest of the day and the next. She wanted Pistachio's bond with Todd to come first. All she would allow Todd to do for now was place a leather strap around her neck so he could lead her, and for Pistachio to get used to being led.

"We have to get her comfortable just being here," she said. "It's a big change. She has to get used to new sights and smells, the pasture and barn and routine and other horses. Mostly get used to you and trust you. Be patient, it will all come. She's a good horse. You made a wise decision."

"With your help!"

"Maybe. But I could see that the bond with you began to form almost immediately. For now, spend as much time with her as you can. She will be your only job for the next few days. You need to be with her from daybreak until sunset. Once she trusts you, you will be her best friend and lifeline. Half our work will be done."

That evening, after tossing two bales of hay down to the floor of the barn from the loft above, Todd and Heather sat down on the lower rows of bales and breathed in deeply.

"I love the smell of a hayloft," said Heather. "Good thing neither of us get hay fever."

Below them, the animals were settling in for the night. In her new stall, Pistachio was contentedly munching on oats after a day as eventful in her life as it was in Todd's.

"Do you really think I can train and break her?" asked Todd. "Oops—I mean train and *bond* with her and eventually teach her to let me ride her?"

"Of course," replied Heather. "She may throw you a few times. You'll get some bruises. But that's part of it. The old bucking bronco stereotype is pretty much a Western movie thing. That doesn't mean horses don't resist having someone on their back at first. If you're going to be a cowboy, you've got to take a few tumbles."

Todd laughed. "I'm hardly a cowboy!"

"With your boots and hat, you're the handsomest cowboy I know! You could walk onto any ranch in California, or Texas for that matter, and nobody would bat an eye or think you out of place. You'll be riding Pistachio all over these hills in a couple years. Don't worry. I'll show you everything you need to know."

Again, it was silent. Neither said anything for several minutes.

"There's something I need to say, Todd," said Heather at length. "I'm not trying to change anything or break up with you or anything—oh gosh—I shouldn't have said that! Forget I said it! You know how I feel . . . I think you do, I hope you do. You've been so good to me, and I know that to some extent the feeling is mutual. I hope that's not too presumptuous to say. What you've given me has changed my life and is a greater blessing than I ever imagined coming to me. But I also know you've only been a Christian a relatively short time. You've made a lot of changes in your life. You left a promising career.

"As you settle into a lifetime of being a Christian and continue to grow, it's possible your outlook could change. That happens. It's natural. You may find yourself wanting to go back into the media in some role, back to the East Coast. You might not want to work on a ranch forever. I know you care for me, but I will understand if we aren't meant to have a future together. I want you to be free to follow whatever God gives you to do, with no strings attached from me. You owe me no commitments if the time comes when God leads you to pursue other things than the life we are enjoying now. I will be blessed for the rest of my life even if there is a change. I never want to hold you back, even if it means being willing to let you go."

She stopped and exhaled a long sigh.

Todd had been listening quietly, staring down at the rough hundred-and-fifty-year-old floorboards of the loft. After a moment he looked up and turned toward Heather. His eyes were swimming. He reached over and took one of her hands. But no words would come.

43

Missions vs. Jihad—Distinct Historic Objectives

THE TEXT, email, and telephone correspondence between Bradon Rhodes and Ginger Forster since Bradon's brief visit to California with Todd was equally surprising to both.

Neither had anticipated it. But as one thing led to another, Bradon full of questions about Christianity and their group, like Todd before him, Bradon found himself learning new ways of looking at life and the world through the eyes of a young woman who was unexpectedly occupying more and more of his thoughts. That their fathers were once best friends added yet more interest to the budding relationship.

Ginger told Bradon about Timothy's lectures and did her best to explain them.

"I'd love to read them," said Bradon when they were talking on the phone. "Have they been transcribed—are they printed and available?"

"Actually, I don't know," replied Ginger. "They're being recorded and videoed, I know that."

"I'd love to have a copy."

"I'm sure I can get you one."

"When's the next lecture?"

"Tomorrow night. Oh—I've got an idea. I'll record it on my phone and you can watch with me live."

"That would be fantastic. I'd have to be someplace alone!" laughed Bradon. "I don't think it would go over too well at the Manor where the walls have ears."

"We all sit together in the front row—Timothy's support team, he calls us. You'll be able to see him just like being there."

☆ ☆ ☆

In spite of his concerted effort to remain objective, Timothy's blunt observations about jihad during his previous lecture had Christian and Muslim students talking passionately on the Sacramento State and Jessup University campuses for the following week.

His fourth lecture focusing on the respective histories of Islam and Christianity turned out to be an even more raucous evening. An honest assessment of many historic corruptions of their ideals, and the negative impact on a true understanding of both Christianity and Islam, was a delicate and controversial topic.

Passions ran high.

☆ ☆ ☆

By Friday evening it had all been arranged. Bradon slipped out of the Presidential Manor. He drove to a secluded section of Rock Creek Park—*not* followed on this occasion by Mike Bardolf!—and awaited Ginger's call.

Bradon greeted the others via Ginger's phone ahead of time—Todd and Heather and Jaylene sitting together, and Ginger with her brother and parents and grandparents. As the hall gradually filled, as Ginger predicted, he felt like he was there with them.

Bradon reflected on how much he had changed since his first awkward encounter with Ginger on Bainbridge Island. Unexpectedly, even weirdly, he found himself more connected to the small group on the other side of the country than with anyone in Washington, DC. Except for his mother, he was a stranger in the Presidential Manor. Knowing that Mike Bardolf was watching him, he almost felt like a foreign agent in the midst of an enemy compound. The whole atmosphere was hostile to his new spiritual awareness.

As he sat in the darkness in his refurbished Mustang, Bradon realized that he was alone in more ways than just sitting in a deserted park at ten o'clock at night. He had no friends at school. Did he have any real friends at all?

Truth be told, he felt closer to the people he had just been talking to on his phone than anyone in the capital—Ginger, Todd, even young Craig, not to mention the Jansens and Ginger's parents.

It was a strange thing to realize, but it was almost like he'd been adopted into a new family—a group of people who had every reason to despise him—yet somehow who actually loved him. That he knew his grandmother was also of that same spiritual family made it all somehow seem so *right*.

His thoughts were interrupted by the sound of Timothy Marshall's voice as his lecture got underway. As he listened he realized why his new friends held the Marshalls in such high regard. The man's knowledge of history and astute insight into the differences between Islam and Christianity were profound. Why didn't they teach these things at Georgetown!

☆ ☆ ☆

Timothy opened by trying to establish an intellectual and historical framework from which to evaluate the histories, looking at the stated objectives of each belief system from the previous week, then attempting to examine where the followers of both religions had diverged from them. This required an honest look at strengths and pitfalls and of the ways in which mankind had benefited, individually and globally, as well as been damaged, by the influences of the two religions.

"The histories of Christianity and Islam," he began after an introductory plea for intellectual honesty and objectivity, "proceed out of their goals and objectives. As I have emphasized, our challenge is to judge and evaluate Christianity and Islam accurately.

"There have been numerous occasions in which their followers *have* reflected Jesus's and Mohammed's teachings.

"Both religions, for example, emphasize caring for the poor. We have seen that alms represents one of the pillars of Islam. Jesus likewise illustrated the great commandments by telling the rich young ruler to sell his possessions and give the money to the poor. This fundamental objective is shared by both Christianity and Islam.

"The historic perversions of Christianity yield a long list: burnings at the stake, excommunications, the narrow-mindedness of its adherents toward viewpoints other than their own, repudiation of scientific advancements, the treatment of men like Wycliffe and Galileo, factionalism, and atrocities too numerous to mention. These, however, are red herrings. Christianity's detractors invariably trot out these perversions to invalidate Christianity. In so doing they only demonstrate their own shallow and dishonest thinking. A thousand such examples do not reflect the teachings of Jesus. They are directly *opposite* to his teachings. They do not represent true Christianity. They are dreadful black marks in the history of the West. But the Crusades don't invalidate Christianity.

"Christianity's history, and the veracity of Christianity, has to be evaluated on the basis of Christianity's *true* objectives and purposes. Included in that purpose is proselytizing the world with the Christian gospel, not by conquest and war but with the *ideas* of Christianity, whose fundamental idea is *love* toward all mankind.

"Christianity's missionary imperative, when lived in accord with Jesus's teaching, has produced literacy, education, health, and advancement. Primitive peoples all around the world have been raised into a higher way of life by Christianity's historic missionary endeavors. Though Christian missions are now viewed by secular progressives as having contributed to white racism and Western imperialism, the charge is obviously short-sighted. Christians have been on the front lines fighting poverty, disease, and illiteracy around the globe for centuries, doing more good in people's lives than is accomplished by all the governmental foreign aid in history. This is a prime example of Christians working toward one of Christianity's objectives, not perfectly but in a generally true direction according to Jesus's teaching.

"The Crusades on the one hand, and Christian missionary endeavors on the other, are perfect examples of using Christianity's history in a *false* way and a *true* way. The many perversions of its truths tell us little about the true essence of Christianity. The lives of selfless, dedicated missionaries tell us a great deal about true Christianity.

"Now comes the hard part—can we be astute and intellectually honest enough to recognize that no parallel with the Christian missionary imperative exists in Islam? That is not a critique, only an honest assessment of historical fact. Islam has not historically sought to help people as *individuals,* but rather to infiltrate and take over *cultures*, and eventually *nations.*

"Islam's imperative is altogether different. It is said today that there are more Muslim missionaries around the world than Christian missionaries. But Muslim missionaries are not missionaries in the traditional sense. Their objective is to take over nations with Islamic culture and ultimately to infiltrate their governments as well. Islam's missionary imperative is to turn native peoples into Muslims. Christianity's missionary imperative is to help them as *individuals.* If they become Christians in the process, so much the better. But conversion is not viewed independently from bringing goodness, health, education, and wholeness to their lives. These are completely different objectives than exist in Islam.

"The ultimate goals of Christianity and Islam are, in one sense, similar—world change. But whereas Christianity seeks to help *individuals*, making their lives better, helping them grow into good, happy, literate, healthy, self-fulfilled people, Islam's goal is to force itself upon cultures and institutions and nations, eventually turning them into Muslim states. There is no such thing as a 'Christian state.' Many have tried to build Christian states. But they have failed because such is not an objective of true Christianity. Jesus's purposes for his followers was neither national nor governmental.

"Islam, on the other hand, is almost *entirely* cultural, societal, and ultimately governmental. That's why its ultimate imperative is defined by that controversial word *jihad*. Conquest of culture is the objective. The individual is not as important as the ultimate goal of spreading Islam throughout the world.

"This distinction sets the two religions at complete opposite poles of ultimate purpose. It is the contrast between an *individual mission to improve lives* and *worldwide cultural and national conquest.* These are *true* pictures of Christianity and Islam.

"We need to be clear about something else. This will be controversial but is vital. I implore you Muslims present to put on your intellectual-honesty hats.

"This vital truth is that Islam's jihadist imperative is *not* the same as the Crusades-red-herring brought against Christianity. It originates with the teaching of Mohammed in the Koran just as the mission imperative of Christianity, with *love* for mankind as its foundation, originates with Jesus. The killing of infidels is not a red herring. It comes straight from the Koran. The history of jihad throughout the long history of Islam gives a generally *accurate* picture of this important aspect of Islam as a whole.

"Violent Jihad cannot be swept aside as a mere fringe idea. Jihad lies at the heart of Islam."

☆ ☆ ☆

Timothy's explanation about the Crusades was so obvious, Bradon wondered how he could not have questioned such a superficial objection to Christianity he'd heard in school many times.

The Crusades don't invalidate Christianity. Christianity's history, and the veracity of Christianity, has to be evaluated on the basis of Christianity's true objectives and purposes.

As the lecture continued, he was also struck by the diametrically opposite objectives of the two religions.

This sets the two religions at complete opposite poles of ultimate purpose. It is the contrast between an individual mission to improve lives and worldwide cultural and national conquest . . . We need to be clear about this distinction or we can never understand this intrinsic difference . . . Islam's jihadist imperative is not the same as the Crusades-red-herring brought against Christianity. It originates with the teaching of Mohammed in the Koran.

As he listened, Bradon realized that he had been indoctrinated into the *religion of peace* narrative about Islam without knowing the first thing about Islam's roots. In spite of his grandmother's influence, he had been equally ignorant about Christianity.

The whole country had been brainwashed with untruths about both religions.

Violent Jihad cannot be swept aside as a mere fringe idea, Timothy had just said. *Jihad lies at the heart of Islam.*

44

Jihad—Every Muslim's Duty

NOTICEABLE RESTLESSNESS spread throughout the auditorium from Timothy's last words. Whether the Muslims in attendance disagreed with his statement or merely considered it an affront for him to say it bluntly, was a question that would probably remain unanswered.

"One of the difficulties in understanding Islam," Timothy continued, hoping the ruffled feathers of agitation would settle down, "is that even most Muslims and certainly most Christians, do not understand the subtle and disguised mechanisms which Islam advocates to further its hidden jihad to undermine the cultural fabric of non-Muslim nations and societies. Mohammed raised armies and simply went to war to achieve his goal of conquest. In recent times, however, cultural conquest has become subtle, mostly invisible. Islam is skilled in the long game. Writing over a hundred years ago in his book on the Crusades, Hilaire Belloc, made the incredibly succinct and prophetic statement, 'Islam survives; therefore it . . . may return. *Our* religion is in peril . . . Islam has . . . preserved its soul.'

"We see clearly the effect of a terrorist attack because it is played on television networks. For a few weeks or months jihad is in the news. Then years go by with few such visible signs. The 'religion of peace' narrative returns. Muslims go on with their seemingly normal and societally integrated lives as if their religious belief system, though different in its specifics, is similar to Christianity. The world becomes convinced that they are just people trying to live peaceful lives. Terrorist activity is written off as an aberration, not reflective of Islam as a whole.

"This is the great deception that even many peace-loving Muslims either do not understand or are unwilling to admit. Jihad remains under the surface as the foundational *modus operandi* by which Islam will eventually dominate the world. It has always been and always will be the ultimate objective. Behind the scenes, the slow, steady, invisible infiltration of every nation's cultural institutions—the media, business, public discourse, technology, academia, and ultimately government—continues its millennium-long inexorable march toward that ultimate goal.

"Westerners do not grasp the fundamental objective of Islam's long game. A hundred years—five hundred years means nothing if that's what it takes. Individual lives meaning nothing in light of the cause. That's why killing is an accepted aspect of jihad. Individual life is not precious. How different this is from Christianity where individuals are *everything.*

"This ebb and flow of jihadist methods, seasons during which violent jihad goes underground, has been in progress a long time . . . not mere decades but for centuries. Consider the situation in which Muslim nations in North Africa sent pirates to demand tribute payments from the United States for safe passage in the Mediterranean. The US ambassador asked what right they had to extort money from the United States. He answered, 'The right is founded on the Laws of the Prophet, for it is written in the Koran, that all nations who do not answer their authority are infidels and it is their right and duty to make war upon them wherever they are found and to make slaves of all they take as prisoners.'

"The words are foreboding—*it was their right and duty to make war.*"

"I use this example to illustrate Islam's long game and the shifting ebb and flow of its tactics. The report of this particular incident was written by Thomas Jefferson over two and a half centuries ago. That's why I say this jihadist perspective is endemic to the fundamental *long game* of Islam.

"It is a misconception that Islamic violence is an anomaly. It may be true that most Muslims are simply trying to go about their everyday business, to provide for their families, and live normal lives. But the fact that many Muslims are good people does not change the essence of Islam's ultimate objectives.

"This forces the question: What is *genuine* Islam? Do we make light of Mohammed's calls for war, terrorism, and beheadings? Should the violent sayings of Mohammed be ignored? If so, what becomes of the essence of Islam based on the teachings of its founder? If Mohammed's teachings are ignored, what is left?

"These dichotomies between the so-called religion of peace argument and the reality of violent jihad always lead to confusion. Even the Muslim world is not agreed on what constitutes *true* Islam. Islam is amorphous. That's why Westerners have difficulty understanding Islam. They view Islam through the lens of more familiar religions like Christianity and Judaism. But this is impossible because Islam is *completely* different at its core.

"Jihadist activism in past centuries has attempted to topple the enemies of Islam by violence, force, coercion, and outright warfare. When accusing the West of imperialism, Muslims are obsessed with the Crusades, making little mention of their own episodes of ghastly violence toward their enemies, nor that the Crusades were in response to their own violent aggression. Mohammed captured Mecca and the surrounding regions by war.

"That is why I say that jihad emerges out of the very origins of Islam. Jihad is essential to Islam. It has been the strategy of countless Islamic conquerors since Mohammed's time.

"In more recent times a new and different method has also emerged, a new *stage* in global jihad, though not a new overall plan. The objective is as ancient as Mohammed. The new method, however, relies on subverting Western civilization from *within*.

"The Muslim Brotherhood inaugurated this new *stealth* methodology and perfectly illustrates Islam's long game. The Brotherhood was founded in 1928 by Hasan al-Banna in an attempt to revive the political aspects of Islam following the decline of the Ottoman Empire. That was a century and a quarter ago. The world was much different then. But the objectives were identical to Islam's objectives of today, and identical to Islam's objectives of a thousand years ago. Times and politics change. Islam's ultimate goals have not.

"Al-Banna stated those goals when he wrote, 'It is a duty incumbent on every Muslim to struggle towards the aim of making every people Muslim and the whole world Islamic, so that the banner of Islam can flutter over the earth and the call of the Muezzin can resound in all the corners of the world: *Allahu akbar!*'

"His words could not be more clear—it is a duty incumbent on *every* Muslim to struggle toward the aim of making the whole world Islamic. This includes nice, peace-loving Muslims. Jihad is *every* Muslim's duty. Eventually that duty will come calling . . . tomorrow, next year . . . in a hundred years. Joining and furthering the jihad will eventually be demanded of every Muslim, because, as al-Banna said, it is a *duty incumbent on every Muslim.*

"Half a century after its founding, the Muslim Brotherhood produced a document detailing a twelve-point strategy for achieving al-Banna's goal of establishing an Islamic government on earth. Its reasoning was cunning and shrewd. Instead of a frontal assault, it advocated deception to mask its true agenda by introducing Islamic law into nations little by little—jihad by *stealth.*"

Timothy paused briefly.

"In 1991 this goal was reaffirmed," he continued. "Mohamed Akram of the Muslim Brotherhood wrote what was titled, *An Explanatory Memorandum on the General Strategic Goal for the Group in North America.* These are his words not mine. He said Muslims 'must understand that their work in America is a kind of grand jihad in eliminating and destroying the Western civilization from within and "sabotaging" its miserable house . . . so that it is eliminated and Allah's religion is made victorious over all other religions.'

"This document ought to send chills up the spines of every American and European. The goal is to *destroy Western civilization from within.* Compare this with Christianity's *individual mission* to bring goodness, virtue, truth, happiness, health, literacy, and self-fulfillment to every man, woman, and child within its reach.

"If they are paying attention, these words ought to be equally sobering to everyday American Muslims. If this is Islam, and if they truly love peace as they say, how will they reconcile themselves to this overarching objective which is considered their duty as well as that of terrorists?

What will they do when the duty is demanded of *them* to help destroy Western civilization from within?

"This is the cunning aspect of Akram's genius. Not merely will individual Muslims act as jihadist moles within Western culture, Islam will become a gigantic, hidden *ideological mole*, whose eventual goal is to infiltrate the entire global structure."

By now the agitation in the hall was rising. It was not exactly a powder keg, but tension was palpable.

"*Allahu akbar!*" came a cry.

A few more shouts followed from throughout the auditorium.

Timothy did his best to continue in spite of the rising din. But it was clear little was to be gained by attempting to continue.

He added a few closing remarks, then left the stage. The hall proceeded to empty as the commotion followed the exodus outside.

45

An Eye in the Sky

"MR. BARDOLF, it's Volker. This Marshall fellow is stirring things up with his lectures on Islam."

"In what way?" said Mike into his private cell phone.

"It's far-right-wing stuff. You and Rhodes may be right—it's got the makings of a subversive movement written all over it. Your pal Bahram should know what's going on. He might want to be here for the next lecture."

"He might be recognized."

"The security's light. Nobody's scrutinizing who's there. It's mostly students, though the Muslims are a definite presence. I know you only sent me out here to see what the lectures were all about. But I'm wondering if you'd like me to do some further nosing around."

"You may be right," said Bardolf thoughtfully. "Yes, I think I would like you to stick around for a while. I want to know everything I can about that group. We're still trying to get a handle on the identity of their so-called prophet or whoever is pulling the strings."

"I'll see what I can find out. The Stewart fellow is still here. Are you still tight with him—should I contact him and see if he'll talk?"

"No, he's a lost cause. We don't want to alert them that you're surveilling them."

"I understand. You could probably have this Marshall arrested under the terms of the Hate Speech Act."

"Maybe. But I should talk to the president about that. Marshall's a friend of his pal Forster. In the meantime, can you get me photographs of the two ranches? If we should have to go in with troops or a SWAT team under cover of Homeland Security, we'll want to know the lay of the land."

"I can do better than that. My two-thousand-foot drone is so small it will never be seen. I never go anywhere without it. I'll get you high-def videos of both places, the layout of the two properties, and hopefully of the people involved."

"It would be good if you were there for one of their meetings. I'd love to have visual evidence of the participants in the conspiracy."

"I'll see what I can learn."

☆ ☆ ☆

Three days later, Todd and Heather were returning from a ride and walk. They had been introducing Pistachio to the trails and woodlands surrounding the ranch. Heather was riding to give Todd's new mare the visual experience of being with another horse with a rider on its back, while Todd walked beside her holding the reins attached to Pistachio's halter. They had not yet put a bit in her mouth. As they went and Heather gave verbal commands to her mount, Todd repeated them to Pistachio along with the corresponding gentle pressure on the reins to right or left, or as needed to indicate faster or slower or to stop altogether.

Midway through the ride, they exchanged places. Heather wanted to reinforce Todd's use of the reins, his legs, his feet, and his voice commands—all of which he knew well enough by now—to make sure they were crisp and precise as needed in training a new horse. The change would also give Pistachio the experience of seeing Todd mount and ride and give verbal commands to another horse. Heather was acutely attuned to the many subtleties by which they were establishing patterns in Pistachio's visual, auditory, and sensory memory.

Neither of them were aware of the tiny flying military grade drone hovering some twelve-hundred feet above them, not only filming their movements but recording their every word. From a mile away, well off David's property, Bruno Volker listened to the conversation as clearly as if Todd and Heather were beside him.

"Do you think there's any chance Mr. Reyburn or Mr. Jansen will run against Bradon's father?" asked Heather as they made their way slowly along the wide dirt trail.

Where he listened, Bruno Volker's ears perked up.

"Not a chance," replied Todd. "You heard them. Both men were unequivocal."

"You know, there is someone else," said Heather, "who might have a chance—maybe not to win but to capture enough public interest to make a difference and stimulate the national debate in good directions."

"Who's that, your father . . . or Mark?"

"No, not them," laughed Heather. "I mean you."

"Me! You've got to be kidding—run for president! I'm a nobody."

"That's exactly what you're not. You're nationally known. You were pretty famous in your day."

Just then the two disappeared beneath a thick canopy of oak and pine and were lost to sight. Volker fiddled with his controls but lost their conversation for several minutes.

But he heard enough to know he had to get this to Bardolf ASAP.

46

Three Stages of Jihad—Stealth, Defense, Offense

TIMOTHY WAS relieved the following week to walk across the stage to the lectern in front of a quiet hall. The raucous end to the previous lecture had worried him. But the atmosphere was calm.

"At the end of last week's lecture," he began, "I quoted Mohamed Akram of the Muslim Brotherhood and his avowed strategy of destroying Western civilization from within. Clearly not all jihadists embrace the stealth strategy. Islam is multi-dimensional. Its overt and subtle strategies work in tandem, ebbing and flowing toward the ultimate goal.

"In fact, the strategy of stealth and the strategy of terrorism actually work in tandem. The stealth method feeds on the outbreaks of terrorism when they occur.

"Terrorism inevitably stirs up hatred on all sides, and precipitates retaliation against Muslims. We saw this after 9/11. This hatred is then leveraged to create a climate in which public figures in the West bend over backward to remind everyone that Islam is *really* a religion of peace, that the terrorists are fringe outliers and do not represent *true* Islam. That narrative, however, ignores the reality that violence *precisely* represents true Islam going all the way back to Mohammed.

"Moderate Muslims are shown yet greater respect and tolerance even than moderate Christians. This furthers the effectiveness of Islam's stealth infiltration. To confirm what forgiving and tolerant people we are, Islam is invited into every aspect of life and culture. And thus the hidden jihad accelerates with the eager help of the very Western institutions it will eventually sabotage and destroy.

"One of Egypt's Islamic leaders early in this century, Ali Gomaa, was considered a champion of so-called *moderate* Islam. His words, however, reveal his stealth radicalism. 'All the moderate Islamic groups in America,' he wrote, 'share the same agenda with the terrorists. What differs is only their methodology . . . there can never be coexistence with non-Muslim value systems . . . our purpose is to embrace a range of peaceful mechanisms . . . on the surface, harmless. Such are among the weapons in the arsenal of the stealth jihadists.'

"His words bear repeating—*there can never be coexistence with non-Muslim value systems.*

"Ali Gomaa described his introduction of revisions into Islamic teaching to make it more peaceful and to mute the more violent aspects of that teaching. 'We accept the revisions conditionally, not as the true teachings of Islam but with the understanding that this process is like medicine for a particular time.' In other words, violent jihad is temporarily set aside for strategic reasons. The goal has not changed, but the tactics have become more subtle and refined.

"Do not miss his words—the temporary peaceful revisions are *not the true teachings of Islam.*

"We return to the objection of Christians wanting to evangelize nations with their religious ideology too. But there is all the difference in the world. To put the contrast between the world imperative of the two religions into its starkest contrast—How many sermons on Jesus's Great Commission end with the words, 'And if they don't accept Christianity, kill them.'

"It's time we were intellectually honest," Timothy went on, "and no longer raise red-herrings like the Crusades as evidence that Christianity is violent and warlike too. Germany may have called itself a Christian nation because it had a state church. But no sane individual would call Hitler a Christian following the teachings of Jesus or Nazi Germany a 'Christian' nation. Muslim terrorists and suicide bombers, on the other hand, *are* faithful Muslims. They are following the teaching and example of Mohammed. In his lifetime Mohammed waged twenty-seven wars. The only violence ever recorded from Jesus was overturning a table and driving the money changers out of the temple. Jesus was a man of peace. Mohammed was a man of war."

Again Timothy paused. The temperature in the room was clearly escalating. A single hand went up. Timothy recognized one of his graduate students, a thoughtful young Christian. He decided to risk responding to a question from the floor and hope it did not start a flood.

"Yes, Bill," he said.

"If all you say is true, and I admit I never knew any of this, then why do we continually hear that Islam is a religion of peace?"

"Your question confirms the success of the stealth jihad," answered Timothy. "It is reassuring to tell ourselves that the people who are kidnapping children and blowing up buildings are not *true* Muslims because they ignore the peaceful elements of the Koran. What gets overlooked is that those peaceful statements in the Koran and in its parallel document, the Hadith, apply only to the first stage or *Stealth Jihad.*

"When Muslims are a persecuted minority, they are told to peacefully coexist with the surrounding peoples. This is where the religion of peace deception originates. This season of peaceful coexistence, however, is temporary, a means to an end. Even when promoting peaceful coexistence, Mohammed was telling his followers to prepare for the time when they would be in the majority and Allah would punish the infidel. He prepared for the second phase of the jihad by secretly building an army. Peaceful coexistence was a deceptive prelude to the war he intended to wage when the time was right.

"In other words, Islam teaches Muslims to *feign* friendship when they are outnumbered. But they are always looking beyond this stealth phase of the jihad to the second phase. When Muslims find themselves persecuted, then the peace-loving approach is discarded for *Defensive Jihad.* At that point they are allowed to attack any individual or nation perceived as a threat or a source of persecution. Such persecution may be nothing more than a criticism of Islamic beliefs. What I am doing here in the eyes of some Muslims would justify violent reprisals. Violent retaliation against the slightest criticism is justified by the doctrine of *Defensive Jihad.* This is *phase two.*

"We observe *Defensive Jihad* in Mohammed's life. When his people grew in power, they began killing those who opposed them. This involved attacking caravans, assassinating critics, and waging war against their so-called persecutors. This has provided justification for much of the terrorism of the last seventy years. Since the United States is considered a persecuting power against Muslim nations, terrorist groups have initiated violent phrase two with a vengeance.

"The third and final phase of jihad is *Offensive Jihad*. When Muslims reach a majority and can come out of the closet and take on their persecutors, opponents, and non-Muslims from a position of superior numbers and strength. At that point all pretense disappears. The true goal, which has *always* been the ultimate objective, emerges from the shadows.

"Islam's mantra then becomes, 'If they will not convert and accept Islam, kill them.'

"At this point, Mohammed's violent sayings make perfect sense. Islam's *Offensive Jihad* is savage and brutal, involving forced conversions, torture, beheadings of those who leave Islam, and the implementation of Sharia law. Mohammed's own teaching and example provide the model. His violence was brutal even by the standards of the seventh century. When his uncle, Abu Lahab, rejected his message, Mohammed commanded: 'He shall be burnt in a flaming fire, and his wife, laden with faggots, shall have a rope of fiber around her neck!' This invective comes straight out of the Koran.

"Obviously there is no parallel with Jesus overturning the tables of the money-changers. The religion of peace argument evaporates in Mohammed's own example."

47

A Stealth Observer

DRESSED IN a nondescript business suit, nothing to give away either his identity or secret objectives—especially among so many robed Muslim clerics and students wearing kufis and hijabs—Hamad Bahram nevertheless timed his entry to the lecture hall for the very last minute as an added precaution against being recognized.

No one so much as glanced twice in his direction as he took a seat in the last row. The only one likely to know him was Forster. He saw him in front, easily recognizable when he turned to speak briefly to his wife.

As Marshall's lecture progressed, he was stunned at the man's shrewd grasp of the essence both of Islam's history and its long-range objectives. Few throughout the country would probably even know about his lectures, or take his views seriously if they did. The likelihood of anything coming of all this was remote.

Still, the man could be dangerous. Marshall's insights were incendiary. If what he was saying became widely known, it would be devastating to his plan. When the time came, he had to be sure that blame fell on Christians.

How could the man be so exquisitely aware of the three stages of jihad? His perception of the unique subtleties of stealth his own father and grandfather used to seduce progressivism and advance their own objectives, was indeed dangerous.

Unwittingly, Marshall had uncovered their entire strategy!

At least he knew nothing definite, no specifics, no timetable.

Bahram wondered how much Bardolf knew about the content of these lectures, or if he had briefed the president. He might take that initiative himself. Though he had to walk warily. Bardolf was dangerous too. He couldn't risk running afoul of him until he had the president's full confidence. But if Bardolf was taking the lectures seriously, it could alert Rhodes to things it would be best for him not to know. He would downplay them to Bardolf, stressing the conspiratorial aspect of the Marshall group and say nothing about the Islamic content.

He knew Bardolf coveted the VP slot. As things presently stood with Rhodes likely to dump Wickes Hardy, such a choice wasn't impossible.

He had to play his cards right between now and then. He was increasingly gaining Rhodes's trust. If only he could get something on Bardolf to undermine his standing with the president.

Yet Bardolf's power in Palladium, now that he had consolidated his position, was not to be toyed with. Mike Bardolf was more powerful than his father, and everyone at Mira Monte knew it. If he misstepped, he could be snuffed out as easily as Bardolf had dealt with the fanatic Hutchins—at least, thought Bahram, if his suspicions were correct.

In the game of power, Mike Bardolf was as skilled as he. The next two years would require him to walk multiple tightropes.

48

A Strange Alliance—Islam and Progressivism

"THERE IS a strange twist in all this," said Timothy as his lecture continued, "which on the surface is baffling to logic. That is the strange alliance between two completely incompatible ideological systems—modern progressivism and the ultimate objectives of Islam. One would think progressivism would love Christianity. As illogical as it seems, however, progressivism has made Islam its ally and set itself to destroy Christianity.

"If the current growth of Islam continues, what we must realize is that the whole world will eventually find itself face-to-face with Islam's *Offensive Jihad*. In the United States and Europe, *Stealth Jihad* has been in progress for decades—harnessing the ideologies of multiculturalism and political correctness. Strategically appropriating the language and processes of Western pluralism, Islamic communities have forged a strange alliance with political liberalism to move ever closer to gaining the supremacy of numbers that will make the shift to *Offensive Jihad* possible. All the while, progressivism is blind to its own folly in furthering the agenda of jihad.

"This alliance between Islam and liberalism is purely strategic. Obviously there can be no compatibility between two such opposite worldviews. But *Stealth Jihad* will do whatever it takes to move Islam closer toward the day when it can seize the offensive and move toward subduing the non-Muslin world by force. Western progressivism has become a pawn in Islam's grand scheme.

"Nothing demonstrates this treacherous alliance better than the idea of *Islamophobia*. The term first began to appear in the mid 1990s, even before 9/11. Finding the idea appealing to its progressive sensibilities, the Western liberal media and politicians gradually redefined Islamophobia and weaponized it to shut down critical debate. This enabled criticism of Islam to be seen as a symptom of irrational fear, from which the subtly shifting definition moved to incorporate hate and racism, which morphed perfectly according to progressivism's playbook to an association with fundamentalist Christianity.

"Connecting progressivism's illogical dots—to be a Christian was to be Islamophobic. All the other phobias of liberalism came along for the ride. Christians came to represent the bull's-eye of all that was backward, bigoted, racist, and evil in our modern society.

"Islam is obviously a religion, not a race. The liberal press chose to obscure this fact by using *Muslim* and *Arab* interchangeably, even though the majority of Muslims are *not* Arabs. This linguistic sleight of hand allowed the media to convey the impression that criticism of Islam was a racist and a particularly Christian offense—a *hate crime*.

"Islamophobia, so-called, became widely considered a form of racist bigotry though the premise of the linkage is illogical in the extreme. All the while, Muslim strategists were laughing in their sleeve. In its irrational rush to brand everything outside its progressive narrative as bigoted and racist, and thinking itself kind and tolerant and embracing of Islam by condemning anti-Islam haters, liberalism has *advanced* Islam's *Stealth Jihad*.

"The next time you hear the word *Islamophobia*, realize this—you have just heard the silent footsteps of Islam's stealth agenda taking another step toward phase three, courtesy of America's progressive liberal machine. After this lecture I will be branded an Islamophobe. Do I strike you as a man of hate? I hope you have been listening more carefully than that.

"If it were *proven* that Christianity was a fraud, that its historical record was complete fiction—if everything I have said was turned 180 degrees on its head—I tell you solemnly I would disavow Christianity tomorrow. How many Muslims are courageous and open-minded enough to examine the texts and historical record of Mohammed and say the same of their allegiance?"

The hall was deathly silent. His words had dropped an unexpected bombshell. Even the agitated Muslim contingent was listening carefully.

"My highest ambition as a man," Timothy went on in a quiet voice, "is to know God as he truly is and to be a good man, to live as God would have me live, to be kind, loving, forgiving, and respectful to those who cross my path—in short to be God's son as one of his created beings. I would hope that such a life's ambition does not make me a bigot, a hater, or a racist.

"I am also a man seeking truth. I will embrace any idea that helps me become a growing and better man. I am also a historian. My lifelong quest for truth has pointed me toward Christianity and the teachings and example of Jesus as the most spiritually and historically reliable path toward the life it is my desire to live. I find truth in his teachings. Thus far my historical research has not led me to the discovery of similar truth in the ultimate objectives of Islam."

Timothy stopped. He was emotionally spent from the outpouring of the past forty minutes. As his listeners sensed that he was through, hands began to shoot up and questions to be shouted down toward him.

As he had on the previous evening, he first took one, then another, and answered as briefly as he could.

But his lecture had at last opened the floodgates of passion within the Muslim contingent. Dozens of hands flew into the air waving to be noticed, most not waiting to be acknowledged. He tried to call on one questioner at a time. But it was a losing battle. He knew he had lost control.

He thought a moment, then bent close to the microphone.

"Hey—*stop!*" he shouted with all the power he could summon. His voice reverberated through the auditorium and brought momentary silence.

He held up both hands and seized the lull.

"I want to do something a little different," he said, slowly lowering his hands. "I have spoken straightforwardly and bluntly. It is clear this lecture has exposed many emotions. I thank you for remaining civil and respectful while I was speaking. I would now like to ask the Muslims among you—and I think several imams from local mosques are with us—if you would select one of your number to come up and join me. I will give him the opportunity to respond to tonight's lecture. I am through for the night. I will not interrupt.

"Before one of you comes, let me add this. I am a human being, a fallible man. Though I have researched Islam and Christianity, I know my perspectives are not perfect. If I have misrepresented Islam in any way, I sincerely apologize. In all humility and honesty I ask you to correct my errors to those who are here this evening. They deserve to be acquainted with cogently presented and historically sound viewpoints if I have spoken untruly or misrepresented a faith I know you hold dear. The floor will be yours for whatever response you feel is appropriate. I believe those in attendance will show you deference and will listen with respect. I am asking all of you to do so."

Heads began turning about and animated discussion immediately spread among the Muslim listeners. It did not take long for a consensus to be reached.

A white-bearded man, tall, robed, with a taqiyah atop his graying head, probably in his late sixties, rose and made his way forward.

49

Husband and Wife

TO TIMOTHY'S great relief, the presence of the imam from Sacramento's largest mosque calmed the hall.

There were no more outbursts. He spoke for fifteen or twenty minutes, in an accent too thick to be clearly understandable. He was visibly angry with Timothy's presentation. He poured out a rambling diatribe against Western aggression and imperialism, singling out the United States and Israel's policies as fully warranting Islam's defensive retaliation. To be fair, he walked onto the stage unprepared and in a high state of agitation. But his remarks did nothing to dissuade his listeners of the probable validity of most of what Timothy said.

Timothy did not notice the tall man at the back of the hall rise and leave as the imam was wrapping up his disjointed harangue, brushing past the young man trying to shove a pamphlet in his face and hurrying from the campus back to his hotel, where he placed a call to his cousin Ada in Iran.

After this night, he was more convinced than ever that there must be no delay to their timetable.

When the imam's ire had spent itself, Timothy joined Jaylene and the others where they sat in the front row. They waited until the hall was mostly empty, then made their exit hoping to avoid unpleasant confrontations.

Dale Birch was still outside the building with his pamphlets as they walked into the warm dusk a little after nine. Thinking it best to ignore his presence rather than call attention to it, they avoided him as they walked to their cars.

As Timothy drove home physically and emotionally drained, he confessed to Jaylene that he was seriously wondering if he should cancel the remaining two lectures rather than provide another open forum for contention, as well as giving Dale Birch more opportunities to spread his divisive message.

"It nearly got away from me tonight, Jaylene. After the inevitable talk that will circulate, by next Friday it could get even more ugly. I said at the outset I would not allow arguing. Yet tonight I couldn't keep a lid on it."

"You handled it as well as was possible," said Jaylene. "At least *you* kept your cool. Hopefully your demeanor will be an example to some of the Christian young people. Unfortunately, your herculean efforts to be objective could not keep Islam's latent hostility from overflowing. I'm not sure you could have prevented it. Muslims are just . . . they're angry, defensive, and closed-minded. How many happy Muslims do you see? They're as angry and closed-minded as liberals. I'm sorry I cannot be as kind and tolerant as you, but that was obvious tonight. Everything you have tried to do was lost on them. But you just stood quietly. You were like Jesus in front of Pilate."

"Well, hardly that," said Timothy sardonically. "But thank you."

"And what a brilliant stroke to bring the imam up! I couldn't believe that!"

"Neither could he!" laughed Timothy.

"I couldn't make heads or tails of what he said," said Jaylene, "except that he was angry, blaming everything on America and Christians and Jews. He hadn't heard a word you said."

"I know," sighed Timothy. "At least people were able to hear his side. So . . . do you think I should cancel the last two lectures?"

"I don't know, Timothy. Only you can determine what God wants you to do. What's the topic of the next lecture again?"

"Doctrine, opinion, and truth. What role doctrine, and indoctrination, has played and continues to play in the transmission of Islam and Christianity. Both religions, each in their own way, use indoctrination, if not outright brainwashing, to plant their teachings into hearts and mind. They would never call it that, and Christians would be furious for me to suggest it of Christianity. Yet how else but by brainwashing with untruths do Muslims convince people that the Koran does not preach war when it blatantly *does* preach war? The higher question I hoped all this would lead to is how we assess the fundamental question of truth: Which is the *truer* religion? Or can both be true in an absolute sense?"

"That could ignite a powder keg."

"I know," sighed Timothy, shaking his head. "Can you imagine posing that question tonight! It would have blown the roof off. Yet that is the culmination of everything we've been talking about—truth. If both sides—I hate to even frame it as *sides*—come itching for religious brawl, I would not want to be the one responsible for it. It would be contrary to the very reasons I decided to do this in the first place."

"What are you going to do?" asked Jaylene.

"I find myself wondering if my stated objective for the next lecture was too lofty a goal. Maybe the whole series of lectures was naïve—thinking Muslims could be objective in a quest for true truth. Questions of that magnitude require an objectivity and wisdom sadly beyond 99 percent of Muslims and liberals. Yet you see it among Christians too when they argue about doctrine. Almost no one is capable of evaluating truth divorced from their own opinions, background, experience, and yes, the *indoctrination* they have received masquerading as sound teaching. The lack of objectivity is a universal problem of humanity."

"But some teaching *is* sound and objective?"

"Of course. You and I have given our professional lives to what we believe is sound and objective teaching. But much teaching is little more than indoctrination, especially religious teaching. Most teaching at the secular university level consists of progressivist indoctrination. Secular academia in our country is no less an institution of propagandist brainwashing than Islam's methodology for the radicalization of terrorists or the propaganda the Russian and Chinese people grow up listening to. Even the Christian students who come to Jessup have been subject to it. We hope to bring objectivity to their lives with our teaching methods. But most young people have grown up in a world of so many diverse indoctrinations and subtle brainwashings influencing how they think, that it is hard for them to escape it."

It fell silent. They did not discuss the evening for the rest of the drive home.

50

Wars, Raptures, Tribulations, and Timetables

FALLOUT FROM the Friday evening lecture and heated debate began immediately.

Discussion in every student enclave throughout the Sacramento area was feverish. Pastors in Christian churches and imams in Muslim mosques spoke of it all weekend, with a multitude of slants and interpretations placed on events.

Knowing that Timothy and Jaylene were probably being besieged by calls after the tumultuous evening just past, Todd asked if they would rather cancel their weekly lunch and Saturday afternoon with him.

"Not at all, Todd," replied Jaylene on the phone. "We need the distraction and to see a friendly face. Please come—Tim is looking forward to it."

Two hours later, as they were finishing lunch, in spite of wanting to put it out of their minds, the previous evening's fireworks continued to dominate their conversation.

"Do you think there will be a war between Islam and Christianity?" Todd asked. "Could that be Armageddon itself?"

"I don't know, Todd," Timothy answered slowly. "Many think so. There are some who think the seven years of the Tribulation began with Ward Hutchins's murder and the election of Jefferson Rhodes. They believe worldwide war is imminent and between now and then the rapture will take place and the Lord will return. It's being written about and preached in many evangelical churches."

"Do you believe it?"

"No," answered Timothy. "I should say, *if* that scenario is in God's divine plan, then I *will* believe it as he reveals it. But at this point I do not believe events are pointing in that direction. If man's church continues to make itself the world's ally, war may not be necessary. Islam will just absorb a worldly complacent church, sound asleep to God's higher purposes."

"What about what you said that according to the Koran Islam will ultimately have to be spread by force. You quoted Mohammed saying, 'Invitation first, call infidels to embrace Islam. If they refuse, then war.'"

"That mindset is but one more example of Islam's hypocrisy. At root, it is a nationalistic political force bent on taking over the world just as Alexander, Napoleon, Hitler, and others have tried. Conquest is not conversion. But with Islam integrating so successfully into societies everywhere, war may no longer be necessary to achieve that goal.

"To answer your question—I don't know. Conquest remains the goal, and theirs is a long strategy. If they can, they will integrate in order to conquer from within. They are happy to *use* democracy temporarily. But the ultimate goal is to establish Islamic law based on the pretense of religion but which in reality is nothing more than a new form of fascism."

Todd let out a long sigh.

"That is truly frightening," he said. "What a terrible future awaits the world if people don't wake up."

"And with China and Russia equally bent on world domination, we may indeed be headed for a nuclear Armageddon—the world powers of Daniel 11 and Revelation 4 and 7 exploding the world apart. Though my lectures are focused on Islam, I am almost more concerned about China and Russia. They've been involved in the long game against America too. Their stealth strategies are as cunning as Islam's, and China has an even longer history than Islam. Few people know that Chinese interests now own between 5 and 10 percent of the land in the continental US, much of it near military bases, major airports, electricity facilities, transportation hubs, and population centers. China is literally poised to take over control of the entire US infrastructure almost without firing a shot. With Islam making significant inroads in China, it is difficult to see a good outcome for America in the decades to come."

"With everything you revealed about Mohammed," said Todd, "and with what are obvious totalitarian regimes of Russia and China, why do Muslims blindly follow Islam? Why do the Chinese and Russians blindly follow dictators? Didn't World War II teach the world anything about totalitarianism versus democracy?"

"They follow for the same reason progressives in our country remain liberal against all common sense and logic and in spite of its ruinous cultural effects. They are brainwashed. They are afraid to admit the emperor of their belief systems has no clothes. Muslims, Russians, and progressives are taught not to question. Questioning is viewed as an attack on the system. Muslims blindly embrace the lies knowing that the death penalty is demanded for apostasy. The so-called religion of peace calls for the death of anyone who turns from Islamic belief. Progressives who wake up to reality are subjected to a kinder, gentler form of death—they are ostracized, condemned, and called hateful and bigoted. Brainwashing keeps everyone in line. Brainwashing is the foundation of totalitarianism and fascism, which all these systems exemplify—US progressivism no less than militant Islam jihadism."

Todd shook his head in amazement to hear Timothy speaking so forcefully. It was quiet for several seconds.

"May I ask another question?" he said at length. "Completely unrelated—though maybe not completely, now that I think about it."

"Of course," replied Timothy.

"You know that Heather and I have been attending church, maybe not on most Sundays but fairly often. She takes me to visit small churches throughout the foothills and in some of the smaller communities around the Sacramento area. She wants me to meet a broad cross-section of Christians. She reminds me that the problem with man's church isn't so much the people but the institutional and organizational structure. She wants us to keep focused on the *true* Church, the body of Christ, which is *people* just like us.

"Though the institutional church of man is not the true Church, the men and women who are the living stones of the true Church are to be found in all the churches of man. Many simply don't know anything else. She reminds me that God keeps sincere believers who are seeking to walk in separation from the world in the churches of man in order to seed the church with the higher truths of the eternal Church. Some are called out entirely, others are called out so they might remain *in* but not *of* man's church. Am I making sense?"

"Absolutely. You have indeed absorbed our perspective of how the church of man and the true Church are not mutually exclusive. They intertwine in wonderful interplay, wouldn't you say, Jaylene?"

"I agree entirely, yes. We always taught Heather that her grandfather's emphasis on separation from man's church is individual and unique. Some must literally separate, as Tim did when he resigned from the board of elders and as Mark did when he left the pastorate. Others feel led to remain. Even recognizing the power of the Ally, they hope to influence the people in their churches who are truly dedicated to lives of Christlikeness. The Church exists within the church. God is strenuously at work seeding the church with members of his high Logos Church."

"I see," said Todd. "Then the question I was getting around to is this. In all these churches, I am continually hearing about the end times and the second coming and Tribulation and Millennium, like you were talking about before. People talk about the rapture like it's going to happen tomorrow. It's a passion. If I was still a non-Christian and heard them talking about flying up into the air, I would probably consider it a cult—the rapture cult."

Timothy and Jaylene laughed.

"You're not so far wrong," replied Timothy. "It's been going on for decades, for centuries. Every generation or two a new wave of end-times hysteria hits and fundamentalist Christians are swept up into it."

"But do *you* believe all that? Do you think we're all about to literally meet the Lord in the clouds—I mean, *actual* clouds . . . *literally* go flying up into the air?"

"Let me respond with a non-answer," said Timothy. "The trouble with all these waves of rapture fever is that nothing comes of them. Eventually the people who believe it with every ounce of energy they possess—they all get old and die natural deaths. No rapture took them off the earth. The frenzy dies down . . . until the next wave hits. The proponents of the new end-times hysteria devise explanations why the prophetic gurus of the previous wave mistook the signs but that why now, *this* new revelation is really and truly *it*.

"And so it goes. Still no rapture. The new prophetic gurus also get old and die . . . until *another* new wave comes along with yet more explanations why the former prophecies were wrong, but this time, defying the lessons of history, this is *really and truly* the time when Jesus will return.

"Generation after generation, gullible Christians continue to be seduced by new rounds of false prophets preying on their fantasies and hopes, preaching new manifestations and signs and wonders and proofs why their new interpretations are *really* the final word, and why they, standing above all prophetic writers who have come before them, understand what no one else was ever capable of understanding. Their hubris is fueled by pompous self-righteousness."

"It does almost sound like a cult."

"Strong words, Todd," nodded Timothy seriously. "You should read Mark's book that resulted from his final messages before resigning his pulpit. He explains the *spiritual* rapture as well as I've ever heard."

"How do you mean, *spiritual* rapture? You mean not literally flying into the sky?"

"Exactly. A spiritual *coming out* of the world, not being *taken out* of the world but *choosing* to come out of the world rather than passively waiting for God to take us out of it. But Mark's perspective is controversial even among our own people. Christians are reluctant to look to the deeper themes of prophecy. The problem is two thousand years old. Christians in first-century Thessalonica were so convinced that the Lord's return was imminent they quit working. The city was in an uproar of anticipation and confusion."

"So what's it all about?" said Todd. "*Why* do Christians keep getting swept up in it when it has obviously failed to materialize in the past?"

"Hubris. They think *their* generation is the most special generation in history, and that *they* are the highly chosen few who will witness the Lord's return. I believe end-times fever is fueled by spiritual pride, plain and simple. The entire premise of most second-coming teachings is founded in a misunderstanding of how God works."

"Which is?" asked Todd.

Timothy glanced toward Jaylene.

"It's exactly what I teach in my Genesis course," replied Jaylene. "My view on the end times is the same as my view of Genesis. God works slowly, through time, and through his natural processes. Like Islam, God's eternal purposes are a long game. His eternal purposes can only be understood spiritually and eternally, not physically and temporarily. The common rapture theology of evangelicalism is a temporal and physical interpretation that by definition is contrary to the way God works. Millions of people suddenly flying into the sky—that's not the way God accomplishes transformation unto Christlikeness."

"It might help you understand what we're saying," added Timothy, "to know that the word *rapture* is not once used in the entire Bible. As most evangelicals define it to mean . . . that Christians will be physically and literally caught up into the clouds. I believe such a physical so-called rapture is an invention of men."

Timothy paused briefly.

"However, there will be an *appearing*," he went on, "a revelation of the Lord, a *coming out*, a removal of God's people from the world. Mark's book explains it in more detail as a *spiritual* coming out of the world and out of man's church. We are part of that revelation and that separation from the world. You are living proof of the great truth. God revealed himself to you and you came out of the world."

"It so completely different," said Todd, "than the people in nearly every church we visit believe."

51

The Kirk Effect

"ON A lighter note," laughed Jaylene, "how is the training going with Pistachio?"

"Slow, but Heather warned me not to be in a hurry," Todd replied. "She says it's progressing on schedule. She tried the saddle on Pistachio's back last week. Pistachio was obviously uncomfortable and fidgeted and squirmed. Then we took it off. I'm loving the process and watching Heather monitor Pistachio's every response as she guides what we do. She's taught me how to use the circular enclosure for *join-up* or *round-pen* training. It's fascinating to watch how horses respond and quietly approach when you relax the pressure after galloping them around the pen."

"We've been watching her most of her life at the West's ranch," said Jaylene. "It's a gift God has given her, there's no doubt about that."

"Yet some of the techniques are things even a novice like me can do. It's not as natural to me as it is to her, yet when I do exactly as she tells me, Pistachio seems to respond similarly. It's as much a learning experience for me as it probably is for her . . . Pistachio, I mean."

They all rose from the table. While Jaylene cleared away the lunch things, Timothy and Todd went outside and walked slowly across to the park opposite their house chatting comfortably.

"What do you think about Charlie Kirk?" asked Todd after some time.

"A courageous young man," replied Timothy. "He was an inspiration to a generation of Christians. I wish I'd had the opportunity to meet him. Why do you ask?"

"Ever since I became a Christian his legacy has weighed heavily on me."

"In what way?"

"I'm not sure exactly. I knew nothing about him before that, only what I'd picked up that he was a right-wing extremist. After learning the true story of who he was and the impact he had, I found myself wondering if his life had more to say to the people of my generation than I'd realized."

Timothy took in Todd's words thoughtfully. He and Jaylene had already made the connection between the two young men.

Turning and retracing their steps, they met Jaylene coming to join them.

"Todd's been asking about Charlie Kirk," said Timothy as they met and she turned and they continued back toward the house.

"There are many who are waiting for the next Charlie Kirk for a *new* generation—for the times we are living in today," said Jaylene. As she spoke, she glanced significantly toward Todd.

"You're not . . . what are you suggesting?" he said.

"Nothing specific. I'm just saying, God raises up new people in every era to speak to their times. And he *has* blessed you with a platform."

"I left the world of politics behind," said Todd. "I have no interest in going back into it."

"God doesn't raise up everyone to speak in the same way. Perhaps he has a different way for you to influence the people of your generation. There will probably never be another Charlie Kirk. But God is continually raising up spokesmen and women to stand for truth in the unique ways their times need. Maybe the next such spokesman won't be speaking on cultural issues, but on preparing God's people for a future that will be much different than most in man's church expect."

"What happened in the aftermath of Charlie Kirk's assassination reveals the limitations of trying to influence the world through culture and politics," added Timothy. "If people aren't turned toward

Christlike-obedience, the impact is not lasting. Where are Trump's attempts to right the ship of America now? Progressivism eventually came storming back to inundate the country with its lies even more pervasively than ever."

"You think the same thing will happen with Charlie Kirk's influence?"

"It already has. Eventually things return to normal. The status quo is a powerful Ally to worldly Christianity. Enthusiasms die down. The status quo silently overwhelms those enthusiasms into long-term ineffectiveness."

"That's discouraging."

"Discouraging but true. That's why revivals never last. The obedience of Christlikeness is usually not at the foundation but some new form of experientialism unique to the new revivalism. Promise Keepers, a men's movement that was all the rage long before your time, swept through evangelicalism with the admirable vision of restoring biblical principles in marriage. But where are those priorities in the church today? I personally know six individuals in the Roseville church where we spent many years with a combined twenty-eight marriages between them."

"You're kidding . . . six people . . . twenty-eight marriages!"

"And all six dedicated Christians. Yet in their lives the model of biblical marriage is in shambles. How much lasting benefit was Promise Keepers? Without a coming out of worldliness into Christlikeness, the power of the world's status quo will always inundate temporary religious enthusiasms."

"You believe this has taken place with the legacy of Charlie Kirk?"

"Look around. Worldliness has never had such a comfortable home as in man's church of the mid-twenty-first century. Right after Charlie's death, everyone was excited and praising God because so many people of all ages were going to church. The congregations of evangelicalism swelled and revival was being proclaimed throughout the land. I remember thinking at the time, if encouraging people to become active in man's worldly church was the premise of the revival, that it was destined to be a short one. I'm not saying going to church isn't a good thing. Maybe it is, I don't know. But how much lasting impact will there be when people are taught feel-good experientialism based on blessings, grace, and what God will do for me rather than the obedience of Christ-likeness? Church isn't the answer. Living by the commands of Jesus is the answer. Bringing people into man's church by the millions will never change the world.

"I feared at the time that all it would do would be to embolden many Christians to follow Charlie Kirk's example to be outspoken about their faith in the political arena rather than following the eternal example of his personal character and his biblical devotion to his family. That was the deeper example which was Charlie Kirk's most significant legacy. But it was altogether lost on both the church and the world. People wanted to emulate his boldness to get in people's faces and challenge the lies of progressivism, which in truth was partially attributable to his immaturity as a Christian. Very few sought to emulate his character, which remained a work in progress.

"Now here we are thirty years later and little has changed. The church of man is still the Ally of the world. Christians are still talking about the end times yet still not preparing themselves for those times with the prayer, *Make me like Jesus.*"

☆ ☆ ☆

After his previous lecture, exactly as Timothy predicted, the charges of Islamophobia were not long in coming.

The first came the next day in a Sunday editorial in the *Sacramento Bee.*

It was given prominence and a headline on the second page of the print edition and led the online posting with the bold words: *Christian University's Racist Homophobic Professor.* It displayed a menacing close-up of Timothy, admittedly grainy from being enlarged, apparently shouting at someone in a white fury, his eyes aflame and the veins in his neck standing out. Neither Timothy nor Jaylene had any recollection of the photo. They puzzled about it all day until that evening Heather recognized the corner of the Bar JG porch in the background.

"I remember that day!" she said. "It was at the gathering last year. Several of us were standing about and Paddy Ayscough had just made some wisecrack—I've forgotten what he said. But you, Dad, roared with laughter. I remember because I'd never seen you laugh so hard. They've used AI to create this picture from one of you laughing!"

Timothy could only shake his head in disbelief.

"How could they have gotten it?" asked Todd.

"Was that when Lionel was there?" asked Jaylene.

"It might not have been Lionel," sighed Timothy. "Honestly, these days I don't put it past them—whoever *them* is!" he added laughing, "to be capable of anything. Everything is saved in the Cloud—that would include every photo on every camera."

"What a horrifying thought," said Jaylene. "I *was* taking pictures with my phone all weekend," she added. "Now that Heather reminds me how Paddy made us all laugh, I *do* recall that time when we were standing around the porch. I'm afraid I took that picture! Oh, Timothy, I am sorry! I'm going to write the *Bee* and demand an apology. I'll demand they publish the real photo!"

"Jaylene, Jaylene," said Timothy softly, "listen to yourself. That's the way of worldly politicians. It accomplishes nothing. People believe what they want to believe. Defensiveness never works. We just have to ride out the storm. This is today's world. Truth doesn't matter as much as perception. This is what Christians will continue to face, at least those Christians who haven't given in to progressivism. We are in the crosshairs. Look what the media did to Charlie Kirk, then Ward Hutchins and Mark. Now it's our turn."

"But I hate it!"

"Christians should hate it. But we have to hate it quietly, the way Jesus hated evil and falsehood, and then, as he did, choose our battles carefully."

☆ ☆ ☆

The *Bee's* article went viral. It was reprinted on hundreds of news sites and was followed by dozens of news articles and postings about the increasing Islamophobia of Christians. None of the reprints, an omission also not mentioned in the original, revealed that the article's author had not attended a single one of Timothy's lectures, and had derived her information from one especially angry Muslim dropout from Sac State with a history of stirring up trouble and who was on the FBI's watchlist.

The Roseville police took the few death threats posted online as a result of the article seriously enough to station a squad car in front of the Marshall home.

52

Calm Before the Storm

THROUGHOUT THE week, as Timothy thought and prayed, gradually a plan came into focus for handling the following Friday's lecture. He went to campus every day to be visible and mingle with students, many of whom wanted to talk to him about the lectures.

On Wednesday he posted notices on the university's bulletin boards. He also wrote a letter to the editor of the *Bee* specifically inviting the article's author to the next lecture as his personal guest and for a one-on-one interview at its conclusion when she would be free to ask him anything she liked.

His letter was not published, nor did he receive a response either from the paper or the article's author.

When Friday came, a similar notice to those he had written earlier was posted on the main entrance to the Christian Humanities Building, as well as on the three doors into the lecture hall. It read:

> LECTURE SIX—DOES TRUTH MATTER?
>
> While I appreciate the interest in the topics I have addressed, and understand the spirited discussion that has characterized our evenings together, at the outset I made the commitment that these lectures would not become a forum for argumentation. Unfortunately I have been unable to prevent it. Therefore, tonight's lecture will be lecture only. I will take no questions. There will be no discussion.

Those who find this unacceptable I encourage not to attend. If the audience is unable to comply, I will immediately conclude my lecture, and campus security will see to the emptying of the hall. In such an event the lecture will conclude on Monday at 5:00 p.m. in the history department lecture hall, where the final lecture will also be held at the same time a week later. Those final sessions will be open only to Jessup students registered for the course.

Thank you for your participation in this important series of lectures and for your cooperation in helping them continue in a respectful and peaceful manner.

—Dr. Timothy Marshall

Friday came. If anything, Timothy's notice only heightened expectation. The Jessup campus was abuzz all day. By late afternoon the campus parking lots were filling up. News vans from most of the local television stations and two national networks began rolling in about 6:00. Half a dozen news crews, journalists, and cameramen were soon setting up outside the building. Several hundred students and members of the community clustered about the doors trying to read the posted notices.

Mixed reaction spread as they read Timothy's notices, from laughter to disgruntled complaints. As the crowd grew, a few turned and left. They had come hoping for fireworks. A thoughtful speech about the nature of truth was not on their agenda for a Friday night. The majority, however, continued inside hoping to find seats.

Dale Birch was beside himself at the crowd. This was his chance to make a name for himself. His only regret was not bringing enough pamphlets!

Few paid him much attention. Laughing as they read his title, most of the pamphlets ended up on the ground, which he scurried to retrieve. He did his best to attract the attention of the reporters, but they brushed him off. The central figure in tonight's drama had become a national figure overnight. They couldn't be bothered with the rantings of a young conspiracy theorist.

Ignoring Birch, the news crews strained for a sighting of the man of the hour, Jessup's now famously labeled Islamophobic professor. They hoped for close-up live images, maybe an angry retort if they pushed him hard enough.

Whatever importune journalist could succeed in rousing upon the infamous professor a reminder of the expression emblazoned in the collective mind of the whole country from the *Bee's* article, would jump into the limelight with his or her fifteen minutes of fame. If they got him on camera before 7:00, they could make the live local news hour.

Their efforts were in vain. Timothy, Jaylene, Todd, Mark, Grace, Craig, Ginger, and even David Gordon—who, though he despised hoopla, came to join Timothy's support base of prayer—had been in the building since 5:30. They entered through one of the unobtrusive rear entrances, observed by no one. They had holed up ever since in the building's faculty lounge, with pizza, French fries, chicken tenders, and cookies.

"Last meal before my public execution," chuckled Timothy with a mordant grin as he saw the women spreading out the smorgasbord.

"Nonsense!" said Grace. "We just want you well fortified. Why shouldn't we enjoy supper together."

"Hear, hear!" chimed in Mark. "We haven't all had a meal together in a while. Consider this a mini gathering of our group."

Even as he spoke, the Wests, Silvas, and two other couples arrived with Heather, who knew the ins and outs of the Jessup campus as well as her parents.

"Welcome to my lynching party!" laughed Timothy. "Jaylene, you didn't tell me this was to be a full scale BCL meeting. I thought we were just hiding out to avoid the crowds."

"We wanted you relaxed and in good spirits."

"You're right about the crowd," said Dewitt West. "News crews, cameras, reporters, and hundreds of people. It's a zoo out there—we saw it as we drove in from across campus."

"I'm glad Heather got you in without being followed."

About ten till seven the group made its way through the back corridors of the building toward the lecture hall. All but Timothy entered through one of the side doors into the front of the auditorium. A buzz spread through the auditorium filled to a standing-room-only crowd. Timothy's family, Mark Forster, and of course Todd Stewart, in whom interest remained high, were all recognized as they sat in the cordoned-off front row. The three sets of double doors at the entry to the hall stood open, pressed with people clustered in the atrium and entryway. Timothy took his place in the shadows of the side stage.

Seven o'clock came and went. The news crews would have nothing of Timothy to air live. Hearing the noise still rippling through the hall, he waited. At last it began to still. When he sensed it quiet enough to begin, Timothy made his way out onto the floor and walked across to the podium.

Before he reached it, he was stunned as the auditorium, mostly Jessup students and Christians from the community, burst into applause. The few shouts of *Racist!* and other invectives from hecklers were drowned out by the outpouring of support for Jessup's now most famous professor. Timothy took his place behind the lectern, slowly raised his head, and looked out. Fully three-fourths of those in attendance were on their feet. The remainder, mostly Muslims in traditional garb, many bearded imams among them, sat silent, stoic, and stern.

Hardly able to contain his swirling emotions, still less to grasp what the unexpected greeting signified, Timothy stood calmly waiting for the clapping to subside. Jaylene's and Heather's faces were wet with tears.

53

Does Truth Matter?

SLOWLY THE hall again quieted. Thinking it best for the sake of his Muslim brothers and sisters of humanity, Timothy did not acknowledge the welcome but began his lecture as dispassionately as possible.

He drew in a breath to steady himself.

"I would like to speak to you this evening," he began, "about truth. After the events of the past few weeks, I found myself reflecting on the fact of the larger question facing us is whether truth even matters. If so, how is something we call *truth*, which has so many interpretations, to be found? These may sound like trite questions. But they really do lie at the heart of the human experience, at the heart of how we each choose to live. It's not just truth itself, it's whether truth *matters*.

"For many, especially in our modern culture, it doesn't matter. The idea of truth gets mixed up with the equally nebulous concepts of *right* and *wrong*. We might also ask whether right and wrong *matter*.

"*Truth . . . right . . . wrong* . . . they've all been on the chopping block of modernism for nearly a century. If you dig deep enough into John Lennon's iconic song 'Revolution,' and nearly all the pop music of the 1960s, you find strains of an unspoken prophetic lyric that has been echoing down through our culture ever since.

"That unspoken lyric of the sixties' cultural revolution was this:

"Right, wrong, and truth no longer exist. Man, it's all an illusion. A rolling stone blowin' in the wind. What's it about? Where have the

*idealistic flowers gone? They've gone to graveyards because the ideals like the flowers are dead. Do your own thing, baby, because truth doesn't matter.**

"You may be a liberal or a conservative, I don't really care. But progressivism's elimination of right, wrong, and truth from the lexicon of human experience and relationship is not a good development. I do not say that as a Christian but a historian. When truth, right, and wrong cease to exist, societies, then civilizations, crumble. That is a historical fact. Yet progressives have been celebrating their demise for almost a century, rejoicing in the triumph of relativism, not realizing that John Lennon and Bob Dylan and Peter, Paul, and Mary were really singing a funeral dirge to their own future. Now that future is here.

"To answer my own question, then, again as a historian, truth *does* matter, just as right and wrong, in an absolute sense, *matter.* They are the mortar holding societies, families, cultures, and civilizations together. Without them, everything crumbles."

Timothy's unexpected beginning held the auditorium, for now at least, spellbound. As he paused for a breath, not a sound was heard.

"Western civilization is in the process of crumbling around us," he resumed after a few seconds, "—invisibly, silently, inexorably. It will continue to crumble unless we as a people, as a nation, as a culture, dare I even say as a planet of humanity, recover the meaning of truth, right, wrong, virtue, and goodness as essential components of life that *matter.*

"However, I did not propose this series of lectures primarily to talk about the planet, but about you and me—about how we individually respond to *truth, right, wrong, virtue,* and *goodness* in how we choose to live and what we believe. Furthermore, we came together to talk about the two religions, Islam and Christianity, and how we assess their claims, their texts, the teachings of Jesus and Mohammed, and their divisive and turbulent histories, in order to decide—*you and me* . . . individually—whether we believe the one or the other of these religions is worthy of our belief and worthy of the dedication of our lives to its cause as representing *truth, right, virtue,* and *goodness.*

---

* Iconic 1960s songs: "Revolution," "Like a Rolling Stone," "Blowin' in the Wind," "What's It All About, Alfie?" "Where Have All the Flowers Gone?"

"There is another significant factor to consider I have not brought up earlier but that is fundamental to the nature of truth. That is the Islamic teaching of abrogation. It holds essentially that later teachings can replace, or abrogate, former teachings. You can see instantly how truth becomes very flimsy on such a foundation.

"Of course a similar principle exists in Christianity, made clear by Jesus in the Sermon on the Mount when he said, 'You have heard that it was said to men of former times . . . but I say . . .' This is abrogation, too, but all toward the good.

"Muslims may complain that I emphasize the Gospels and ignore the Old Testament, which, they might say, is just as violent as the Koran. Christianity, however, is not based on the Old Testament, but grew out of it as Jesus elevated former teachings into new realms of goodness, kindness, and love. Christianity abrogates the *bad* in order to replace it with the *good*. It is abrogation moving in a good and positive direction.

"Islam turns this sequence on its head by saying that many of the peaceful verses in the Koran have been abrogated and replaced with violent ones. It is abrogation moving in the wrong direction. This mirrors Mohammed's life, in which he first tried to convince people to join him, and later used force to convert them, even to murder those who refused. As an example, Koran 9:29 and its brother verse, 9:5, are collectively known as the Sword Verses. According to mainstream Islamic jurisprudence, these verses abrogate 124 verses calling for peace and tolerance. Many Muslim clerics thus use the principle of abrogation to ignore verses in the Koran about peace. This does not prevent them, however, as most modern Muslims do, using sleight of hand with various proof-texts to show that Islam is really a peaceful religion. Clearly, as I say, this makes ultimate truth a flimsy proposition in Islam.

"Putting all this together, I would therefore propose to you tonight two series of questions. The first is: *Does Christianity represent truth, right, virtue, and goodness*?

"Do I want to follow the teachings of Jesus as revealed in the Gospels of the New Testament?

"Do I want to dedicate myself to the objectives and purposes of Christianity as taught by Jesus, whether or not consistently lived by its flawed human followers through history?

"Do I believe in the principles and methodologies and ultimate worldwide objectives of Christianity?

"Do I want to be a truthful, good, virtuous person who lives by what is right and treats all humanity as a truthful, virtuous, good person should as those ideas are embodied in Christian teaching?

"Or the related series of questions:

"Does Islam represent truth, right, and virtue?

"Do I want to follow the teachings of Mohammed as revealed in the Koran, and as clerics in later years have abrogated passages about peace with the Sword Verses?

"Do I want to dedicate myself to the objectives and purposes of Islam?

"Do I believe in the principles and methodologies and ultimate worldwide objectives of Islam?

"Do I want to be a person who lives by and treats all humanity by the ideas embodied in Islamic teaching, including the Sword Verses?

"Progressivism, though in our time favoring Islam, would say that *both* religions can be true, that our answers to these questions is relative and comes down to personal preference. That is progressivism's great lie—that *absolute* right, wrong, and truth *don't* exist. We all choose what is right, wrong, and true *for us*. It's all relative and individual. Two opposites can be true. Black and white are intrinsically no different. By this illogical lie, *both* Islam and Christianity can be true.

"What they are really saying is that *neither* is True, with a capital T. Neither of them represents *objective* Truth.

"In the matter of choosing clothes, certainly black and white, or red and blue, are personal preferences. Right and wrong don't enter it. In the matter of choosing a religion to which to dedicate one's life, however, right, wrong, and truth *do* come into it. It's not like choosing clothes or deciding what to have for dinner. In matters of religion, there are *absolute* truths—truths that matter—truths in the upper case. *True* truths."

Timothy paused again. He arrived at the crux of his lecture. The next few minutes would determine how the evening unfolded.

"At last we come to the most fundamental question of all," he went on. "It's a very controversial question. It's emotional and highly charged. Please, I implore you—hear me accurately. Do not judge me too quickly.

I am attempting to speak to you as an objective historian not a partisan. I hope you can do the same—hear me as objective listeners.

"All right, then. That fundamental question is this:

"Can Islam and Christianity be equally true?"

Rustling and squirming through the hall was audible. Timothy quickly went on.

"Do the Koran and Gospels of the New Testament present equal *truth, goodness, right,* and *virtue*?

"Do the lives of Jesus and Mohammed equally reflect *right, goodness, virtue,* and *truth*?

"Will my humanity as a man or woman grow equally in *goodness, virtue,* and *truth* living by the principles and purposes of either Islam or Christianity?

"Those are enormous questions. Very personal questions. In one sense, we hear what progressives are saying. These questions can only be answered individually. We have to *individually* decide how to address those queries. But not because both are equally true or untrue, but because we have to individually probe deep within ourselves, deep into our hearts and brains, relying not in the indoctrination we may have received but relying on our own logic, intelligence, reason, awareness of history, and our common sense to decide what is *really* true.

"The individual decision we make is not because one is as good as the other, like choosing the color of a shirt. The individual decision is:

"There is a truth, a *real* truth, a real right and wrong, a true uppercase absolute *Truth* that matters? Where will I find it?

"For example, if it could be proven—I mean really *proven*—that Jesus was not such a good man as he is portrayed, that he had illicit involvements with women, perhaps even that he killed those who disagreed with him or criticized him, and that he never actually rose from the dead, the *true* Truth of Christianity would be gone in an instant.

"Game over. Christianity would be exposed as a fraud. End of discussion.

"Of course millions would continue to pretend to be Christians and go on as before. But on what basis? Where would be the *truth* of their belief? Many good principles might still exist in the teaching. But it would be a new religion. Everything about Jesus's sinlessness, his compassion, his tenderness toward women, his dying for the sins of the world and rising from the dead, and appearing to five hundred witnesses after his death, the entire basis for Christian salvation—all that would be gone, exposed as a lie.

"An objective man or woman, confronting that evidence, would have no choice but to conclude that Christianity based on Jesus as the Son of God was not a *true* religion. He or she might embrace the new religion formed on the basis of his teachings as a mortal man. But it would not be Christianity as formerly taught."

Again Timothy paused. Did he dare go ahead? He had come this far, he couldn't stop now.

"I realize that many of you here tonight are Muslims. I would like you to notice something. I have just spoken what to many Christians will sound like blasphemy. I have raised what probably many of the Christians here are shocked to hear me say.

"Yet did you hear a single outcry? They listened to me respectfully. Why did they listen? Because most of them recognized the truth of what I said. If these things were indeed *proven*, Christianity would be undone. Truth matters. They understand that. They see that the premise I just stated is true.

"What about the other side of it. I challenge you Muslims—are you equally objective to ask hard questions of Islam? If it could be *proven* that Mohammed owned slaves, had fifteen wives, advocated beheading and ordered the beheading of teen boys, approved of sex with children and had sex slaves of his own, personally committed theft, torture, and murder, encouraged rape, and ordered his followers to kill apostates and infidels—would those allegations make a difference in *your* perspective of the truth and goodness of Islam as a religion? Would you still view Mohammed as a worthy model and example of truth and virtue whose life and teachings you aspire to emulate?

"In the face of such allegations, would truth matter to you?"

By now many eyes in the hall were riveted in the direction where most of the Muslims sat together. A notable agitation was stirring.

"There is this difference," Timothy continued. "These things I have just mentioned *are* in fact historically documented from Mohammed's life.

"So where does a religion based on his teachings, his life, his example stand given these historic realities? Are Muslims objective enough to face them, to look them in the face, and with open-minded intellectual honesty ask of their religion and its teachings, does truth—"

Suddenly one of the bearded imams rose to his feet and thundered in a loud commanding voice, with outstretched arm pointing toward Timothy:

You infidel! You blaspheme the holy prophet!

At almost the same instant the entire contingent jumped to its feet shouting:

Infidel . . . infidel!

Allahu akbar . . . Allahu akbar!

One of the young men reached inside his robe, and with the words *Allah be praised* sent an orange in the direction of the stage. Seconds later a barrage of apples, more oranges, and assorted missiles, harmless in themselves, were being hurled in Timothy's direction. They had obviously come prepared.

The auditorium erupted in shouts. Within seconds they became screams of pandemonium.

A general panic broke out. In confusion and terror, hundreds scrambled pushing and shoving for the exits.

Police outside heard the screams and ran toward the doors to see what had caused the disturbance. But the human tide pouring out was against them.

As calmly as he could, Timothy turned and walked toward the side stage. More fruit and now a few eggs landed on the stage around him, also with rocks echoing off the hardwood floor. Just as he disappeared into the wings, a bottle shattered, spraying fragments of glass and beer after him.

By then Jaylene and the others were on their feet and ran for the side entrance. Those seated near hurried to follow them. That door and the back corridors of the building were quickly as clogged with yelling and shoving to get out as was the atrium in front.

54

Explosive Repercussions

THE FIRST hint the news crews in front of the building had of trouble was seeing the doors burst open with screams and shouts and a panicked flood of humanity pushing and squeezing to get outside.

Within seconds cameras were rolling, reporters scrambling to organize their thoughts into what impromptu commentary they could think of, though none knew what had caused the frantic rush from the building.

Equally astonished at the sudden exodus, Dale Birch forgot his momentary annoyance when the reporter he was talking to suddenly turned and ran from him.

Any crisis, whatever the cause, was red meat. Pamphlets in hand, he eagerly dashed toward the fray.

Leaving the building in mass hysteria, two or three hundred people were now running in every direction. Though no one actually *saw* any danger—only missiles being lobbed toward the podium—the shouts simultaneous to everyone jumping to their feet, created a herd response. One thought was paramount—get out!

As if the hysteria was self-fulfilling and itself caused what followed—impossible as that was, though had they remained calmly in their seats, the outcome may have been different—a sudden explosion of gunfire echoed over the Jessup campus.

Complete pandemonium erupted. The screams became screams of terror.

Shots continued. Several policemen sprinted out of the building, one fell . . . shrieks came from those nearby . . . more innocents fell.

Repeated gunfire rang out . . . single shots spaced a second or two apart.

Victims continued to fall . . . the crowd in full panic stumbled over their bodies.

The policemen were too surrounded by the crowd to return fire . . . guns drawn they tried to get free of the mob but could not isolate the shooter.

In the midst of the mayhem, police were yelling, "Stay inside the building!" Those attempting to get out were soon overrun by others trying to get back inside to safety.

Shouts in the distance sounded above the fleeing crowd:

Allahu Akbar . . . Allahu Akbar . . . Allahu Akbar!

Police sprinted in the direction of the voice.

More victims fell to the ground . . . Dale Birch's pamphlets flying about and strewn underfoot.

☆ ☆ ☆

Deep inside the Christian Humanities building, Timothy had just met Jaylene and her entourage, which now spread back the entire length of the corridor. Realizing they were safe, the following throng slowed and followed the Marshall contingent around corners and down a flight of stairs toward the outside.

Suddenly everyone stopped dead in their tracks.

"What was that?" said Todd, taller than most of the rest and glancing behind them at those who followed.

The muffled reports came in rhythmic succession.

"There's only one sound like that in the world," said Dewitt West. "That's gunfire. We need to stay where we are!"

Timothy made a rush for the outer door. Whatever it was, he was the captain of this ship! Jaylene had to physically restrain him for a few seconds, aided by Todd, until Timothy relented.

☆ ☆ ☆

In front of the building after ten more terrifying seconds of measured shots, two final explosions sounded, seemingly louder than the rest.

Then as suddenly as they had begun, no more shots were heard.

Shrieks, cries, and wails of grief came from among the fallen. Dale Birch, the young man who would change the world, lay dead in a blood-soaked pile of his ill-omened pamphlets.

Shouting and running for the parking lots continued, hundreds heedless of the cries behind them. The building began to empty again, as police fanned out in search of the gunman.

After a hundred simultaneous 9-1-1 calls, sirens from ambulances, police, and emergency vehicles whined in the distance racing toward the Jessup campus.

Thirty seconds went by . . . then a minute . . . then two minutes.

As the crowd thinned, it became clear that the shooting rampage was over. Shell-shocked reporters and their crews, the entire episode caught on film by those few cameramen with the presence of mind to keep their cameras rolling while scurrying for cover, tried to regroup. As they resumed recording, still fearful for their lives, the journalists glanced about every second or two as they tried to get their game faces back on.

Timothy, Mark, and Todd were the first out the back door. They raced around the side of the building.

Their steps slowed in horror. Spread out in front of them was a scene of devastation resembling a war zone. Tears filled the eyes of all three.

Timothy grew faint.

"What have I done!" he wailed in disbelief, then collapsed unconscious in Todd's arms.

☆ ☆ ☆

Three hundred yards away, Bruno Volker picked up his shell casings—he never needed more than one per shot—tossed them into his case, snapped it shut, took one last look about to be sure not so much as a speck of dirt could draw attention to this place, then began the short walk to the bus stop.

Public transportation was always best in such circumstances. Well disguised, with no car to trace and no chance of being recognized, a city bus guaranteed anonymity.

Two hours later, he was on a coast-to-coast red-eye back to DC.

55

Denver Stone

FNC'S DENVER Stone hadn't quite *seen it all*, as the saying goes. He'd seen enough, however, to make him a firm believer in original sin. He hadn't covered a shooting since the ACH assassination eighteen years ago. He'd prayed never to have to cover another.

Now he was about to go on camera to cover thirteen killings that had all taken place within two minutes. A lump sat in his gut. This would be one of the hardest on-camera reports of his life.

It was just after 11:00 EST. Much of the east was already in bed. It was still prime time in the other three time zones. His report would be seen by millions. He'd give anything to be spared the spotlight on this night.

"This is Denver Stone, FNC News speaking to you from our Nashville headquarters," he began three minutes later. "A horrifying scene is still unfolding at this hour in California. An unidentified gunman opened fire on the campus of Jessup University where a lecture on Christianity and Islam was being held. An unexplained disturbance during the lecture sent listeners rushing for the exits. As hundreds poured from the building, the gunman began his methodical rampage. The shots were fired singly, luckily not with the spray of an automatic weapon. They came in measured cadence as if each victim were targeted, though that is not known. By the time the police on hand for the controversial lecture series were able to return fire, thirteen lay dead outside the lecture hall, including one policeman and the gunman positioned fifty yards away. Only seven additional victims were wounded, a remarkable fact, all of whom are being treated in Roseville's Sutter hospital. I have Jan Davis from our local affiliate in Roseville on hand.—Jan, what can you tell us?"

The coverage broke to a young woman, microphone in hand, standing in front of Jessup's Christian Humanities building. Though the crowd had obviously thinned, several dozen people were still about, a number of ambulances, police cars with lights flashing, multiple news crews, dozens of police and investigators, and, most chilling of all, multiple medical examiner wagons still retrieving the bodies of the dead. A white police tent was being set up as an on-site command post.

"As you can see behind me," Davis began, "the scene is still fluid and somewhat chaotic. Police have locked down the Jessup campus. All the wounded have been taken to Sutter Hospital. Half the covered bodies have yet to be removed from the scene. The gunman is also dead, though has yet to be identified. All I have been able to learn is that he is white and is thought to be in his mid-twenties. I have not been able to learn the type of weapon used, or—"

She stopped abruptly, glancing about.

"Wait just a minute. There seems to be—"

She hurried off, followed by her cameraman. Other reporters were doing likewise, scurrying toward a police spokeswoman. Within seconds the woman had half a dozen microphones in her face.

"There is little to report beyond what you already know," said the lead investigator. "Without detailed ballistics, nothing can be ascertained with reliability but a team of investigators have widened their search to include the possibility of a second gunman who may still be at large. I must emphasize the word *possibility*, and that—"

"On what basis?" one of the reporters asked.

"Multiple witness statements, confirmed by several policemen who were in the thick of the melee, indicate that many heard a distinct change in the final shots. This is mere speculation as the scene was frenzied and confused. Nevertheless, police are being called in from around the Sacramento area to conduct a search surrounding Jessup University. The campus borders much rugged terrain as the valley gives way to the foothills. A fugitive on foot would be able to disappear easily. Helicopters are on their way and will be combing the area as long as daylight lasts. We know nothing for certain. However, we want to alert viewers in the Roseville and Rocklin communities to stay inside their homes, and to report any suspicious activity."

She turned back toward the police tent. Questions continued to be shouted from the reporters hurrying after her.

The television screen returned to Denver Stone.

"Thank you, Jan," he said, "we will stand by for what further information you have for us. Tonight's ill-fated event," he continued, "was sixth in a series of lectures comparing the two world religions of Islam and Christianity by Jessup history professor Dr. Timothy Marshall. From early sources, as far as is known, the initial lectures were attended by a generally respectful crowd, though by the third and fourth lecture the discussions became more combative, though with no hint of what would lead to this evening's tragedy.

"Dr. Marshall, an outspoken Christian with several books to his credit, has a reputation as an objective historian, well respected in his field across ethnic and philosophical lines. During his lecture last week comparing the histories and world-missions of the two religions, a few of those I was able to speak with said that he was more blunt about Islam's jihadist ambitions than his Muslim listeners were comfortable with. His critics, which are numerous, say that his pretense of open-mindedness was but a smoke screen for an attack on Islam masquerading under a cloak of objectivity. The charge of Islamophobia has been circulating for the past couple weeks, which could have led—"

56

The Vultures Descend

TODD DROVE the Marshalls home. Timothy sat in the car in a stupor, eyes staring vacantly. Jaylene and Todd led him into the house attached securely to both arms. He was unsteady on his feet and his face was white.

At Jaylene's request, their friends followed the Marshall car. "Timothy is going to need us all around him," she whispered to Mark, Grace, and Dewitt. "This will devastate him. He will be a long time recovering. He needs all who love him close, not just family but all of you too. The great tribulation of his life may have come."

They nodded soberly. They would be there for their friend in every way they could.

They now sat in the Marshall living room watching television coverage of the event. Against Jaylene's pleading that he be checked out at Sutter after fainting outside the building, Timothy sat among them. He heard almost nothing of what was said. He sat disconsolate, eyes down and blinking back tears, unable even to glance at the television screen. He had not spoken another word since the wail of horror from his lips at sight of the carnage.

It did not take long for the paparazzi, smelling blood in the water, to dispatch their second-string news teams to the home of the suddenly infamous right-wing Christian professor. Already some of their colleagues on the left-leaning networks were pointing none too kind fingers of accusation at Timothy for instigating the shooting with his inflammatory rhetoric, labeled by some as hate speech.

Realizing, however, that this was where the real red meat of the story might be found, most of those second teams were intercepted en route, told to get to Jessup for mop-up operations, and their first teams sent to the Marshall home.

Within minutes of getting Timothy safely inside, seated, and sipping absently on a glass of water, the initial vans began rolling up. Suspecting the truth, Heather rose and drew the curtains and blinds, then walked through the rest of the house making sure they were closed in the other rooms. Even as the group watched Stone's report on FNC, the increasing noise and lights from film crews outside was impossible to ignore.

It wasn't long before a knock came to the door. Everyone glanced around. Who should answer it?

Jaylene rose. She took two or three steps toward the door but was stopped by Todd's hand on her arm.

"I've got this, Jaylene," he said with a smile. "Until this is over, I am the official spokesman for your family . . . for all of you," he added, glancing around the room. "I hereby appoint myself! None of you say a word to the press. Don't open the door to anyone but me—I'll use a single knock followed by two more in succession. Make sure all the lights in the house are off except here. Turn off the overhead—leave one lamp on. Lock the door behind me."

Jaylene's eyes filled. She embraced him. "Thank you, Todd," she whispered.

Todd walked toward the front door. After a few steps he stopped and turned.

"And pray that I will keep my cool and reflect the spirit of Jesus," he said. "These people are vultures. I know. I used to be one of them. Pray that they will see something different in me."

He opened the door narrowly, slipped through quickly, and shut it firmly behind him.

At sight of their former famous colleague, a dozen reporters with microphones in hand rushed forward bombarding him with questions.

Todd said nothing, merely smiled and continued walking slowly, though half of them were blocking his way. He persisted forward, not exactly shoving them aside but not to be deterred. When he was across the lawn, onto the sidewalk, and twenty yards further away from the house, he finally stopped to face his importune entourage.

Questions again assaulted him. He stood silent. It took a full minute for them to realize he would say nothing as long as the shouting match continued. Finally, it quieted.

"Back away," he said calmly.

Instantly a dozen shouts silenced him. He waited another twenty seconds.

"Back away," he repeated. "When you are at a respectful distance, I will answer questions one at a time."

A few began to step back, though more shouts silenced Todd yet again.

From windows in every house up and down the street of the residential neighborhood, curious eyes peered out. Heather's was among them.

"You should see Todd!" she said. "He led them away from the house. He's way down the sidewalk."

"Can you hear what he's saying?" asked Craig.

"I don't think he's said anything yet. He's just standing there until they quiet down."

"Good for him," said Mark. "The Charles Reyburn strategy."

"I believe also the Mark Forster strategy," added Dewitt. "As I recall you used it with singular effectiveness during your first press conference at the Presidential Manor a while back."

"I suppose I did," rejoined Mark.

☆ ☆ ☆

"All right then," said Todd. "You, young lady," he said to one of the more reticent of those surrounding him standing behind the others, "you have not shoved a microphone in my face nor shouted at me. So to you goes the first question. The rest of you should learn from her example that being a journalist does not require you to be rude. I'm sorry, I don't know your name."

"Lora," said the girl, who could not have been more than twenty-one or twenty-two and represented a small new station in Dorado Hills.

"All right, then, Lora—what would you like to ask me?"

"Thank you, Mr. Stewart. Is Mr. Marshall in the house with you?"

"He is."

"What is his mood?"

"He is devastated, sick over this, as are all of us . . . as is the whole country. He is sitting with tears in his eyes as we speak."

Several shouted questions drowned out the last of Todd's answer. He went silent again. When it again died down, Todd nodded once more to young Lora.

"Does he feel responsible for what happened?" she asked pointedly.

Todd thought a moment, then drew in a deep breath.

"I'm afraid he does," replied Todd slowly. "I hope that feeling is short-lived. But he is a sensitive man. That initial reaction probably cannot be helped."

"*Is* he an Islamophobe?" asked another. The quiet tone of the question, and that the small group remained silent awaiting his answer, prompted Todd to answer it.

"Let me ask a question of you all," said Todd. "A show of hands will suffice, no shouts or objections. How many of you attended all Dr. Marshall's lectures?"

No hands went up.

"How many of you attended *one* of his lectures?"

Still no hands were raised.

"How many of you are familiar with Dr. Marshall's credentials as a historian?"

No hands.

"How many of you did your due diligence on Dr. Marshall before coming here this evening? How many of you know anything about Dr. Marshall?"

"A reporter is under no obligation to—" began one of the more insistent young men in a defiant tone, taking a step toward Todd.

"Back!" said Todd loudly. "You can't intimidate me. I've been where you stand. I know the game. But I've also learned a thing or two over the years. I've learned that respect for your subjects is the most important aspect of being a good journalist. If you want to be a hack fine—go be one somewhere else. If you want to treat me with respect and Dr. Marshall with the respect he deserves as a renowned historian, then I will speak to you as the family's spokesman. But if I find one of you twisting or misrepresenting my words, that will be game over between you and me. I will be straight and honest, but I will put up with no twisting of the facts."

Whether the small group was intimidated was doubtful. Few liberal journalists were intimidated by much of anything. But Todd's bold self-confidence, probably somewhat garnished by his reputation, opened their eyes a bit wider than was customary.

"Dr. Marshall is one of the most objective and honorable men in the ranks of professors in all California," he went on. "His father was an equally renowned educator, as is his wife. Had you attended his lectures, you would have been treated to an objective analysis of Islam and Christianity presenting the evidence, pros and cons, of both religions in a more even-handed way than I can imagine any other Christian or Muslim presenting it. He did so as a knowledgeable historian.

"He neither justified the Crusades nor quailed from exposing the dark side of Islam's jihadist agenda. He was blunt in speaking about jihad—yes. What would you have him do, gloss over the truth? If you cannot report his courage to do so with the same objectivity he displayed in his lectures, then I have nothing more to say to you. Leave the charge of Islamophobia to the childish responses of the uninformed or to Muslims who do not have the same courage and open-mindedness that Dr. Marshall exhibited in his lectures."

He paused, leaving half of those surrounding him stunned at his bold words.

"For those of you who want to explore tonight's tragedy on a mature footing of mutual respect, I will come back out in an hour and speak to you again. You might use that time to begin your due diligence on Dr. Marshall. The rest of you who are unwilling to play by my rules might as well leave."

Todd turned, and with a few stray shouts following him returned to the house, reached toward the door, but was admitted by Heather who saw him coming before knocking, and disappeared inside.

57

A Microcosm of Christ's Body Knit Together in Prayer

REPORTS OF the shooting on the campus of Jessup University spread like wildfire. As those gathered in the Marshall home sat dumbfounded, reeling from the events of the previous hour, watching reports from the scene where they had all been a short time earlier, by ones and twos some left the room for more secluded parts of the house to telephone others of the Brotherhood.

Their messages sent throughout the country were similar, "We are all in shock but okay. Timothy is despondent. He has not spoken. None of us have ever seen him like this. Pray for him! Pray for the families of the victims. Pray for Christians and Muslims everywhere."

Across the country the news flew.

Most regular television programming was interrupted by live reports from California, in which Timothy was featured. He quickly became the story's sub-plot, the eye of the storm, the personality, the *Christian*, around whom opportunistic journalists quickly began to frame a narrative of cause and effect, and around whose neck they could hang a millstone of blame. With exquisite skill, their questions required no answers.

They would point no fingers of accusation. They would only report. Shielding their hypocritical bias, they would innocently pose a series of disingenuous questions laced with the implications they wanted their viewers to draw.

"The whole country is asking tonight," they began:

Is Jessup University a secret hotbed for Christian racism?

Is Dr. Marshall an Islamophobe?

Were the Marshall lectures a thinly disguised attack on American Muslims?

Should Dr. Marshall be arrested for inciting terrorism under the Hate Crimes Act?

Should Jessup University be shut down?

Thankfully no one in the Marshall home, whose television was tuned to FNC, heard the most outrageous commentaries from irresponsible journalistic opportunists. But their scandal-mongering innuendoes were heard by millions and made hundreds of hearts of the Brotherhood at once both sick and angry in a turbulent mix of emotions between the Old and New Adam.

☆ ☆ ☆

If confirmation was needed that the earthly body of Christ was neither housed in buildings, overseen by professional clergy, nor defined by elaborate systems of theologically contorted doctrines, that confirmation came through the mysterious operation of prayer interweaving its unseen strands among the invisibly connected hearts of that body. Prayer—linking them not only with one another, but also lifting their petitions, their heart-cries, their sighs of pain, their inarticulate groanings for which they could form no words, and the myriad dimensions of the otherworldly love—bound them together in the eternal realm of the heart of their mutual Father, whose sons and daughters in a worldwide and eternal family they were.

The men and women loosely linked in a fellowship unofficially identifying themselves as brothers and sisters of the common life of God's Fatherhood and Jesus's exampling Sonship, or "Brethren of the Common Life"—a fellowship with no leader, no buildings, no doctrine, no membership, no times or seasons, no regular meetings, no budget, no organization, no venerated texts but the Gospels, and no agenda other than to live the commands of those Gospels as Christ's followers in but not of the world—were all well aware of Timothy's lectures on Islam and Christianity. The *Master's Helps Newsletter* had announced it weeks before.

The invisible worldwide web of prayer by which those of this unseen network upheld, sustained, loved, and shared life together in ways known only by the Father in whose heart all their prayers resided, had kept Timothy at the center of its collective focus ever since. Their brother had stepped into the crosshairs. He needed their prayer, and guidance from on high, more than ever. He had walked onto the battlefield in full view of a hostile and virulently anti-Christian country, placing himself at the forefront of a war becoming less and less invisible with every passing year.

Little had they known how soon he would desperately need their prayers all the more. His future, his faith, potentially his life, would depend on the daily reality of Psalm 91.

☆ ☆ ☆

In Idaho, where they could not believe what they saw and heard on their television screen, Matthew and Sarah Gardner wept for the friend who had reached out to them so many years ago. In a palpable sense, they owed the continuation of their ministry to this man who had become one of their closest friends. Either one of them would have taken his place and subjected themselves to the attacks in an instant if they could protect him from the onslaught of the world's accusations.

Oh, Lord, Lord . . . Matthew prayed, *fill dear Timothy's heart with your love. In a depth of despondency I cannot imagine, step into the cauldron of his suffering with him. Give him reassurance in his grief that you feel every accusation, share his pain, that you are upholding him, even deepening his sonship in this testing fire of tribulation. And may we never forget the families who have lost loved ones, whose grief is even greater than Timothy's. In this terrible hour, turn hearts toward your Fatherhood.*

☆ ☆ ☆

Where he watched in Laramie, Harvey Jansen had some idea what Timothy was going through. The odium hurled at him from the press, stinging as it was at the time, was nothing like this. *God . . . be his Father!* were the only words that came to his lips. They were enough.

The overspreading Fatherhood of the universe is always enough when we give ourselves to it.

Beside him, Harriet's thoughts were with Jaylene. She knew a wife's suffering to hear an honorable husband called a fool, a bigot, a racist, and worse. She did her best to shake off the anger rising at the words she just heard on the news. She reached for the remote, turned off the television, then closed her eyes. The faces of Jaylene and Timothy filled her mind. She drew in a deep breath.

Comfort my precious sister, Jaylene, Lord Jesus. Give her wisdom and grace to be what Timothy needs at this moment—a helpmeet, a prayer-warrior, a companion, a sustainer, an encourager, a sister, a friend.

☆ ☆ ☆

Where they watched in Kansas, Gerald and Rebecca Stevens did likewise, turned off their set, and sat hand in hand in silence. As they lifted their brother Timothy and all who had been at the fateful lecture into God's hands, their prayers found no audible words. Their silent thoughts of love and shared heartache were their prayers.

☆ ☆ ☆

As of one accord, where they sat together in their home in Texas, Geoffrey and Martha Powell began praying aloud.

You gave Timothy wisdom and courage to prepare these lectures, prayed Martha, *to speak the truth boldly. Now give him courage to face this valley of grief with equal fortitude.*

After a brief silence, Geoffrey continued. *Gird up his loins to be your man as the attacks come, and in the humiliation of being falsely accused, remind him of Jesus before Pilate, that accusation cannot be met with defense but in the quiet confidence which is our strength. Strengthen him in silence.*

☆ ☆ ☆

Where they watched in Kentucky, Charles and Regina Reyburn, closed their eyes, and wept. Charles's voice, as he began to speak a minute later, was nearly inaudible.

Lord God, our precious Father, may all of us suffering with our brother at this time of his tribulation above all be your sons and daughters. Timothy has done so much for us. How dear to my memory is the moment we first laid eyes on one another. The bond of brotherhood was instant. He had come to me, a stranger, in my hour of need. He had come merely to say, "I am your brother, and I will be a brother to you." Oh, God, may I be a brother to him! Show me what I can do to ease his pain, to share his grief, to stand with him against the enemy's attacks. Show me, Holy Spirit, how to be what you want me to be for my brother.

☆ ☆ ☆

Where they watched in Albany, Trevor and Violet Langdon prayed silently for several minutes. At last the quiet was broken by Violet's voice.

Oh Lord, she prayed, *don't let Timothy's present valley of discouragement cause him to lose his vision. So many of us need his writings. We need him to continue strong and bold to communicate your deep truths. May his writings henceforth take wings to new heights of insight into your purposes and methods, and what you would say to your people and do among your sons and daughters. Comfort the families of the fallen.*

☆ ☆ ☆

Where they watched in horror, anger, despondency, and heartache, Court and Stella Masters waited but moments before both were on their phones—Court to Dewitt West, Stella to Grace Forster. They would not immediately intrude too close into the Marshall circle, but they must know what they could do. After praying together, Court was on his computer in search for last-minute flights. Cost was no object. The Brotherhood was under attack. He must be there. By 10:30 the following morning, he was on his way to California.

☆ ☆ ☆

At his home in the nation's capital where he watched the coverage of the shooting, Congressman Alfred Nason fell to his knees.

Lord Jesus, he prayed, *may this incident redound to your glory and further your purposes, giving wings to the truth Timothy has spoken to be spread throughout the country. From an audience of a few hundred, may millions hear Timothy's clarion call to truth. May I display a tenth of Timothy's courage to be your man in the halls of Congress. Give me opportunity to take my stand alongside my brother in the war for truth.*

☆ ☆ ☆

Only a mile away in Washington, DC, hearing of the shooting on his car radio returning from the school library, the first thing Bradon Rhodes did upon reaching his apartment, was turn on the television. Unexpected personal sensations rose within him as he watched a replay of the events unfold. The moment the cameras cut to the scene outside the Marshall home, curtains drawn and few lights on, instinctively he knew that Ginger was inside the house, probably with the rest of her family. The whole idea of prayer was still new and strange to him. Yet all at once, as if a force from inside suddenly erupted and began speaking through him, unplanned words came tumbling from his mouth.

God, I pray for Mr. Marshall, Bradon heard himself say. *Give him strength to endure everything that is being said about him and to know they are lies. And be with all those gathered with him right now, Ginger and her parents and Mrs. Marshall and all their friends. I know they are there and are probably praying too. Please join my prayer to all of theirs.*

Bradon fell silent, in awe at what he had just done. He sat staring blankly at his television, watching absently as the camera panned away from the house to a small group of reporters a short distance away.

There was Todd being interviewed!

A surreal sensation swept over him. He felt almost like he was *there* with Todd. In a weird way, he *was* there! Todd was his friend. In their short acquaintance, Todd had changed his life more than anyone he ever knew.

His heart ached to be there, to share this with them all—awful as it was—to be with Todd with Ginger, even Mr. and Mrs. Marshall as little as he knew them, to be able to shake Mr. Marshall's hand and look into his eyes and say, "I know who you really are."

A sense of detachment swept through him. Washington, DC—this center of gravity of the political world where he now sat—was suddenly cold and lifeless. But there, in that house in Roseville 2,500 miles away in California, a *family* was gathered sharing this crisis together.

Then followed a startling, incredible, astonishing thought. They were *his* family too!

This wasn't just about Ginger anymore. It was bigger than that. Though he was a continent away, he wanted to be there, he wanted to be *with* them . . . to be part of the family gathered inside that house.

Without understanding all it signified, he somehow knew that the center of gravity of his life had shifted on its axis.

He sat several minutes, trying to absorb the rush of thoughts unmaking everything he thought he had known prior to these last few months. He then reached for his phone.

His mother's private number went straight to voice mail. He punched in the official number instead. The next voice he heard was the Presidential Manor operator.

"It's Bradon Rhodes," he said. "I would like to be connected to my mother."

It took two minutes before Marcia Rhodes answered.

"Hi, Mom . . . are you watching the news?"

"Yes, it's terrible. I'm sick about it."

"Could you call me back on your encrypted cell?"

Bradon ended the call. His phone rang twenty seconds later.

"That's better," he said. "I don't want to be recorded."

"What I was going to say," said the First Lady, "is that I'd like to call Jaylene. But your dad's watching me like a hawk. My friendship with Grace Forster has him suspicious."

"I wish I could be there with them," said Bradon.

"I know what you mean."

"But don't tell Dad what I said."

"This will remain our secret."

☆ ☆ ☆

Around the world, news of the shooting made headlines everywhere, highlighted as one more example of America's lawlessness, gun culture, and racial acrimony. News sources in the Middle East emblazoned Timothy's face as the instigator of the incident, accompanied by various captions and headlines: *Hate-monger, Islamophobia grows in US, The new American terrorism.* Anti-American riots broke out in Iran, Syria, and Iraq, with Timothy burned in effigy in at least six cities. Iranian spokesmen called for reprisals against the new wave of America's persecution of Muslims, and for the death of Timothy Marshall.

☆ ☆ ☆

When Leon and Alita Morales heard the news in Ecuador, Alita's prayer was simple yet profound, a prayer for all seasons, for all people, for all circumstances: *Encircle Timothy with your arms of love.*

☆ ☆ ☆

When Richard and Jessica Constable heard the news in London, Richard's heart went out to Timothy as personally as had Harvey Jansen's. Richard had walked in Timothy's shoes. He had been falsely accused of heinous things. He still regularly received hate mail. Such a trial was probably coming to shake Timothy's world to its foundations. Spontaneous prayer poured forth from a brother suffering for a brother.

Oh, Lord God! My poor dear brother is your man in this critical hour. Timothy has taken the truth his father gave the world in his writings into the public square with boldness, humility, and courage. Out of his grief, and perhaps the guilt he may feel for this evil done, raise Timothy to strength upon strength to stand in your truth, as a man of God bearing his father's mantle. And shower your love and comfort abroad in the hearts of those who have lost those they love.

Richard's voice stilled, hardly realizing the import of the words coming from his lips. Beside him, Jessica was already writing down his prayer, silently asking the Spirit for remembrance. Timothy had to know what his friend prayed for him.

☆ ☆ ☆

When they heard the news in Scotland, Moira and Alexander Campbell remembered how personally Timothy had reached out to them, encouraging them in their first efforts to open their home and begin sharing with other hungry men and women. At this moment, the memory of their trip to California to meet Timothy and Jaylene was full in their hearts. They might not be able to give a full return for what they had been given. But they could pray. Maybe that was the most important thing of all they could do for Timothy right now.

Heavenly Father, said Moira softly, *in this time which must be more terrible for Timothy than I can imagine, what I pray for him most of all is wisdom. I'm sure he must be filled with doubts about what he has done. He is probably questioning many things. But he will endure. With Jaylene's help, he will continue to be an example to the rest of us. But he will need your wisdom now more than ever, wisdom to know your heart, wisdom to sense your guidance during a season filled with doubts, wisdom to respond to the attacks with the grace of Jesus, wisdom to write what you have for him to communicate to your people.*

Hardly aware of the words pouring forth from her mouth, Moira fell silent, closed her eyes, a great sense of release flooding through her that God had given her the words to pray, she had given them back to him, and he would send the answering fulfillment of his purpose, having allowed her to share in its birthing, into Timothy's heart.

☆ ☆ ☆

When Monika and Fynn Sievers heard the news in Germany, Fynn's voice as he began to pray was scarcely above a whisper:

May Timothy feel your presence, dear Lord. I do not pray for you to remove his pain until you would remove it. You may have a work for it to accomplish in his heart. But through the pain, as he listens for your voice, may he feel your presence with him, around him, and in him.

☆ ☆ ☆

When they heard the news in Poland, Grigor and Anya Popov gathered their small group of brothers and sisters as soon as they could meet and spent the evening in specific prayer for Timothy and Jaylene. Anya shared the principle of prayer arrows she had learned from Jaylene. As Grigor then prayed, his prayer became a model for all their prayers:

Though a world separates us, in you we are side by side, joined as one. As I launch my prayers up into your heart, heavenly Father, send your answering arrows of light, comfort, strength, courage, wisdom, encouragement, confidence, and peace down into the heart of my brother Timothy Marshall.

☆ ☆ ☆

The moment Paddy and Charlene Ayscough heard the news in New Zealand, Paddy immediately closed his eyes and words of prayer poured from his lips.

Strengthen Timothy through this, even as he is doubting that he has heard you. Enable him to hear your voice even more clearly. May he speak the words you give him with clarity and boldness. Raise him to new regions of understanding into your eternal purposes.

☆ ☆ ☆

One of the most poignant responses to the shooting took place in a solitary apartment in Sacramento where a young man in his thirties sat watching in horror as the events played out in front of him. As the camera zoomed in on a body lying face down on the pavement in his own blood, a portion of paper could be seen beneath him—one of the few not retrieved. He recognized it immediately.

It was the Birch pamphlet!

The watcher's head fell forward. He buried his face in his hands, his face hot and red, his eyes blinking back bitter tears.

Though no other human being ever heard them, in an overpowering flood of guilt, the very words Heather's father had cried such a short time before burst from his lips,

"What have I done!"

A low knocking had begun on the door of Lionel Holt's brain. In truth, it had not just begun for it is always tapping out its quiet call to wakefulness. For the first time, however, its soft echo found a crack to enter. The sound had not yet reached deep enough to be heard in the region of his heart. Whether it would penetrate that far was now up to Lionel.

What would he do? Would he heed the knock? Would that barely perceptible voice from on high get deep enough inside him to begin the transformation into sonship?

☆ ☆ ☆

A week later a letter arrived at the Marshall home addressed to Timothy. Jaylene and Heather had been screening all the mail for obvious reasons. But when they saw the name on the envelope, they knew Timothy would want to open this one himself.

Dear Tim,

I know this must be a terrible time for you and I am hesitant to intrude or to bring up the past. But I want you to know that your life and example have had a profound impact on me. Because of you I have been reading Dad's books. I regret more than I can say that I did not recognize the stature of the man he was earlier in life. But one is never too old to learn, they say. I think I have finally begun to grow spiritually into the sort of man he and Mom taught and trained us to be. I thank you for your influence in helping me embark on that spiritual journey, even if I am a little late in life to be doing so. I am reading your books too—you sound just like Dad! His gift was obviously passed on to you!

But what I really wanted to tell you is that after what happened, I found myself praying for you. I wanted to share what God put on my heart to pray. I am continuing to pray this for you every day.

"Heavenly Father, I pray for and lift up my brother Timothy to you. I cannot imagine his suffering at this time. But I know you honor his integrity, his life lived for you, and his courage to be a man of truth. Show him at this time how much he is loved by many around the world he doesn't even know, and how deeply he is loved by those nearest and dearest to him whom he does know. Most of all, fill him with the awareness in his suffering that you love him most of all and are holding him in the palm of your hand. Bring light back into his life to help him through this time of darkness."

You have been a good brother, a faithful son to our parents, and an important influence my life. I know you are in God's hands in this time of trial. I love you, Tim.

Woody.

58

Picking Up the Pieces

THE IDEA of Timothy delivering a seventh and final lecture was obviously out of the question. He was too despondent to think and hardly spoke for days. His classes were cancelled for the following week.

However, Jaylene had his notes for his proposed seventh presentation. It had been slated to draw the previous weeks to a conclusion with a discussion of *truth and lifestyle*. Flowing out of their overall purposes and objectives, how Islam and Christianity were intended to be lived practically and consistently in the day to day. Timothy had hoped to ask what such practicality might have to say about how one chooses and places faith in a belief system representing *truth* beyond learned doctrines. He hoped by then that the group would be capable of an intelligent discussion focusing on that question.

It was now clear, even if the final lecture went forward, that such a discussion would be impossible.

Based on Timothy's notes, Jaylene considered delivering the lecture herself, hoping to put the lectures and shooting into perspective. After advice from their friends and Jessup's president Travers, however, and in light of ongoing threats and sporadic violence throughout the Sacramento area, the decision was made to cancel it. The police would probably have done so anyway.

An announcement was made in the *Sacramento Bee* and posted on campus, adding that further information for those registered for the course, their final assignments and exam, would be handled through

Dr. Jaylene Marshall's office. Full credit for the course, after final papers and exam, would be given in spite of the cancellation.

Funerals and services for the victims began within the week and continued for another ten days. Mourning replaced violence throughout most of California's northern valley region. The national news, as it always does, moved on from the twenty-four-hour news cycle. Local news crews continued to be seen outside the Marshall home, however, still hoping to be the first to land an interview with Dr. Marshall in person.

The man at the center of the firestorm had not been seen since the incident.

Meanwhile, the press managed to get hold of the complete transcripts of the six lectures. They were disseminated throughout the country.

Just when the country began to breathe and move on after most of the funerals, the publication of the transcripts hit the media and ignited more controversy than anything since the Pentagon Papers and the infamous WikiLeaks documents. Had Timothy's lectures been published in a book, they would have topped *The New York Times* bestseller list. As it was, they were online everywhere and were being spun and given every conceivable political and spiritual slant possible.

Except for the far-right, which thought Timothy had not gone near far enough in his condemnation of the evils of Islam, most Christians universally proclaimed what were inaccurately being called "the Islam Papers" as the most fair and balanced presentation and contrast of the two religions ever produced. The Muslim community, on the other hand, lambasted Timothy as an Islamophobe of the worst kind, one who hid his bigotry behind the pretense of objectivity. The papers were nothing but a thinly disguised anti-Muslim manifesto of misinformation, lies, and hate.

The news media predictably followed the Muslim narrative—inflaming passions, inciting Muslim violence toward churches and synagogues and Christian and Jewish businesses, justified in the eyes of much of the country as a reasonable response to Timothy's hate speech. Excerpts were carefully chosen, quoted over and over and out of context, putting Timothy in the worst possible light.

Calls for his arrest continued.

☆ ☆ ☆

Like most of the country, Hamad Bahram also read the transcripts. His response was more thoughtful than that of his fellow Muslims. They filled him with an undefined angst, a deep concern that, after the initial emotional reactions on all sides subsided, the country would dig deeper into Marshall's frighteningly astute articulation of the truth.

"This man knows too much," he said to himself after laying aside his printed copy of the lectures. "He *understands*!"

He leaned back pensively. Without knowing it, Marshall could expose his own agenda. He understood what few Westerners ever grasped. The papers were dangerous!

It would obviously not be possible to put a lid on the thing now. The genie was out of the bottle.

It might be that he would need to accelerate his plans. The fool Marshall may have unwittingly and single-handedly triggered phase three.

59

A Summit of Brotherhood

LATE OCTOBER 2051

IT WASN'T on the scale of a BCL gathering such as had been held at the Gordon and Forster ranches. Its importance to that Brotherhood, however, was the equal of anything those gathered at the Jansen ranch in Laramie had ever been part of. All eighteen realized a Rubicon had been crossed.

Harvey Jansen initiated the summit. Arranging with Court Masters for a private video call through his new secure server with Charles Reyburn and Mark Forster three days after the shooting, he first wanted to know how Timothy was holding up. Mark's firsthand reports confirmed what the other suspected—that Timothy's dark night of the soul had come. More than ever he needed a surrounding group of friends in his life.

The sixteen who would be traveling to Wyoming cleared their schedules. Nothing was more important than this. They arrived at the Jansen ranch in the last week of October—Timothy and Jaylene and Heather Marshall, Todd Stewart, Mark and Grace Forster, Charles and Regina Reyburn, Court and Stella Masters, Dewitt and Pearl West, Congressman Alfred and Catherine Nason, and Matthew and Sarah Gardner. The three Marshalls and Todd would stay at the ranch. The other couples had rooms booked at Laramie's Best Western.

They came with no agenda other than to be together.

Conversations were quiet, thoughtful, personal.

No one counseled Timothy with platitudes.

No cheap spiritualities were heard among them.

When they prayed, the focus was for all of them, the whole group, Christians everywhere, the country. Timothy knew they had gathered for him. He listened and absorbed. But no words of prayer fell from his lips.

They took walks, a few rides, drives about Laramie, into the mountains and back. It was a quiet time of retreat for them all.

Timothy said almost nothing their first day together. He was cordial, pleasant, obviously appreciative, keenly aware of the love being showered on him.

But his soul was in pain and his spirit quiet. His grief remained too profound for words. He had to walk those inner valleys alone.

Hugs and quiet smiles were numerous. Words were few.

All sensed that in this desert of Timothy's personal desolation, the mettle of his spiritual manhood was being honed, purified, and strengthened for yet greater works as God's man. Though nothing was said, nor would be said, henceforth they recognized that the mantle of the father had passed to the son through the valley of this great shadow in his life.

Unable to leave the ranch because of two young foals needing constant care, and wanting Todd to experience such an important time with the others, David remained at home, saying as much to Mark before his departure. "When Timothy wins through this," David said, "he will be a different man. Whatever direction his future writings take, I believe they will be profound, probably prophetic."

It was obvious that Timothy was weak, vulnerable, suffering, and at the lowest ebb his faith ever experienced. Yet in that weakness he rose in stature in the eyes of these, his closest brothers and sisters.

They gazed upon him—sometimes from a distance as Timothy walked alone in the precincts of the Jansen ranch—almost with awe at what was in progress in the heart of this man they loved. They saw the spirit of the father in the son.

Even Jaylene realized that he had entered the depths of his own private Gethsemane, where she could not follow. She knew what prayer he was praying there. It was the same prayer their Lord had prayed.

And thus the others not only watched Timothy from afar, their perceptions were equally keen in holding Jaylene up in prayer. They had some inkling into what deep regions her own faith was also being drawn. The bond between this man and this woman lay at the heart of the ever-widening fellowship of the unofficial Brotherhood. That bond would surely be tested in new ways.

On the evening of their second full day together, seated in the expansive Jansen living room enjoying the pies the women made earlier in the day, a lull fell in the conversation. Unexpectedly it was Timothy who broke it.

"I know I've not been very sociable or talkative," he said quietly. "I'm sure you understand. I want you to know how much I truly appreciate you all. Thank you for planning this, Harvey—it had to be you!" he added, casting Harvey a smile.

"Guilty as charged," nodded the host.

"I know it took some doing to get you all here," Timothy went on. "It means the world to me. Just being *with* you, my dearest friends. I begin to feel hints of life returning. It will be slow. I am utterly confused by what has happened, tormented by guilt, as how can I not be. Had I not given those lectures, all those people would be alive. I know you will say I am not responsible. But I *am* responsible. My words precipitated the shooting. There is no way around that fact."

He paused. The room was silent for a minute or two. None would fill the speaking silence with ill-chosen words.

"The hardest part," Timothy went on at length, "is that I genuinely prayed long and hard, not only about embarking on the lectures, but in my preparation for every one. I felt *led* by the Holy Spirit every step of the way. Yet . . . now this.

"Did I misread God's leading? That question probes to the bedrock of my faith, to God's sovereignty, to how one hears God's voice. I wake up in the middle of the night seeing the bodies and the blood. I have no answers. My faith feels as if it is hanging by the slenderest of threads. I am a babe scarcely able to walk who has been set in the middle of a dark forest not knowing where to turn, not even knowing if light exists in *any* direction out of that darkness."

Again he paused. His eyes were full of tears. The others waited. They needed say nothing. God would care for his son. God would bring the light to the forest of his doubts when those doubts accomplished their work.

Beside him, Jaylene took his hand. Timothy drew in a shaky breath. Most of the others were blinking back tears of their own.

"I didn't mean to go off on all that," he said with a smile. "I'm sure you know something of what I'm feeling. Yet good is already coming out of it that I want to share. Perhaps it's the light in the darkness, though it's still hard to see.

"You've probably noticed how Jaylene has been busy writing in her notebook, yesterday and today, as you've prayed or afterwards. I don't want anyone to be intimidated, but she has been writing down your prayers."

Looks and glances and nods and smiles spread about the room, as if silently asking Jaylene if it was true.

"He is right," she said. "I have been doing exactly that."

"There is a good reason for it," Timothy went on. "Almost immediately after the shooting, we began to receive messages on all the social media sites, and quite a few by old-fashioned mail. They were uncannily similar, some version of, 'This is what I have been praying for you' or 'I was led to pray this for you.' Then usually followed the words of their prayer.

"It was the most extraordinary thing. I cannot believe it was accidental. It obviously *wasn't* accidental. God was leading them not only to pray for me, but to share their prayers, and often using similar language. Maybe that's not surprising since they are being led by the Spirit."

Comments and nods and *amens* went around the room.

"They began coming one or two a day, then more. At first, from friends and others in the various fellowships, then from many of our foreign friends. Then they started coming from people we didn't know, some signed but others with no name at all. Most said some version of the same thing: 'God led me to pray this for you.'

"The magnitude of it worked on me. God was using his people to sustain me in prayer! God was thinking about me! God was speaking a clear message—*I haven't forgotten you, Timothy. You are encompassed about not only by a great cloud of witnesses of those who have gone before, but a countless brotherhood of men and women who are upholding you in my love.*"

As they listened, Heather and Jaylene were weeping. Most of the others were wiping at their eyes.

"I can't tell you what that did for me. God was speaking to his people on my behalf."

Timothy paused, blinking back his own tears.

"Jaylene saw me one day sitting reading over some of the prayers that had come. Reading the words, realizing not only that people were praying these things for me but that God had prompted them to do so, was the most extraordinary feeling. That's when she had the idea of typing them up and keeping track of them."

He pulled out a small notebook. "This is what she has put together for me so far. There are over fifty prayers in it—imagine . . . for *me*! I find myself reading it throughout the day. You've probably seen me carrying the book about. I can't describe the feeling."

"I wondered what it was!" said Mark.

"Now you know," rejoined Timothy. "My own personal journal of prayers from God."

He smiled.

"That's the most extraordinary part of this of all," Timothy added. "Paul says in Romans 8 that the Holy Spirit intercedes when we don't know what to pray. None of the people who have written were probably planning to pray for me. As they said, God prompted them to pray. *God gave them the words!*"

He shook his head almost still in disbelief at the idea of it.

"These prayers in this notebook are *God's* prayers for me. The stupendous reality is God's Spirit has been interceding for me! Using his people to pray *his* prayers for me.

"I can hardly get my head around that! He sends a prayer out through the Holy Spirit into the brain and heart of someone like Grigor Popov—whose prayer in this notebook is unbelievable!—prompting him to pray it back to God. The prayer has thus gone full circle from God's heart into

Grigor's heart and back again. Then Grigor shares it with me, and I am able to receive it coming again from God's heart into mine.

"The multiple dimensions of this unbroken cycle of prayer are beyond understanding. It makes me wonder if all true prayer originates in the heart of God to then flow out among his people and be spread through all mankind and be lifted back into God's heart.

"Then I realized that these prayers are not only for me. They are God's prayers for all his people, especially his remnant people. These are God's prayers for you as well as me—universal prayers originating in the heart of God and that are continually flowing out from his Father heart into his world, and into the hearts of those who are tuned to his Spirit to receive them and send them back to God as their own prayers, whose answers were already sent in prompting them to pray in oneness with God's own purposes. They reflect universal prayers to and from God's heart into the hearts of his humanity."

They all sat trying to absorb the magnitude of what the great truth signified. Jaylene was writing as fast as she could to get down Timothy's thoughts.

A silence in the Jansen home fell as a hush of holy awe, each communing in their own way with the Spirit dwelling within them all which bound them in the eternal brotherhood of God's family.

60

Unexpected Invitation

A WEEK AFTER their return from Laramie, the telephone rang in the Marshall home. Jaylene answered it.

"I'm calling to ask if I might speak with Dr. Marshall," said the voice on the line.

"This is Mrs. Marshall. He's taking no calls just now," replied Jaylene. She thought she vaguely recognized the voice. "I'm sure you understand."

"I do understand. I know these must be very difficult times. If you could tell him Phil Simons called. I will leave you my number. When and if he is so inclined, perhaps—"

"Hang on just a minute, Mr. Simons."

She carried the portable phone into Timothy's office.

"You might want to take this," she whispered, handing him the phone.

Timothy looked at her animated face with no idea what her expression signified.

"This is Timothy Marshall," he said.

"Hello, Dr. Marshall, it's Phil Simons. Thank you for agreeing to speak to me."

"Well, this is a surprise, although I don't think I even want to ask why you would be calling me."

"You probably guessed it. I would like to have you on my program. You're in the news. Everyone is talking about your Islam Papers just as they were Dr. Reyburn's book a few years ago. You and he are friends, I believe."

"We are."

"I assume you saw my interview with him."

"I did."

"I hope you felt our exchanges were respectful enough that you might consider my request knowing that I would do my utmost to show you the same courtesy."

"I appreciate that. You were forceful with Charles, occasionally hinting at liberal edginess. But we recognize the ultra-liberal environment of our times. Charles felt it was a fair interview, and I agree."

"So you'll come on my program?"

"Not so fast," said Timothy. "After what has happened, the stakes are high. I'm sure you understand my reluctance to do anything that might inflame a delicate situation."

"I understand completely. I share your concerns."

"Nor would I consent without your assurance that you read my lectures in their entirety—every word."

"That's fair. I would agree to that."

"Additionally, I will not have my words twisted or misrepresented as the media has been doing continuously since the incident, parroting both the progressive and the extremist Islamic narratives. I will not defend myself with debate or argumentation. But neither will I tolerate outright lies. All this anti-Muslim nonsense is absurd. The media's promulgation of it is irresponsible."

"So you're not an Islamophobe?"

"That you ask the question, Phil, betrays that you *haven't* yet read my lectures. I would have assumed, before even making this call, you would have familiarized yourself with my approach. I am as unracist and unbigoted as any man you will ever meet."

"What better place to make that case than on my program?"

"I have no interest in making a case. My case was made in my lectures."

"It's obvious that most of the country has gotten the wrong impression of your views."

"That's true, and it's the media's fault, not because I didn't make myself clear."

"You don't want a chance to explain yourself on national television?"

"Not really. I doubt it would do any good. I am only calling on you, if I should agree, to be responsible in your questioning."

"You want only softball questions?"

"Of course not. I was pretty blunt in my lectures. I don't mind you playing hardball, if you do so with accuracy, respect, and a responsible representation of what I clearly said in my lectures. No twisting. No innuendos. One word, one question like what you asked a minute ago, laced with the underlying assumption that I *might* be Islamophobic when you should know full well from my lectures that the question is absurd and should never be asked—one misrepresentation of my motives, one twisting of what I have plainly said, and I would consider the interview over."

"What journalist would agree to such one-sided terms?" said Simons.

"None I can think of," laughed Timothy. "You'd do well to keep your distance from me!"

"Well, I must say, you drive a hard bargain. Let's say, provisionally, that I could agree, *would* you come on my program?"

"Possibly. I would have to pray long and hard first. If you agree to be well versed in what I said in my lectures, to have done your due diligence, to represent my perspectives fairly, and to present me as an objective historian not a right-wing kook, then I *might* agree. However, I do not think either of us ought to pursue this any time soon. Time needs to pass. Healing needs to take place. The country needs to put this terrible incident behind it and attempt to place it into perspective."

"Next spring perhaps?"

"At the soonest. That will give us both time to reflect further. By then you may have changed your mind and not want me!"

"I doubt that will happen," said Simons. "If I make a commitment, I stick to it."

"Well, you have my terms. You read my lectures thoroughly. You tell me honestly beforehand if you believe you can represent me fairly, without a hint of the negative portrayal that has been swirling for the past two weeks. If you do not believe you can do so, you must tell me. You do not have to agree with every point I make. By insisting on a favorable interview climate, I mean only that you would approach it with the assumption that I am intellectually honest, that I was attempting to get at the truth in my lectures, and that the characterization of the lectures dominating the public narrative in recent weeks is not worthy of honorable journalism."

61

Grand Canyon

November 2051

IN MID-NOVEMBER, Heather and Todd drove south to Arizona to visit Todd's mother, as well as to see Heather's grandparents and her aunts and uncles and cousins on her mother's side of the family in New Mexico.

Mrs. Stewart saw the difference in her son immediately. A light shone in his eyes that could not entirely be explained by the obvious connection with his young lady friend.

Meeting Heather for the first time, though Todd had sent pictures, his mother was hardly prepared for just how short she actually was alongside Todd. More than a foot separated the tops of their heads when they stood side by side.

With Heather's bright smile and sunny countenance, it did not take long for Mrs. Stewart to fall in love with her. She was, as Todd recognized the moment he met her, one of the most authentic individuals he had ever known. Seeing how contented and comfortable Heather and her son were with each other was a revelation. They were so much further ahead and prepared for a life together than many young people.

Todd's mother was full of questions about Heather's family and the background involving her grandfather and the Marshall family writings and Heather's correspondence work for their group. Looking up the three Marshall authors prior to the Thanksgiving visit—Stirling, Timothy, and Jaylene—Todd's mother was astonished to find some three dozen books between them.

Proud of her son, and assuming that Todd's background with NBC made him a well-known personality wherever he went, she gradually realized that Todd had been grafted into something of even more widespread impact, with a history going back more than fifty years. In their circles, it was the Marshall name that was known and revered among thousands who never heard of Todd Stewart. For the first time she understood much of what Todd had written her about and how important he considered his partnership with Heather in continuing the legacy of her parents and grandparents and their writings.

It was with a sense of marvel and quiet joy that Heather listened to Todd explain his new walk with God and his work with David at the ranch. As he told his mother about his time in the Shenandoah hills and his prayers, she could not keep tears from welling up in her eyes. It was the most moving testimony of a changed life she had ever heard. That she had a role in it filled Heather with nothing short of awe at what God could do.

After hearing Todd's story, Mrs. Stewart expressed eagerness to read what Todd called Heather's "Essence of Christianity" letter. A copy had already been sent to Bradon Rhodes. And now a second request!

☆ ☆ ☆

After a visit with Heather's grandparents and various aunts and uncles and cousins of her mother Jaylene's side of the family, they began making their way back to California, taking an extra day to detour to the south rim of the Grand Canyon. They spent the night in the Grand Hotel in Grand Canyon Village. Heather was surprised that they were able to get two rooms on the spur of the moment so close to Thanksgiving, especially on the same floor just down the hall from each other. What she didn't know was that the reservations had been made two months in advance. After an early dinner in the hotel dining room, they went out walking along the spectacular rim in the descending dusk of late autumn. Though Thanksgiving was warm at Todd's mother's, a decided chill was in the air at 7,000 feet. At this time of year, snow could come anytime.

They sat on some large rocks a short distance off the path. A near full moon was inching over the horizon, a globe of white amid the pinks and reds of the sunset. Overhead the canopy of blue gradually faded into the blackness of night.

Away from the noisy hotel, the evening was quiet and still.

"This has to be one of the most stunning views anywhere in the world," said Heather. "The first time I came here with my parents—it was on the far side, on the north rim—I was only seven. My mom loves it here. Her whole family were geologists—well, you know . . . you met them! She was working on a series of lectures for a class on the dating of the earth. She said it always struck her as remarkable how the Grand Canyon was used as evidence by both sides in the dating debate—as validating a four-billion-year-old earth, and a six-thousand-year-old earth. Everyone looks at the same evidence, she says, and interprets it differently."

"So what theory does she teach?" asked Todd.

"She tries to lay out the data as objectively as possible, then tells her students to write a paper in which they are required to formulate their own new theory to explain the evidence, without parroting back any of the existing theories. They can use elements of them, but they have to come up with new ideas of their own. She does that with everything she teaches—always forcing her students to think for themselves."

"Do any of them come up with genuinely new theories?"

"My mom is sometimes surprised. She doesn't expect revolutionary new geologic revelations. But the process of forcing them to think that way gives them an understanding of the science involved that they couldn't get any other way."

"That's exactly what she does with me," said Todd. "I've never been so stretched in my thinking as during my weekly visits with your folks. What an amazing man and woman! Between your dad's perspectives of history and your mom's of science, weaving their knowledge through the tapestry of God's outworking of his purposes for creation—it's a graduate-level learning experience. They never try to indoctrinate me. It's just as you say—forcing me to think for myself, weigh ideas and options, thinking of implications and logical consequences, always basing conclusions on the character of God and the Bible and common sense. It's such a novel method of approaching knowledge and truth."

Heather laughed. "That sounds exactly like my dad and mom . . . and my grandfather."

"And *you*!" rejoined Todd. "All you Marshalls speak with a consistent voice."

It fell silent. They continued to stare out over the vast open space of the canyon, its depths now crisscrossing ribbons of pitch black. Todd reached over and took Heather's hand.

"I have something I want to say," he began. The tone of his voice was different. Heather's heart began to beat more rapidly.

"I know we've talked about the future. I suppose some people would consider our relationship strange—we talk about *everything*. I want to share everything with you and I want to know everything about you and everything you're thinking. There's no one else I want to be with. You're my best friend. I love you, Heather. I want to spend the rest of my life with you. And I want to make it official."

By now Heather's heart was racing!

"I know this is not the way it's done, but here we are and I don't care. But I'm telling you now—Heather Marshall, I love you and I want to marry you. You are the one I've been waiting for all my life. So now I am asking you—*will* you marry me?"

Heather turned to face him. The light of the moon shone in her eyes, which were swimming in liquid.

"Oh, Todd . . ." she began, then started gently to weep.

Todd waited.

"I hardly know what to say," said Heather softly after a few seconds. "You know how much I love you. But all I can think . . . all I've been able to think since . . .well, you know, since we began growing close . . . is why me? You are famous and tall and handsome. Somebody told me you were voted one of Washington's most eligible bachelors. And look at me—I'm a nobody. I can't even walk straight. I'm not pretty. Of course, you know my heart but I just . . . it's still impossible for me to believe that you would want to be with me, seen with me . . . that you could love me. Little old me!" she added, laughing lightly. "Do you really love me, Todd?"

"Heather, Heather—how can you ask!" replied Todd. "You are the most integrated, wise and mature young woman I've ever known. All you say about me is superficial and external. It's who we are *inside* that matters. I'm not tall and you're not short. You are beautiful. You light up every room you are in with your quiet, contented spirit. You radiate. We're two souls whose hearts have met and become one. It's that inside *you* I love with all my heart, I cannot get enough of. I will spend the rest of my life trying to catch up to the inside true woman I love. That woman is *you*, Heather. I want to continue loving you and learning from you and growing with you and experiencing life with you. Yes, yes, how else can I say it—I love you!"

Todd exhaled a long breath from the outpouring that had been building inside him.

They sat for two or three minutes as their spirits calmed. A major turning point in their lives had come. Heather's eyes were full of tears. She had never heard, never even imagined hearing anything like what she just heard from Todd.

"I love my mom," Todd began again, his voice now calm. "I think you saw that. Yet I feel I am joining *your* family more than the other way around. I feel almost like I am becoming a Marshall, if you know what I mean—being drawn into an amazing legacy God is using to influence so many people. How privileged I feel to be with you. Yes, Heather, I really and truly love you. I want to call you my wife. You didn't answer me. So again, will you marry me?"

Heather smiled then drew in a deep breath. "You know I love you, Todd. There is nothing I want more. Of course I will marry you."

They sat for several minutes in the moonlight. Darkness came rapidly at this elevation at this time of the year.

"I'm afraid I don't have a ring," said Todd at length. "Somehow, it just didn't seem—"

"Don't even think about apologizing, Todd," interrupted Heather. "I do *not* want a diamond ring. Can you even see me wearing a diamond! I'm a horse gal, not a diamond ring gal. Buy me a new saddle, not a diamond!" she laughed. "Honestly, I never expected to be married. But whenever the thought flitted through my brain that *maybe* I would marry, all I could think was that I didn't want to wear a big diamond on my finger. I would be much happier with small simple matching bands."

"Sounds good to me. I suppose it will save me some money too! Though come to think of it, how much *do* saddles cost?"

Heather laughed. "A lot! But I was joking."

"Whatever you want. I want you to be happy."

"I am happy, Todd. I am happier than I have ever been. You have made me the happiest girl in the world. It's a fairy tale—me, Heather Marshall, engaged. Can you believe it! Or . . . *am* I engaged? *Are* we engaged, Todd?"

Todd laughed. "I don't know. This is new territory for me too. I guess we are if we agree we are."

"I agree!"

"Then by common consent—Todd Stewart and Heather Marshall are hereby engaged."

He leaned over and kissed her lightly.

"Sealed with a kiss," he said. "I am happy too."

"Do my parents know?" asked Heather.

Todd nodded. "I talked to them before we left."

"What did they say?"

"I asked them when they thought it would be acceptable to formalize my intentions, as it were—that I wanted to marry you. They were very gracious and basically said that anything was fine—I could talk to you, propose to you whenever I felt the time was right. They said they were delighted with how Christopher's Plan had worked and that I had their complete blessing. They did add that they felt it best we continue as we are and not be in a rush with our plans. I said that was fine. I know I still have a lot of growing to do as a Christian."

☆ ☆ ☆

They arrived back in Sacramento two days later. They drove straight to Timothy's and Jaylene's to share their news with Heather's parents and then to the Circle F to tell Mark, Grace, Ginger, and Craig. While there, Todd telephoned his mother and then Bradon to tell him, then handed his phone to Ginger. She disappeared with it into her bedroom for the next fifteen minutes.

When Todd finally reached home at the Bar JG about 9:00 that night and told David of his engagement to Heather, the old man simply smiled a peaceful smile as if he had known it all along.

As long as you remember that if you get involved in politics, you have to be very careful that your leader is for Allah. You don't get involved in politics because it's the American thing to do. You get involved in politics because politics are a weapon to use in the cause of Islam.

—New York Imam Siraj Wahhaj

☆ ☆ ☆

Muslims must understand that their work in America is a kind of grand jihad in eliminating and destroying the Western civilization from within and sabotaging its miserable house.

—Mohamed Akram

of the Muslim Brotherhood, in *An Explanatory Memorandum on the General Strategic Goal for the Group in North America*, 1991

PART 4

THE SHINING CITY ON A HILL . . . R.I.P.*

SPRING–FALL 2052

* A phrase often used by Ronald Reagan to describe the historic exceptionalism and uniqueness of the United States among all nations of the world. It echoes the words from a sermon by John Winthrop in 1630 onboard the ship *Arbella* en route to the new world where Christian pilgrims were just beginning to establish what would become the greatest light for freedom, democracy, and Christianity ever seen in the world.

62

Long-Awaited Alignment

THREE-TERM VICE president Elizabeth Wickes Hardy had enjoyed a singularly undistinguished career as the perennial second-fiddle of the executive branch in US affairs. Current president Jefferson Rhodes paid as little attention to her as had his predecessor Akilah Samara. Rhodes and Hardy were as much strangers as their reelection campaign neared as they had been, much to Hardy's chagrin, when Rhodes defeated her for the nomination in '48 and named her his running mate.

Now it appeared she was poised to run for an unprecedented fourth four-year stretch, unless he decided to dump her after one term. If not, after serving sixteen years, though she would only be sixty, it would be unlikely she would ever be viewed of presidential stature. Her "turn" would have come and gone. She wasn't sure she could endure the humiliation of losing again.

In the meantime, the most vital aspect of her position in the government, as was true of all vice presidents, was that she represented the readiest pathway to the Oval Office—a fact not lost on Hamad Bahram. It had taken a century for the stars to align such that Islam's lofty goal might at last be attainable. Now, thought the scion and fourth generation of US Bahrams, he himself stood on that historic threshold.

His grandfather being a first-generation voting member in Palladium and intimate of founder Slayton Bardolf ensured that the Bahram name was known and respected throughout Palladium. But it was his association with the future bearer of the illustrious Bardolf legacy that had thrust his name into the upper echelons of power as the new chairman of the Presidential Religion Commission.

He knew Mike Bardolf had spoken of him to the president. If circumstances could be engineered to necessitate President Jefferson Rhodes appointing a new vice president, one never knew. He had the feeling Bardolf coveted the office for himself. But the man was sometimes impossible to read.

As the year 2052 opened, the presidential campaign got underway, though without much drama. The Republicans still had no viable candidate. The chief name being floated was Texas Senator Dindinger, though he, like Reyburn insisted he was not a candidate and entered no primaries.

The biggest news of the new year concerned leaked portions of the president's Freedom Bill. The controversial legislation encountered stiffer headwinds winding its way through Congress than Rhodes had expected. As its provisions came to light, his ratings began to slip in the polls, though he continued to play the conspiracy card to bolster his insistence that the bill was imperative.

When he first read the draft of Mike Bardolf's Manifesto at Mira Monte a year before, Hamad Bahram realized that the time could well be approaching to bring his grandfather's daring strategy to fruition.

Fools like Domokos, Bardolf, and Rhodes with their utopian progressive dreams would never know any more than Obama and AOC that they had been mere pawns to bring Sharia law to the West. Their liberal agenda to replace white Christian America with feminist, black, homosexual America had achieved its purpose. Yet in eroding America's core idea, Clinton and Obama and Biden, AOC and Perez and Samara and Rhodes, and all their lackies in Congress and the media, had no idea that they were creating a moral vacuum that Islam stood poised to fill.

He smiled when he thought of Mike Bardolf, the little man with grandiose ambitions of power. He would join Obama and Domokos and the others on the scrap heap. As useful as it had been for its purposes, even Palladium would eventually be swept away by the Caliphate.

When Mike Bardolf asked for his suggestions in working the Manifesto into its final form as the foundation for the Freedom Bill, he cringed anew to read it. He knew, however, that he must continue the deception a little longer. Doing so enabled him to add Islam-tolerant provisions to the document. It was a case of keeping your friends close and your enemies closer.

Christianity, feminism, and homosexuality were Islam's mortal enemies. But Christianity was the *greatest* enemy. Islam would never dominate the West until Christianity was eradicated. As distasteful as it was to play along with progressivism's moral depravities, once the Caliphate was in place, they would be eliminated. Bardolf hardly batted an eye with his proposed changes to the bill. Nor had the president objected when the document was prepared for Congress.

When the time came and the nation trembled, it would turn to the highest placed Muslim in the administration to soothe world tensions and restore peace and stability.

Thanks to Jefferson Rhodes, everything was in place to ensure that Christians would be blamed. He could not have envisioned a more perfect scapegoat scenario than Rhodes's and Bardolf's obsession with a homegrown Christian conspiracy!

Once he was in control of the Oval Office, he would place minarets atop the Capitol dome and the King Monument and the Presidential Manor, and change the name of the Trump Ballroom. He would replace Lincoln's statue and change the monument to the Mohamed Shrine. Then he would call on Muslims throughout the country to come to Washington, whose name would also in time be changed, to march in celebration of the new era. The Islamic caucus in Congress was already stronger than that of the Republicans. With Congress behind him and the power of the executive order, the country would follow his lead and rejoice to leave the dark ages of Christianity's influence. In power for so long, the liberals would never know what hit them.

A trip to Tehran was in order. His position as chairman of the Religion Commission gave him all the cover he needed. He would meet with Islamic leaders to discuss innocuous matters about worldwide religious unity which wouldn't ultimately mean a thing, all out in the open, making himself a visible international figure in full view of the president.

Meeting with his cousin to finalize their secret plans would have to be kept from getting too much attention. But a visit could easily be explained on the basis of family ties.

Shepherding the Freedom Bill through Congress, Rhodes continued to pressure Speaker Black and Senate Majority Leader Aswad, using the Alinsky rule to exaggerate the threat of a Christian conspiracy and gain public acceptance of the bill's more radical provisions.

In May, after strenuous lobbying by the president, the Freedom Bill passed and was signed into law.

63

The Interview

May 2052

DURING THE weeks prior to Timothy's and Jaylene's flight to New York for the interview with Phil Simons, he and Charles Reyburn had several discussions about what Timothy should expect. They were not exactly coaching sessions. Timothy did not want his responses scripted or rehearsed. They made no attempt to anticipate the issues Simons would raise. He needed to be himself, spontaneous, relaxed, and confident, Charles told him. "If your spirit remains calm," he said, "God will give you the words he wants people to hear."

Nevertheless, being prepared for the experience was important—the lights, women fussing with makeup, being treated like a celebrity, walking out in front of a potentially hostile live audience, TV cameras zeroing in too close for comfort, and trying to ignore the monitor. The atmosphere was intimidating to one who had never faced it before.

"You appeared completely at ease during your interview," said Timothy. "You looked like a seasoned pro."

Charles laughed. "I'd never experienced anything like it in my life! All the while as I sat in the green room, I had to keep *centering down,* as Thomas Kelly says. When I walked onto that stage, I was terrified. I kept saying, *Lord, communicate through my words what you would say to these people here—and to your people everywhere.*"

"A simple but remarkable prayer," nodded Timothy.

The sessions with Charles helped put Timothy at ease, along with insights into Simons's mannerisms, body language, how he responded to certain things which he hoped would help him gauge his own responses.

"One thing I find almost peculiar about the man," said Charles, "is, liberal though he must be, he seems to respect straightforward, even blunt answers from conservatives like us. Don't be afraid of how he might respond. If you come across as sincere and honest, he will give you the benefit of the doubt. I said some challenging things. I think he appreciated I wasn't afraid to do so. If you don't have a good answer, he will respect an honest *I don't know* more than trying to fake it with stock responses like politicians do. He has those kinds of people on his program every night. My takeaway is that he respects straight-shooting sincerity. Speak calmly and graciously but with confidence that you are standing on truth."

"I will consider you my mentor," nodded Timothy. "You were amazing with Simons."

Charles laughed. "I don't know about that. I just tried to remember that my demeanor was more important than my words."

"Keep *centering down.* That is good counsel."

When Timothy and Jaylene walked into the studio two hours before air time, they were already more than overwhelmed by the Big Apple—a limo meeting them at JFK, a luxurious four-star hotel, a walk through Central Park on the morning of the interview, remembering *Sleepless in Seattle* at the top of the Empire State Building, an early dinner, before being taken from their hotel, again by limousine, to the network headquarters.

Simons came from somewhere in the building to welcome them personally. They chatted about logistics. He was personable and expressed genuine appreciation that Timothy agreed to the interview. He quickly put Timothy and Jaylene at ease about how the evening would go. Timothy was then prepped by staff, endured the process of being made up while Jaylene watched from the wings. Then both were taken to the green room to await the countdown.

Twenty minutes before zero hour, Jaylene was escorted to her seat in the front row of the sound stage. The seconds ticked by.

Simons came onstage to rousing applause and music from his live band, cracked a few jokes, gave his opening monologue, bantered with the audience, until finally the moment of truth was at hand.

"Ladies and gentlemen," said the king of late-night television from his familiar host-chair, "we have with us this evening a man whose name will be familiar to most of you—Dr. Timothy Marshall from California."

Sporadic applause trickled almost reluctantly through the studio audience, obviously not with the customary enthusiasm shown to Simons's guests. Mingled with it were a few *boos*. Jaylene cringed where she sat, afraid for what it portended.

Simons waited for it to die down, then sat a few seconds in the ensuing silence.

"I am not surprised by your response," he said at length. "Though I must say I am disappointed. Dr. Marshall and his wife, Jaylene, also *Dr. Marshall* and who is with us this evening, are professors of history and anthropology. Their careers are distinguished. Between them they have authored a dozen books. They are highly respected educators in their respective fields. Dr. Timothy Marshall is altogether undeserving of the negative reports and accusations swirling through the press in recent months. Your tepid response shows clearly that you have been influenced by that negative press. I will say categorically here and now that most of what you have heard is absolutely false.

"I say that knowledgeably," Simons went on. "One of the conditions of his agreeing to this interview was for me to read his series of lectures that has been in the news in recent months. Probably like many of you, I was guilty of misjudging Dr. Marshall after the incident at Jessup University last October. Once I read the transcripts of his lectures in their entirety, I was stunned at the immaturity of my preconceptions. I found Dr. Marshall's research, observations, and conclusions to represent the most balanced and insightful comparison of Islam and Christianity I have ever encountered. I was embarrassed for how shallow and unthinking had been my impression of one I now consider a man of stature and integrity. I immediately began reading for a second time.

"I have never made a secret of the fact that I am not a religious man. But Dr. Marshall's lectures have forced me to think about many things in a new light. He is a man of honesty, open-mindedness, intellectual integrity, and kindness—a man whose life quest is to find and know truth. How many of us would say that of ourselves? As a result of knowing this man, I am now asking some of life's most fundamental questions for the first time. I realize I have been floating through life without stopping to ask what life means. I am embarrassed that it has taken me so long to face that fundamental question. Dr. Marshall is a man I have come to respect, admire, and honor for his life's quest.

"Please, then, I ask you to give the welcome he deserves to Dr. Timothy Marshall!"

The applause this time, though not ear-splitting, was suitably enthusiastic as Timothy walked into the lights, crossed the stage, shook hands with Simons, and sat down.

"Welcome, Dr. Marshall," said Simons. "I must say, it feels odd to address you so formally. After our few conversations, and after reading your lectures twice and another of your books, as well as your wife's fascinating book on Einstein and Genesis, I feel I know you both quite well."

"By all means then, I would be honored for you simply to call me Timothy if you are comfortable with that," replied Timothy with a smile. "And I appreciate your taking the time and effort to read the lectures."

"I had to," laughed Simons. "You made it a condition of your coming on."

"True. But you did so thoughtfully and sincerely. And reading it twice! That is more than I expected. That is going the extra mile!"

"An allusion from the Sermon on the Mount, as you reference in your second lecture on the texts of Christianity."

"You *did* read carefully!"

"I tried to. But as I read through the second time, I found myself reading not simply to prepare for this interview, I found myself confronting many wrong preconceptions I had harbored about Islam and Christianity. Your lectures *changed* me. It is not that I am planning to become a Christian or a Muslim—though I suppose," he added laughing, "this is how such things begin."

"Everything begins with how we think," nodded Timothy, "*if* we have the courage to do so. It is one of the hardest things in life to do with honesty. Many people never learn to truly *think*. But that's where the quest for truth begins."

"Well I *am* thinking in new ways about both religions. Who can tell where it will lead! And thanks to you, I am confident that I am thinking more accurately about both. As familiar as we think we are with Christianity and Islam, many of the impressions those of us who espouse belief in neither are pretty much dead wrong. At least that was true in my case. I am at last in the process of rectifying that."

"Then I am delighted," said Timothy. "The purpose for which I gave the lectures in the first place has been achieved. I would not, however, have us lose sight of the terrible tragedy of that day. I cannot talk about it in anything but a sober tone of heavy sadness and heartache. Obviously, it is a grievous stain upon the lecture series that they ended in such senseless killing. Not a day goes by that I do not pray for the families and friends of the victims. I will live with that sense of responsibility for what happened for the rest of my life."

"Do you blame yourself, Timothy?" asked Simons. His voice carried not a hint of accusation. From his tone, it was clear Simons shared Timothy's pain. It was not an interviewer's question; it was a heartfelt and deeply personal question.

64

The Ultimate Effect of Eternal Goodness

THE STUDIO was deathly silent, awaiting an answer to the question that, in one form or another, had been on the minds of everyone in the country for six months.

As much as they had prepared for this moment, knowing the question had to come, that it came so suddenly at the beginning of the interview jolted Timothy on stage and Jaylene where she sat.

Give him your heart and mind at this moment, Lord Jesus, Jaylene prayed. *Give him the words you would have him say in response.*

Timothy smiled sadly and thought for several long seconds.

"*Blame* is a hard word," he finally replied. "Yet in a way, it is the only word that will do under the circumstances. I ask myself that question every day. Am I to *blame* for what happened?"

He paused briefly.

"There is a burden of responsibility I will always carry for that day," Timothy went on, his voice soft and with the hint of a quiver. "But it is a pain that quails alongside that of many others, and I would not ask to have it removed. My own pain reminds me to lift into God's heart those who have suffered so much more."

He paused again and drew in a deep breath. His emotion was palpable. Everyone throughout the sound stage could not help being drawn into it. There had never been a Phil Simons interview like this.

"If you don't mind my asking," said Simons, "what does that mean . . . lifting them into God's heart?"

Timothy smiled. Every camera zoomed up close. Around the country, millions of mesmerized viewers were watching the face of this quiet man, waiting for him to explain the eternal mystery of prayer to a nation that had forgotten how to pray.

"In short, Phil," replied Timothy slowly, "it simply means to *pray*. Yet so often when we pray, we don't know what to pray. Can you fathom the grief I feel even trying to pray for those dear people who lost loved ones that day? I can never know their anguish and grief. I do not know all the circumstances of their lives that have been forever changed. How can I possibly pray?

"But *God* knows them, knows me, knows us all. He holds all of us in the loving heart of his eternal Fatherhood. He holds our pasts, our futures, in his heart as an ongoing present, an eternal *Now* in which his infinite love is alive. I cannot explain how that can be or how it works. But God is our good and loving Father. His heart is infinite to hold not only the past and the present, but also the pain and grief and heartache of the past and present in that eternal Now."

He paused again.

"So when I don't know what to pray, I lift the person or situation in my thoughts into the realm of that eternal heart of the Father's love, knowing that he knows the need, feels the pain, knowing that all pasts, presents, and futures are equally alive to him in that Now where he dwells. *God, hold your dear one close to you in your heart*, is sometimes all I can pray. *Wrap your arms of love around them and be a Father to them.*

"That day of tragedy is alive with God too. The loved ones who fell are alive in his heart because all pasts and all presents are alive in his heart. When I lift another, in prayer, into the heart of God, I believe that something holy and eternal is at work to further God's purpose to reconcile, heal, and bring together all loves in eternity.

"He is a Father whose purpose is to reconcile and unify *all* loves—incomplete loves, lost loves, fragmented loves, painful loves, loves cut short by death. They will all be brought into oneness and be made whole and complete, transformed into *fulfilled* loves in eternity. This is what

I pray when I lift the victims and their families up into the heart of God, asking him to accomplish his purposes in every life touched by that tragedy."

Simons had no immediate reply.

"I hope you do not misunderstand, Phil," Timothy went on. "I do not say that as a trite panacea. These are hard things. Pain is hard, the world's suffering is hard to understand, death is hard, life is hard. We are weak human beings. There are no panaceas for suffering. The world's suffering, for many, is reason not to believe in God. For me suffering is one of the reasons I *do* believe in God, because I believe strongly that all things will come right in the end.

"Only an infinite Father-Creator can bring them right. As I say, for me suffering and grief and pain and heartache prove the existence of an eternal heart of Love at the pulsating center of the universe, not disprove it. I realize many of your viewers will call such a statement ridiculous and brand me a religious fanatic. I cannot help that. I can only paraphrase Martin Luther and say, In faith I believe it, I stake my life upon it . . . and here I stand."

"Know, Timothy, that I would never call what you have said ridiculous."

"I do know that, Phil. And having said it, I remain a mortal man struggling like all mortals to make sense of the mysteries of life. Of course, bitter tears often return with the stark reminder that had I not scheduled my lectures, those people would be alive today. I cry out to God as many do—*Why, God . . . why!* But the playing out of events is not one-dimensionally cause and effect. I am but one piece in a complex interweaving of circumstances that on that day resulted in a great tragedy. I bear my part in it, yes. I will not shy away from the word *blame* if others want to use it. But as a Christian I also believe that God's sovereignty exists on a higher plane than we can perceive and that he is at work in human lives in ways we have no comprehension of."

"Surely you are not saying that what happened was God's will."

"Of course not. I do not believe that for an instant. But when bad things happen outside his will—the *causes*, so to speak—God is yet able to raise the *effects* of those bad things into the higher plane of his purposes and bring about good through them. In the complex interplay between cause and effect, God's most significant activity is in the world of *effects*. He does not cause bad things, nor is it his will such things happen. Yet he brings good to grow out of them.

"Goodness is the fruit of the rootstalk of God's essential being. God desires to grow the fruit of goodness throughout his universe. But it is an eternal objective not a short term one. Goodness requires eons to be perfected. It is that I was speaking of before. In the *Eternal Now* of God's heart, he is tirelessly and energetically working toward his ultimate purpose to reconcile, heal, and bring together all things in eternity, to transform all incomplete loves into fulfilled love. That is the ultimate good, which, as I said, I believe God will bring right in the end."

"Let me be sure I understand you correctly—you are saying that good can come of what happened at Jessup last October?"

"I believe so, yes. God can bring about good in lives even through tragedy. That does not make the tragedy his will, it only confirms that God is always at work to grow good *effects* out of *causes* we may never understand. He grows the fruit of good in the lives of those who allow him to do so and who look for the good as he grows it."

65

The Deep Waters of Suffering

"COULD GOD have prevented the shooting?" asked Simons.

"You ask really good questions, Phil," answered Timothy. "No wonder your show is rated number one."

Simons nodded in acknowledgment but did not reply.

"What you ask plunges deep into theological waters that have plagued mankind for millennia," replied Timothy. "Why doesn't God do this—or that? Why is there suffering? Why does my wife or husband have cancer? Why didn't God stop Hitler? Everyone asks those questions. We ask them every day.

"There are two overriding reasons, in my opinion, why people reject Christianity—*hell* and *suffering*. They cannot accept the idea of hell and they do not understand, if God is loving and all-powerful, why so much suffering exists in the world."

"What would you say to them?"

"About hell, I decline to comment. It is a complex theological question. About suffering I do have an answer. It is a simple one: I don't know."

"An interesting answer—a non-answer," smiled Simons.

"But an honest one," rejoined Timothy. "*Could* God have prevented the shooting? I don't know. What we do know is that God *doesn't* prevent suffering. I don't know why. He placed free will into the heart, brain, soul, mind—however you want to describe it—of humanity. From all we can tell, it seems to be a hands-off free will. Many Christians disagree with me on that. But the evidence suggests to me that God *doesn't* generally step in to manipulate events. Therefore, bad things happen.

"His most important ongoing work exists in human hearts. That's where he is growing the fruit of goodness—in hearts. He doesn't grow that fruit by making events turn out to our liking—always pleasant and happy.

"Events are not God's primary concern. Hearts are. In that unseen arena, I believe he is continually active and energetically attempting to grow the fruit of goodness in the hearts of those who allow him to do so."

"You said earlier that God raises up the effect of bad things to bring about good, if I am representing you accurately," said Simons. "This is a mystery to me. You say he *doesn't* prevent bad and suffering, but he *does* bring about good."

"Again, an astute question, Phil. You've put your finger precisely on the answer—it is a *mystery*. I don't know *how* it works. I don't know why God does the one and not the other, why he concerns himself primarily with *effects* rather than *causes*. But somehow, in the midst of its mystery, that is the equation told by the New Testament account."

"In other words, God allows pain and suffering?"

"I suppose in a way. I do not prefer the word *allow*. It carries the implication of purposefulness, as if God chooses it. That would be a misrepresentation. God doesn't *decide* to inflict pain and suffering. If he does not *prevent* it, neither does he *choose* it. If setting the history of humanity in motion by investing it with free will means that God has *allowed* suffering to infect his creation without preventing it, then I suppose that is an accurate word. But he still doesn't choose it. God hates what Hitler did and hates what terrorists do and hates what happened on the Jessup campus six months ago far more than we hate it. But free will has consequences that, in a manner of speaking, even determine what God can and cannot do.

"We call God all-powerful, omnipotent. Yet there are some things God chooses *not* to do, some areas of life in which he chooses *not* to exercise his omnipotence. One of those is preventing bad things happening. This is the great human mystery—why an omnipotent God chooses *not* to exercise his omnipotence to prevent bad and suffering."

"Do you have an answer?" asked Simons.

"No. That mystery baffles me no less than it baffles every atheist who uses it to deny there is such a being as God at all."

"Do you have an opinion?"

Timothy smiled.

"You are probing the depths, Phil," Timothy nodded, still smiling thoughtfully. "Your questions are forcing me to think on my feet about deep and eternal mysteries."

He paused. Simons waited.

"Yes . . . I do have an opinion," said Timothy at length. "I believe it is a sound, deeply researched, and prayed opinion forged over more than forty years of walking with God and trying to understand his character and his ultimate purposes. But I cannot prove its veracity other than to say, I believe it. It remains my opinion, my *interpretation* of the mystery of bad and suffering in the world and why God, as it were, allows it and does not prevent it."

He paused again and drew in a deep breath.

"For reasons and in ways that will remain a mystery as long as we are in this life," Timothy went on, "I believe that such things are intrinsic, perhaps even *necessary* for the growth and development and triumph of the ultimate goodness God is slowly bringing to fruition in his universe. In short, they are for our best. We cannot see that but God does. The bad and suffering we cannot understand are being drawn up into God's heart too, to be used—possibly as nothing else *could* have been used to the same effect—in the final making right of all things. They are intrinsic to the reconciliation, unifying, and transformation of all heartaches into the fulfilled loves of eternity. How . . . I don't know. We would have God prevent them. One day he will tell us, 'I could not grow you into the fullness of your personhood as my son or daughter in any other way.'"

Simons sat a moment staring down and slowly shaking his head.

"I've never heard anything like that," he said softly. "It will take time to process."

"I may have been speaking in circles," rejoined Timothy, "and I apologize for that. These are deep waters, Phil. All I can say, in summing up, is that God doesn't prevent suffering, but he will bring good from it in the lives of those who allow him to."

"Well—thank you for attempting at least to explain it, though it remains a mystery. I almost hesitate to ask, but I know there will be viewers who want to know *how* good can come to the families of last October's victims when their loved ones are dead?"

"That is a deeply personal question. You would have to ask them. But of the families I have met and spoken with—"

"You've met the families?" asked Simons in surprise.

"I made a commitment to myself that I would contact all the families of the dead and wounded and ask if they would meet with me. I felt it important that I personally express my grief and sorrow."

"What has been the response?"

"As you would expect. Some were angry and asked me to leave. Some were cool, listened to what I had to say, but it went no further than a brief, strained conversation. But most have been courteous and respectful. As Jaylene and I have visited the families, we have had some rich times of tears and prayer and healing. Several of the families have even become part of our fellowship. Obviously there remains great pain but slowly most of the families are trying to find good where they can—God's fruit of goodness, eternal good transcending the pain of the here and now, the good of knowing their loved ones are alive with a Father who loves them and is holding them close. That process is a deeply spiritual and highly individual process."

"What did you say to them?"

"Nothing more than to share my own grief, to convey my deep sorrow and my sense of responsibility for what happened, and to tell them they and their loved ones are in our prayers. They are not forgotten. We speak their names and talk of memories. Certainly, it is no time for trite platitudes."

Nothing was said for several long seconds.

"Well," said Simons, "I must say this has been most unexpected and thought-provoking. I think this would be a good time for a break. Timothy, stretch your legs a minute or two while the network gets in its all-important commercials. For those of you watching at home, we will return shortly."

66

TRUTHOPHOBIA

AFTER A brief interlude with Jaylene at the edge of the stage, Timothy returned to his place beside the host as the band transitioned back to the interview.

"I thoroughly enjoyed our first segment together," Phil Simons began. "I admit that most of what you said was beyond me. I can see that I will be reading more of your books in the future. If you don't mind, however, I would like us to shift gears somewhat and talk about your lectures, and where our country is headed."

"Of course," replied Timothy. "And I apologize if I went too deep into the theological weeds before."

"Not at all. It was fascinating. I opened those doors with my questions. I'm glad you felt the freedom to respond in such depth. Those are not perspectives I've heard Christians articulate before. But shifting abruptly—do you mind if I ask you a political question?"

"I don't mind if you ask, though I may choose not to answer."

"You sound like a politician!" laughed Simons.

"Heaven forbid!"

"So what do you think of the new Freedom Bill?"

"Have you read it, Phil?"

"Actually, no."

"I have. It's classic liberal sleight of hand. It takes *away* freedom. It is the *opposite* of a freedom bill."

"Plain spoken."

"That has been the liberal M.O. since Saul Alinsky's *Rules for Radicals.* Mask the true agenda by pretending things are not what they are. For fifty years progressives have been touting freedom, tolerance, equity, and justice, while systematically targeting certain groups with their intolerance, injustice, racism, and bigotry."

"You're charging progressives with racism, intolerance, and bigotry?"

"Of course. It's hardly a secret."

"You say they target certain groups—what groups?"

"Phil, you're an intelligent man—you can't be oblivious to what's been going on for years against whites, Christians, men, nuclear families, and those who believe in biological gender, not chosen gender. All these groups have been subject to ruthless persecution and have had their freedoms taken away. What have progressives been saying about me for the last six months? How tolerant have they been of *my* views, *my* Christianity, *my* ethnicity, and gender?

"Hilary Clinton's infamous statement of 2025 about the damage being done to our country by white men of a certain religion rings with racism, bigotry, intolerance, and anti-Christianity. Yet she was held up as a paragon of virtue by the Left. But I don't want to get into all that. Charles's book said everything that needed be said. To return to your question, the so-called Freedom Bill is a hoax. Yet so thoroughly does the progressivist agenda have an unassailable stranglehold on the country that it is now the law of the land. It's become much worse since Mrs. Clinton's assessment. As much damage as her intolerance, hypocrisy, and self-righteousness did, they were nothing alongside the outright *hatred* toward Christianity so widespread today. Charlie Kirk's assassination was but the beginning of violence against Christians and churches, as events of the last twenty-five years have shown. The intolerance and bigotry of progressivism has morphed into a level of malice that is truly dangerous."

"A blunt assessment."

"Do you think I overstate it? Did you happen to watch the roundtable discussion on your own network last month on the future of religion in America?"

"I did."

"Were you not disturbed by the tone of the guests and your colleague who was moderating it? The Muslim cleric, the self-described druidic priest of the Church of Satan, the three atheists, and the head of the president's Religion Commission, Dr. Bahram, were all afforded complete courtesy and respect, while the Catholic priest and evangelical pastor were excoriated mercilessly. The lies about Christianity that have been endemic in the cultural discourse for fifty years, calling Christians bigoted, backward, racist, exclusivist, and patriarchal are easily seen as unfounded and absurd. Any objective, rational, individual who loves truth can see through them.

"What has changed, however, is the narrative attributing violence, cultism, treason, armed resistance, brainwashing, child abuse, pedophilia, female subjugation, misogyny, systemic oppression, and so many other true *evils* to Christianity. These unbelievable accusations have been such a persistent part of the progressive narrative that they have filtered down into the general public mind. All this was on display in the round table last month—complete with film clips and interviews with abused women and children rescued from their cultish churches, blacks denouncing the Christian church as the most segregated institution in America. It was a terribly biased and untrue presentation.

"Every belief system and institution has outliers. Everyone understands that. But to paint all of Christianity with that brush is unconscionably false, especially the charge of segregation. Yet the average man and woman on the street, getting their so-called news from such biased sources, comes to view Christianity as a truly dangerous influence in society that ought to be outlawed.

"A massive ground-shift in morality, redefining terms like 'racism' and 'acceptance' along with gender and even right-and-wrong, has created a chasm between those who have gone along with progressivist thinking and those who have not. Once the generation that remembered the unifying values of pre-1960s America died off, those holding to traditional morality are as strange to today's audience as an Amish farmer would have been to their parents.

"How else can you explain rational thinking people actually thinking it a *good* thing for Christian parents not to have the freedom to teach their own children as they want to? A *freedom* bill? What freedom do

Christian parents have in the way they raise their children? But people now accept the progressive narrative that Christianity is a malevolent force. Children need to be protected from it. From there to the idea that Christianity ought to be outlawed is an easy transition. Based on this progression of falsehoods begun in the last century and now culminating before our very eyes—it may not be long before Christianity is declared a terrorist movement."

"But *why*, Timothy? How can it have come to this given the Christian roots of the nation?"

"That is the great mystery, Phil. It is incredible how people could believe a religion preaching goodness, virtue, kindness, and love could be so hated. It's irrational. There is no explaining it other than what Paul wrote in the first chapter of the book of Romans in the New Testament."

"I'm sorry, I'm not as up on my Bible as perhaps I should be—what did he say?"

"He said because they did not honor God, their thinking was futile and their foolish minds became darkened."

"Paul is even more blunt than you!"

"He says it like it is. I couldn't agree more. Progressivism has darkened the minds of three generations. How else can you explain the antipathy toward millions of Christ-followers who are trying to bring light and truth and goodness to the world, who are trying to live good and Christlike lives, and the parents among them who are trying to raise and teach their children to live good and Christlike lives?

"I have no answer, Phil. Christianity is the one goodness, the one source of light and truth in the world, and the world hates it. Maybe that's the answer. The world hates anyone who claims to be trying to live by a higher standard of righteousness. The world hates the idea of *righteousness* itself. It assumes that anyone who claims to be trying to live a righteous life must, by definition, be a hypocrite. By extension, all of Christianity must be a sham and therefore evil. Meanwhile, Islam—whose founder was a murderer, misogynist, and man of war is hailed as a religion of peace. If you can make sense of that, Phil, you are a more perceptive man than me."

Simons shook his head and exhaled slowly.

"You speak bluntly, as always. And you feel this misperception of Christianity is at root in the current political discourse."

"I'm sorry if I was too blunt," replied Timothy. "But yes, I would agree that the misperception of Christianity is a significant factor in the political divide that has consumed our nation for most of this century. However, I'm not really as politically minded as you might think. In our fellowship we are keenly aware of what is going on in the world around us. But politics does not represent the true focus of our deepest interest."

"Your *fellowship*—what is that exactly?"

"Simply a loosely affiliated group of Christians joined together attempting to live by the principles taught by Jesus. Even to call it a *group* is somewhat misleading. That's why I used the word fellowship."

"Is it a church?"

"Not as commonly defined. We are part of the Church, yes, but we are not a church per se. We do not meet on Sundays. There are no regularly scheduled meetings at all."

"Interesting. What has been the continuing impact of your lectures?"

"Predictably I continue to be lambasted. But a surprising number of requests have come for copies of the lectures and requests for permission to use them in high school and college courses. We are in the process, through Jessup, of printing the lectures in a small pamphlet to be used for that purpose, which will include discussion questions and documentation of all the points I made, with detailed quotes from the Bible, the Koran, and the Hadith."

"Will you teach another course based your lectures?"

"I don't plan to. My presence would only stir up controversy."

"Do you mind if I wade into some controversial waters?" asked Simons. "Feel free not to answer if you are uncomfortable. But millions around the country are interested in what you said that may have led to the shootings. I realize that most of the press about you has been critical. I would like to give you a chance to respond to your critics. Let me phrase it like this. Could you give the country tonight a two- or three-hundred-word summary or encapsulated version of your lectures? An elevator speech, as it were. You've got the audience in an elevator. You have until it reaches the top floor to recap the primary points of your lectures for those listeners."

"That is a tall order, Phil. How many floors does the building have?"

The studio audience broke into unexpected laughter.

"How many would you like?"

"Could it be the Empire State Building, which Jaylene and I visited yesterday?"

"Granted!" laughed Simons.

The sound stage grew silent as everyone waited. Again, the cameras zoomed in on Timothy's face as he thought quietly for ten or twenty seconds.

"All right," Timothy began, "while standing waiting for the elevator doors to open, let me say I realize that what I say may not be acceptable to a majority of Christians *or* Muslims. I may not even be able to please a few of the people *some* of the time. However, I believe that anyone who is prepared to be intellectually honest and open-minded and who is willing to put aside their biases, preconceptions, and learned religious doctrines for the time it takes us to ride up to the observation deck—they will see the logic and common sense in what I say."

A long pause followed.

"Islam and Christianity are worldwide religions with millions of followers," Timothy resumed. "Most of these, in my opinion, have adopted the perspectives they hold on the basis of teachings they have received—in many cases which is little more than indoctrination, in extreme cases, brainwashing. They are taught about their religion by opinionated, subjective, and illogical mentors and instructors, and given teachings that are often not representative of true Islam or true Christianity. Most Christians and Muslims have not personally thought through the tenets of what they believe for themselves. They take what they are taught without questioning it.

"In my lectures I attempted to address this problem by challenging those present to examine the lives and teachings of Jesus and Mohammed. I challenged them to examine the texts of the Koran and the New Testament Gospels. I challenged them to examine the purposes and objectives of both religions.

"Inevitably the controversial histories of both religions came into the discussion. I emphasized that atrocities committed in the *name* of Islam or Christianity may not be true representations of those religions.

I stressed over and over we must base our findings on the teachings of their founders and texts, not on false representations of their followers.

"In spite of many overlapping priorities and objectives, when we dive deeply into the texts, purposes, and histories of Islam and Christianity, we discover major differences. In Christianity we find an overriding mission to improve and bring fulfillment to the lives of *individuals*. In Islam we find an overriding imperative to take over *nations and cultures* with the values and ultimately the law of Islam. Those distinctions are factually verifiable by the teachings and texts themselves. I am a historian. I would ask those who are listening not to condemn the messenger but to look at the facts objectively.

"These two distinct objectives we find furthered by Christianity's historic missionary endeavors to bring goodness into the lives of *individuals* and by Islam's historic three-phase jihadist objective of *worldwide conquest*.

"The rancor directed at me for laying out these distinctions is perhaps understandable. I would only ask, 'Where am I wrong? Where have I misrepresented either Christianity or Islam?'

"I have been branded an Islamophobe—a man fearful of Islam. I would rather say that I am a man in search of truth wherever it leads me.

"I challenge all who are listening not to be afraid of truth. *Truthophobia* is our great enemy. Truthophobia is rampant in our world. It is rampant in religion, it is rampant in politics. Where I have erred in my perspectives about either Islam or Christianity, I apologize and invite anyone listening to point out my error and help me progress further toward the truth.

"I hunger for truth. I hope you listening will say the same. I hope you will escape the subjective, illogical, and often false influences of the truthophobes clustering about you with their political and religious opinions. I challenge you to leave truthophobia and press toward real truth, *true* Truth."

Phil Simons sat unmoving and silent, as did everyone in the live audience.

At last Simons drew in a breath and exhaled slowly. "Having read your series of lectures twice, I can attest to that being an accurate and thought-provoking summary. I encourage all who are listening to me to read Dr. Marshall's lectures."

He paused and glanced toward Timothy.

"I cannot thank you enough for being with me tonight, Timothy. You are a straight-shooter, a deep thinker, and an honorable man. I'm not sure if this is appropriate," he added, "but a final question occurs to me, if you don't mind."

Timothy merely nodded.

"Islam considers Christians and Jews infidels, and thus enemies of Islam," said Simons. "Do *you* consider anyone an enemy of Christianity?"

"Any individual—no. Christianity's only enemy is hatred of truth and refusal to live by truth."

67

Persecutions Grow

June 2052

TODD ARRIVED at the home of Timothy and Jaylene one Saturday in early June for a midday meal. Heather joined him on this day. Her parents wanted to talk to them about their upcoming marriage later in the year. It was time to begin making definite plans.

They immediately saw more serious matters than the wedding on the minds of Heather's mother and father.

"Mom . . . Dad, what is it?" said Heather as she and Todd walked into the house where she had grown up.

"We've just received the *Christian Free Press Newsletter* in the mail," replied her father. "Our phones have been going off all morning. People are calling from all over the country. We've also been on the phone in a conference call with Mark, Court, Charles, and Harvey."

"What's it about?" asked Todd as they sat on the couch.

"The provisions of the so-called Freedom Bill passed by Congress two weeks ago are coming to light," replied Timothy. "Court and Stella are preparing their next newsletter, and wondering how they should address it."

"Is it bad?"

"Worse than bad," replied Jaylene. "It's obvious why they kept it a secret."

Timothy handed the newsletter to Todd. He and Heather read through it together.

Shaking heads and a few exclamations of outrage proceeded as they read.

"I can't believe any of this," said Heather. "It's too shocking to imagine . . . the Koran included in new Bibles . . . gay and Muslim tolerance standards for churches . . . are they kidding—attendance by government officials required for all church services to monitor sermon content . . . Christian groups required to register with a Religion Compliance Committee! How can they get away with this? Are they actually going to monitor what can be talked about in Bible studies! What about freedom of religion?"

"The Bill of Rights is gone, remember," said Todd. "I reported on it myself six years ago."

"But they could never enforce all this!"

"If they actually go through with it," said Timothy, "and use the National Guard to close churches, they *will* be able to enforce it."

"That so-called Church Compliance Agency might as well be called the Gestapo," said Jaylene heatedly. "How are they going to choose the compliance officers—the Koran quoted in churches equally with the Bible—how could they monitor that?"

"Easily enough if there's a compliance officer sitting there taking notes or recording the service. They will probably also use AI video surveillance."

"Isn't that an invasion of privacy?" said Heather. "And church taxes raised to 50 percent on all income! What will they do next, require every church to hire gays and lesbians on their staff?"

"It may come to that," sighed Timothy. "This bill may be just a beginning. On the phone Charles said he heard that applications by the tens of thousands are already pouring in for the compliance officer positions. Preference will apparently be given to minorities, gays, avowed non-Christians, and Muslims to monitor Christian churches to ensure they do not try to cheat the new regulations."

"It is unimaginable," said Todd, shaking his head, "—strict regulations on Christian publishing . . . newsletters, blogs, books all subject to review by the Compliance Agency . . . books with Christian content banned from public and school libraries. I don't even know what to think. And of course, no parallel restrictions on Muslim mosques that can continue to teach jihad and as much anti-Christian and anti-American venom as they like."

"So much for the pamphlet of my lectures," said Timothy.

"How did this possibly pass?" said Heather in frustration. "Are there no Christians in Congress."

"Not many," replied Todd. "At least not serious ones."

"Mark said he was going to call Justice Trent this evening to get her read on the constitutionality of the bill," said Timothy. "But with the Court so stacked in favor of the progressive agenda, the justices won't block it."

"We've got to resist the darkness with heightened awareness," said Timothy. "The darkness doesn't look like darkness anymore. The masses have been adjusting to it for decades. My father's Brief warned exactly of this. I often heard him say, *Don't let your eyes adjust to the darkness.*"

"It is all so shocking," said Jaylene to Heather and Todd, "Charles and Harvey plan to meet with Senator Dindinger to discuss whether they should reverse themselves and mount a campaign after all. They are flying to Texas as soon as they can arrange it."

"Now *that* is big news!" exclaimed Todd. "But isn't Senator Dindinger on record saying the same thing as Charles, that he won't run under any circumstances?"

Timothy nodded. "The difference is that he is a politician. He will be at the convention in August. He's a senator. The convention will nominate *someone*. It will be an interesting discussion between the three men!"

"If anything could change any of their minds," said Heather, "it seems this bill would. What do you think they'll do, Dad?"

"I don't know. These provisions change the entire landscape for Christians. It would appear that the homeschooling mandates last year were only the beginning."

"Will the church go underground, like it was under Communism in the last century?"

"Probably many will. But the government seems to anticipate that. Many Christians won't be willing to risk imprisonment. I've never heard the tone in Charles's voice I heard today. It was righteous indignation."

"This reminds me of *1984*," said Todd. "It makes me wish I was back in the media. *Somebody* definitely ought to mount a campaign."

"Why don't you run, Todd?" said Jaylene.

Todd broke out laughing. The expression on his future mother-in-law's face, however, was deadly serious. The room quieted.

It was Heather who spoke next. "I said the same thing to him, Mom. But though Todd would never say it, let's face it—the country would never elect a man with a crippled wife. And we're not even married yet. People would want him to change his mind and marry a trophy wife."

"Don't even think it, Heather," said Todd, reaching over and taking her hand. "Not even as a joke."

"It wasn't *entirely* a joke. I know *you* wouldn't do that. But if you were in the public eye again, people would think it. You know how they are."

"Once people know you, they love you. And all that's beside the point," said Todd. "The idea of me running for office is the craziest thing I've ever heard!"

He started laughing again. None of the others joined him. Their faces were serious.

"Times change, my boy," said Timothy. "It may be that this Freedom Bill will alter how we view our role in the affairs of the world. The future of the church, and perhaps the Church as well, is at stake. It's times like this when I wish my father was here," he said. "His Brief disavowed politics as the arena for Christians to spread his kingdom in the world. In light of this threat, what would he say? I honestly don't know."

68

The Ally Responds

WHATEVER DIRECTION the conversation might have taken was interrupted by the sound of the doorbell.

Jaylene rose and went to the door.

She opened it and saw the young minister of Foothills Gospel Ministries. "Rev. Carmichael!" she said in surprise. "Hello—won't you come in?"

"I, uh . . . hoped I might have a word with you and your husband," said Carmichael, obviously nervous.

He tentatively followed Jaylene into the house. He was twenty-eight and Foothills was his first pastorate. His selection as head pastor was a mystery at first, though when it was learned that he was Stoddard Holt's nephew, the choice made sense. After assuming the pulpit, he had been well briefed on the Marshall, Forster, and Gordon family histories in the church, and had met Timothy and Jaylene who occasionally attended. Prior to today he had never called on them personally.

Timothy rose as they entered the room.

"Anthony!" he said offering his hand, "how nice to see you. I don't think you know our daughter Heather and her fiancé Todd Stewart. Heather, Todd, meet Rev. Anthony Carmichael."

Handshakes went around among them.

"I, uh . . . don't mean to intrude," began Carmichael when they were seated. "I didn't realize you had company. But in all honesty, I have heard of you, Mr. Stewart, and I know of you too, Miss Marshall. So I suppose what I have to say pertains to all of you."

He hesitated somewhat awkwardly. The others waited.

"It's just that there is talk in the church about the group you started, several years ago as I understand it. Many consider it a cult. There is concern in the congregation, and it is proving a disruptive influence."

"What kind of concern?" asked Timothy.

"That false teachings are infiltrating the church body. Given your history at Foothills, naturally the congregation is divided in the matter."

"Do you know what we do when we meet?"

"Not specifically. Only what I've heard from . . . what I've heard."

"Mostly we discuss the ideas in some of my father's books on scriptural topics. The commands of the New Testament, as one example. I'd like to give you one so you can determine for yourself if they contain dangerous ideas."

"I would rather not read anything of your father's. I've been warned about his writings."

"Don't you want to find out for yourself?"

"I need to protect the flock from false ideas. I would rather not be tainted by delving too deeply into them."

Where Jaylene sat in silence, her face was taking on a gradually brightening shade of vermillion.

Timothy and Rev. Carmichael continued to talk for another five minutes but without achieving a meeting of the minds.

At length Carmichael rose.

"I should go," he said. "Given the situation, I think it best if you attend no more services at Foothills."

Timothy and Jaylene stared back dumbfounded. They hardly believed what they heard.

"We *are* members," said Timothy slowly. "You are aware of that?"

"Yes. But as you have not been active for some time. I would like you to withdraw your membership. Your presence is confusing to some of our members, and, as I said, cannot help stirring up controversy. I think it best."

By now speechless, Timothy rose and led him to the door, then returned to the living room, where his wife and daughter sat with steam coming out of their ears.

"What was *that* about?" asked Todd. "Am I missing something here, or did he just tell you to stop going to church."

"That, my boy, was the Ally," replied Timothy. "You have just seen a visible representation of the Ally in the lowercase church going on the attack against the uppercase Church."

A long discussion followed. Gradually Heather and Jaylene calmed. When they sat down to eat half an hour later, the petitions around the table included prayers for Foothills and its people, including Lionel and Edith Holt, and the prayer that young Anthony Carmichael would be receptive to the Spirit's arrows of light when they were launched from on high into his heart and brain.

An hour later Timothy and Todd wandered out into Timothy's workshop while mother and daughter cleaned up the kitchen.

"I haven't seen Diane for a while," said Heather. "How's she doing?"

"Not so well, I'm afraid," replied Jaylene. "I went over to visit with Pearl last week. Poor Diane, I don't know that she's lost her faith exactly, but she has certainly lost her belief in prayer. I've never seen anyone so discouraged. She's just going through the motions with the home schooling. After the horrible things planted in the children when they were away, she doesn't see any use in it. Pearl is doing what she can. Diane is even talking about giving up and sending the children to public school."

"Oh, gosh!" exclaimed Heather. "She doesn't blame God for what happened?"

"Not exactly," replied Jaylene. "But it's made her cynical about prayer. What does prayer matter, she says. Jesus said if we ask he will grant what we ask for. We're told to obey the commands, to take the Bible literally, so what do those words mean? It's obviously not true—that's what she thinks, that Jesus made a promise that isn't true. As she sees it, they prayed good prayers for their children, prayers for protection—prayers that *weren't* answered. Their children have been damaged. Their family was stolen. She is a shattered young woman."

"That's heartbreaking," said Heather, shaking her head. "Though I have to admit I went through some of that after my snake bite."

"You were just a girl."

"I know, but I understand how deep doubt can go. What did you and Pearl say?"

"What could we say? Diane has heard all the pat answers—that sometimes the answer is no, that God's purposes are higher than we can see. None of that matters to her. Her children's minds are full of sexual images they were forced to look at by those horrible women who took them. The damage is done. I didn't have anything to say. I'm not sure I understand those words of the Lord's either. She is right. I've looked it up in every translation I can find. He says as clearly as it can be, *If you pray it I will do it.* What are we to think when that doesn't happen?"

Timothy and Todd walked in laughing together.

"How about some rice pudding?" asked Jaylene. "Then let's talk about something that's not so depressing!"

"Todd and I were talking about the possibility of another gathering," said Timothy. "We both think it's time."

"Wouldn't it be risky, after what happened last time, and now this unbelievable Freedom Bill?" said Jaylene. "We'd be making everyone a target."

"We were thinking we could make it different than before so there's no possibility of any conspiracy or cult talk."

"*Different* . . . how?" asked Heather.

"By throwing it open, inviting the Holts, Rev. Carmichael. Let Lionel take all the pictures he wants. We'll even have Mark send the president an invitation! We'll *prove* there's nothing underhanded going on."

"What a thought!" said Jaylene.

"I've got an idea!" exclaimed Heather excitedly, glancing at Todd with an expectant expression. "Let's have an outdoor wedding at David's ranch! We'll make our wedding the gathering."

"I love it!" said Todd. "It's perfect. Our Christian friends will celebrate with us. Then we'll have a gathering for the rest of the weekend. We'll just postpone our honeymoon a few days."

They both glanced at Timothy and Jaylene.

"Would you really want Lionel and Edith at your wedding?" laughed Timothy.

"Please," moaned Heather, "not Lionel!"

"Or the president!" added Timothy.

"The president would be pretty great," said Todd, laughing. "He used to like me, though that's probably changed since I came under the influence of you religious radicals," he added. "Wouldn't that make a media circus of it! He would never come—not to a gathering of Christians, not after this Freedom Bill. He has as good as declared war on Christianity. But being blatantly public about the event ought to quiet the ridiculous talk of a secret cult."

"I guess the next thing is to ask David!" said Jaylene. "You were planning on October anyway. That will be the perfect time for another gathering! The summer will fly by quickly. That's only four months away. We had better start making plans!"

"By the way," said Timothy, "have you thought about who's going to marry you?"

"Mark, of course!" replied Heather. "He's still a licensed minister."

69

Campaign

August 2052

WITH THE summer nominating conventions behind them and the presidential campaign officially beginning its final phase, Vice President Elizabeth Wickes Hardy's upcoming trip to St. Louis was planned to serve a dual purpose—ring the opening bell in the initial trading session of the new Midwest Stock Alliance, as well as tout President Rhodes's new Freedom Bill as the cornerstone of their campaign platform. The Rhodes-Hardy campaign did not need to campaign, of course, but it was still useful to go through the motions to keep approval ratings high.

At the Republican convention the previous month, the delegates nominated Senator Dindinger, who reluctantly agreed to act as a placeholder until another candidate came forward. He would not campaign, he said. The Republican ticket, Dindinger and Cynthia Dominguez, congresswoman from Puerto Rico and a complete unknown, was scarcely on the country's radar.

The Freedom Bill had encountered more pushback during the last year than either its architect Mike Bardolf or its primary mouthpiece, the president, anticipated. Some of its provisions were radical even for liberals. Two or three Supreme Court Justices had taken the unprecedented step of commenting on its potential constitutional overreach, wondering how soon it would take for lawsuits to begin working their way through the legal system. That these included his former friend Justice Linda Hutchins Trent, whom everyone considered a faithful Progressive, raised more than a few eyebrows and infuriated the president.

Jefferson Rhodes did not like criticism. But he managed to keep his emotions in check, put on a smiling face, and hoped to ride it out, smooth ruffled feathers, get people accustomed to the changes, and encounter as little rough water as possible as the election neared.

In truth, he was annoyed at Mike for aiming so high and incurring opposition from his own party. Especially just before an election. But to back down now that the bill was law would betray weakness. Therefore, they would deal with the fallout as best they could.

In light of the Republican woes, noise continued about a Reyburn candidacy to replace Dindinger on the ticket, or, failing that, a write-in effort. In the latter case, it was unlikely he could even get 5 percent of the vote. Yet his book continued to be in *The New York Times* top ten. The man was a menace. In spite of Reyburn, however, the Rhodes-Hardy team was poised to amass a victory even greater than their previous record-breaking percentage.

In the enclaves of the two California ranches, the idea of Todd replacing Mrs. Dominguez on the Dindinger ticket was talked about behind closed doors, though only when Todd was not present. Everyone knew the congresswoman was no more anxious to run than Senator Dindinger. Like him, she had only agreed as a temporary measure.

When the Todd scenario was mentioned to Charles Reyburn and Harvey Jansen, both men nearly exploded with enthusiasm at the prospect.

When he got wind of the fact that people were talking, Todd wrote a brief response for Heather to circulate as she felt appropriate.

> *Either we are serious about following Jesus's example or we aren't. Some time ago I heard Charles Reyburn make a simple but bold statement when he was being pressed to run for the presidency. He said, "If Jesus would not run for office, how can I?" or words to that effect. Jesus is likewise my example, and my response is the same.*

70

Stratagems of Power

September 2052

HAMAD BAHRAM and his cousin Ada had numerous lieutenants to carry out their orders. Both were too well known to be seen traveling either to Iran or to the US. By now Hamad was high enough in Palladium, and with his position in the administration and with Mike Bardolf's imprimatur, he could function with near impunity. Getting things in or out of the country was not a problem. Palladium had operatives at all the major airports and virtually owned the TSA. The three suitcases that came in through Kansas City, Indianapolis, and Minneapolis reached their St. Louis destination without incident.

Through layer upon layer of secrecy, none of those who handled them surmised what role they were playing in history. In spite of, or perhaps because of, every possible high-tech security system imaginable—a system designed and operated by one of Palladium's subsidiaries—eventually they were situated safely in the basement of the new Midwest Stock Alliance building in St. Louis.

Bahram planned his own moves so carefully as to have orchestrated a meeting of his commission, as he now considered it—at the Presidential Manor to precisely coincide with the vice president's speech opening the new investment center for minorities and immigrants at 9:00 a.m. Central time.

He had by then so skillfully learned to manipulate the master manipulator that Mike Bardolf scarcely realized to what an extent Bahram had been worming himself into the president's focus. His commanding 6'3" dark-skinned presence and his mesmerizing voice and calm demeanor wove a spell over the president, that gradually began to eclipse Mike's own. A few private meetings, brief but purposeful, when Mike was away from the Manor, accomplished their work. Rhodes felt the man's aura without realizing he was being seduced.

Exchanges and looks revealing the president's heightening fascination, even awe, of Bahram, caused Mike to wonder if he had been wise to bring Bahram so close to the inner circle. By now, however, events were moving too rapidly for even Mike Bardolf to stop.

Bahram wanted to make sure he was at the Presidential Manor at the critical time, and that chief of staff Randall and most of the other Manor staff and assistants were otherwise occupied in the capital. It was vital that he be in position to step in at the critical moment with more aplomb than Al Haig had demonstrated during his spotlight moment in 1981 after the Reagan shooting. He must be seen in a leadership role at the president's side. Getting all the pieces in place on the intricate board for the end game took some doing. But he was as skilled in the use of the vast Palladium network as was the heir of the Bardolf name. Even Palladium's League of Seven did not know it had been comprised of mere pawns in the centuries-long patient alignment of pieces on this global chess map.

The meeting of the Religion Commission in the Roosevelt Room of the Manor was well underway. President Rhodes would come in for a few remarks a little before 10:00 Eastern.

71

The Midwest Stock Alliance

VICE PRESIDENT Hardy stepped to the microphone in St. Louis about ten minutes before 9:00 a.m. Central Time. She began her predictable remarks about the vibrancy of the US economy and the historic step represented by a new stock exchange whose emphasis would be on the strong economic band bisecting the country, with emphasis on new investments from emerging minority and immigrant markets and immigrant offshore venture financing. She was especially careful to avoid any turn of phrase that hinted at "capitalism."

Her remarks were timed to exquisite perfection as she watched the second hand on the giant clock on the opposite wall gradually approach the zero hour of nine o'clock.

At thirty seconds Hardy paused.

"And now," she said, picking up the large bell on the podium in front of her, "it gives me great pleasure . . ."

On the floor the waiting stockbrokers began to chant down the seconds.

Ten . . . nine . . .

"to announce . . ."

Eight . . . seven . . . six . . .

"that the new Midwest Stock Alliance . . ."

Three . . . two . . .

72

Catastrophe

IN WASHINGTON, DC, scarcely displaying more emotion than if he were about to fall asleep, Hamad Bahram was addressing the commission specifically as pertaining to the growing and healthy influence of Islam and Hinduism across cultural lines in the United States, expressing his regret that Christianity continued to resist the inevitable progress of—

Suddenly the door crashed open. Anson Roswell ran in shouting, grabbed a remote from where it sat beneath the television in the far corner of the room and turned on the set.

"There's been a bombing!" he cried, then ran out.

By the time the chilling image came onto the screen, shouts and yelling could be heard throughout the Manor. There was no doubt what those in the room were watching on the screen—a white mushroom cloud rising over St. Louis. Remarkably, the Gateway Arch was still intact and visible in the foreground.

Half the room emptied. Those who remained stood, white-faced in horror, eyes glued to the television.

The entire Manor erupted in chaos. Sirens screamed outside. Assuming an attack on Washington was next, eyes throughout the city were riveted on the sky while tens of thousands scurried for wherever they thought they could find safety.

As the rest of the commission ran through the door, the president ran out of the Oval Office. He was flanked by two Secret Service agents, with Mike Bardolf hurrying behind them.

"Mike, come with me!" Rhodes cried to Bardolf, "they're taking me to the bunker. The country's under attack. It's nuclear. We've got to get out of the city!"

At the door of the Roosevelt Room, tall, stately, and serene, the form of Hamad Bahram stood calmly as one awaiting orders.

"Don't worry, Mr. President," he said, stepping forward. "I'll take care of everything here. Go with the president, Mr. Bardolf. You must be safe. The president needs you at his side. I'll take charge here."

Bardolf glanced around, for one of the few times in his life uncertain what to do.

"It's that Christian conspiracy group," said Bahram, following alongside as the agents hurried the president along the hall toward the exit. "I'll call Director Parva for an update immediately."

As emergency protocols were frantically implemented, Mike Bardolf had no choice but to submit to the very Secret Service agents technically responsible to him. He felt suddenly and strangely not in control.

By the time they were over the city in Marine One, reports were coming in that the bomb had detonated the instant the vice president rang the opening bell, almost as if she set it off. The new financial center complex in downtown St. Louis was reduced to rubble in seconds. Though no official report was yet available, it was impossible Vice President Hardy or anyone in the building could have survived.

Planes scrambled from Edwards and were already prowling the air above the capital. Numerous protocols instituted after 9/11 had never been used before this day. Concerned that more attacks were imminent, suddenly the country was depending on those protocols.

Within five minutes the Pentagon had mobilized the armed services to high alert. The country's airports were instantly shut down, planes turned back from runways. All en route flights were rerouted to the nearest possible airports. National Guard troops were quickly mustered for St. Louis within the hour. The early warning system continued to scan the skies for incoming missiles. NATO, too, was on high alert, along with US allies around the world.

Had it been a coordinated ICBM attack, multiple warheads would surely have been exploded at various sites around the country almost simultaneously. That no more attacks were reported after ten minutes was hopeful.

Speculation ran rampant. Most talking heads on the television networks were thinking of North Korea, China, Russia, Syria, Iran, or the rogue Taliban state of Afghanistan.

73

Cut Off the Head

OVER THIS complex turn of unexpected events, the probing mind of Mike Bardolf roamed like a searchlight. All his instincts told him that something untoward was in the wind, blowing from unknown directions.

He had lost his grip. Events were spiraling out of control, and he was not in front of them. His active brain was on fire, attempting to regroup and figure out what to do next.

Churchill's timeless words never went out of date: "Never let a crisis go to waste." As the magnitude of this new crisis was borne in upon him, his brain flew into high gear, turning over many things like a computer on overdrive.

Bahram's final words about the possibility of a Christian conspiracy had lodged in his brain, exactly as Bahram had intended.

There was no way a small renegade group of Christians led by fools like Mark Forster and his "Prophet" could have laid their hands on a nuclear device or would have had the resources to develop a so-called suitcase or car bomb with nuclear capability. In spite of his blustering accusations to the president, they could not be behind this.

Unless . . .

These days, who could tell? Court Masters might have the necessary connections to pull something like this off. Yet that too seemed unlikely.

What if they were in on it with some rogue foreign power, playing the role of the inside man, so to speak. This had international terrorism written all over it. The Christian group was known to have cells around the world. Why not point the finger at Forster and the rest—use the incident to take them out once and for all. A move against them on the heels of the bombing would be easy to disguise. The proximity of events in the public consciousness would link them whether there was anything to it or not.

And who could tell—it *might* have been them.

Before they had landed in the secret location deep in the Shenandoah mountains, a devious plan was taking shape in Mike Bardolf's brain. Cut off the head and the rest of the organism would wither and die. Where there is no general, the people perish—hadn't he heard something like that? Maybe Churchill again.

It was time to cut off the head. Eliminate the Prophet.

Uncharacteristically for one who always thought of every angle, it had not yet occurred to him that one of the president's first agenda items when they were safely underground, after addressing the nation, of course, would be to appoint a new vice president.

By day's end, however, he *had* thought of it. Might this be his opportunity to move one rung higher up the ladder?

He wouldn't mention it, thought Mike. It would be unseemly for him to give the president a short list of candidates with his own name heading it.

Best let the president himself suggest it.

74

News Recap

IN THE foothills of California, the large living room of the Forster ranch was filled with fifteen or twenty people who had come for an early dinner to follow the still-unfolding events of the day and to pray for the nation. Like most in the country, they sat glued to their televisions. They were not alone. Mark had spoken with Linda, Court Masters, and Charles and Regina earlier. After speaking with his mother, one of Todd's first calls was to the Jansen ranch.

Because of Todd's history with NBC and his interest in his replacement, they tuned in that evening to Mason Templeton's report, with sidebars from other sources giving a balanced perspective.

Templeton was reviewing the days' events preparatory to an address to the nation by President Rhodes scheduled for 6:30 Pacific time.

". . . no motive for the explosion has yet been determined," Templeton was saying, "nor has any terrorist organization claimed responsibility. But as radar picked up no satellite or missile activity from the direction of the Pacific, over the pole, or from the Atlantic, a missile attack by North Korea, Russia, China, or the Middle East can be ruled out.

"The blast site and surrounding blocks are still burning at this hour. Investigators are unable to get close enough to begin poring through the rubble of what was the newly constructed Stock Alliance Trade Center. Experts say the nature of the blast and mushroom cloud, and absence of incoming missile images, indicate a bomb on site. That fact, along with the challenges of getting a device of such magnitude through border security, has prompted speculation that the bomb was of US origin—homegrown, as it were, by rogue terrorists or a militia group.

"Rumors have again surfaced about an end-times fundamentalist group obsessed with end-of-the-world cataclysms. Some are calling it the Tribulation Cult, though nothing definite about the group is known. Since the president made the country aware of a religious movement associated with the still-unconfirmed Reyburn presidential campaign, investigators have been unable to uncover specific evidence of a conspiracy against the government, though this event will certainly inflame the rumors."

Glances around the room were serious. No one spoke.

"To recap," Templeton continued, "this morning at seconds after nine o'clock Central time, as Vice President Elizabeth Wickes Hardy rang the first clanging tones of the opening session of the new Midwest Stock Exchange, St. Louis and its surrounding suburbs were rocked as a terrific blast shook the ground. The tremors were felt up to a hundred miles in every direction, accompanied by a blinding light reportedly seen from as far away as Denver and Chicago. A white mushroom cloud rose instantly from central St. Louis. It is immediately obvious that more than one hundred years after Hiroshima, the United States has finally been attacked on its own soil by a nuclear weapon.

"Eyewitness accounts obviously come from some distance away. They all tell the same story—a blinding flash of light, an earthquake, then a second or two later depending on the distance, a deafening explosion followed by a hot blast of wind knocking many to the ground. The eerie sight of the mushroom cloud—familiar to all from movies and film clips—struck awe and terror into all who saw it. The following, taken by a tourist just outside the city videoing the Gateway Arch, is the best image we have been able to obtain thus far."

Templeton paused as the video played onscreen. Exclamations and a few screams could be heard from the family surrounding the man holding his phone, followed by the sound of the explosion, then the picture wobbled as the ground shook beneath him. Gasps went around the Forster living room as they watched.

"Within seconds, downtown St. Louis was filled with thousands frantically running and screaming, dust and ash and debris raining down, the scene reminiscent of New York five decades earlier. Within minutes streets were clogged, cars and cabs and city buses trying to get as far away as possible, though making it impossible for police and fire and ambulance vehicles to get to the scene. Fallout detection is being monitored throughout the city. Right now the blast and burn victims are taking priority, but radiation protocols are also being put in place.

"The mass exodus continued all day and into the evening. Police, fire, and other first responders in protective suits were finally able to get close enough to do their work. The National Guard is on hand in force, helping to locate more injured and dead. Hospitals are full to capacity, mostly from fire-related injuries and falling debris. Central St. Louis was mostly a ghost town as dusk descended. Highways and country roads in every direction remain bumper to bumper into the night.

"The Stock Alliance Center was essentially incinerated, along with surrounding adjacent buildings. The damage to the blocks surrounding was limited to fire which is slowly being contained. Whether bodies will be recovered is unknown. Vice President Hardy and an estimated three thousand others thought to be in the Alliance Trade Center building were killed instantly. Estimates of casualties in the surrounding blocks range from twenty to a hundred thousand. No one knows what the scene will be when the firefighters are able to get the multiple blazes extinguished. Emergency response teams around the country from multiple government and private agencies and organizations are en route to St. Louis as we speak.

"In the nation's capital, fighter jets were immediately scrambled at word of the explosion. They continue to blanket the Eastern Seaboard as the military remains on high alert. No more attacks have come, but the country remains on edge.

"One of the curiosities experts have not yet been able to answer is why the blast, obviously nuclear, was so limited in scope, only a fraction of the devastation caused at Hiroshima. Added to this is the apparent low fallout being registered. As yet no one has an explanation. Scientists are privately scratching their heads wondering why St. Louis was not completely flattened, and why, dreadful as is any loss of life, the death toll was not higher.

"The president was rushed to the underground presidential bunker constructed a decade ago at an undisclosed location. Select members of his cabinet, congressional leaders, and Supreme Court justices were likewise rushed to other secure undisclosed locations.

"The Presidential Manor has issued no statements yet, nor has there been word when President Rhodes will appoint a new vice president to serve out the remainder of the term. At this time Speaker of the House Ross Black would be second in succession to the presidency. He is safe out of Washington, though he has issued no statement at this time."

Templeton paused.

"Ah . . . yes—I have just received word that the president is about to address the nation. We will go live to the presidential bunker."

75

Presidential Address

THE PICTURE cut away to Jefferson Rhodes sitting at a desk with flag and presidential seal behind him. To all appearances he could have been sitting in the Oval Office.

"My fellow Americans," he began, "it is with a heart of profound grief that we come together to mourn our newly fallen in this unthinkable horror which has been inflicted upon our nation. As our prayers go out to the families of the dead and injured, we mourn the loss of a great public servant, Elizabeth Wickes Hardy, whom it was my privilege to serve with as a trusted colleague and friend. We are filled with indignation and will not rest until this attack on America is avenged. If indeed, as now seems likely, this outrage came from within, we must never cease our vigilance to root out treasons and all lingering remnants of Trumpism, still alive after more than thirty years, doomsday prophetic hysteria, and the religious zealotries that encourage violence and which have been the cause of nearly every major war of the last five hundred years."

As he listened behind the lights and cameras, Mike Bardolf was pleased. The script he had written planted exactly the suspicions and innuendos he intended. The president's tone was perfect. By tomorrow, the media would be talking about the Christian conspiracy mentioned in the president's speech a year earlier, connecting precisely the dots Mike wanted them to connect. He did not allow himself to betray the slightest hint of what he was thinking. As the president's assumed second in command, his every move was watched. Premature as it was, he was already being treated differently in the bunker, many assuming they were addressing the next vice president.

"There is no place in our modern world for the bigotry and fanaticism of religious extremism," the president went on, not hesitating over Mike's words which everyone assumed were his own. "We will spare no efforts to root out every militia and terrorist cell, whether here or abroad, to ensure the safety of all Americans. The recently passed Freedom Bill will give us the tools to fight this underground guerilla war against conspiracies of treason and revolution that have arisen in our midst. It may well be that this shocking crime was orchestrated as an attempt to undermine those efforts, if not to take down our very government.

"Such conspiracies will never succeed. I promise that the perpetrators—whether homegrown or originating on foreign soil—will be brought to justice. But for now let us remember the fallen, and join our hearts and thoughts for the families . . ."

The president went on for another ten minutes. Then Mason Templeton resumed his coverage.

76

Reaction in the Foothills

"I'VE HAD enough," said Mark, turning off the television.

Sitting beside Grace, he let out a long sigh. "What I feel we need to do most," he said, "is pray for Jeff, for the country, for those who are suffering, for the grieving, and that God would bring healing to all. Thousands of families have lost sons, daughters, mothers, fathers, brothers, and sisters today. My heart has been weighed down all day for Derrick and Paula. I don't know where they live in relation to the blast, but they are certainly in the middle of the tragedy. Even if they are safe, they will surely have friends who have been impacted and probably killed. We need to pray for God's sovereignty to somehow be active and present in this catastrophic time of loss, uncertainty, and fear."

"We've been trying to call them," said Jaylene. "So far no answer."

Mark nodded thoughtfully. "This is a major turning point for the world, not only for the US," he went on. "Who can tell but what many have long predicted has begun. As you know from my book on prophetic themes, I'm not one to invest every world event and political development with end-times overtones. So I would not predict that this suddenly heralds the return of Jesus. He said, *There will be wars and rumors of wars . . . but the end is not yet.* Too many jump the gun and ignore that last phrase.

"However, I do believe I can say that the progressivism of the past hundred years may finally be reaching its natural culmination and that this surely does signal the end of America as we know it—the end of what our founders established in 1776. Progressivism has steadily eroded those historic foundations so thoroughly as to make this catastrophe possible."

He smiled a melancholy smile.

"And where he sits as the heir, however unworthily, to Washington, Adams, Jefferson, Lincoln, FDR, Reagan, and Trump, poor Jeff desperately needs our prayers," he added. "Though he would disavow it, I probably know him in some ways, even after all this time, better than he knows himself. I could see in his eyes and in his voice as I watched, that he is terrified. This is not what he envisioned. He expected a smooth ride—progressivism marching to its appointed destiny with Jefferson Rhodes riding its crest as a white knight."

He paused thoughtfully.

"I suppose what I just said was a bit doomsday. I hope I am wrong. Maybe this will have just the opposite effect. Sixty-three years ago, in the span of twenty-four hours, the toppling of the Berlin Wall suddenly revealed the bankruptcy of seventy years of Communism. Those in the Kremlin who assumed they were on the way to defeating the West reeled in shock. They never knew that their system had been decaying for decades. This may be just such a moment. Ever since John Lennon sang of revolution, for eighty years the liberal progressivism of this country has blithely assumed that it, like Communism's leaders, represented the wave of the future.

"Suddenly a shocking reality is upon them. This moment may prove the beginning of the unraveling of the bankrupt progressive utopian dream. We have no idea who caused this or why. Yet events produce results no one can predict. This may prove to be the equivalent of the toppling of the progressive Berlin Wall. Is it possible that this event will call America back to its Christian foundations?

"Perhaps it will not. This may be the beginning of birth pangs, when wars and rumors of wars awaken a spirit of antichrist in the world. Greater tribulations may soon be upon us. We cannot know. But I do know that Jeff has no clue what to do. He will put on a brave front. But he is suddenly a babe in the woods. I don't mean to be presumptuous, or to exalt what I might be able to do if I were there, but I cannot help feeling, just when Jeff needs me most, when he needs his friend, that he has shut me out of his life.

"Oh, Lord," said Mark, breaking into prayer, "find some chink in the armor of Jeff's heart that has long been closed to you. Break through with a flash of truth, an arrow of light that will cause him to say, *Oh God, help me in my hour of need.*"

He fell silent.

Grace reached over, took Mark's hand, and began to pray. "*There are so many to raise into your presence, heavenly Father,*" she said, "*though we do not know their names, you know every one. Even nameless we lift them into your love. Oh God and we pray especially for our dear brother and sister Derrick and Paula Hanson and their family. Wherever they are at this moment, keep them in your care. And for Jeff and Marcia and Bradon, and for Jeff's mother, Sandra.*

"*Give Jeff wisdom at this time, Lord. Keep him and Marcia in your heart. It cannot be other than your will that we have been friends all these years. Surely you have a purpose, yet unfulfilled, to work in the Rhodes family. Send arrows of light, as Mark said, into all their hearts.*"

As her mother prayed, Ginger's thoughts gathered around Bradon. His face filled her mind. All day, though the nation's center of grief focused on St. Louis, everyone was aware of the potential for more attacks. Obviously, the Presidential Manor loomed large in those fears. Not hearing anything all day, with every passing hour, her anxiety mounted.

Protect Bradon, Lord, Ginger whispered inaudibly. *Wherever he is, keep his thoughts on you.*

The California nucleus had been in touch with many of their fellow BCL groups. Prayers for their brethren and the nation were being raised in Florida, Kentucky, Australia, Kansas, Texas, Washington, Poland, Idaho, Arizona, Wyoming, New York, England, Scotland, Germany, Georgia, from an untold multitude of homes.

All the prayers of God's faithful joined an invisible multitude around the world, his praying men and women encircling the globe with a surrounding interconnected network of petitions raised into the heavenlies. As with one voice, these thousands of prayers contained a single entreaty—for God to accomplish his purposes on the wayward planet on which he had planted his humanity, that his men and women might grow to become his sons and daughters.

Diane Statler sat rigidly at Rod's side. The catastrophe in St. Louis was incapable of melting the ice in her heart. She did not enter into the time of prayer. What good would it do? What good did anything do? If she had ever believed in prayer, she believed in it no longer. That was probably why her own prayers weren't answered—she had no faith. She did not pray *believing.*

To her doubt and despondency over the past year was added a deepening sense of guilt that what had happened to their family was because she did not have enough faith. It was *her* fault that God had not answered their prayers for protection. How could she care about the vice president or the president or anything else? Her children were scarred for life. She would never care for anything again. All the love and care they had poured into their children were water down a sieve into a barren sandy desert. Where were their prayers now? Where were Jesus's promises about answered prayer? If her faith wasn't enough for God to answer, why should she make a mockery of it by continuing to pray at all?

Thus she sat beside her husband like a statue of stone. All the while Rod was desperately trying to cling to his own faith but finding it almost as difficult as did Diane. The innocence and purity of their family had been destroyed by people who claimed to care about their children and had then done everything they could to destroy them. He doubted he would ever be able to forgive them.

More prayers, broken by long silences, continued around the room.

When the others heard Todd's voice, a few ears perked up. Neither he nor Heather were much given to praying in public. When friends or groups came together to pray, neither spoke aloud. On this occasion, an impulsion swept through him to give voice to the stirring within him.

"I pray for the people of St. Louis, for the president and his family, and for our friend Bradon," Todd began. *"Only you, Lord, know the full scope of what this day means, and what is its eternal significance in the hearts and minds of your faithful men and women. Your purposes are higher than we can see. All we can do is pray that you will accomplish those purposes through this tragedy, not only for the nation but your purposes for us all. And may we be your willing and obedient co-sharers in your work."*

He paused briefly, then continued. *"Accomplish your purposes in me, Lord Jesus. Create in me a pure heart. Purify me in your will and make me* *ever more faithfully and obediently your son. Use this catastrophe to turn Christians as well as the world to you. Deepen within all our hearts the constant prayer—accomplish your purposes in us, heavenly Father. I pray for my colleague Mason Templeton and for President Rhodes, and for my one-time mentor though I believe him to be a man of evil, Mike Bardolf, who came to my mind as we have been praying. These are men I know. If I pray for them, as our brother Rees Howells* prayed, may I be willing to be the instrument you use to answer my own prayers. I am willing, Lord. Use me if you can, if you will, in these men's lives. Strengthen your remnant to stand as a beacon of truth during this time. Raise up your remnant-body in unity as a testimony of light to a world in which darkness has reigned too long."*

He fell silent. The torrent was unexpected and full of emotion. Todd sat back, spent.

Timothy and Jaylene could not help glancing at one another with wide eyes. Jaylene imperceptibly mouthed the single word, *Wow!*

David, likewise, was not a man of public prayer. Following Todd's outpouring, his was the next voice they heard.

"*This moment,*" he prayed, "*is but a symbol of what has been the fate of our nation for generations. As grievous as it is, use it, heavenly Father, to bring your people and this nation back to you. May this become a moment of national repentance by the unthinking masses for allowing themselves to be deceived by perversions of truth which have undermined America's national character. May the vision our brother Charles wrote of so forcefully be realized. May this nation repent of its sin and return to its roots—roots established in your Word and in your truth.*"

☆ ☆ ☆

When the group broke up about 11:00 p.m., Mark and Grace and Craig, Heather and Todd, and Jaylene, Timothy, and David were left alone. Ginger had finally been able to reach Bradon, for whom it was now after two o'clock in the morning, and was in her bedroom on the phone.

---

* Welshman whose story and unique approach to prayer was told in the 1952 classic by Norman Grubb, *Rees Howells, Intercessor.*

"Everything has changed," said Timothy as he continued to talk quietly with the others. "As we were praying, the feeling came over me that this terrible moment is a sign that God's people must know the cost of what may be coming. If they do not stand now, will they ever be capable of standing against the world's great lie. With these thoughts also came the strong sense that it may be time for my father's Brief to be more widely distributed. Persecution may come to the remnant rather than national repentance. The president's words, for those with ears to hear them, threw down a gauntlet. With respect to your friend, Mark, I believe Jefferson Rhodes was declaring war upon serious, believing, obedient, command-following Christianity. We must continue to pray urgently, as you and Grace prayed, that God will open his eyes. Yet we must also gird up our loins for battle. We will pray for *repentance*, but we must prepare for *persecution*. And as we prepare for next month's wedding and gathering, I believe it is time we tell those who have been with us for some time about the Benedict Brief."

Todd glanced at Heather with an expression of question.

She smiled and nodded, then glanced over at David.

"Maybe it's time you tell Todd about the Brief on your drive home," she said.

David nodded. "He is about to join the family, it is definitely time."

Todd and David finally left for the Bar JG around midnight. At Grace's invitation, Timothy and Jaylene decided to stay the night at the Circle F, and return to Roseville in the morning.

77

AFTERMATH

A PALL SETTLED over the nation unlike anything it had ever experienced. Even 9/11 could not compare. The closest similarity was the bombing of Pearl Harbor which galvanized the country for war.

These events of 111 years later, however, were likely to create division—not the unity that had followed the Japanese attack. Nor could the combined loss of 5,500 lives from the incidents of 1941 and 2001 be likened to what was, after three days, estimated to be 17,000 dead in St. Louis from the initial blast, with injuries three times that—though both numbers would climb. Neither could it be predicted how many deaths and illnesses in future years would be linked to its fallout. That America's homeland had been invaded added to both anger and angst.

In what skeptics were describing by the vague term "divine intervention"—though Christians hailed it as the answer to millions of prayers—the wind shifted uncharacteristically toward the northwest almost at the very moment of the explosion. It took the mushroom cloud and residual particles on a course, if the trend continued, that would cause the fallout to miss all major North American population centers, miraculously skirting a narrow corridor between Des Moines, Minneapolis, and Bismarck before drifting west of Hudson Bay and over the vast Northwest Territory of Canada. Hopefully there it would dissipate over the North Pole, though the long-term impact on the steadily thickening ice pack was obviously worrisome. Unless another brief global warming trend reversed the cooling begun in the early 2030s, experts were hopeful that the fallout would be buried in the polar ice cap indefinitely.

The mood of the country was mixed, ambiguous, uncertain, fearful. No one knew what to think, especially about the president's none-too-subtle blaming of Christian conspirators for the event. Confirming the president's warning of doomsday fanatics, evangelicals predictably proclaimed the beginning of the Great Tribulation, and—though with conflicting interpretations of sequences—the imminent return of Christ. In spite of the new publishing guidelines, a new spate of prophetic books—many written by AI—were begun within hours that would roll off the presses in five or six weeks. In accordance with government regulations, Amazon and Google were scrambling to filter out news and reports of the many wild supernatural interpretations of events, and would do their best to suppress sales and keep listings off their search engines.

Most confused about the events were progressives. They had not anticipated this. They fully expected their agenda to bring peace and light and happiness and goodwill to all mankind. With America's imperialism and bigotry and white supremacist history on history's scrap heap, with its borders open, its wealthiest citizens being taxed at 90 percent, poverty and welfare a thing of the past thanks to guaranteed living income and free housing and health care for those at the lower end of the scale . . . who could possibly want to inflict damage on the *new* United States of America. Their matrix of global unity and goodwill had no place in it for war and destruction.

The only answer to the calamity that made sense, as the president obviously believed, was that the attack was internal, indicating that half a century of progressive policies had still not completely eradicated every pocket of evil, backwardness, and hatred in the country.

Within days following the attack, the focus of speculation—NBC's Mason Templeton giving the most visible voice to the theory, fed by his "inside information from highly placed confidential sources"—was that the attack had indeed come from within. A Christian conspiracy originating deep in the heart of America was the likely source. As it served the progressive anti-Christian worldview, most liberal pundits jumped on the bandwagon.

Hearing the vocal evangelical wing of Christendom prophesying their diverse end-times scenarios, biblical prophecy was again ramped up for ridicule in the national press. Wherever it had originated no one knew, but after being heard on nationwide television from Mason Templeton, the term Tribulation Cult gained traction, and was increasingly associated with those responsible for the bombing.

A resumption of the Antichrist Sweepstakes from 2048 was up and running in Las Vegas within days, US President Jefferson Rhodes, Russia's President Golubev, and China's Premier Jiang heading the initial list.

To further the narrative, Mason Templeton began to receive leaked memos from his confidential sources in the FBI indicating that there were rumors that the underground conspiracy group was stockpiling weapons. Incendiary bombs were said to be included in the group's arsenal.

Evangelicals who believed in biblical prophecy were portrayed not only as misguided simpletons but as dangerous to the country, likened to David Koresh, leader of Waco's Branch Davidians, and Jim Jones of the People's Temple.

Film clips were regularly replayed from the president's speech of the previous summer warning of a vast right-wing conspiracy of religious zealots intent on undermining the progress the country had made since the Obama Progressive Revolution.

"We must cut off those sinister and evil forces before they can gain a foothold," the president was now saying.

After his strong address to the nation and his handling of the crisis, he was being hailed as a strong leader whose words and programs against what he called "this new evil among us" must be implemented fully and without delay.

"And still," Mason Templeton concluded his most recent broadcast, "the president has offered no hint about his potential pick to replace Vice President Hardy for the remainder of the year, nor what will be the impact of his choice on November's election."

78

CONSPIRATORIAL PLOT

THE PRESIDENT had used his warnings of a year earlier to push through the Freedom Bill. In the wake of the St. Louis bombing, criticism of the bill quieted. The bill and its architect were viewed as prophetic. The president's ratings soared.

Rhodes . . . a prophet, smiled Mike Bardolf to himself as he prepared another leak to get into Mason Templeton's hands. That would be an interesting twist, he mused—take out the Christian group's prophet and replace him with *national prophet* Jefferson Rhodes.

A *prophet* in the Presidential Manor, he smiled at the irony. He wondered how the "prophet" angle would play with Muslims.

Though the country remained on high alert, as days went by no signs of additional attacks surfaced. Released from the bunker, Mike Bardolf met privately with Bruno Volker to hammer out details for his secret follow-up stratagems based on the videos of his surveillance mission in California. All that remained was to assess when the time was right, then give the word.

The limited nature of the damage at St. Louis had physicists and politicians baffled. That the crater in the middle of the city was so small, only destroying three or four blocks, and initial reports indicating radiation almost negligible, remained ongoing mysteries. It was obviously a new generation of device—lethal yet curiously not designed to wipe out catastrophic numbers. The loss of life and economic devastation was incalculable. Yet when compared with the Hiroshima and Nagasaki casualties of 200,000, the St. Louis numbers were miniscule. This was obviously a new kind of bomb. Who could tell how it would ultimately change the approach to war.

Everyone had been talking about twenty-first-century weaponry as capable of wiping out life on the planet. Now it appeared that a new breed of tactical weapon had surfaced with the potential to alter the strategic thinking of nations and movements. *Less* lethal, it could in the long run prove *more* destructive by removing the built-in deterrent implicit in the end-of-the-world scenario.

One thing the experts agreed on was that no backwoods underground militia group could possess the expertise or materials to develop such a sophisticated weapon. The facilities, financing, science, and obtaining whatever new material was the basis for this bomb, would be impossible to keep from detection.

The underground conspiracy theory, however, served progressivism's anti-Christian agenda so perfectly that the majority of the country gradually came to believe conservative Christians responsible.

The term Tribulation Cult, with its sinister end-of-the-world religious vibe, fit in perfectly with the Koresh-Jones narrative. The mythology of such extremist groups played right into Mike Bardolf's hands, especially when he leaked hints that a mysterious "prophet" associated with one *branch* of the cult—a word he emphasized for its subliminal effect—was an unknown man by the name of *David*. What else could it be but a resurgence of the "Branch *David*-ians," now gone nationwide and with the sophisticated backing to have produced a bomb.

Then surfaced rumors that outspoken Christian Harvey Jansen, vowing to get even with President Rhodes for his humiliation of 2048 and a closet Trumpist, had orchestrated the event in hopes of succeeding where the January 6, 2020 conspiracy failed. He was, even now, preparing a large following to march on Washington and seize the Presidential Manor by force.

The next phase in the development of the story was that Christians—long frustrated that world events had refused to march to their end-times drum and the rapture and subsequent Great Tribulation had not ushered in the millennial reign of Christ on earth—decided to take matters into their own hands and precipitate another world war themselves.

Jesus had tarried too long. They would force their Messiah's hand.

79

Presidential Reflections

MIKE BARDOLF walked into the president's private office two days after their return to the Presidential Manor.

"I've been thinking," he said, "this bombing might give you just the opportunity you need to enact even more stringent measures."

"What kind of measures?" asked Rhodes.

"I've been working an addendum bill to follow the Freedom Bill—specifically targeting Christians, cults, militia, and right-wing groups suspected of not complying with the mandates of the Freedom Bill. I've drawn up a proposal I'd like to leave with you."

"We're pressing our luck with the bill as it is," began Rhodes. "Not everyone's happy about it. I'm not sure—"

"That might have been true a week ago," interrupted Bardolf. "But your star is riding high again. It's the perfect time to press our advantage, go after these wacko groups for good. The country's in the palm of your hand. Seize the moment."

"All right, I'll look at it," rejoined Rhodes with a hint of irritability.

Bardolf turned to go.

"By the way," said Rhodes after him, "is Dr. Bahram in the Manor today?"

"Not to my knowledge. I can get in touch with him. Why?"

"I want to thank him for how well he handled things here after the bombing when you and I and the senior staff were off the grid."

"I'll pass along your gratitude."

"I think you misunderstand me, Mike," said the president testily. "I want to talk to him *myself*. Personally."

"I'll see to it, Mr. President," said Mike, then left the office, an indefinite uneasiness creeping into his mind.

Jefferson Rhodes still sat alone ten minutes after Mike Bardolf's departure. He had been glancing over Mike's so-called addendum. Actually, it was good stuff. Mike was one who knew how to go for the jugular, no doubt about it—outlaw Christian gatherings of five persons or more . . .require all Christian home groups to register with the Compliance Agency . . .

He chuckled at some of the ideas in Mike's addendum. They were so outrageous, so intrusive, trampling on religious freedom like a modern inquisition! Who but Mike would dare propose such measures? Mark and his crowd would go ballistic!

Let them! He would throw the whole lot in jail and keep them there this time.

Yet something was bothering him.

It was Mike's manner. He was getting cocky, as if he were running the show. It annoyed him particularly today. Mike was getting above himself.

The president tossed the file onto his desk and leaned back in his chair, thinking hard. Everyone was badgering him about a VP pick. He had been given a dozen lists of names. Every constituency in Washington was pushing its favorite. But the choice was his, no one else's.

Mike Bardolf had his detractors, he knew that. Many saw him as an opportunist. There was no doubt he got things done. He had connections, he knew people. He had been his right-hand man for years. He was actually the perfect choice. The senators and congressmen would squawk. But most of them were hacks. Mike was a doer. The instant the dust settled, Mike's name stood out prominently as Hardy's logical replacement.

Yet in recent months Mike's presumption had begun to irritate him. They had reached too high with the Freedom Bill. As president, he'd taken more heat than was comfortable, at least until this St. Louis thing.

Now this latest . . . this anti-Christian addendum.

He glanced at the folder on the desk in front of him. The bill gave him plenty to quash the right-wing fringe. There was no need for an addendum. Why give his opponents more ammunition to use against him just when the country was getting behind the Freedom Bill?

Mike's ideas were good. But he was too arrogant, too brash, too sure of himself. Sometimes you had to show a man like Mike who was boss.

He thought another minute or two, then opened the drawer on his right, took out a sheet of blank paper, and set it in front of him. He reached for the pen in the desk stand and wrote on the top of the page.

VP Possibilities

Obviously Mike was still a strong contender, along with the two most powerful persons in Congress. Again he set pen to paper.

Mike Bardolf
Speaker R. Black
Majority Leader N. Aswad

After another minute, he added,

NY Governor S. Obama
Georgia Governor W. Boone

Three more names followed:

Conn. Senator C. Clinton
Texas Congresswoman A. Lawless
Ca. Congresswoman M. Feinstein

He sat back and scanned the list thoughtfully. An admirable group. But except for Mike, routine. No fun in that. They would all feel entitled.

He sat for ten minutes. Slowly a smile spread over his face. He leaned forward and added a ninth name.

Professor H. Bahram

Continuing to peruse his completed list, his smile widened. The lifelong politicos would expect to be considered. They would think it their "turn."

Why should he carry the water for *their* ambitions? Why not pick an outsider? Why not do the unexpected? Shake things up before the election.

He wasn't a politico, but Mike was probably the most ambitious of them all. His ambitions were different. But in his own way, he was just like the rest. A climber. An opportunist. He *wanted* it.

Truth be told, he was put off by Mike's overconfidence.

He began to chuckle lightly. Mike was a valuable asset, but maybe it was time to knock him down a peg. He needed to know he couldn't count on getting everything he wanted.

Rhodes circled one of the names, then set down his pen, looked at the list for several seconds, crumbled the paper tightly, threw the wad into the waste can, then broke out laughing at the thought of watching the others squirm.

He was in no hurry to make an announcement. He would enjoy letting them sweat a little longer.

80

It's a Go!

MIKE BARDOLF was anxious to move quickly with his plan to capitalize on the bombing. He wanted to link what was coming with St. Louis in the public mind. Yet he had to gauge the national mood. And the president's.

As for the public, the timing couldn't be better. His proposed follow-up provisions to the Freedom Bill provided perfect legal cover. The country wouldn't bat an eye.

The hold-up was Jefferson Rhodes. If they waited too long, the opportune moment with a public hungry for payback would pass.

Something peculiar was going on with the president. Why was he dragging his feet? He could usually read him like a book. He assumed that Rhodes would jump on his new addendum and push it through without delay. But in the last few days, he had grown uncommunicative, almost distant. When they spoke, he was cool, irritable.

After delaying more than another week, Mike decided to wait no longer. He would force the president's hand. This was no time to get cold feet. They must press their advantage. If Rhodes was too timid to act, no one would make that accusation against Mike Bardolf.

He thought another moment, then picked up his phone.

"Bruno," he said, "the time's come. It's a go. Day after tomorrow . . . late, after dark. I want nothing left . . . make sure he can't get out alive."

81

Hard Day's Work

Early October 2052

TWO WEEKS after the St. Louis bombing, with the country still reeling but gradually breathing again, thousands of funerals and memorial services being conducted and planned, David Gordon and Todd Stewart had been working hard most of the day.

Todd was now so comfortable in the saddle—though he had not yet ridden Pistachio— he was out much of the morning rounding up a dozen cattle being sold from two of the pastures and herding them back to the ranch where they would be picked up the next day.

He and David spent a good bit of the afternoon driving into Grass Valley and loading several dozen long 4 x 4 and 4 x 6 beams and 8 x 6 x 6 posts onto David's flatbed for a new corral and the beginnings of a barn addition he had planned, along with sand, lime, and cement for the project. By the time they arrived back at the ranch, they were spent. They wearily agreed to unload the supplies the next day.

They unhitched the flatbed next to the barn and returned the pickup to the front of the house.

Todd had not seen Heather for two days and was looking forward to an evening together. She had been in Dorado Hills where tensions and anxiety were still high and many of the care home residents needed extra attention. Much of the local BCL group continued to meet nightly with Mark, Grace, Timothy, and Jaylene at the Circle F, praying for the country and its leaders, the families of the fallen, and their brothers and sisters in other groups throughout the country.

Heather drove into the Bar JG a little after 6:00, just as David and Todd were calling it a day.

"You two look beat!" she said, meeting them walking toward the house after closing up the barn for the night.

"I am worn out," laughed Todd. "David was determined for me to ride that Sorrel when rounding up the cattle. I don't know how you people stay in the saddle so long."

"There's no place a lover of horses would rather be," rejoined Heather.

"Those long days in the saddle are a thing of the past for me, I'm afraid," said David. "I can't say I don't miss it. But a couple hours at a time is about all I'm good for these days. I'm bushed. In fact, I'm going to pass on the prayer meeting tonight. This young fella's working me too hard!"

"I think you've got it backwards, David!" laughed Todd.

"Well, we make a pretty good team, I will admit. But I think I need to take it easy for the evening and hit the hay early."

"You don't mind if I go?" said Todd. "I haven't seen this little lady for two days!"

"Of course not. Give everyone my best."

"Do you want to ride over with me, Todd?" asked Heather. "I can bring you back later. I'm spending the night at the Forster ranch."

"Sure, that'd be great. Let me grab a quick shower," he added then ran toward the house.

82

Wings of Angels

TODD AND Heather arrived at the Forster ranch a little before 7:00. Ginger and Craig had been staying at the ranch since the bombing, not frightened exactly but taking comfort being with their family and out of the city.

"I got a letter from Bradon today, Todd," said Ginger as Todd and Heather sat at the table. The others were mostly finished with supper. Mark and his father were outside. "He'd written it before the bombing. The mail's so slow now with airplanes still grounded, though I've talked to him on the phone since. He said to tell you hi. He's still full of questions."

"I remember how I was when Heather and I were first writing," smiled Todd. "This strange thing called Christianity was so new. From my talks with him, Bradon seems to be growing rapidly. One of his biggest challenges," Todd added, chuckling, "is keeping the books you're sending him out of sight in the Manor."

Ginger laughed. "He's said that to me too. He's putting fake covers on them."

"I thought he'd planned to get an apartment of his own."

"He thought about it, but decided with the expense of law school it would be best to stay where he is for now. He's more in the spotlight at the Manor but like he says—free room and board staying with the folks!"

"He's an amazing story. Why does spiritual hunger come to some people and not others? Why Bradon?"

"What about you?" rejoined Ginger. "Why Todd Stewart?"

"I guess you're right. I'm used to it now. But what a change it was for me at first too. For some reason, both of us began to ask if there was more to life. Thanks to the young women God brought along to stimulate that question, we both began to get unexpected answers."

"I would never have guessed what God was going to do in Bradon's life from our first conversations in Seattle."

Just then the Wests and Statlers walked in. They were followed a few minutes later by the Laynes and Faith Silva. More gradually trickled in.

"David not coming tonight, Todd?" asked Dewitt, glancing about.

"We had a long day. He decided to read and make an early night of it."

By 8:00 some twenty or more were seated in the Forster living room. Gradually a spirit of prayer descended on them.

"We need to pray for David," said Todd.

"Is anything wrong?" asked Mark.

"Oh, no. He's as wonderful and wise and witty as ever. It's only that sometimes I sense that he's tired—not just physically. I don't know what I mean exactly—almost like he's weary of the battle. The world and the state of our country and the church . . . it's all weighing him down with a weight almost too heavy to bear. The bombing in St. Louis hit him hard. I know he is grieving for the loss of life, but also that such is the state of our nation. He feels it all deeply, even personally. Seeing how Christians are so misunderstood, how the Christian message is twisted and turned into evil . . . the things said recently by the president and others. He *feels* it in the depths of his soul on behalf of the Lord."

Todd paused and thought a moment.

"If I can say it like this," he went on, "I think he feels the *weight* of the Great Lie. It's not just that Christians are being blamed. There's nothing new in that—Nero did the same thing two thousand years ago. It's that truth is being mocked, that the whole country, deluded by progressivism for so long, is so willing to believe the lies. The pain he feels is draining his spiritual energy. I think he is discouraged, almost defeated, feeling that there's no use, no one is listening, that the world is not going to change. It's sad to see such a great man sapped of the very vision, speaking for myself, that has given me so much strength. I'm sure many of you would say the same."

Nods and comments and *amens* went around the room.

"He is a great man," Todd added. "But he is tired of the fight."

A silence, heavier than *mere* quiet, descended—a *spiritual* silence, pregnant with import. The prayers lifted out of it were borne on the wings of the Spirit praying what none of them could formulate in words of their own.

"These are perilous times," said Dewitt West softly. "David is not like other men. I have often wondered why such a wonderful man was not married. I believe in a sense, God preserved him for himself, for the purpose of keeping David's focus over a lifetime on growing ever deeper, year after year, in his understanding of the nature and character of God. God called David to a life of solitude, almost as some of the great monks of old, so that he would understand God, and would so thoroughly assimilate Stirling's understanding of God's ways as to be able to pass that intimate wisdom on to us, and to future generations.

"Stirling had a family and five children and lived a life active among men. David has lived an entirely different life. How and why God chose these two men to walk such different paths for a common purpose is a mystery. Now here we are, the next generation to whom this legacy is passed. None of our lives follow the pattern of either of these men. But through us their legacy will go on."

Again, a deep Spirit-silence settled over them, as if giant wings of angels were quietly enfolding them into the heart of all things.

83

Hearts of Love

AS THEY prayed, David dozed off in his chair, the open copy of his well-worn Kempis still on his lap.

Dusk fell. The house grew dark.

Still he slept, not even turning on the lamp beside him.

☆ ☆ ☆

Through the darkness of the foothills four miles away, Todd's and Dewitt's words plunged deep into the hearts of those who heard them. Their hearts were heavy to realize the sobering reality that the man they had all looked up to for strength for so long, like Stirling before him, would not be with them in the flesh forever. Such was the way of God's truth—it went on through the generations—and all flesh is like grass, as Peter said.

"Oh, Lord, our Father," prayed Timothy, *"we lift up our treasured brother and friend David to you. Hold him in the palm of your hand, Lord God. Give him not only physical strength, but internal spiritual strength to continue strong for the battle. We depend on him, Father. Give him many more years among us as our leader and friend and as a prophetic voice. Invigorate him during this season of discouragement. Strengthen him to continue wearing the mantle of your servant Stirling Marshall for as long as you give him breath. And build into each one of us Christlike hearts to faithfully follow his legacy when the time comes."*

Gradually the others lifted up prayers for their beloved brother—some silent, some whispered, some audible but all flowing out of hearts of love.

84

Sounds in the Night

A SUDDEN SOUND jolted David awake.

All was darkness around him but his senses were immediately alert. Lights flashed intermittently through the windows.

He jumped to his feet and hurried through the blackened room to his kitchen and looked out.

The sound of three or four engines roared toward the house. Whoever they were they were not trying to sneak in unseen or unheard.

The first SUV reached the house. Even before fully skidding to a stop, its doors flew open. Four large men in military camouflage hit the ground and sprinted toward the house, large fuel cannisters in their hands, rifles slung over their shoulders.

David could make out only black shadows running toward him. This was no friendly visit!

He spun around and ran out of the kitchen and across the floor of his great room.

It took but seconds for the following two vehicles to empty. In twenty seconds the house was surrounded.

85

Light in the Darkness

TODD AND Heather left the Forster home a little after eleven and walked slowly out into the peaceful night. A chill was creeping through the foothills. But as long as they were together, they did not feel it.

"How old is David?" asked Todd.

"Eighty, I think," replied Heather. "Or almost. He's nine years older than my dad."

"An amazing man for that age."

Thoughts of David sent Todd's gaze absently in the direction of the Bar JG, his home for the past year.

Suddenly his eyes shot open.

"Heather—look, do you see—what can that be!"

A glow of light shown above the trees and hills.

"It's coming from David's!" she exclaimed.

Without another word, they sprinted for Heather's car. Moments later those inside the house heard them racing along the driveway away from the ranch. Where he sat in the passenger seat, Todd hastily called Mark on his cell to tell him what they had seen. Neither Todd nor Heather spoke for the remainder of the four-mile drive. A terrible premonition filled their hearts.

When they came into the clearing and raced under the Bar JG sign, there was no evidence of the intruding vehicles, only David's pickup in front of the house. The entire landscape was lit up like day.

David's house was engulfed in flames shooting a hundred feet into the air.

Gradually Heather slowed. She stopped fifty yards from the house. They jumped out and tried to walk further but met only the blast as from a furnace. The heat was too great to continue.

They stood gazing at the horrifying sight. Tears filled both their eyes. They could do nothing. No one could survive such a holocaust.

They saw no sign of David. The horses and cattle were frantic with sounds of terror. They had backed away as far in their corrals and paddocks as they could get. There being not a breath of wind, the barn some two hundred feet away, Todd's car parked in front, seemed safe.

"Oh, Lord Jesus!" whispered Heather, then fell weeping into Todd's arms.

Suddenly a tremendous sound rocked the ground beneath them. Heather dared not look. Over the top of her head as he held her, Todd saw David's pickup explode into a bright ball sending debris high into the air.

At nearly the same instant, the front wall of the house collapsed inward. Half the roof came crashing down over it sending a flurry of cinders into the night sky.

The other walls, and what remained of the roof soon followed.

86

Horrifying Reality

TODD AND Heather spent the night of the fire at the Bar JG, sitting in Heather's car, snuggling together under several blankets, alternately dozing, then waking to the horrifying reality, Heather weeping anew, Todd in a stupor. He did not even try to comfort her because he could not comfort himself.

The fire engines and full crew from the Grass Valley Fire Department did not leave the scene until after 3:00 a.m. By then the blackened ashes of the one-hundred-fifty-year-old ranch house lay in a thoroughly drenched blackened heap. They had remained two hours after the fire was out to make sure no hot spots erupted. Fire in the dry California hills could all too easily be sparked into a conflagration. Two men remained on guard with one truck for the rest of the night to ensure that no chance spark spread to any of the outbuildings or grass of the surrounding pastures or trees.

Mark and his family, Heather's parents, the Wests, and the others who had been praying at the Circle F, had hurried over after Todd's call and arrived even before the fire brigade. They all left the tragic scene about the same time. None got much more sleep than Heather and Todd.

☆ ☆ ☆

In the first light of day, shortly after 6:00, a car drove up beside Heather's. The sound brought her and Todd out of a fitful doze. They glanced over. It was Timothy and Jaylene.

No words were spoken as all four got out. Heather hurried around the car, breaking into sobs, and was embraced by her mother and father. Todd drew in a deep breath of the chilly morning air pungent with the overpowering smell of ash and smoke, then left them and walked slowly toward the remains of what had been his home for the past year. He had loved this ranch house! He loved David—the closest man to a true father he had had in thirty years.

The devastation in his heart was not for the house. It was for the loss of something far more precious—a spiritual giant, a father, a mentor, a friend.

Slowly he walked around the smoldering ruin, the smell of wet char burning his nostrils, not daring look too closely. Fire investigators and the coroner would be here by mid-morning to pore through the ashes. He didn't want to be here when they did. He did not want to see what they might find. He took no notice of the two firemen still on guard.

He did not know that all the land surrounding him, the property on which the house once stood, everything he gazed on as he looked about, had been left to him in the will David had executed with his attorney in Grass Valley a month before. That fact would come out soon enough. Even then, it would pale beside the loss of the great man himself. Nor could he avoid thinking about David's library of books, and even his own small collection of treasured volumes that had made such a difference in his life, and the Bible Heather had given him. They were the *first* such treasures he had ever owned. They were irreplaceable.

He circled the house and slowly made his way back to the two cars.

Jaylene embraced him. "Oh, Todd, I'm so sorry! I know what he meant to you."

"To us all," said Todd in a choking voice.

"Why don't the two of you come back to the Circle F?" said Timothy. "There's nothing more we can do here. There will be much to process and do. There will be a lot on your shoulders, Todd, my boy—reports to fill out, police, fire, insurance claims, clean up. I don't even know where David kept his important papers. You need to get some rest."

Todd nodded. He didn't want to think about that right now. But he knew Timothy was right.

After two or three minutes of silence, the four stared, still dumbfounded at what was a scene of deeper desolation than any of them had ever known, for Timothy, equaling the loss of his own father. Without another word they piled into the two cars and drove slowly away.

☆ ☆ ☆

The somber mood at the Forster ranch continued all day. As befitted the unofficial wake, food began to arrive in abundance, though no one felt like eating. There were phone calls with the police and fire department, most of which Mark and Timothy handled. David's insurance agent called. Timothy provided what information he possessed so the paperwork could begin.

With no idea how central he was to events, Todd was too shattered to face anything. Nor did anyone else know about the will. David's lawyer was out of town and knew nothing of the fire.

The next day passed much the same. The only thing of note were assurances by the Marshalls and Forsters that Todd had a place to live at either of their homes.

87

A Door Is Opened

ON THE third day, at last Todd began to breathe.

"I need to go back," he said to Heather after breakfast. "I have to see to the animals. I should have gone over yesterday, but I couldn't face it. We also have those cattle that were to be picked up yesterday. I need to make a call about that too."

He let out a long sigh.

"Mostly," he said, "I just need to *be* there. I need to feel the spirit of the place, David's spirit. I appreciate the offers, but I may want to fix up one of the old bunk rooms in the barn to stay for a while. You taught me well—a ranch doesn't take care of itself!"

"I'll go with you," said Heather. "We'll see how the animals are and what else needs to be done."

They drove up the Bar JG drive half an hour later both feeling a stab of fresh pain to see the black ruins in front of them. Heather drove to the barn and parked next to Todd's car, covered in ash.

Sounds of horses, cattle, goats, chickens, and three pigs let them know that their animal friends did not take kindly to being ignored, even with enough grass to keep the four-footed among them alive. As for the chickens, they always managed to survive.

Not even glancing in the direction of what had once been the house, they walked to the barn and opened its wide doors. Heather noticed all the water troughs, both inside the barn and out nearly full.

"At least they've had plenty of water," she said. "Though it doesn't look like they were very thirsty. I'm surprised the troughs aren't empty."

They walked into the darkened barn, still and silent. Ghostly memories of the gathering of a year and a half before rose in their minds' eyes. This very place was so full of life, so full of the Spirit of God moving among his people.

Now the slanted beams of light pouring in from the east, dust particles bouncing on the sun's thin rays, seemed desperately trying to enflame the emptiness with life. But there was no life left.

"His spirit is here," said Todd softly. "That's why I need to be here. I *want* to be here. I don't think I can be at peace, for a while at least, unless I'm here."

"Are the old bunk rooms in back fit to live in?" asked Heather.

"I don't even know. I only saw them once when David was showing me around. They're mostly full of junk. Let's go have a look."

He led the way deep into the darkest part of the barn, through a wide door into the storage area where much of the small equipment was kept. Brushing away cobwebs and threading their way through stacks of lumber, rusting old implements, and cabinets containing paint cans and small tools and a century's miscellany of farm life, they came to two doors opening out of the back of the storage room.

"Here we are," said Todd, leading Heather through the door on the right. "Looks like no one's been in here in decades," he said, squinting in the darkness as their phone lights panned around in the dark.

"Doesn't look like much of a bunkhouse," said Heather. "It's too full of junk. You can't stay here!"

They stood, gazing about as their eyes adjusted. It was deathly quiet, the wood floor thick-packed with the accumulated straw and dirt of many years. In this corner of the huge barn, not even the few rays managing to penetrate gave enough light to see clearly.

Suddenly a creaking behind them split the silence.

Heather's heart leapt into her throat.

They spun toward the sound. In the corner of the room, movement caught their eyes. Something beneath it was disturbing the straw on the floor.

In terror, Heather clutched at Todd's arm and began to back away. The day of her snakebite rushed back upon her. With it came a lifetime fear of wild animals suddenly frightened out of their hiding places. Especially giant rattlers!

Below the blanket of straw, the floor was moving!

Dust flew into the air. A 3 x 3–foot trapdoor, hinged on one side, slowly lifted. Light from below burst into the room.

Muffled steps sounded as first a head, then shoulders, and finally the torso of a man's figure emerged. He threw back the lid of the clandestine tunnel into the earth and climbed up out of his hiding place.

"David!" shrieked Heather, running forward to embrace the poor man before he could even get his feet well planted on the surface of the barn floor.

Academia in the United States is famous for supporting the Soviet system. This is a great paradox, when the capitalist world supports and actively nourishes its own destructor. Maharishi Mahesh Yogi was a spiritual leader, or a charlatan, depending on your point of view. The Beatles were trained at his ashram in India. Mia Farrow and other useful idiots from Hollywood followed. They returned to the United States zonked with marijuana, hashish, and crazy ideas of meditation: Just sit down, look at your navel and meditate. Due to some strange logic and cosmic vibration, things will turn out all right by themselves. This is exactly what Marxist–Leninist propaganda wants—to distract Americans into believing in nonexistent global harmony. Obviously, it's more beneficial for the Soviet Union to have Americans duped with such nonsense so it can capitalize on the naïveté and stupidity of Americans.

These are the useful idiots—a term attributed to Lenin of academics, intellectuals, and students as the catalyst for the ideological subversion of America—dissidents like Jane Fonda and civil rights defenders who idealistically believe in the beauty of Soviet Communism. They are all instrumental in the subversion and destabilization of America.

The main emphasis of the KGB is not intelligence, but in what we call ideological subversion or psychological warfare, changing America's perception of reality. It's a great brainwashing process which goes very slow.

The first is to educate students in your country with communist ideology, pumping Marxist–Leninist ideas into their soft heads without being challenged or counterbalanced by the basic values of Americanism. Even if you expose them to authentic information, even if you prove that white is white and black is black, you still cannot change their basic perceptions. The facts tell them nothing. Even if I shower them with information, with authentic proof, they will refuse to believe it.

The next stage is the destabilization of America's economy, foreign relations, and defense systems. In such sensitive areas, the infiltration of Marxist–Leninist ideas in the United States is unbelievable. I could never have believed it when I landed in this part of the world that the process would go so fast.

The next stage is to precipitate a crisis with a violent change of power. This is what will happen in the United States if you allow these fools to promise a paradise on Earth.

Most Americans think they are living in peacetime. This is false. The United States is in a state of war—undeclared total war against the basic principles and foundations of the American system. The time bomb is ticking. A disaster is coming closer when you will say goodbye to your freedom. Understand what is going on. You have precious little time to save yourself. Americans don't like to listen to things which are unpleasant, but I have defected to tell you that it's a question of the survival of the American system.

—Yuri Alexandrovich Bezmenov

Edited and adapted excerpts from the 1984 interview between Soviet defector Bezmenov and with G. Edward Griffin

PART 5

AMERICA TAKES A RADICAL TURN

2057

FOUR YEARS AND THREE MONTHS LATER

88

The Stealth Coup Is Realized

January 2057

WHAT JEFFERSON Rhodes, president of the United States for another minute or two, was thinking as he watched his two terms drawing to a close, it was impossible to say. After his resounding reelection four years earlier and a second term boasting 70 percent approval ratings, he wistfully wished a third term might be possible. But it could not be. The torch must be passed.

Basking in the glow of the world's approbation, he little perceived that for eight years he had been a pawn in the hands of forces bigger than he could conceive of—not Palladium alone, nor the progressivism that had used him, as it had two generations of presidents before him, to advance its God-mocking agenda.

Deeper than both, and of more sinister roots than the blindly foolish liberal movement it would soon sweep away, rose the specter of the ancient Prophet's grand vision of conquest. Yet that dark shadow was unseen, its danger unfathomed, by the very nation it was poised to swallow into its centuries-long design.

The new president had been elected by the same miscalculation that swept a dangerous political neophyte into office in 2008, a majority of Americans showing their tolerance and openness for diversity with no clue that they had allowed a Trojan horse to infiltrate their country. America would never be America again. It might continue to go by that name for a season. But never again would it be what it had once been.

Like Clinton and Obama and a succession of liberal presidents after them, Jefferson Rhodes had no conception of what he had done to undermine the fabric of America, making it ripe for the invisible coup now at hand. Beside him stood the architect who would don the Prophet's mantle and usher in a new era in the history of the world whose momentum only Armageddon could likely stop.

Whether the Almighty would intervene was a question in the months and years ahead that would occupy the books, sermons, and prognostications of an increasing number of self-appointed prophetic gurus. They would likely, however, be as unseeing of history's eternal themes as had been their prophetic predecessors for a century.

Rhodes glanced to his side at the man standing three inches taller and gazing straight ahead, his expression stoic, at the multitude spread out across the Mall.

The Chief Justice of the Supreme Court stepped forward in front of both men to administer the oath of office. The vice president laid his hand on the leather-bound book held in front of him, a seventeenth-century copy of the Koran. Following the lead of the chief justice, he began:

"I, Hamad Mohammed Bahram, do solemnly affirm that I will faithfully execute the office of President of the United States . . ."

Where he watched among congressional, cabinet, and other dignitaries, the venom on Mike Bardolf's face was impossible to hide. Not only had Rhodes passed over him for the VP slot on the '52 ticket four years ago going into his second term, Bahram led him throughout the previous spring in the primaries leading up to the Democrat nomination. The man used his years as vice president to carry out a deviously effective public relations snow job, positioning himself as Rhodes's undisputed heir apparent.

Bardolf and Bahram hated each other, not as mere political rivals, but as two alpha males, both of whom knew that only one of them could survive at 1600 Pennsylvania Avenue. Watching Bahram's speech accepting the nomination at the convention the previous August, Mike knew that his days at the highest echelons of power, the unseen crafter of Viktor Domokos's sweeping vision and progressivism's final triumph, were over.

Nor had he long to wait after the election for it to be made official. He was told by Bahram days later that there would be no place for him in the new administration. It would be appreciated, he added, if he would vacate his office in the Manor well before inauguration day, the sooner the better.

Mike's seething reflections only made the words over the loudspeakers all the more bitter to hear.

". . . to the best of my ability, preserve, protect and defend the Constitution of the United States . . . *so help me Allah.*"

The single word-change in the final invoking of the deity, after a brief intentional pause, was only one of the new president's gambles on this day. The nation's previous nominally Muslim presidents had kept to the traditional *God* when taking the oath. Though none used a Bible, they had not gone so far as to introduce the Koran into the proceedings. On this day, the crowd did not see the Koran. But the *Allah* jolted many ears.

It was obvious that a new era in America had dawned.

Then it was done. After rounds of handshaking, congratulations, and cheers from the crowd, new President Bahram began his inaugural address.

That he was not the first Muslim to occupy the Oval Office raised no more qualms in the nation's collective consciousness than it had the previous November, when it had given him an enormous landslide victory.

After half an hour of platitudes that sounded like a rewrite of his predecessor's two boring inaugural speeches, the new president paused.

Suddenly over huge loudspeakers heard from the Capitol to the Presidential Manor and throughout the Mall, came the high piercing intonation of Islam's public call to prayer. The huge crowd listened, surprised but quiet and respectful. When the loudspeakers went silent, still the throng waited, not quite sure what to think.

"What you have just heard," Bahram said, his deep penetrating voice echoing over the multitude, "is called the *Adhan,* or call to prayer, for Muslims. I know many of you and many in the country do not profess the Islamic faith. But prayer is good, no matter to whom we pray. It is my hope that by installing minarets in our major cities, and throughout the capital—which will comprise my first executive order today—we will come together as a people to pray.

"For those of you without a specific faith of your own, let me explain and teach you the words you have just heard. They recite the core principles of Islam, though of course you are free to personalize them to suit your own beliefs.

"First in Arabic:

"*Allahu Akbar, Allahu Akbar, Allahu Akbar, Allahu Akbar, Allahu Akbar. Ash-hadu an la ilaha illa Allah, Ash-hadu an la ilaha illa Allah, Ash-hadu an la ilaha illa Allah. Ash-hadu anna Muhammadan, Rasulu Allah, Ash-hadu anna Muhammadan, Rasulu Allah, Ash-hadu anna Muhammadan, Rasulu Allah. Hayya 'ala-s-Salah, Hayya 'ala-s-Salah, Hayya 'ala-s-Salah. Hayya 'ala-l-Falah, Hayya 'ala-l-Falah, Hayya 'ala-l-Falah. Allahu Akbar, Allahu Akbar, Allahu Akbar. La ilaha illa Allah, La ilaha illa Allah.*

"You will see all the phrases are repeated. The seven individual phrases are translated as follows: *Allah is most great. I testify that there is no god but Allah. I testify that Mohammed is the messenger of Allah. Come to the prayer. Come to salvation. Allah is most great. There is no god but Allah.*

"Now I ask you Muslims here today to join me in reciting the Adhan. The rest of you I hope will join along as you are able and will come to know the words of our prayer and make it your own."

89

Dangerous Defection

1984

SEVENTY-TWO YEARS EARLIER

FOUR TOP-RANKING officials of the USSR—the chairman, defense minister, and the heads of the KGB and its press agency *Novosti*—were summoned by Foreign Minister Andrei Gromyko for a private meeting in the Kremlin in the inner sanctum of the general secretary's office.

"So what is this all about, Andrei," said Konstantin Chernenko, general secretary of the Communist Party of the Soviet Union. "You said it was urgent."

"It is about our nemesis Yuri Bezmenov," replied Gromyko. "According to my agents in the United States, he has surfaced."

"Where?"

"It turns out he has been living in Canada under the cover name assigned by the RCMP, Tomas D. Schuman. My sources have traced him to the US, though his exact whereabouts is unknown."

"Can we take him out? You have enough agents in the US, to find him, Viktor," said Chernenko, turning to the head of the KGB, Viktor Chebrikov. "Send over that young assassin you were telling me about—Putin, wasn't it?"

"It may be too late for that, Comrade Chairman," said Gromyko. "Bezmenov has just concluded a major television interview. It is more than troubling—it is explosive."

"In what way?"

"He publicly exposes our entire strategy to infiltrate the American Left. If his interview gets into the mainstream American media, it could set our objectives back decades."

"What did he say?" asked Defense Minister Dmitry Ustinov.

"He has laid bare our four-phase agenda of ideological subversion."

Pavel Naumov, head of *Novosti,* chuckled.

"I hardly think it a laughing matter, Pavel."

"Have you forgotten what Comrade Lenin said about useful idiots? He could not more perfectly have anticipated the America of the late twentieth century. American academia and its student population of hippies will pay no attention to his warnings. Neither will the masses. They are all useful idiots together. That is why we make use of them to achieve our objectives. I strongly counsel against Bezmenov's assassination. That would only focus undue attention on his interview."

"But there must be reprisals or we could face wholesale defections."

"Relax. It will blow over. It will change nothing. Let their left-wing zealots spout their noble ideals while the moral fabric of America crumbles. Soon they will not know right from wrong and won't care. They will never see their danger. The four stages of our program will continue. We can be patient. The brainwashing will have its result. America will fall into our lap without need of your tanks, guns, or ICBMs, Dmitry," Naumov added, glancing toward the defense minister. "The American Left will bring about its own collapse."

"Are you not overly optimistic?" said the general secretary.

"Not at all. Everything is working to perfection. We will continue to use their student protesters, their Malcolm X and Angela Davis, their leftist intellectuals and professors and feminists—useful idiots exactly as Comrade Lenin said. Their Reagan is no idiot. He *understands*. But he is an anomaly. His warnings about our strategy, along with Bezmenov's, will fade and be forgotten. Take my word for it, Andrei, they will elect a black man president, and elect communists to their Congress in our lifetimes. Democracy will kill itself. Communism will survive and be victorious in the end."

90

The World Will Tremble

January 2057

IN A private enclave of the Standing Committee of the Political Bureau of the Central Committee of the Communist Party of China and the National People's Congress, the seven most senior members of the state council were engaged in momentous and confidential discussions. On today's agenda was their decades-long master plan for the takeover of the United States.

The mandated purpose of the Committee was to set policy for the larger Politburo. Chinese Premier Jiang, also General Secretary of the Central Committee, had called the private meeting immediately at the conclusion of the inaugural speech of the new US president which he had watched live on television two weeks earlier.

In those moments, Jiang realized, everything changed. President Rhodes had personally invited him as a special guest of honor to his inaugural fete on Seattle's Bainbridge Island seven years earlier. No invitation had been forthcoming on this occasion from incoming President Bahram.

It was not being snubbed for the inauguration that concerned him. None of the heads of state of America's European allies had been invited. What worried him was what the change portended. He had not been sufficiently wary of Bahram, nor mindful of the potential danger his election could mean to their plans.

Suddenly it was all too clear. He had been caught unprepared. He had allowed himself to grow confident by years of easily manipulating

American presidents and their policies to China's advantage. With Bahram's election, a sea change had taken place he had not anticipated.

As today's meeting got underway, Jiang hoped his six colleagues on the Committee had had time to gather the information he had assigned them. On his part, he had accumulated several files of illuminating data—illuminating and alarming. He was not a man frightened by many things in the world. He ceased being frightened of America once Trump faded from the scene. But this man Bahram *did* frighten him.

"As I shared with each of you privately," Jiang was saying, "I fear we have allowed ourselves to become complacent. We have assumed that our long-term strategy for infiltrating the American economy would proceed invisibly and successfully without interruption. America's complacency and the ease with which we have acquired such a large percentage of its land, manufacturing, banking, energy, media, and technological holdings, has lulled us into the assumption that our ultimate victory was assured. This supposition was bolstered by our 85 percent control of American goods and services and the fact we hold 90 percent of America's two hundred trillion–dollar debt. We could collapse the entire American system overnight with one signature in my hand calling that debt due. Such has not been our intent but rather to join the powerful economic American engine with our own and this we have successfully done."

He paused and glanced around the table. His expression was not one of triumph over the successes he had just summarized but of grave concern.

"It is suddenly obvious, however," he went on, "that all this is not enough. We have failed to consider what in the end may be an even more strategic factor in the eventual domination of America. We have not paid sufficient attention to winning the minds and affections, and the religious and psychological devotion of the American *people*. Over the last century we have gained control of their *systems*. But we have not won their *hearts*.

"It is now clear that in that all-important battleground, Islam has beaten us, as the Americans might say, at our own game of stealth infiltration. While we have been buying land and taking over businesses, technology, media, manufacturing, Islam has been infiltrating hearts and minds. As I watched the inauguration of the new US president, it suddenly dawned on me that Islam's strategy is global in a way I had not foreseen. While we have focused upon America to our east, we have not sufficiently recognized the more serious threat has been growing in the west.

"Islam's stealth global strategy is aimed at us too!

"I believe that we must entirely rethink our strategy. We have to recognize that all nations are stealth targets for Islam's global domination. That includes the People's Republic of China. We must take steps to prevent it taking us over from within as invisibly as they are now poised to complete their takeover of America."

He turned to his right.

"Comrade Zhao, do you have those statistics I asked you to gather?"

"I do, Comrade Chairman," replied Zhao.

"What is the current percentage of Muslims in China?

"Approximately 5 percent."

"How many Muslims does that make in China today?

"Approximately 80,000,000."

"That is a staggering number. And ten years ago?"

"The percentage was only 3 percent"

"And at the beginning of the century?"

"It held steady at about 1.5 percent until about 2020 and then gradually began to grow."

"So Islam is growing in China?"

"*Very* rapidly."

"And Comrade Liu, do you have the corresponding birth rates?"

"The birth rate among non-Muslim Chinese women is two point zero births per woman. Among Muslim women, that rate is just under three births per woman."

"No wonder Islam is on the march in China. And the Muslim birth rate worldwide?

"It varies from country to country, but it ranges between two point zero and three births per woman. Islam is growing worldwide in births far more rapidly than any other religious or demographic group. Muslims account for some 60 percent of all world births. Islam is expanding exponentially everywhere."

"How do those statistics compare with trends in the United States?" asked Chairman Jiang.

"It is much the same story, though with an even greater acceleration."

"Please explain."

"In 1950, there were fewer than 27,000 Muslims in the United States. By 2000, that number had risen to nearly three million. After 9/11, remarkably there was a spike in American favorability toward Islam, such that the Muslim population had doubled by 2025. All the while Christianity was in steep decline."

"And today?"

"Approximately 17 percent of Americans identify as Christians, while an incredible 43 percent identify as Muslim. Among those who identify as having no religious affiliation, Christianity has 15 percent favorability, while Islam boasts between 70 percent and 75 percent favorability."

"These are stunning statistics. Thank you, Comrade Zhao. It becomes clear why Mr. Bahram is the new US president."

The Chairman paused.

"These statistics do not lie," he said after a moment. "If these trends continue, all the nations of the world will tremble at the global power of Islam. We have to make sure China stands alone and that we are not overrun as the Americans have been. If it takes military might to do so, we must not ignore that reality.

"That is why I firmly believe that our global strategy must change. We must be prepared for war against militant Islam. Its takeover of the United States did not require a full military jihad because their stealth tactics were shrewd and successful. But Islam's history is one of military jihad when other measures do not succeed. We must prepare ourselves to prevent the success of Islam's global jihad of both stealth *and* open warfare if it comes to that.

He turned to the man in full military attire to his left.

"General Wang," he began seriously, "what I am about to say must never leave this room." He paused and glanced at the others, then back to the general. "I want you to begin clandestine strategic planning," he went on. "I am speaking of a revised potential military objective in the direction of Iran."

A few sharp intakes of surprise went around the table.

Ignoring them, Jiang continued. "What are your current deployable numbers, General?"

"Six million."

"And America and Russia?"

"One million and three million."

"With our superiority, you should easily be able to disguise gradual changes toward alternate first strike objectives."

"Do you seriously think, Comrade Chairman," said Wang, "that Iran poses such a threat?"

"I do. The event in St. Louis demonstrates their willingness to employ tactical nuclear weaponry. We must be prepared."

"It has not been ascertained that the Iranian government was behind the attack."

"Perhaps not. But Bahram was involved, we can be assured of that. It placed him in the presidency."

"He would not dare move militarily against China—not with America's feeble military in such decline."

"Not overtly, nor soon. If my instincts are correct, however, it may become necessary for us to make a first move before a Muslim is sitting in my chair and China has been taken over from within just as has America. It is well known that Islam's design was always to topple the West. We must now recognize that its jihadist strategy is broader. It is global. The time will come when China will also be in Islam's crosshairs. We must be attentive to the subtle shift in the world balance of power that Bahram's election may signify."

The discussion around the table became animated.

"You have said little, Comrade Wu," said the chairman at length, turning to China's Minister of Banking and Finance.

"You have given us much to think about, Comrade Chairman," replied Wu. "I am only quiet in considering the financial impact of these changes. But I am confident, with our control over America's major sectors, that we could, in a sense, successfully wage a two-pronged war—financial and military—even against an Islamic America."

91

The Sharia Declaration

2057

SEATED AT the Obama desk in the Oval Office in the Presidential Manor, President Hamad Bahram perused the document laid out before him. The desk was fitting, he thought. More than any other man, Obama had paved the way to make this historic day possible.

No one but he would ever see these papers he had been working on, revising and adding, since the day Jefferson Rhodes selected him his running mate. On that day he had known that the presidency would ultimately be his. It would require finesse and continued stealth to bring it all to fruition. The ancient jihad had taken a giant stride forward on this day. But there was still much to do.

Its ultimate objectives, here and globally, must remain hidden a while longer while Islam continued to multiply in China, South America, Russia, Africa, and Europe. The chessboard of Islam's ultimate victory spread around the entire planet. Its intricate pieces had to be positioned at the right place and time and under the right circumstances, exactly as he had successfully engineered here.

South America and Africa were already in his camp. Russia remained fraught with questions. China could prove most difficult of all. He hoped no more St. Louis events would be necessary in the near future, but he was not ready to rule them out. All that would come later per the *Terminus*. Though North Korea and its Kim dynasty of imbeciles was a constant irritant and might eventually simply have to be eliminated.

First, he had to consolidate his hold in the United States. That entailed introducing the principles of Sharia so gradually they would go down easily in the gullible American mind.

For that he would depend on his able vice president, Shelly Jones. He had earmarked her for the second slot as much for her name as her political acumen. Her background, speech, family, education, and political history were as American as apple pie. Everything about her would be beyond suspicion. The moment he heard that the congresswoman from Minnesota had converted to Islam, he had been watching her. Scheduling a private meeting last year, assessing how far she was willing to go to fulfill Islam's hidden jihad, he had been more than satisfied.

She was the perfect prototypical "American" to gently educate the nation's women about the role of women in Islam. She would head off progressive and feminist objections by presenting it as a joyful role not a subservient one—the only true path to fulfillment. She would win women over by the force of her personality and enthusiasm for new ways, innocuously introducing the hijab and a few other Islamic customs. Who would argue with a woman named *Jones*? Hard core feminists might raise a ruckus for a while but their leaders would be identified, dealt with, and their voices silenced. Permanently.

Bahram had used his position as vice president to put most aspects of his master plan into place on the chessboard, identifying dozens of visible born-and-bred American Muslims like Jones who would be loyal to him, ready at a moment's notice to become active pieces moving in concert toward checkmate. He had never forgotten the words of former New York Imam Siraj Wahhaj from late in the previous century, "If six or eight million Muslims unite in America, the country will come to us." They had easily ten times that number now. The ultimate checkmate was as good as a *fait accompli.*

Thanks to the forerunning influence of the "Squad" back in the 2020s, he had a majority of Muslims and Muslim sympathizers in both houses of Congress, along with four pro-Muslim Supreme Court justices.

Meanwhile, he continued to develop his secret Sharia Declaration outlining his full strategic agenda, including short-term, intermediate, and the long-term objectives embodied in *The Qur'an Terminus* he had shared with Jones a few months earlier. No other eyes but hers had seen the *Terminus*. He needed to be sure she was fully committed.

Not wanting to be a mere figurehead, he asked Rhodes a few months into his second term to be given carte blanche to bring to fruition a comprehensive peace accord in the Middle East. With the collapse of Trump's peace initiative after Trump's death, status quo tensions and animosities returned. The president had no objection. Thus he had used his vice presidential platform as a smokescreen for travel to the capitals in the Middle East, secretly drawing leaders from other Arab nations into his orbit, hinting that the elimination of Israel would be at the top of his priorities once he was in occupation of the Oval Office.

It was obvious that progressivism as a political and cultural force in America had to be eliminated as essential to Sharia law. Christianity was the far more dangerous threat. But it was as good as dead already. US liberalism, however, was still thriving and had to be systematically extricated from the American landscape. The progressives would never know what hit them until it was too late.

He had to smile at the simplicity of his stealth strategy, the reality that at its root progressivism was a daring con perpetrated on the unthinking masses who would go where they were led and believe what they were told to believe. They had believed liberalism's lies for nearly a century. They had been brainwashed about the evils of Christianity, and with the idiocy of the LGBTQ agenda. The country went along though 90 percent of the people didn't believe a word of it. They had duped four generations of Americans into accepting homosexuality, same-sex marriage, and gender choice as normal. None of the fools bothered to ask how a civilization believing such lunacy could sustain itself.

Creating the illusion that half the country was gay or lesbian or trans, the masses were subtly pressured to go along. They must demonstrate that they were good and open-minded people. In reality the figure was less than 5 percent, possibly half that. The con had allowed a miniscule population of deviants to control the narrative of the cultural agenda and destroy the fabric of the nation.

Now it was his turn. He would reeducate that same gullible 95 percent to accept Sharia law. Progressivism had eliminated Christianity as a cultural force—Islam's most feared enemy, the only enemy with the power to defeat Islam. As a result, he only had to fight the battle on one front not two.

The gay minority would be his first major target. After the LGBTQ voice was silenced and with Shelly skillfully reeducating women about their role, gradually other elements of Sharia would follow.

He identified Northampton, Massachusetts, and Burlington, Vermont—two of the country's most liberal small cities—as future gay utopias to which he would invite all groups under the LGBTQ umbrella. There they could live in perfect freedom. All who relocated there would be offered perks and financial incentives and tax breaks. Non-gays would be equally compensated to relocate elsewhere, with the ultimate aim of both entire cities being LGBTQ friendly.

When the announcement was made during his second month in office, new president Bahram was hailed by the LGBTQ world as a worthy successor to the enlightened administration of President Rhodes. Along with the announcement, Bahram issued an executive order that 2057 IRS forms would include LGBTQ preference boxes, each with a designated minority tax credit which would be applied, along with a 50 percent tax credit for all same-sex married couples whether filing individually or jointly.

He explained this in a major press conference. In order to make certain that all individuals identifying as LGBTQ were treated equitably and were provided all the services and financial benefits due them under the Minorities Act of 2043, it was necessary to compile a national data base of all LGBTQ individuals. The gay community was effusive in its praise, never pausing to consider the potential sinister implications of such a file of names.

The transition to Sharia would not be without bumps along the way. But progressivism had shown how easily the masses could be made to believe anything.

If we were united and strong, we'd elect our own emir and give allegiance to him . . . if six or eight million Muslims unite in America, the country will come to us.

—New York Imam Siraj Wahhaj

(Served as a character witness for the mastermind of the 1993 World Trade Center bombing)

☆ ☆ ☆

We are now fifty years into the [Muslim] Brotherhood's 100-year plan to entrench themselves into key institutions in the United States and other Western societies to undermine and destroy our democracy. . . . This is . . . a transnational ideological project that adapts itself to Western systems while working to undermine them. The Brotherhood has learned to use the very freedoms of democracy as tools to erode it from within, exploiting the tolerance and openness of liberal societies as strategic vulnerabilities.

—Dr. Charles Asher Small

Founding director of the Institute for the Study of Global Antisemitism and Policy, 2025

PART 6

A NATION REMADE

2052–2057

FOUR YEARS EARLIER

92

The Second Rhodes Term

October–November 2052

PRESIDENT RHODES'S delay in filling the vice presidential slot on his ticket after the death of then-VP Elizabeth Wickes Hardy in the St. Louis bombing was of no great concern for his reelection bid of 2052. With the GOP a distant memory, his victory was a foregone conclusion no matter who was on the Democrat ticket. The few printed ballots in use had already gone out, but everyone knew Hardy would be replaced.

That he waited until a week before the election was more theater than anything. He decided on Hamad Bahram soon after the bombing. But he wanted to forestall any unpleasantness with Mike Bardolf until as close to the election as possible. Mike was a powerful man. He didn't want him causing trouble.

With the country still reeling from the nuclear attack on American soil, the Rhodes-Bahram ticket swept into office with 70 percent of the vote over Senator Dindinger of Texas, whose reluctance to run and refusal to campaign carried through the election. Even his home state gave him only 32 percent of their vote.

Rhodes did his best to placate Mike, assuring him that he would retain his Presidential Manor office and would be given increased power during their second term. He tried to soften what he knew Mike considered a profound insult by reminding him how insignificant most vice presidents turned out to be.

Had either man been clairvoyant enough to read Hamad Bahram's mind, they would have shuddered at how clueless were the president's instincts about both men he considered for the ticket. In truth, in spite of their years together, he knew Mike no better than he knew Bahram.

☆ ☆ ☆

Proceeding with the culmination of the liberal agenda with nothing to hold him back, President Jefferson Rhodes had no inkling, in thus remaking America into a progressive paradise, that he was in fact laying the foundation for its ultimate *unmaking*. With every new triumph, as he considered them, waiting in the wings his vice president smiled inwardly. His titular boss was perfectly aligning all the dominos. When his own time came, they would fall as predictably as clockwork.

The only thing Hamad Bahram truly feared was Christianity. Not pretend Christianity, but the real thing.

Jesus *frightened* him. Not a dashboard Jesus, a dead Jesus on the cross of the Catholics. Not the imaginary Jesus of evangelicals whose teachings they barely lived and whose life they had no desire to emulate.

The *real* Jesus was the only real threat to his plans. His *true* followers—men and women willing to lay down their lives to obey his teachings and emulate his life—represented the only potential force capable of preventing Islam's worldwide domination.

Thanks to the good Mr. Rhodes, however, that threat was nearly gone. Progressivism had done his work on behalf of Islam without knowing it. He only had to keep an eye out for pockets of resurgence, flare-ups of the ancient "gospel passion," as he once heard some fanatical Christians call it. He knew the fool Bardolf had a particular loathing of Christians and was also watching for danger signs. That part of it Bardolf could take care of for him if the need arose.

☆ ☆ ☆

In the aftermath of the St. Louis bombing, investigations produced nothing concrete other than shadowy unsubstantiated links to various terrorist organizations. Mike Bardolf had done his best to link it to the West Coast Christian conspiracy he had been pushing. But Rhodes didn't believe it for a minute. He suspected Mike in the fire that had apparently taken the life of the old Gordon fellow. He shuddered to think that Mike could have gone so far off the rails as that. The shooting at the Christian college connected with Mark's group was equally worrying. In the president's darkest moments, the thought even crossed his mind that Mike might have orchestrated the St. Louis bombing in order to implicate Mark's group. There were times he wondered what Mike might actually be capable of.

But Rhodes didn't ask too many questions, though he made it clear to Mike to lay off the Christian conspiracy talk and take no more action against any Christian group.

By the time of the election, central St. Louis was well on its way toward being rebuilt. The city and nation would recover. But the country remained in shock to know that terrorism could strike a major blow anytime. Bahram's stepping up with such cool aplomb and handling the fast-tracked recovery plans for rebuilding the city with such efficiency, he was the obvious choice to replace the unfortunate Ms. Wickes Hardy.

With his second term secure, Rhodes lost interest in Mike's obsession with Christians. That outspoken Senator Dindinger had been so soundly defeated told him that Mike had been making too much of the Christian threat. Congressman Nason, one of the Marshall group's politicos, had also been defeated for reelection. He hadn't heard so much as a peep from any of the principal players in the thing—Jansen, Reyburn, Linda, Mark, the Marshall fellow.

The whole conspiracy notion had been blown out of proportion. He shouldn't have been so worried. Let them have their meetings and gatherings, he thought. No one cared.

93

The Fellowship Rebounds

Early 2053

ENTHUSIASM RAN high when word began to circulate through the network of BCL groups around the country via Court and Sheila Masters's newsletter that another gathering was scheduled in the spring of 2053 at the Circle F ranch in Grass Valley.

After the shocking events that had taken place at the previous gathering a year and a half earlier, followed by the shooting at Timothy's Jessup lectures and the fire that had destroyed the Bar JG ranch house and, everyone assumed, caused David Gordon's death, there had been great uncertainty about the future of the fellowship.

The fire was immediately identified by the authorities as arson, but no leads surfaced nor arrests made. It was obvious to everyone connected with the BCL fellowship, however, that they were under attack. Ever since the raid in April of 2051, every home school family in the BCL network was terrified they could be next.

Announcement of another gathering was therefore greeted with a curious mingling of conflicting emotions. Most were relieved to realize that the fellowship was to all appearances still alive and well. Their enthusiasm, however, was tempered by some trepidation that there remained a possibility of a repeat of what had happened last time.

Thankfully, with the election past and Jefferson Rhodes riding high, the conspiracy talk died out. Anticipation was heightened by two additional pieces of information that went out in January's edition of *Master's Helps Newsletter.*

The first announced that the gathering would also be the occasion for the wedding of Stirling Marshall's granddaughter Heather Marshall to Todd Stewart, to which all were invited.

To this was added the announcement that on the day following the ceremony, those capable of wielding a hammer or saw or who could carry boards or help cook meals, were invited to participate in an old-fashioned "house raising" at the Bar JG ranch. The debris from the fire had been cleared away. Plans had been drawn and approved according to Todd's specifications as new owner of the ranch. The concrete foundation would be poured and the underground pipes and electrical lines all in place by April.

Formal wedding invitations went out in early February. The invitation list included President Rhodes and his wife, Vice President Bahram, Justice Linda Trent, and a number of other Washington dignitaries whom Mark had met during his brief tenure on the president's Religion Commission. Invitations had also been sent to some of Todd's former colleagues in the media. If even half the East Coast invitees accepted, the occasion could prove a noteworthy media event with the potential of a brief mention on national news,

Everything possible was done to make sure the event was public and fully out in the open. Nearly a hundred invitations also went out to members of Foothills Gospel Ministries. That list included Edith, Stoddard, and Lionel Holt, and Rev. Anthony Carmichael.

All the while, David remained safely beneath the radar, comfortably ensconced in the underground bunker he had constructed for precisely the purpose of potential persecution to their fellowship. During all the months of his secretive work several years earlier, he'd had no idea that he was creating his own ark of safety, accessible from ranch house and barn, that would save his own life from the very threats he had seen on the horizon.

Until they could learn more about why he had been targeted, it was the consensus of the Marshall-Forster-Stewart triumvirate of leadership that David should remain out of sight and allow the assumption to persist that he had not survived. When and how the truth should be revealed remained a matter of prayer. For now, David's safety was their top priority.

Todd was suitably awed, dumbstruck, and humbled to learn that he had been named David's heir. Though technically David's will would not legally be enforced, its terms, revealed by David's attorney who likewise thought David was dead, were soon known throughout the fellowship.

That Todd, as was supposed, was now the new owner of the Bar JG, it was natural for him to continue the work of the ranch as much as possible on his own—though obviously with Heather's help and that of Mark and Bob Forster. Temporarily staying at the nearby Forster ranch, with Mark's and Robert's help, the storage end of David's barn, which had miraculously survived the windless night of the fire, was remodeled into a modern and serviceable two-bedroom apartment for Todd's use during planning and construction of a new house on the site of the former home built by David's great-grandfather in the early 1900s. Built directly on top of the opening to the underground bunker, the barn "bunkhouse," as it was called, allowed David to spend most of his time above ground as he and Todd got the ranch back in working order. Together they drew up plans for the new ranch house. If visitors happened by other than the Forster and Marshall clans, it was an easy matter for David to disappear back down into the bunker.

No indication of further danger to the group surfaced. The severity of recent events, however—arrests, children taken from their parents, the St. Louis bombing, the shooting at Jessup, the fire—gave clear evidence that a new era had dawned. In addition to making plans for the gathering, the wedding, and the rebuilding of David's house, the discussions during the months of David's isolation were often serious. David, Todd, and Heather were frequently joined in the barn's newly constructed "bunkhouse" for prayer with those few who knew David was still among them—Mark and Grace, Ginger and Craig, Bob and Laura, and Timothy and Jaylene.

Recognizing the reality that there were hundreds, probably thousands, around the world who looked to them for leadership in how Christians should respond to the changing times and the increasing persecutions that were sure to come, their conversations and prayer drew them to consider deep and important questions about what were God's purposes for his people in the days and years ahead. Mark's and

David's unconventional perspectives on prophecy were often part of their bunkhouse discussions.

At the center of their thoughts was the conundrum whether or not they as Christians, and those looking to them for guidance, should make concerted efforts to withdraw from the world in more definite ways. Were isolationist steps called for, or even inevitable—looking for properties or locations where Christians could band together off the grid.

Yet where? What about those for whom such measures were not possible? Most families could not afford to uproot their lives, leave jobs, buy new homes, and undergo the complexities of relocating?

Was escapism the answer?

It was clear—and it always brought laughter and no little amazement that he was able to pull it off under all their noses!—that David had been led, in a sense, to a one-man isolationist response by building his bunker. He could not rationalize having done so other than to say that he had felt the urging to do so. He did not believe in isolationism as a strategy. Yet the bunker had saved his life.

From the bunker, the discussion occasionally returned to David's idea of rebuilding the run-down bunkhouses in the hills used by his grandfather and great-grandfather in the previous century. His idea was not to turn his ranch into a Christian community but to provide safe haven, should the occasion arise, for those in temporary need when danger was imminent, exactly as his bunker had for him.

"In many respects," said David on one occasion, "the remnant will increasingly become an underground Church. I have little doubt of that. Yet we cannot imagine that we can entirely hide from persecution. However, neither should we court it. We need to find ways to be wise as snakes and innocent as doves. I believe that God may have uses to make of this land he has provided in our two ranches—not as an escapist utopia, but perhaps as a place to offer occasional haven, respite, encouragement, and safety."

The consensus seemed to be that special forms of isolation might be called for in unique situations when lives were threatened. The examples of the ancient monasteries of the Middle Ages and the underground Church during the years of Soviet persecution were ever before them.

Lives had been saved and the remnant in the countries behind the Iron Curtain enabled to survive. God's true Church had been forced underground and remained strong with the help of those temporary and imperative measures.

As a global Christian strategy, however, wholesale isolation from the world in scattered survivalist Christian communes was not only impossible, neither was it consistent with Jesus's teaching.

He had said, *Flee to the hills.* Yet Christ's more enduring command, exemplified by his own life, was to engage in discipleship and servanthood with a world and people in need. Balancing the two strategies presented serious Christians with the enigma of the ages. Always, therefore the fundamental question returned to inform their prayers—how to live *in* the world but not be *of* the world.

In the midst of the discussions, David often grew quiet and thoughtful. The others knew deep currents were flowing within him. He had gone through the fire and emerged as a man, though reborn in a sense, yet with one foot on the river's edge—sensing the beckoning of eternity.

More than ever before the others were aware that Stirling Marshall's mantle had passed to his son and his protégé. In awe they realized that in David they were in the presence of a great man—attuned to the eternal whispers of the Spirit—a humble man to whom God may be preparing to reveal a new word to his remnant Church.

94

Invitations Arrive in Washington

WHEN JEFFERSON Rhodes received his personal invitation to the Marshall-Stewart wedding, an uncharacteristic smile of fondness came to his lips.

Well . . . young Stewart, he thought, *good for you. So you're going to marry the girl and cast your lot with all those Christian fanatics. A courageous thing to do. I knew you were something special when I first laid eyes on you. More power to you and the girl, you young rascal.*

His reflections spiraled back through the years to the days of Pine and Pike and his visits to the foothills of California, to Camp Pinecroft and the Forster ranch.

Those were good times. Mark was a good friend. He'd probably misjudged him . . . misjudged the whole thing. Mike Bardolf's suspicions were toxic. He shouldn't have turned on Mark like he did. He regretted it now. He ought to apologize. Mark wasn't such a bad guy.

Even the old duffer Gordon was probably harmless enough. All Mike's ridiculous conspiracy talk. What had he been so worried about? He should never have listened. *The Prophet!* The guy was no prophet. He was just an old man on a ranch who happened to be Mark's neighbor and a Christian.

Too bad about his place. The poor guy. Maybe he'd gotten out, though there was no sign of his having survived. He ought to have sent a sympathy card or some acknowledgment to Mark and his family. He'd have to remember to do that.

And a wedding gift to Stewart and the girl.

He smiled again. Wouldn't that knock them all out of their saddles—for him to *accept* the invitation and show up!

As if reading his mind, his wife walked into his office. She was holding the same invitation that came separately to her.

"I see you got the invitation," said Marcia.

Jeff chuckled. "I was thinking what a stir it would cause for me to accept," he said.

"I want to go, Jeff. I want to see Grace Forster again. Why don't we both go?"

"It was just a fleeting thought. How could I possibly get away? There's no way."

"Who says?"

Jeff shrugged noncommittally.

"I'm sure Bradon will go. Maybe even your mother."

"You're probably right. But I'm not sure I want to be associated with that group."

"Why?"

"You know—they have pretty radical views. It wouldn't look good."

"What are you worried about, Jeff? The election's over. You've got nothing to prove to anyone."

"I'll think about it."

"You've got no objection if I go?"

"And if I did?" smiled Jeff wryly.

"You're right," laughed Marcia. "I'd go anyway!"

☆ ☆ ☆

One of the responses to the invitations was addressed to Heather and Jaylene with *Private* written on the envelope. In spite of the joy of their plans and anticipation of Heather's big day, what they read brought tears and heavy hearts to mother and daughter.

Dear Heather and Jaylene,

You have both been such good friends since I first wrote you what seems like many years ago. I need to confide in you a great grief that has come to my life and ask for your prayers.

From out of the blue, Trevor announced to me last week that he was cutting off ties with you and the BCL fellowship. I knew he had questions about church involvement, especially when I quit attending our church. But that was years ago and I thought he was fine with us pursuing our individual priorities. I had no idea how serious his reservations had become about what David espouses about the institutional church. We have had a new pastor for about a year. He has asked Trevor to become more involved in leadership, but I fear his influence has not been healthy for Trevor.

Last week Trevor told me he believes the BCL group is a cult, and requested that I cut off all further contact. I tried to talk to him, but he said I had to decide between him or the group. He even hinted, if I do not cut off ties with you and start going to church with him every Sunday, that he might leave me.

I cannot believe he would do that. He was visibly angry. He said he would not be married to a woman who was involved in a cult.

I am devastated, as you can imagine. I have never been so heartbroken in my life. He's a completely different person than the man I thought I knew.

Obviously, I will not be able to attend your wedding. I am so sorry to burden you with this. But I felt you needed to know. I love you both, and everyone in the group, so much. Thank you for all you have done for me. I hope God will make it possible for me to see you again sometime.

Please don't write back. Trevor checks all the mail and my emails and texts.

Sincerely,
Violet Langdon.

95

The Wedding Gathering

April 2053

THE APRIL gathering at the Forster ranch, like that of two years earlier, was scheduled for Friday through Sunday. The wedding would take place on Saturday, with a wedding feast to follow. The house raising would get underway on Sunday, with those who could do so staying on a few more days to help get the roof and exterior walls completed.

Todd and Heather would not leave on their honeymoon until the workers were on their way home—whether that was two or three days or a week. Todd was not about to turn down all the help he could get to move the construction as far along as possible. One of Court Masters's friends, Denver Phillips, was coming with Court and Sheila to supervise wiring the house and getting the electrical systems functional.

Once completed, and the walls and roof were secure and the interior was well begun, the newlyweds would be off to Scotland, where Todd had wanted to take Heather from almost the day they met.

The atmosphere was festive as arrivals began pouring in late Friday morning. Knowing the president had been invited eliminated most concerns about reprisals, threats, or arrests. His attendance was doubtful, but that wife, mother, and son would be present added to the anticipation of a joyous weekend.

The occasion proved to be a great BCL reunion. Most of those who had attended the gathering in 2051 determined not to miss this one, with the exception of their international friends. Of those, only the Constables from London and Sievers from Germany were able to make it.

The greetings and tearful reconnections with old friends in the Spirit continued all day Friday. No activities were planned other than hundreds of spontaneous conversations, happy and animated. The only agenda was experiencing the fellowship of one small slice of God's Church, living in the reality of what was a foretaste of eternity when that Church would be revealed in its fullness.

The time was obviously tinged with undercurrents of sadness about David and his ranch, along with the keen reminder that they were living in increasingly dangerous times. Their friends Derrick and Paula Hanson, who had perished in the St. Louis bombing, were also on everyone's minds. They had lost three of their own.

Todd's mother, Theresa, from New Mexico was treated almost as royalty. Unaccustomed to the outpouring of love showered on her, she was overwhelmed into occasional speechlessness, especially to see how greatly her son was loved. Meeting a Supreme Court justice and the country's First Lady only added to her dazed awe. She had stepped into a dream. Throughout the afternoon, her eyes often filled with tears she was unable to account for.

As for David, it was all he could do not to rush out from his imposed sepulcher, rush over to the Circle F, and jump out of his pickup with arms wide to embrace the brothers and sisters he loved. But he submitted to the wisdom of those who cared about him, and knew this was best for now. His face was wet with tears to see the faces and watch the many hugs and reunions taking place a few miles away on his television screen from the cameras Mark had installed about his property.

Given that the grounds had been set up for the wedding, there were no trailers or tents spread about the property on this occasion. With such a momentous event planned for the following day, the exodus from the Circle F began after the outdoor potluck supper at 5:00. By 7:30 or 8:00 most had returned to their homes and motels, though a few quiet conversations continued for several more hours.

Todd invited his mother to bunk with him in the newly outfitted Bar JG barn-apartment, which he assured her was modern and imminently comfortable. She said she would rather book a motel in town. In spite of his protestations to the contrary, she insisted that he should not spend the night before his wedding having to worry about his mother.

He therefore returned to his "bunkhouse," as was thought, to spend Friday evening alone, but in fact to spend it in lively conversation and laughter with his adoptive mentor-father as he recounted to David the events of the afternoon.

Heather spent the evening and night with her parents in the home where she had grown up in Roseville. Never having expected such a day, Timothy and Jaylene were feeling none of the pangs of coming separation from the daughter they loved, only joyful thankfulness that God had brought such a young man of character into their lives who had fallen in love with their daughter.

All evening, mother and daughter fussed with Heather's dress and the many feminine details of her trousseau that suddenly loomed so important in the midst of Heather's excited nervousness, while Timothy kibitzed from the sidelines.

☆ ☆ ☆

On Saturday morning, keeping to protocol, Heather remained in Roseville, dressing and getting ready with her mother, until driving to Grass Valley—Jaylene in her new burgundy and white dress, Timothy dignified in his tux—about 11:00. Heather was quickly spirited away by Ginger, her maid of honor, into the depths of the Forster house. There she would be kept out of sight, with Grace and Jaylene coming and going and with endless minor adjustments to coiffure, dress, shoes, bouquet, and all the rest, until the moment of truth arrived at noon.

Todd's preparations, meanwhile—involving all the intricacies of getting a tall man into his tuxedo and his tie and cummerbund and other paraphernalia just right—remained under the supervision of Mark, Timothy, and David at the Bar JG bunkhouse. Though he would have to watch the ceremony on his monitor, David was able to enter into the joy of the preparations and send Todd off with his blessings. As he watched the three men go, David's eyes glistened with thankfulness. God had not chosen to give him a wife. But in these latter years he had honored him with a treasured son of the heart.

Upon their arrival at the Forster ranch, sans David, Todd was whisked away to another room in the house, where, with Theresa and his best man, Bradon Rhodes, in attendance, he awaited the zero hour.

Outside, Timothy as father of the bride and unofficial host of the day, greeted the flood of arrivals, aided by Craig and Dewitt West gradually showing the guests to their seats. A surprising number of local RSVPs had been received from members of Foothills for the Saturday ceremony. Timothy arranged for the catering service handling the afternoon meal also to supply three hundred folding chairs which were set up with a carpeted aisle down their center, spreading away from the house.

Word had gone out to the BCL for string musicians to identify themselves. With music for the "Wedding March," "Pachelbel's Canon," and several other classical pieces sent out ahead of time and practiced among them by video link, the string sextet comprised of Clarence Nason, Harriet Jansen, Regina Reyburn, Sarah Gardner, Sheila Masters, and Geoffrey Powell, seated to the right of the raised altar overspread with arched arbor, began playing at 11:45.

Seated in the first several rows were Harvey Jansen, with an empty chair beside him where Harriet would join him; Charles Reyburn likewise beside an empty chair for his wife; Linda Trent with her husband Cameron; Marcia and Sandra Rhodes, wife and mother of the president, respectively; Eloise and Truman Hutchins, Deidra Hutchins, Fynn and Monika Sievers, Richard and Jessica Constable, Gerald and Rebecca Stevens, and the Gardners, Powells, Nasons, Dindingers, and Masters, with more than two hundred locals and guests from around the country spread out behind them.

At five minutes before noon, with Theresa Stewart on his arm, Craig Forster brought the mother of the groom down the center aisle and seated her in the front row. Two minutes later he returned with Jaylene Marshall, beaming as he seated her opposite Theresa next to Timothy's four brothers and sisters and their spouses.

At twelve o'clock on the dot, Mark, Todd, and Bradon emerged from the house, walked down the aisle and took their places on the platform. They turned to face the assembly. The music stilled. Silence overspread the ranch.

Seeing the door of the house open, unofficial concert mistress Regina Reyburn nodded and the "Wedding March" began. Ginger Forster in her yellow floor-length dress, clutching a bouquet of white roses, descended from the porch and slowly began her measured walk along the carpeted aisle. Behind her, Timothy came out of the house with Heather on his arm and followed onto the carpet. Heather's white dress, exquisitely tailored, could not technically be called a gown with its old-fashioned Western style. Its lace, trim, and fringe on the sleeves would have been entirely fitting with boots and cowboy hat, though she agreed to short-heeled pumps and a small tasteful shoulder length veil though nothing covered her radiant face.

Todd's heart nearly leapt into his throat at the sight. He had to blink hard to keep the tears in his eyes from overflowing. Heather's calm, happy, peaceful expression was breathtaking. Her radiant smile glowed as if completing and fulfilling at this moment what he had beheld in its incipient form on the shores of Puget Sound. He knew it was a smile meant for him.

As the bride and her father passed, the guests slowly rose. They continued to the front, then stopped. Timothy took Heather's hand and helped her up onto the raised platform, then stepped back. To his right and left, Jaylene and Theresa remained standing as the crowd sat. The two women stepped into the aisle beside Timothy.

"My dear friends, and friends of Todd and Heather," began Mark, "we have come here today to celebrate an occasion of great joy. Who gives this man and woman to be married to each other?"

"We do," answered Theresa, Timothy, and Jaylene in unison, then resumed their seats.

Heather stepped forward to Todd's side and turned to face their guests.

"On behalf of our two guests of honor, welcome to you all," Mark continued. "They wanted me to tell you that they are honored for you to share this day with them and that—"

In the distance the long mournful low of a cow echoed over the scene.

Laughter erupted through the crowd.

"You see! Even the animals sense the momentous events of the day and are rejoicing with us!" laughed Mark. "What I was about to say is that Heather and Todd want you to know that this weekend is not so much about them as it is about the body of Christ that God is developing and maturing and drawing together. Their marriage is a symbol of the greater unity of love among God's people that will continue to flourish in the world and will culminate in eternity. They are privileged to be part of that flourishing work of God with you and with all those God draws into it."

He paused, glanced about with a smile as if waiting for another bovine comment, then went on.

"With those few words, then," he said, "let us get on with the purpose for which we are here as Todd and Heather vow their mutual love to one another . . ."

96

Rich Fellowship

FOLLOWING THE festive ceremony, and after greetings and the expected hubbub, Todd and Heather excused themselves. They drove over to Todd's temporary digs at the Bar JG, ostensibly to change clothes for the afternoon, which they could have done at the Forster ranch but in reality to see David. He was waiting for them with tearful hugs and congratulations.

"We were thinking of you, David," said Heather. "We knew you were with us in spirit. We felt your presence in our hearts."

"I'm glad to hear it. You were certainly in mine. I am proud of you both. I eagerly anticipate seeing how God is going to use the two of you in the years ahead. I will be watching you and the others all afternoon. It's not quite as good as being there, but I am nevertheless enjoying it immensely."

"Be prepared, David," said Todd, "Mark and Court and Timothy and the rest of the men should be rolling in tomorrow morning between eight and nine so we can get an early start on your new house."

"*Your* new house, Todd, my boy!"

"All right—*our* house!" laughed Todd. "I hope we will share it for many years to come. Though Heather and I are in something of a quandary about just where we will live—here at the ranch or in Dorado Wood."

"All I can say is that it would bring more joy to this old man's heart than I can say to share the new ranch house with you, even if only part-time. I do understand that the Marshall home is the family home where much of your work gets done, Heather. That said, the Bar JG will belong to the two of you before too much longer. I am eighty-two you realize."

"And the liveliest eighty-two I know!" said Heather.

"There will be time to talk about all that later," rejoined David. "You two need to get back to your guests."

☆ ☆ ☆

Heather and Todd were the obvious center of attention for the rest of the day, doing their best to personally greet all of nearly three hundred guests. Not everyone who came knew them personally. Most who attended from Foothills did so out of courtesy to Timothy and Jaylene and Mark and Grace, or, after hearing about the strange goings on at the Forster ranch since Mark's resignation from their pulpit, out of mere curiosity.

Todd enjoyed renewing acquaintances with many of his former media colleagues. They too were curious about this strange group Todd had become involved with.

By day's end none of the skeptics could see what all the fuss had been about. This was the liveliest, friendliest, most gracious group of men and women they had ever been with. Even Edith Holt found little to complain about, almost shocked by the kindness shown her. She would doubtless be on her phone most of the next day, though what gossip she would have to spread was hard to say.

After the lavish catered buffet lunch, Todd and Heather scarcely able to eat for the constant press of well-wishers, the crowd slowly thinned and the huge temporary parking lot in the nearest pasture slowly emptied of cars. By four o'clock, only some hundred and twenty-five or so remained, predominantly from various BCL groups, including most who had attended the 2051 gathering.

As on that occasion, gradually the conversations quieted, became more personal, small groups of three or four walking off together. Others clustered about the newlyweds. Six or eight might be seen sitting apart from the others in spontaneous prayer. Then different small groups formed and reformed as the network of interconnected relationships ebbed and flowed by the Spirit's invisible moving among them.

The day was warm. Gradually chairs were moved and shifted and drawn together until most of those who remained were seated in a makeshift circle of randomly spaced concentric circles, all talking and sharing as one. Everyone wanted to hear from Todd and Heather. Many questions were also addressed to the First Lady, to Charles Reyburn and Harvey Jansen about the state of the country. Justice Linda Trent was also a focus of interest and questions. Court and Sheila Masters were known to everyone from the newsletter. Curiosity was also high about Bradon Rhodes and Ginger Forster where they sat together. It was obvious to everyone that they had been together all afternoon for more reasons than being best man and maid of honor for the day.

The fellowship deepened as night gradually fell.

About 8:30, Todd finally rose. "While we would love to stay for hours," he said, "we all have a long day ahead of us tomorrow. I for one, and I think I speak for my new wife as well, am exhausted. It has been a wonderful day. But I think it is time we bid you farewell until tomorrow."

He turned to Heather and offered his hand.

"My dear," he said, helping her to her feet.

Todd's car was parked next to the house. After hugs for their three parents, they walked to the car. A minute later the taillights slowly departed down the long drive. No whoops or shouts followed them, nor cans tied to the bumper. Quiet hands waved farewell. An abundance of tears trickled down many cheeks, not all of them on the faces of the women. None of them had ever been to a wedding like this.

Silence descended over the Forster ranch. A gradual exodus made its way to the remaining parked cars.

Theresa Stewart left with Timothy and Jaylene, accepting their invitation to stay with them for the remainder of her time in California.

Todd and Heather drove to the house in Dorado Wood, where they began their life together as Mr. and Mrs. Todd Stewart.

97

A Ranch House Goes Up

BY COMMON consent and by Todd's appointment, Court Masters and Dewitt West were put in charge of organizing the house raising. Court and Sheila and their friend Denver came to California a week early. By the day of the wedding, they had everything planned and in place.

Builders, contractors, plumbers, additional electricians, roofers, and handymen skilled in every trade whose acquaintances Court had made through the newsletter, volunteered to be part of the project. The barn was filled with the windows and doors ordered in advance, piles of sheetrock, tools, boxes of nails and screws and brackets, set up with a table saw, large radial saw, several smaller chop saws, grinders, sanders, a drill press and lathe, cordless nailers and drills, two long work benches, and other supplies—all of which Dewitt West brought from his own ranch or arranged to borrow from friends around the area.

Fortunately, power to the barn was not disrupted by the fire, with 120V and 240V. Everything was ready for the crew to hit the ground running.

Pallets of 2 x 4s, 2 x 6s, roofing tiles, and stacks of plywood, trusses, and floor joists were piled around the foundation. Dewitt had overseen the installation of the underground plumbing and electrical pipes, conduits, and wires over the previous month. The floor joists and rough flooring would be the first order of business.

Pickups and cars began rumbling into the ranch about 8:15.

Within an hour, sounds of power saws and hammers, an occasional shout, laughter and much animated conversation, filled the air. Floor joists and flooring starting from one end was followed almost as soon as there was room with the first appearance of walls laid out on top of the plywood floor, then hoisted into place. Court and Dewitt busily scurried about, blueprints in hand, like two conductors managing a fifty-piece orchestra, conferring now with one now with another. It was a case where the more chiefs the better, with ample Indians to shoot or pound nails once the chiefs made sure everything was exactly where it was supposed to be.

Nearly everyone who remained at the Forster ranch into the previous evening was on hand. Fifteen or twenty women set to work with tables and food and brewing gallons of coffee outside the barn for breakfast to get the workers on their way. More arrivals came with additional supplies throughout the morning. Half the ladies were busy in the Forster kitchen and several other local homes supplementing the leftovers from the wedding buffet with additional casseroles, stews, soups, pies, cakes, and cookies. By the time lunch rolled around, there was food enough for twice the number of workers on hand.

Everyone had come in work clothes and was anxious to help. Those who didn't know what to do were handed brooms, hammers, or paint brushes.

A crew of ten or fifteen, men and women side by side on their knees, worked their way methodically across the flat expanse of the plywood floor making sure each plank was secured to the joists below along the network of parallel chalk lines with its full complement of fifty or sixty nails. Two or three men stayed ahead of them slapping fresh 4 x 8 sheets down into position, sawing off overhanging ends or making corner and angle cuts as necessary.

Two rows of sawhorses sat between the barn and site of the new house with lengths of siding to be primed. There a second army of painters outfitted with cheap overalls were coating the boards of dry fir, which were then carefully carried into the barn to dry.

Side by side Todd, Heather, and Timothy were among the flooring contingent talking amongst themselves. More than a few glances of amazement were cast in the direction of First Lady Marcia Rhodes on her knees beside her son wielding a nail gun, driving the nails home, displaying as much skill as half the men. On her other side, Linda Trent did her best the old-fashioned way with hammer, with an occasional tip from Mrs. Rhodes. Ginger and Craig Forster knew their way around tools and moved across the plywood sheets with care and precision.

Not to be left out, her skill also observed with initial surprise, Harriet Jansen took control of the yellow DeWalt chop saw in the barn, supplying the framers with one-to-two-foot lengths of 2 x 4 bracing pieces. Jaylene penciled down the exact length of each and delivering them to the framers, returning with a new list of lengths needed.

By the time the beehive of activity paused for a coffee break about 10:30, sweat pouring off faces as the day began to warm, the loose sheets of plywood floor were nearly down and nail lines chalked, though it would take several more hours to be completely nailed off.

Then work resumed until lunch. Managing to keep out of the way of the kneeling army of nailers, framing crews laid out both exterior and interior walls, Court and Dewitt carefully inspecting each as they took shape for positioning of doors and windows.

From his underground bunker, David watched in awe to see the first walls going up on the site of his former home. The outline of the new house slowly began to reveal itself. Two sides of walls stood in place with long boards stretched to the ground temporarily holding them in place.

Surprising everyone with his carpentry expertise, after the first of the walls were in place, Charles Reyburn was up on a ladder in conference with Bob Forster measuring and marking positioning for the ceiling joists and roof trusses to follow.

Nothing brings people together quite like hard work and a common purpose. New and unexpected relationships formed throughout the day. Mark renewed his acquaintance with Ward's father, Truman Hutchins, and a new bond formed between them. Theresa Stewart and Marcia Rhodes found themselves unexpectedly sharing many things in common. Before the day was over, Theresa was invited for a visit to the Presidential Manor. Harvey Jansen and Cameron Trent likewise hit it off, the former presidential candidate and the wife of the Supreme Court justice who was bravely nailing away on the floor in spite of sore knees.

By mid-afternoon, with fatigue setting in and the entire floor nailed off and the exterior walls in place, all that remained of what Court and Dewitt had hoped to accomplish was hoisting and securing the roof trusses in place with the telehandler forklift they'd rented. It was a somewhat technical as well as dangerous procedure. But with the six or eight experienced builders on hand—everyone else, weary and glad to observe and help pack up the food—it took only another hour to erect the trusses and complete the outline of the new building.

As the men responsible for the final capstone of the day's efforts climbed down to the ground, exclamations of wonder, amazement, and pride in what they had accomplished settled into a contented silence.

It was just after 4:30.

"All right, everyone—a good day's work," said Mark. "I think we're all pretty impressed with ourselves. I know I am!" he added as laughter spread among the others. "And thanks to Court and Dewitt for their supervisorial expertise in directing our efforts."

"Here, here!" shouted several of the men, accompanied by applause and more exclamations.

"Well then," Mark went on, "supper at our place at 6:30. That will give you time to rest a bit, return to homes and motels and shower and relax."

With the new friendships the day had spawned and the deepening of old ones, the fellowship that evening was among the richest many present had ever experienced. For those immersed in the bubble of the nation's capital like the Trents and First Lady, being part of the rich dynamic of normal, hard-working, friendly people, was not only eye-opening but a tonic to their souls.

The work crew the next day shrunk to about fifty. That was enough to see the roof and walls mostly covered in plywood, the interior walls in place, and the interior wiring well begun. Tuesday's agenda called for the roofing tiles and exterior windows to be installed, the wiring completed, and interior drywall well underway.

By Wednesday most of the out-of-towners had to be on their way home, satisfied that Bob, Dewitt, and Court, who would stay on as long as necessary, with the help of the neophytes Bob, Mark, Craig, and Timothy would be able to complete much of the remaining interior work and oversee the local inspection process until it was necessary to hire carpet, tile, cabinet, counter, and kitchen and bathroom fixture installers.

That afternoon, Timothy, Jaylene, and Theresa drove Heather and Todd to Sacramento International Airport for a short flight to Phoenix. There they would board an overnight flight to London, thence to Aberdeen, and their two-week honeymoon in Scotland.

98

Reincarnation of the Domokos Vision

2053–2056

WELL AWARE that his wife, son, and mother were in California for the Marshall-Stewart wedding, Jefferson Rhodes could not prevent his mind straying over the weekend in the direction of the California foothills where he had spent happy times as a teen with his BF Mark Forster.

His thoughts wavered between fondness and annoyance. He liked Todd Stewart. Remembering the plain little girl he had been introduced to on Bainbridge Island, however, he could not help wondering what had possessed Todd to give up a job as one of the country's media stars to join Mark's group of cowpokes? He could have dazzled any girl in the country. Yet if the reports were accurate, he was now spending his days shoveling manure!

Such reflections, however, did not derail the focus of Jefferson Rhodes for long. Riding high in public approval and in his own estimation, he proceeded during his second term with the implementation of the provisions of the Freedom Bill, many of its provisions implemented by the sweeping, though constitutionally ambiguous, powers granted to his twelve so-called Freedom Commissions.

☆ ☆ ☆

As what amounted to a consolation prize at not becoming the nation's vice president, Mike Bardolf was given oversight over the commissions. He determined to make the best of it. His first order of business was to make sure the commissions were filled with the most progressive men and women possible, many of them his fellow Palladium colleagues.

Though still stewing at his boss for elevating Bahram above him, the reality was that he was in a position to carry out his plans more effectively than if he were vice president. He was free to operate virtually with impunity. The president had never been a detail man and asked few questions. He would never forgive him, but the fool Rhodes actually had done him a favor.

Under his leadership, the Constitution commission began plans immediately for initial drafts of a new US Constitution according to the provision of the Freedom Bill.

A debate arose in the committee whether to change the country's name and redesign its flag to reflect a more international and less nationalistic vibe. The discussions and potential names floated and flag design under consideration were kept strictly behind closed doors. Not a whisper was leaked to the president.

Linking discussions about the constitution with the Unification and Expansion Commission, Mike set up several steering committees. The first was tasked to explore the best methods, timetables, and strategies to gain public acceptance of unification with Mexico and the Central American countries, and to develop a plan to establish the borders of new states to be added to the United States.

The second prioritized initiative was to work with the U.N. and representatives of other countries to assess proposals, then to draft a World Constitution, to which all nations would, in time, subordinate their individual governing institutions.

A bill was introduced in the Senate—its rough draft also penned by Mike and passed through channels to the appropriate personnel—to ban Christian churches and Christianity in general, mandating religious questionnaires to be sent to every household requiring the disavowing of belief in Christianity, with severe penalties for not responding.

This was one of Mike's more daring initiatives which he allowed to proceed into the public arena, almost as a trial balloon to see how ready Congress, the president, and the country, were for radical change.

The bill was squashed in committee, though narrowly.

Regrouping, Mike turned his attention toward other means to monitor churches and Christian groups for compliance to the standards and guidelines he instructed the commission to establish.

He intended their measures to be supplemented by vigorous new mandates enforced by the Education Commission. In order to bolster the gender choice mandate, prior to entry into second grade, all children would be required to identify their chosen gender and give themselves a chosen name. Affidavits would be registered with the Department of Education, ensuring home and charter school compliance.

Ongoing noncompliance would result in removal of children from homes deemed unfit educational environments and placed in government housing where their proper education would be closely supervised. Though preliminary steps in enforcement had been met with such stiff resistance and enforcement temporarily eased, steps would now be taken to resume monitoring and step up compliance.

The commission was also tasked with establishing more stringent protocols, programs, curriculum, teacher training, and testing, based on a secularist worldview, inculcating tolerance, hate eradication, gender and marital-lifestyle choice, multiculturalism, and instilling a personal awareness in white students of the destructiveness of systemic white racism, and to eradicate the last vestiges of Christian or supernatural myths from the educational sphere. Mandated high school and collegiate courses would be expanded to include multicultural and social justice ethics to replace math and science requirements, all courses taught bilingually in Spanish and English. All teacher contracts would henceforth include a legally binding "belief clause," disavowing belief in God, Christianity, or supernaturalism.

Moving on to the Medical and Wellness Commission, Mike's instructions called for an expansion of the provisions of the Freedom Affirmation Bill and Youth Rights Act. This would include elimination of the requirement of parental permission for gender reassignment surgery for children eleven and older. Transgender surgery would continue to be publicly funded according to the terms of the Gender Neutrality Act.

To its provisions would be added 50 percent public funding for biological birth-males to be implanted with uterus and other necessary organs enabling them to bear children and carry them to term and for biological birth females to be implanted with organs and provided hormone treatment enabling them to produce sperm and impregnate an identified female of either biological birth-gender. Gender reassignment surgeons would be immune from lawsuits or prosecution for any cause. Pre- and post-surgery gender affirmation therapy would be provided at public expense.

Cut-off period for post-birth abortions in cases of mental or physical handicap would be increased. Recognizing birth certificates as living and changeable documents, the Commission would mandate that birth certificates be changed to include a "Temporarily Assigned Gender" specified by the attending physician or government midwife, but with "Chosen Gender" options available to mother, with or without father's consent. These options would be available to any child after age ten, their choices legally binding, and would supersede temporarily assigned gender choices.

The commission would prepare a recommendation to the president that research be accelerated into isolating various "proclivity genes," especially the religion gene and conservative gene, with the objective of increasing predictability of culturally destructive influences. Parallel research would also be expanded to determine the most appropriate means to turn off such genes within the human response system, using worldwide vaccination dissemination through insect RNA and DNA modification technologies, with the goal of bringing all races, cultures, and societal groups into uniformity.

Recognizing the drain of the aged on the financial health of the nation, Mike began privately drafting a bill to mandate euthanasia on the terminally ill, those with irreversible dementia, and those unable to care for themselves. Under the auspices of the Medical and Wellness Commission, medical professionals were consulted about establishing age parameters for useful life, and a list of terminal conditions which should not be prolonged after confirmed diagnosis.

The commission would authorize a governmental panel with decision making authority concerning life-sustainability feasibility parameters for individuals over the age of ninety, and younger when disease or conditions proved incurable.

It was also increasingly imperative to mandate societally beneficial abortion protocols on the basis of genetic predispositions as determined by mandated DNA testing of all couples applying for marriage licenses, and all fetuses.

All the commissions were instructed to incorporate into their recommendations ideological and linguistic conformity according to the Linguistic Reform Bill of 2037 but encompassing all modes of expression, rendering terms contrary to the accepted worldview gradually obsolete.

Christian nomenclature, in particular, would be subject to a program of term redefinition to be taught in all schools, organizations, and churches. The definition of sin, as but one example, would be stripped of its archaic presuppositions and replaced with racism, sexism, bigotry, hate speech, homophobia, and patriarchy as its defining essence. Repentance for such social sins would be encouraged through the Education Commission, stripped of all association of sin with Christianity.

The Religion Commission would work to spread through all religious groups a new perspective of religion that exalted racial groups of color, sexual minorities, and encouraged the leadership of women. A revised religious morality would be emphasized and materials prepared and spread through churches, mosques, synagogues, and other religious organizations and institutions.

To ensure a society free of oppressive ideologies, mandatory reeducation programs would target those found expressing dissenting views. These programs would be carried out through the workplace and enforced, if necessary, by removal to reeducation centers. There all remnants of non-conforming thought would be eliminated. The consciousness of its subjects would be aligned with the mandated perspectives and instilled through whatever means proved necessary, including incarcerative, electric, aquatic, hypnotic, and drug and deprivation therapies.

Mike tasked the Literacy and Publishing Commission to expand the provisions of the Literacy Management Initiative of 2036. The ban on Christian content without equal attention to alternate points of view had grown too lax. Underground publications by authors known to be noncompliant, though considered a felony and punishable by fines, confiscation of assets, and imprisonment, had not been enforced with sufficient vigor.

The current guidelines established by the previous administration for the publication of Bibles would be expanded. A new edition of the Love Bible would be produced and brought up to current terminology of usage, presenting parallel teachings throughout from the Koran.

To formerly mandated literary protocols would be added an AI-based program of monitoring all books offered for sale, whether new or used. Those found by AI to include substantial Christian content, or reflecting an overtly Christian worldview or by authors known to profess Christianity, would be banned from sale.

The duties of the Literacy Compliance Agency would be coordinated with the Technology Commission to scan all new publications for imbedded noncompliant content before filing barcode applications. Publications without a compliance barcode—including private newsletters and online mailings—would not be allowed to be sold by retail or online outlets or given away for private use.

All publishing facilities, public or private, including private homes where literature originated for distribution, would be required to register with the Literacy Compliance Agency and would be subject to unannounced inspection.

An even more sinister component of Victor Domokos's far-reaching vision, which, for now Mike kept to himself but planned to set in motion the moment he became president in the next cycle was to take control of reproduction.

Through his surgeon general he would issue a directive: Couples would be required to apply for governmental authorization to conceive. Future pregnancies would be effected *in vitro* in a carefully controlled hospital setting. Those conceiving on their own would be subject to fine or imprisonment. Unauthorized pregnancies would be aborted. By then his administration would be in control of the entire medical complex. All doctor visits, every procedure, every shot, every pill would be monitored. Home births and unauthorized midwives would be banned. Illicit pregnancies among the poor would be aborted.

A secret identifying DNA would be implanted into every man's sperm prior to the *in vitro* procedure. Every child born would thus have an identifying DNA marker that could never be removed and that could be tracked throughout their lives. This same technology would be implanted into the general population via vaccines, medications, and prescriptions. Slowly the entire population would thus be implanted with identifying DNA.

The identification of a religious-predisposition gene would provide the cornerstone of Mike's far-reaching plan to engineer the demographics of America's future. Couples applying for a government-sanctioned *in vitro* pregnancy would be thoroughly tested and monitored. Any couple whose blood and DNA samples revealed the presence of the religious gene would be secretly deemed at risk for Christian influences. In such cases the husband's sperm would not be used. The mother would instead be impregnated from a sperm bank of more acceptable donors. If the mother also had the religious gene, the sperm of a man with supposed homosexual markers—though the science of the identification remained dubious—would be used to impregnate her to counteract it.

The inventory of the governmental on-hand sperm bank would be gathered exclusively from non-Christians, atheists, and homosexuals. In every way possible, predispositions against Christianity would be maximized to mitigate potential parental Christian influences. The goal would be to despiritualize and desexualize all newborns with genes orienting them *against* Christianity and *toward* gender neutrality. Homosexuals and lesbians desiring to procreate would be allowed to do so without regulation.

Mike had already begun drafting what he called the Propagation Directive. Its implementation would begin during his first year as president in 2057. To avoid suspicions about the paternity of newborns, racial and other physical characteristics would be closely followed. No observable deviations from genetically expected eye and hair color, height, build, skin tone, musculature, and personality would be apparent. In cases where sperm substitution was deemed necessary, such measures would make it impossible to discover the fathers were not the true fathers. It went without saying that all DNA testing laboratories would be under their control.

☆ ☆ ☆

Unbeknownst to Mike Bardolf, however, even more to President Rhodes, Islam was quietly infiltrating more and more segments of society. All Mike's efforts to entrench progressivism permanently into the fabric of the national culture were being invisibly thwarted by the rising invisible tide weaving its ancient deceptions into the soul of the American consciousness.

All the while, now with an office in the executive mansion and with the president's ear, Hamad Bahram continued to lay the groundwork, traveling the country in preparation for what he was now confident would be his ultimate takeover of the government.

99

THE PROPHET RESURFACES

THOUGH REPORTS coming from Washington were not encouraging, no new threats against them had surfaced. Mark, Timothy, and David concluded that it would be beneficial to try to have yearly gatherings of the BCL fellowship. From the increasing mail received, it was clear that many around the country and around the world felt isolated in their day-to-day lives and depended on regular contact with like-minded Christians. Even relatively infrequent contact gave them a sense of inclusion in a larger fellowship, and was truly a lifeline.

During the previous election, Charles and Harvey had developed a close friendship with Texas Senator Dindinger. The three began discussing the possibility of their hosting gatherings in either Kentucky or Texas or Wyoming. Doing so would relieve Mark, Grace, Timothy, and Jaylene, as well as Todd and Heather, from having to plan the complexities and logistics of food, lodging, and scheduling. Though weather was always a factor, they agreed that spring was the best time of year.

As a result of their conversations, during the holiday season seven months after the wedding celebration in California, the *Master's Helps Newsletter* announced that a BCL gathering would be held at the Jansen ranch in Laramie, Wyoming, during the second week of May 2054. Land was plentiful. Tents, campers, and trailers would all be welcome. Laramie was not a large city, with a population of some 40,000. It was recommended that those preferring to stay in motels book their accommodations early.

By the time April rolled around, the new Bar JG ranch house had been completed and David had been back in residence for several months. Todd and Heather were splitting their time between the Bar JG and the Marshall home in Dorado Hills. David decided the Laramie gathering would provide the occasion for him to come out in the open.

There would be no announcement or fanfare. He would simply show up at the gathering as if it were a matter of course. Questions would be inevitable. They would simply say that he had managed to get out of the house, had survived the fire but needed time to recuperate. He would use his age as an excuse, saying that he had not been up to participating in the previous gathering or house raising. The existence of the bunker remained confidential.

As might have been expected, the rejoicing, hoopla, and fuss made over him when the first of what turned out to be some hundred guests arrived at the Jansen ranch and saw David sitting calmly on the porch with Harvey Jansen, was boisterous and enthusiastic. David took it in stride.

Everyone was anxious to hear details about what had happened. Asked by Harvey to kick off the gathering that evening by addressing the fellowship, David confined himself to speaking about the increasing danger of the Ally and its infiltration into America's churches. He then read from Stirling Marshall's Benedict Brief, which he and Timothy mutually felt led to begin making public. The times were dire, and they felt the remnant Church needed the prophetic truth that Timothy's father had written for such times as these.

The weekend was memorable, with many highlights and new relationships. Todd and Heather, now married, took on the stature as representing the new generation of leadership within a fellowship that had no leaders—only brothers and sisters in an expanding remnant Church.

☆ ☆ ☆

Increasing concerns, threats against Christians in the news, and disturbing reports from around the country, pointed to the reality that the respite following the president's reelection had been but a lull in the steady effort not merely to sideline Christianity but to eradicate it.

When the BCL gathering was held in Texas the following year in April of 2055, hosted by Senator Dindinger and his wife, those concerns were on everyone's minds. The attendance was down considerably.

The news from Washington—where Senator Dindinger was aware how the provisions of the Freedom Bill were impacting more and more policies at the grassroots level—were not encouraging. He was also privy to many of the add-ons surreptitiously infiltrating the bill's implementation being mandated by what was, in effect, no longer the president's, but Mike Bardolf's twelve commissions.

The senator's report to the group was alarming. Discussions about how Christians should respond to threats likely to increase dominated much of the weekend.

There were no easy answers other than renewed prayer, vigilance, and preparing for the worst. It was clear that tribulations and persecutions loomed on the horizon against those who took command-discipleship seriously.

David remained mostly silent all weekend, taking in every word. He was obviously deep in prayerful thought.

Returning to California without the exuberance that had followed previous gatherings, a month later Senator Dindinger's warnings were confirmed. Mark and Todd, on their respective ranches, became aware of faint and peculiar humming sounds. It took some detective work, moving to different places on their ranches, finally with binoculars scanning above them, to realize that the Bar JG and the Circle F were being surveilled by drones.

With the help of Court Masters, whose FBI experience and continued monitoring of technological advances kept him well-apprised of the latest in high-tech equipment, both ranches were installed with drone blockers that would effectively disrupt audio and video and render the drones useless. Yet the realization that they were being watched was concerning.

So as to put none of their families, or any of those in other BCL cells in danger, it seemed best to hold no gathering in 2056. They must try to keep the wider fellowship under the radar if possible.

100

A Momentous Election Approaches

IN SPITE of the cautions, disturbing reports, and urgings for vigilance shared in the *Master's Helps Newsletter,* the hunger for deeper reality in their spiritual lives spread like leaven from person to person, from couple and family to more couples and families. The unofficial, leaderless, doctrineless movement known as the Brethren of the Common Life—though recognizing itself increasingly separated from the organized churches of Christendom, and monitored by multiple governmental agencies, continued to grow around the world.

As Stirling Marshall's Benedict Brief was more openly shared, it ignited the passionate fire within thousands—perhaps which would grow to millions, fed and energized by times of tribulation which could not extinguish that ancient fire—to be known simply as *owned* men and women, given wholly to a single purpose, to live by the commands of their Master as sons and daughters of their heavenly Father.

Getting wind of the *Brief* again through his lackey Bruno Volker, Mike Bardolf went to the president with renewed exhortations to take aggressive action against the Marshall-Forster cult, using the c-word repeatedly in Rhodes's hearing. Not only, however, was Mark's childhood friend no longer worried, that his son and mother were now involved precluded him making an issue about it.

"That's yesterday's news, Mike," said the president. "There never was a conspiracy. I shouldn't have listened to all that. You made a mountain out of a molehill. I don't want to hear any more about it. I just hope you didn't order that fire at Gordon's place, though I wouldn't put it past you. If you were involved, I don't want to know! I'd have to have you arrested."

"My sources tell me the Gordon fellow is still alive."

"Who cares?" rejoined Rhodes heatedly. "He's just an old man. He's no prophet. Drop it, Mike. I mean it!"

Fuming not to be taken as seriously as he once was, licking his wounds, Mike redoubled his efforts to learn more about the nationwide cells Volker and the operatives his Enforcement Committee had files on. Simultaneously he began planning his candidacy for 2056. He assumed Bahram would also run but dismissed his chances. For now he'd have to lay low about the Marshall group. He couldn't afford to cross swords with the president. He would need his support in the primaries, especially if his own vice president was also running.

All the while, under his very nose, Mike's obsession blinded him from the true threat to his future, to Jefferson Rhodes's legacy, to Viktor Domokos's sweeping progressive vision, and to the underpinnings of the United States of America itself. That threat did not originate but was now preparing for its culmination just down the hall in the office of the vice president. In truth it had originated just short of 1,500 years earlier. And its fulfillment was nearly at hand.

Neither Jefferson Rhodes nor Mike Bardolf was remotely cognizant that Hamad Bahram was laying the groundwork for the systematic dismantling of the entire progressive house of cards they had built.

With the conventions of 2056 approaching, anti-Christian rhetoric mounted again. Pressure increased once more on Charles Reyburn, Harvey Jansen, and Senator Dindinger to run for the Republican nomination. Numerous voices also entered the discussion calling for Todd Stewart to step forward.

Hamad Bahram was not as uninformed about the activities of Mike Bardolf as Mike was about him. He knew the *Bardolf* name carried significant weight in Palladium. With its many tentacles throughout the country working on his behalf, Mike would be capable of mounting a credible threat to his own nomination. The nomination could come down to which of them had the president's backing. It might even come down to the convention. Would Rhodes back his vice president, or the man who had been his right-hand since long before his presidency?

As the question revolved in his mind, a cunning plan began to form that might subtly win the president's favor on behalf of the Bahram-Jones ticket. A closed-door meeting with the congresswoman he had selected as his running mate followed. They didn't especially need the Christian vote in November. But he knew the president's son was somehow involved with the group in California. It would behoove him to know if there was any substance to the cult-conspiracy rumors, as well as adding a less-than-subtle play for the president's support.

As the result of his conversation with Ms. Jones, Bradon Rhodes received a telephone call out of the blue.

"Hello, Bradon," he heard when he answered. "This is Congresswoman Shelly Jones. I assume you've heard that Mr. Bahram has invited me to join his ticket should he receive the nomination at the upcoming Democrat convention."

"Yes, I was aware of that," answered Bradon.

"I've heard good things about you," Jones went on. "I'm calling to ask if you would like to join my campaign staff."

Stunned, Bradon was speechless.

"Bradon . . . are you still there?"

"Yes . . . sorry—I don't know what to say. This comes as a complete surprise."

Jones laughed. "I understand. Why don't you think about it? Come by my office tomorrow afternoon, say about three, and we can talk about it. It's Saturday so my staff will be off but come right in. I'll tell you what I have in mind."

He had never been a political animal. Yet how could he not be intrigued, thought Bradon. He couldn't imagine what she would want with *him*. No doubt because of his father. Political or not, the Rhodes name was something he would never escape. What would be the harm in seeing what it was all about?

He arrived at the congresswoman's suite a few minutes before three and walked in. No staff was present, as she had said. The outer reception area was empty. He looked across the room. The door to her private office was ajar. She'd said to come in.

He opened it the rest of the way and walked in. The office, too, was empty. Uncertain if he should sit down and wait, he wandered toward one of the two chairs sitting across from her desk, unconsciously glancing over it.

His eyes widened at the sight of two documents in Arabic spread out over the desk! He knew Congresswoman Jones to be a third-generation American. What could it mean? Had she converted to Islam!

Sudden chills swept through him—a preternatural premonition of something untoward in the wind. Without pausing to think about the ethics of it, he grabbed his phone from his pocket, snapped two pictures, then turned and hurried out of the office, leaving the door behind him just as he had found it. His mind was racing at the implications of what he had seen.

When the congresswoman rushed in five minutes later, she found him seated calmly in the outer office. He was thankful that the delay had allowed him to begin breathing more easily.

"Bradon," said Ms. Jones, walking breathlessly in and offering her hand. "I am sorry about this. I had an unexpected bit of committee business I had to attend to. I hope you didn't think I stood you up."

"Not at all—no problem," replied Bradon.

"Come into my office and we'll have a talk."

As she led him inside and walked to her desk, her face blanched momentarily as she saw the papers she had inadvertently left on the desk. She quickly covered them over as she sat down, took a deep breath, and recovered her poise.

The result of the meeting was Bradon's promise to consider the congresswoman's offer.

Two weeks later, Bradon was on a flight to California to show Timothy and Mark what he had seen in the congresswoman's office.

101

The Qur'an Terminus

TIMOTHY AND Mark listened to Bradon's story with sober expressions. He then handed them each a copy of the pages he'd photographed which he'd printed after his arrival at the Bar JG where he was staying.

"I don't mean to make light of this," said Timothy after a few seconds, "but it's all Greek to me, as the expression is. I have no clue what it means."

"Nor do I," added Mark. "I must admit the existence of such a document, in Arabic, in the congresswoman's office, concerns me. I'd heard she had converted to Islam a few years ago. That's no doubt why Vice President Bahram chose her as his running mate. Sad to say, conversion to Islam is not so unusual these days. High-profile conversions have become a daily occurrence. But that she is communicating with someone in Arabic, which must be for the purpose of secrecy—that is possibly worrisome. Though technically this document is obviously the property of Congresswoman Jones and we have no right to possess it, I would be most curious to know its content. It may be innocent enough—a grocery list, for all we know."

"Was I wrong to photograph it?" asked Bradon.

"I don't know," replied Mark. "You acted on impulse. I cannot fault you for that. Maybe it was wrong—I can't say. But the fact is, it has come into our possession. We have to decide what to do about it. What do you think, Timothy?"

Timothy sighed. "I don't know either. Notwithstanding the right or wrong of what Bradon did, the fact that we *do* have it now may indicate that God allowed it to come into our possession for a reason. That is probably questionable theologically," he added with a light laugh. "Still, I have the sense that it may be important for us to know the content of this document. The innocence of doves is sometimes a difficult tightrope to walk when also sensing the need to be shrewd as snakes."

"Do you have a colleague who could translate it?" asked Mark.

"I do. Retired, like me. He was Jessup's premier Middle Eastern expert for years. I think we should pray seriously about the best course to follow. If we three are unanimously agreed —your prayers will be as important as ours, Bradon—then I will talk to him. However, if one of us feels a check or hesitation, then we do nothing. Agreed?"

The other two nodded.

"Until then," said Mark. "Not a word of this to anyone. You haven't said anything to Ginger, have you, Bradon?"

"No. I didn't tell her I was coming. I wanted to talk to the two of you first."

"Well, then," laughed Mark, "she's in for a surprise! Grace and Craig will be excited to see you too. Our place for supper later?"

"That would be great. I'll be there."

☆ ☆ ☆

Ginger was so delighted to see Bradon that she asked few questions. Sleeping in the barn bunkhouse at the Bar JG, he spent the following days alternating between the two ranches and helping with the work of both.

When he and Mark walked into the Marshall home in Roseville after Timothy's call five days later, they had no idea what to expect. He'd indicated nothing in his phone call other than that he'd heard from his colleague. Timothy led them into his office. Not even Jaylene knew what it was all about.

"I have a translation of the document," began Timothy when they were seated. "It is titled *The Qur'an Terminus.*"

"What does that mean?" asked Bradon.

"My friend said it denotes Islam's end game, the finale, the culmination of the Koran's teachings. The terminus and climax of what Islam has been pointing to for a millennium and a half."

Mark and Bradon let out subdued exclamations, though not entirely of surprise.

"It was written and signed by none other than Vice President Bahram," added Timothy. "I'll let you read the translation. It speaks for itself."

He handed them each a single typed sheet. As they read, the eyes of both widened in astonishment, disbelief, and obvious alarm.

THE QUR'AN TERMINUS

Our hour approaches. The final destiny of Islam is at hand.

The inheritors of the mantle of our great Prophet Mohammed in these last days will not be fulfilled merely because Christianity as a religion loses its potency. Upon those of us who are privileged with the sacred honor to bring all things in the holy Qur'an to their appointed culmination lies the duty to exterminate all Christian races—its evil forebears the Jews, the northern Europeans, and the Americans. Organized Christendom is in chaos and has lost its influence as a world force. But this is not our ultimate victory. Though we will continue buying derelict churches and cathedrals in the name of Allah and converting them to mosques, and though we will eventually take over the Vatican and send the pope into exile in the triumph of our beloved Islam, this is not yet the end.

If the efforts of our new Islamic administration in Washington fall short of achieving full Sharia law, and the transformation of the former United States into the Muslim States of America, then more stringent measures will be undertaken, as foreseen by the Prophet.

According to the Mohamed Protocol, we must be vigilant for the right moment to send the word forth to all Muslim cells and groups and mosques. Our network must be so thoroughly embedded in every nation, with seamless untraceable communication links, that Muslims throughout the world can be secretly notified to begin working their way back to their homelands in the Middle East, Africa, Indonesia, and Asia. This great exodus of faithful Muslims, while raising curiosity, will not be sufficient to alert the decadent West to the scope of what awaits it.

If milder measures have not been successful, we will, as necessary, wipe out those populations that have been incalcitrant in their opposition to Islam—their cities, schools, libraries, governments, monuments. When the time is right, tactical nuclear strikes will be carried out as necessary—against the United States, Israel, and western Europe primarily if we have not successfully yet taken them over from within—employing devices whose radioactivity is of limited scope. The limited half-life of the new radioactive isotopes will prevent the globe as a whole from contamination. Within ten years, the earth will be free from radiation.

The result will create virgin new lands whose soil, plant life, forests, fields, pasturelands, and farming regions will again be verdant with life. These regions will await being reclaimed and repopulated by the faithful followers of Allah and his Prophet. A new world order will emerge, ushering in the new golden age of Islam throughout the earth.

H. Bahram.

It was silent for several minutes.

"What do we do with this information?" said Mark, voicing the question on all three of their minds.

"I honestly don't know," replied Timothy, shaking his head.

"What if he is elected president?" said Bradon. "Don't we have a duty to the country to expose him?"

"I'm not sure we do, Bradon," said Mark. "I very much doubt it rests with us to try to influence the election."

"Even in the face of something this potentially horrific?"

"That is a far-reaching question. I have no answer. Did Jesus try to protect his people from a future under emperors like Caligula and Nero? I think all we can do for now is watch and pray. If more is required of us, we have to trust that God will reveal it."

"One thing I do feel would be appropriate to pursue," added Timothy, "is to spread the word among our fellowships to begin collecting and preserving books and Bibles and a wide range of the historic English literature. Whatever may be the wider implications of this document—and the possibilities are frightening—I am certain that if Islam continues on its present course, the books and writings of our heritage, especially Christian and Jewish literature, may be in peril. Look at what the Nazis tried to do."

"Wisely spoken, Timothy," nodded Mark.

As a result of their conversation, though the document giving urgency to the effort was not mentioned, a massive literature preservation movement began. Spreading through the BCL network at first, it became a worldwide underground effort to gather, preserve, and protect as much of the literature of the past, old translations, histories, and especially spiritual books and as many Bibles as possible.

"It came to be known as the Alexandrian Project, in memory of the Alexandrian library which was tragically lost to history. It drew its parallel from the monks and monasteries of the Middle Ages, whose heroic efforts had preserved the sacred texts of Christianity. Individual groups undertook to establish their own secret sites, where, all taken together, repositories of important books grew and were safely stored.

Meanwhile, at the two ranches in the California foothills, plans moved forward, as David had suggested earlier, to begin rebuilding the former bunkhouses in the hills above the Bar JG. Purchasing materials a little at a time from different outlets, as David had done for his bunker, and storing the timbers, plywood, electrical and plumbing materials, windows, and roofing, in the two barns, everything was transported into the hills by night, taking various routes so that no worn roadway would become apparent. When the construction got slowly underway, no loud power tools were used, nor hammers and nails but screws and nearly-quiet battery drills. No other ranches were nearby, yet they wanted to take no chances of their work being heard. They remained concerned about drone surveillance. Solar power would be used for electricity, heat, and hot water.

Knowing that he was responsible for bringing the Arabic document to light, Bradon could not help wondering if he ought to have done something differently? And what should he do about Congresswoman Jones's offer? With what he knew, he could obviously not actively support her campaign. However, might her offer give him the opportunity to learn more? But could he use such duplicity, even if it was in the cause of truth?

For weeks after his return to Washington, his nights were restless, filled with confusion, unanswered questions, anxieties, and fears.

The only leading he received was to write Congresswoman Jones a brief letter stating that he appreciated her offer and was praying about it. As no decision had become clear to him, however, he doubted he would be able to accept her offer before the election.

Bradon was still young in his faith. Every question, revelation, insight, and sense of God's leading was new. Likewise, each one expanded his knowledge and experience as a growing Christian. In spite of the many uncertainties surrounding what he had discovered and the obvious dangers it portended, as the election neared, he began to sleep more easily, and found peace stealing over him about the future.

He had thus been given a major new lesson in the deepening process of learning what it meant to walk with God:

He did not need to know the answer to every conundrum ahead of time.

God held the uncertainties, and their answers and resolutions, in his hands. For those who walked as his sons and daughters, that was enough.

If only Muslims were clever politically, they could take over the United States and replace its constitutional government with a caliphate.

—Siraj Wahhaj

New York imam invited to give the opening prayer before the U.S. House of Representatives in 1991

PART 7

THE TRIBULATION CULT

2057–2064

102

The Muslim States of America

2057–2060

NEW PRESIDENT of the United States Hamad Bahram wasted no time after taking the oath of office in January of 2057 and explaining the *Adhan* to the stunned, somewhat bewildered, and surprised inaugural crowd.

Having orchestrated in advance the dissonant blaring of the Islamic call to prayer on the minaret over the National Mall, he was in the Oval Office three hours later, perusing the more complete agenda he had shared with only one other individual, along with the far-reaching Qur'an Terminus accompanying it—new vice president Shelly Jones. She would be instrumental in implementing the agenda and gaining its acceptance by America's women. As he perused both documents, he was filled with a sense of fulfillment that his appointment with destiny had finally arrived.

His cabinet appointments had been made long before, during his vice presidential tenure—most, like Jones, with harmless Anglo-Saxon names yet every one committed to Islam and ready to begin instituting initially innocuous elements of Sharia law into their agencies. The twelve Rhodes commissions would be disbanded and merged into the machinery of the government bureaucracy, there to weave Sharia invisibly into its foundational fabric. The first order of business for his cabinet heads would be to systematically weed out deep state progressive partisans and replace them with Muslim loyalists, remaking every agency from the ground up with those committed to Allah's cause.

Setting the documents aside, he began signing the stack of executive orders he had prepared ahead of time. All appeared bland to the unseeing eye. In concert with his cabinet, they had been carefully crafted to lay the groundwork for more consequential measures—instituted by executive order and legislated into law by his allies in Congress in the months ahead.

It would have surprised the liberals throughout the country who considered him one of them, that the two US presidents he admired most were FDR and DJT. They were do-ers. Both men had stormed into office, cleared the desks, and began reshaping the country from day one. Roosevelt and Trump were, along with Lincoln, the nation's strongest and most transformative presidents in the country's history.

Not that he cared about US history more than was necessary to keep up appearances, sprinkling his speeches with enough Americanisms to play his expected role. In truth, his real heroes were from further east on the global map, and of far deeper antiquity than *any* American president.

He had been only sixteen at the time of Donald Trump's first inauguration, but that was old enough to vote for him in 2020 and 2024. He'd watched Trump's bungling of his first presidency and the lessons he'd learned, and followed the early tidal wave of activity early in his second term with growing fascination. Both examples exercised a profound impact on him. Like Trump in 2025, he knew he might have limited time to do what needed to be done. He had to follow the same model and act fast. By the time the country realized what was happening, the dominos would be toppling.

It had been easy enough for progressives to undo the Trump-Vance years by perpetuating Trump Derangement Syndrome and making it stick to conservatism in general well into the next decade. Once the pendulum swung back in its favor, progressivism roared back with a vengeance. The recent reign of the fool Jefferson Rhodes crowned the apparent success of liberal lunacy, and set the stage for the triumph of Islam over the decadence of the West.

Though most of Trump's moves had been reversed, Bahram had built safeguards into his own agenda to prevent that from happening.

That was the beauty of Sharia law—it was self-perpetuating. The changes of his presidency would *permanently* re-make America and the West into such an Islamic colossus that not China, not Russia, and certainly no rebirth of progressivism or fascism could stand against it. Once in place, Sharia would be impossible to dislodge.

His presidency represented the culmination not only of his father's and grandfather's clandestine plan to use progressivism and Palladium to infiltrate and gain power, but also the centuries-long plan of Islam to defeat Judaism, Christianity, and the entire West. Having played the game for their three generations, he was himself now in a position to bring it all to fruition.

He'd like to have met Trump. But back in those days of the 2020s, liberals—which included most of his own colleagues in the political sphere—had so thoroughly lost their heads in apoplectic TDS that he didn't dare attempt a pretext for a meeting. But the man's example lived on. This day's flurry of executive orders was but the first step.

The national debt would provide the thin edge of the wedge toward full implementation of Sharia law. Several of his initial financial orders would lay the groundwork for what he had privately set in motion with certain high-ranking Chinese officials close to Premier Jiang during his vice presidency. That was for China to call its US debt due. Decades of congressional refusal to rein in progressivist spending now had the national debt at the tipping point.

Though still negotiating the best timing—whether immediately or two or three years into his presidency, or perhaps even in his second term—once the Chinese move was made, Wall Street would go into a panic. With the nation in crisis, Sharia law would be accepted to avoid a repeat of 1929. He would then renegotiate with the Chinese before any lasting damage could be done. Wall Street would quickly bounce back, he would be hailed as having prevented economic collapse. Islam would be on its way to becoming the law and the religion of the land. As long as Jiang didn't double-cross him.

☆ ☆ ☆

In the following months, Bahram and his cabinet appointees established Muslims throughout the government. His four years of stealthy operations were set in motion so invisibly that even a year later few progressives suspected that their agenda was in peril. His election swept a majority of Muslims into both the Senate and House, bolstered in the 2058 midterms to ensure the success of his master plan, after which Muslims were in charge of most governorships, statehouses, local government, federal agencies, and judgeships.

The most daring of his proposed moves, which Bahram anticipated would be sufficient to kill progressivism in its tracks, was also one whose timing remained uncertain. Its initial announcement would feign an ultimate triumph of liberalism. In the guise of being a friend of the LGBTQ community, his cunning plan to identify all gays, lesbians, and trans in the country would begin by inviting them to submit applications for the incentives available to those relocating to the two designated LGBTQ communities of Burlington and Northampton. The questionnaires and applications went out late in his first year in office.

Progressives gleefully expected a hundred million applicants. When less than a million applications were returned, the few remaining pockets of conservativism in the country loudly proclaimed vindication of their contention that the number of gays, lesbians, and trans in the country had always been wildly exaggerated.

Bahram didn't care about the numbers. He knew that the LGBTQ agenda was a mirage and a fraud. He had always known it. A tiny minority of sexual deviants had dictated the direction of progressivism for nearly a century. As long as the most militant gays and lesbians and trans could be coerced to flock to Vermont and Massachusetts expecting the utopia of their dreams, after he had them all in one place, they could be eliminated en masse in accordance with Sharia law.

Many, of course, would survive, but they would be forced into hiding and would be weeded out over time. In the meantime, the soul of the deception would be dealt a death blow. The country would be stunned by the sudden deaths. Legitimate explanations would be prepared ahead of time—a fast-acting gay-virus more lethal than AIDS, a gas leak, a massive accidental explosion whose poison gas was sufficient to wipe out those living within hundreds of square miles. He might use a combination of all three, ensuring that blame pointed to the gay community itself.

In the aftermath of the catastrophe, martial law would be declared. With Congress, the Supreme Court, and the FBI behind him, the country would fall in line with the new realities.

With the subsequent outlawing of homosexuality in all its forms, the rescinding of all same-sex marriage certificates, and the arrest of gay couples identifiable by tax returns, and the arrest and execution of all trans "persons" identifiable by medical records, and the imprisonment of the doctors who performed gender-modification surgeries, the ensuing fear would put a stop to the lunacy for good.

In anticipation of his eventual presidency, Bahram had been thinking for several years about what to do about Palladium when his time came. After his election he decided on a radical course, though realized that it was not without risk to himself. He decided, however, to go ahead.

At the next scheduled meeting of Palladium's entire membership, he called a major news conference from the small town of Mira Monte. Admitting his own membership for the purpose of unmasking and dismantling it, he publicly exposed Palladium, whose headquarters sat behind him as he spoke, as a sinister subversive organization of danger to the country. With the FBI on hand and having been issued its orders, a contingent of a hundred agents swooped in and placed the 141 active members of Palladium's Hundred-and-Forty-Four who were on hand under arrest. In addition to himself, the two Bardolfs on the League of Seven were not present. The perfectly-timed raid was conducted with such lightning speed that most were behind bars before they knew what hit them. The Mira Monte compound was confiscated and became Bahram's western Presidential Manor.

He was conflicted about what to do with Mike Bardolf. On the one hand, he could be invaluable as knowing the inner workings and behind-the-scenes machinations of Washington probably better than any man alive.

On the other hand, he knew that Mike hated him and lusted for the office that had been denied him. Two Alpha males thrust together—it never worked. He would be a dangerous adversary.

Keep your enemies closer was a shrewd policy as far as it went. But he suspected Mike in more than one assassination. He didn't want to be the next.

As if in confirmation of his instincts, Mike turned out not to be at Mira Monte at the time of the arrests. He had got wind of the impending raid, warned his father to stay away, went into hiding, and had not been seen since. Bahram immediately set FBI searching for the man who, until a short time ago, had virtually run the entire bureau.

Next on President Hamad Bahram's agenda was the emasculating of militant feminism. Women needed to return to their subservient place, where they would be happy and fulfilled when not trying to usurp the role of men in their lives.

Vice President Jones's massive reeducation campaign about the role of women would be effective toward that end, and would be expanded to include an indoctrination blitz against all the idiocies of progressivism, Judaism, and Christianity. Progressivism and religion would become pariahs, their former leaders seen for the fools they were. How ironic that progressivism had done its best to successfully eliminate Christianity. Now they would go to the grave as one—two opposites hating each other, sharing a tomb as the corpses of their ideas decayed together in the graveyard of history.

Fearing for their own lives, the gullible citizenry—as unthinking as the millions who had swallowed the lie of progressivism—would goose-step into line behind him just as had the gullible Germans behind Hitler. With mosques in every town and city, Sharia law would gradually transplant all former Western ideologies as the accepted outlook of enlightened Americans.

The one exception he was mulling over concerned those denominations, churches, and other factions within the broad array of Christendom that had been thoroughly secularized into progressivism. These might actually prove useful.

He was not opposed to making use of those elements of the Rhodes Freedom Bill that could serve his ends. Maintaining some pretext of freedom of religion might preserve the illusion that the populace still had religious choices. The churches of Christendom, gutted of their essential foundations and happy to embrace Islam as its brother religion of peace, could serve that end admirably.

☆ ☆ ☆

It went without saying that one of the ultimate objectives of the Bahram administration would be the removal of Israel from the map of the world. Whether he would make such an attempt in his first or his second term—or perhaps even in a third term once the nation's new constitution was in effect—would depend on how the geopolitical balance of power shaped up during his administration.

In the first two years of his presidency, during frequent goodwill trips to the Middle East, Bahram privately assured leaders of all the Arab nations that he would take action at an appropriate moment. However, if they should choose to act in concert with a joint bombing of Israel, even with tactical nuclear weaponry, such action would not be resisted or condemned. When the dust settled, the United States would enter Israel with troops, declare martial law to prevent escalation of war, and establish Israel as an occupied territory, partitioning its land and dividing the spoils between the nations of the Arab world. Israel as a nation would cease to exist.

At whatever point circumstances resulted in a move against Israel, he would follow such action by bringing the nations of the world together to implement the centuries-long vision of a new-world-order. The Caliphate would be based on an alliance between what would become known as the Muslim States of America and the united Arab nations. With the Middle East and former US united, the UK and Europe would fall in line and move toward Islamic leadership and law. He'd had people in those countries at work behind the scenes for years. It was only a matter of tipping over the first domino.

The wild cards he had to keep an eye on were China and Russia.

One priority which Hamad Bahram shared with progressivism was rewriting the record of Western civilization. His vision was different in underlying focus, however. Whereas liberalism's intent had been to strike Christian and white influence from the historical record by emphasizing the role of blacks and native peoples, his objective was to incorporate a foundation of Arab and Islamic influence, with the beloved Prophet as its chief cornerstone.

Whereas the Freedom Bill had only sought to secularize history and remove Christianity's role, his motive was to reeducate younger generations by a slow process of inoculation, interpreting history as an inexorable march of the grand truth of Islam to its appointed destiny as the world's religion and revelation of Allah to mankind.

☆ ☆ ☆

Meanwhile, throughout the world, small pockets of Christianity continued to grow and expand, within and outside the institutional church. A new flurry of underground prophetic books managed to find ways to circumvent the prohibitions against Christian publications. Most of these proclaimed that the rapture and Tribulation were at hand, many naming President Hamad Bahram the antichrist.

☆ ☆ ☆

As the election of 2060 approached, on Bainbridge Island, Jefferson Fitzsimmons Rhodes was paying little attention to the transformation of the country under his successor. He was too preoccupied writing his memoirs to worry about where the country was going.

Unknown to either man, Mike Bardolf was not content to go quietly into the night. He had been moving about the country under assumed names, never staying in any one place for long. As he traveled, he was feverishly at work on a book of his own, reprising the Domokos vision in an attempt to reignite progressivism, exposing President Bahram for the fraud he was, and reestablishing his own reputation in the process.

His father's suddenly declining health, however, brought him home for a brief perfunctory visit.

A small news item appeared on the wire services and was printed in most of the nation's newspapers on the eve of President Bahram's second inauguration in the first week of 2061:

> Former presidential aide and Deputy Director of the FBI Michael Bardolf was found dead at the Bardolf family home in Colorado Springs yesterday. The death has been ruled suspicious by the police, though no details are known at this time. Bardolf first rose to prominence as assistant to legendary political financier Viktor Domokos. He is the author of Domokos's biography and is survived by his father, Loring Bardolf.

103

A Stirring

SPRING 2061

DAVID GORDON woke early. He glanced at the clock on his nightstand. It was 4:30. Pitch black. All was quiet.

He was alone in the house. Todd and Heather were in Dorado Hills for the night. He came awake with the unmistakable sense that God's Spirit was speaking. Something was at hand. The sense of expectancy grew as he lay in the darkness.

He'd turned ninety a few weeks before. He felt fit mentally and spiritually. At this age, however, you could never tell how much longer you had. Men were mortal, after all. Not many were privileged to match Moses's 120 years!

Was God stirring him, as he had his mentor Stirling forty years earlier, toward some culminating end-of-life message? He had been feeling movement in his spirit ever since his birthday, a sense that a turning point had come, that he must quiet his soul and listen, that something was coming into focus in the Spirit realm that God would have him understand, and perhaps communicate to his brothers and sisters of God's family.

But who was he to think he had a word for Christ's body? He was an insignificant man who had lived an insignificant life in all the ways by which the world judged significance. Even as he posed the question, he knew none of that mattered. If God was speaking, he had only one duty. That was to listen, and to hear the Voice aright.

He rose, showered, put on the coffee, and sat down with his Bible in the quietness of the morning.

Lord God, my Father, he silently prayed, *what do you have to reveal? What word would you convey? Spirit of Jesus, speak into my heart.*

The morning advanced. It was a warm day. Though he did not often ride these days, there was only one place where he could feel completely one with the life God had given him to live. That was in the saddle.

On the back of his favorite horse—though those favorites had changed over the years—he was perfectly in harmony with his heritage, with his father and grandfather, and with the land that had come to him as an inheritance he treasured above all earthly things. Even the loss of his home paled beside the land.

The *land* . . . his *inheritance.*

It was an inheritance of the generations that had come before—a good land, in the words of the ancient text, a land flowing with milk and honey, a land where he lacked nothing. He had been blessed beyond measure.

By ten o'clock he was slowly heading into the hills on the back of old Dusty, his faithful equine friend of twenty years. He was in no hurry, his spirit quietly reflective as the years of his life replayed themselves on his memory.

The death of Stirling Marshall had left a great void in his life. He had wondered at the time how life could go on. Yet it did go on. Much had happened since. The world changed. The country had changed. The church had changed.

God had privileged him to see what he knew in his heart was the birth, or a *rebirth,* of his remnant true Church, a remnant born anew in every generation to preserve and pass God's truth into the future when the church of man—as it often did throughout history—had lost its way.

In a sense, he was now standing where he had never expected to stand, in the shoes of Stirling Marshall, gazing back over his own life, and at the same time gazing ahead and asking God what he had for him to do and say before his own end came. Humbling though it was to realize it, he knew that many looked to him to clarify what was happening in the world, to speak wisdom in uncertain and dangerous times.

He smiled as Todd's face rose in his mind's eye. What a transformation God had wrought in that young man—a spiritual son to him in his later years, sharing life with dear Heather, a spiritual daughter, too, if it was not too presumptuous for him to claim a small part of her along with Timothy and Jaylene.

He had never considered that the inheritance he had received would be passed on *as* an inheritance. Yet God had brought into his life a true son in the Spirit to receive it.

Whatever God was stirring within him, he knew that it was meant for Todd most of all. What a remarkable thing, that Todd had been spiritually grafted into his lineage and the lineage of Stirling Marshall as well.

With such a spiritual patrimony, what things God must have planned for Todd and Heather!

Oh Lord, his spirit cried out as he rode, *what do you have for me to give that young man and young woman?*

David reached the first of the cabins they had secretly built high above the Bar JG in a thick grove of pines where it could not be seen from the air.

He dismounted and walked inside, gazing at the sparse furnishings. His thoughts went back to the bunker which still only a handful of people knew about. He had not known the purpose for which God had led him to undertake such a madcap project. Yet it had saved his life. Would this cabin and the others in various stages of completion through the hills save lives among God's persecuted people in the future?

He could not know. Usually the leading came without knowledge of the ultimate purpose. One merely had to obey and let God determine the outcome.

He walked back out to the porch and sat down on the bench-slab of oak, breathing in the pleasurable fragrance of the surrounding forest warming in the heat of the sun.

"What do you have for me to communicate to your people?" he whispered. *"If my time is short, what is the final message you have for me—for Todd, for Heather, for others of your Church?*

"Is this all there is to it, finding ways to keep out of sight, hiding books, evading detection, underground meetings? Are those strategies important for God's people at certain times?

"If so, what links them to the commands? What are the underlying foundational connections to the commands that reveal your purposes? The Bible's commands surely represent your marching orders for your

remnant Church as they have revealed your will for your people in all ages. How do the commands inform whatever strategies you lead your people to follow?"

He drew in a deep breath, rose, remounted, and continued through the woodland.

After some twenty minutes he came upon the trail connecting the Bar JG and Circle F ranches. He turned Dusty up the slope and found himself at length cresting the summit of Rustler's Butte.

Again he dismounted, tied Dusty to a nearby scrub oak, and walked to the lookout point. Below him spread portions of both ranches, with the land—*his* land—rising from the valley floor.

Moses returned to his thoughts. At the end of his life he too stood on a mountain gazing out on the land that would become the inheritance of his people. This was *his* land of promise that God had preserved through the years for him.

Suddenly a flash of light stabbed into his brain.

He was standing overlooking the land of an inheritance at the end of his life exactly as at the end of his life Moses stood overlooking the land of Israel's inheritance.

Moses may have prayed a similar prayer. Moses also had a final message to give to God's people. That final message of the great man of God was all about the God's commands!

Moses left his people with a single clarion message—*Live by the Bible's commands.*

With that realization, David knew that God had given him his answer. Moses held the key!

☆ ☆ ☆

Back at home an hour later, the book of Deuteronomy open before him, David began reading through the message God had given Moses for his people. Excitement stirred within him. This ancient book contained not merely a message for the people who heard Moses deliver his final exhortation. This was God's word to his people in *every* era. It was the message for God's people now in *this* era too.

More than three thousand years had not changed God's intent. The word of God to his people was timeless.

104

Two Men

FALL 2061

THE GATHERING of thirty or forty men and women in the underground bunker beneath the new ranch house of the Bar JG ranch outside Grass Valley, California, was strictly by invitation only. They entered through the steep stairway descending from David's new master bedroom above.

Select leaders from BCL groups around the world had been privately notified. Plans for the meeting were made out of the spotlight by Todd and Heather. To further deflect potential curiosity, a BCL gathering was held two weeks prior in Texas which *had* been publicly known, was widely attended, and had attracted some media attention.

Expecting no group gatherings again so soon, those individuals arriving surreptitiously in north-central California a short time later attracted little notice.

The stirrings David felt leading to his ride up to Rustlers Butte several months earlier had not diminished. These were pivotal times for Christians throughout the Western world. He remained convinced that the answers many of God's faithful were seeking about how to respond to the times lay in casting their gaze *back* rather than *forward*, toward antiquity rather than with prophetic scenarios about the future.

Timothy Marshall, now gray and only nine years David's junior at eighty-one, had been feeling almost identical stirrings. It was heavy on his heart that change was coming to the worldwide body of Christ. Whether or not he would characterize those times of change as preparatory for the Lord's return, he was not one to make such a claim. He knew millions of Christians around the globe expected that very thing. But they had been expecting it for a century.

He knew God's people must prepare. The sense was deepening within him, however, that those preparations would be in much different ways than most had been led to expect. He, David, and Mark were in agreement that the coming tribulation would be no Hal Lindsey or *Left Behind* tribulation. It could well be a tribulation that those wedded in allegiance to man's church would never realize was upon them.

If his own time was short, or if a season of tribulation was indeed at hand when God's remnant people would be tested, pruned, and purified as if by fire, then as Stirling Marshall's son he must give to that remnant a word, perhaps as his father had done with his Benedict Brief.

More than sensing an urgency to speak, however, Timothy was hungry to hear what the Spirit was showing his father's protégé and his own dear friend and spiritual mentor to many.

The two men of God were being stirred in prayer by a single Voice.

When Timothy approached David with the request that he follow his father's example—giving God's people an expanded version of the Benedict Brief for new times, or perhaps with some new challenge God was showing him—David smiled knowingly.

"I sense that such has been on your heart as well," he said with a smile.

"It has," nodded Timothy. "But I am more anxious to know what God is showing *you*."

"No less anxious than I am to hear from you. You are Stirling's son. His mantle is upon you."

"I have always seen that mantle resting on your shoulders."

"Perhaps that privilege has come to us both," said David, smiling again. "I concur that the Spirit is stirring. Perhaps the time is coming for us *both* to speak."

Timothy thought back to a conversation he and Jaylene had had with Todd several years before when, almost by accident Todd had used the term "rapture cult." As a relatively new Christian, he had raised the same questions that were on the minds of many who were watching the alarming changes in the world since the half-millennium mark. The St. Louis bombing had exploded a renewed wave of second-coming frenzy.

Timothy was concerned that the prevailing lexicon of end-times teachings was leading thousands, if not millions, away from the bull's-eye of God's purposes. He had tried to help Todd recognize that the "coming out" of the world was lifelong, not something God would accomplish in the twinkling of an eye.

That perspective needed to be transmitted to the entire body of Christ. With a Muslim president in the Oval Office, a new US Constitution pending, and all indications pointing to continued crackdowns on Christianity, the threats of global crisis under the Islamic and Chinese juggernaut were sweeping Christians into a new wave of rapture fever.

Perhaps it rested with him and Mark and David to put these new perilous times into perspective. Bringing Mark into their plan, the three agreed to seek God's guidance about a joint address to the BCL leadership.

As a result, Timothy spent two days alone in the hills in one of the secluded cabins. David remained in the sprawling rebuilt ranch house where he had lived mostly out of sight for the past seven years, which he shared with Heather and Todd and his godson and adoptive grandson, their five-year-old son David Marshall Stewart. Both men had remained serious, prayerful, and reflective in the weeks leading up to the private meeting which was now at hand.

105

Passing the Torch

THE UNDERGROUND compound—warm, comfortably furnished, even cozy in its own way—was silent with a deeper quietude than could be felt above ground even in the most isolated location.

In front of the group, which was squeezed tightly together on chairs and couches, some on the floor, Timothy was the first to speak.

"You all know," he began, "that David, Mark, and I asked you here on what we consider perhaps the most serious business ever to bring us together. We realize the time and expense involved for you to get here, and we appreciate the effort. We have what we believe is a word from God for you to take back and transmit to those among your own groups and fellowships who look to you for leadership. Most of you have been with us for years. You know our hearts. You know we would not make such a claim frivolously. In a sense, we are passing on to you the torch of our combined hundred and seventy years on this earth—speaking for myself and David in particular. Mark is the young kid of our trio! He will be carrying that torch with the rest of you for many years to come."

He briefly explained how he and David had individually experienced similar stirrings about the future.

"The recent elections and the massive changes that have come to the country and world," Timothy said in conclusion, "have many in man's church, yet again as at so many times in the past, proclaiming the approach of the end times and the Lord's return. I'm sure many in your groups are being swept up into that prophetic enthusiasm. We have called you here to give you a long-range and eternal perspective. Of course we need to prepare. We need practical strategies as we face difficult challenges. But for the remnant of God's people whom he is calling out of man's church, those strategies will be much different than for those who are in man's church. We three are convinced that the answers lie in taking a longer view that perhaps looks back instead of forward."

He paused and turned to his right.

"And with that, I will turn it over to my friend and a man I know you all revere as much as I do.—David," he said with a smile. "I am as eager to hear what the Spirit has been showing you as I know everyone else is."

David nodded and smiled, though his countenance was noticeably serious.

"I turned ninety earlier this year," he began after a long silence. "The passage of every decade is momentous as we journey through life. I remember thinking after turning fifty, *Well, I'm halfway there!* Suddenly forty more years have passed. When one turns ninety, it is likely there will be no more decade transitions. Ever since I have felt a strong stirring that God has been speaking. I knew it was important for me to convey what I am seeing."

He paused and drew in a deep breath.

"All those ninety years ago, I was born the year after Hal Lindsey's *The Late Great Planet Earth* was published," David went on. "I came *into* the world just as millions of Christians were anticipating being raptured *out* of the world. The years of my youth were years of feverish second-coming passion in the evangelical church. I was just turning thirty when the *Left Behind* phenomenon took up where Hal Lindsey left off and reignited that fever. During those decades there were literally hundreds of books by best-selling authors proclaiming that the Lord was coming soon, that the antichrist was alive on the earth, and that the events predicted in Revelation and Daniel would take place in our lifetimes.

"I was caught up in it too. I attended a conference at Arrowhead Springs in southern California as an enthusiastic teen. I heard Hal Lindsey speak. All of us listening were mesmerized, myself included. The rapture, the Great Tribulation, the beginning of the millennial reign of Christ on earth—these were all going to take place in our lifetimes. We *knew* it! We were absolutely convinced that we would not live to see the year 2000. We were *utterly* certain everything Hal Lindsey predicted would happen—and soon.

"It is no secret in retrospect, of course, that none of it took place. The author of *88 Reasons Why the Rapture Will Be in 1988*, after the book sold four-and-a-half million copies, said that he had made a computational error in calculating the years. The following year he released a new 1989 version.

"The authors of this flood of prophetic books became famous and wealthy. But where are they now? All those authors are dead. Hopefully they are with their heavenly Father, but they were *not* raptured.

"The fact is, they were all false prophets. According to Deuteronomy 13 and 18, false prophets were to be put to death. But the gullible Christian public continued to swallow everything they said. No one minded that they were false prophets. That is exactly why you will get no specific predictions from me. I look to *trends*, but I am not fond of predictions.

"Neither will it be a secret to any of you that rapture fever has continued through the decades. Millions truly believe that they could be snatched into the clouds at any moment. With all due respect, because I know he was greatly loved by many of you, even Mark's best friend of many years Ward Hutchins perpetrated this imminent rapture delusion.

"My lifetime has almost exactly paralleled this era of prophetic fever, the roots of which can be traced to Israel's nationhood and return to its homeland in 1948, and was ignited into flame by Hal Lindsey's book in 1970.

"I have been watching and observing all this time. I have been studying the Scriptures. I have been asking the Holy Spirit to reveal truth to me. Your series of sermons before you resigned your pastorate, Mark," said David, glancing to Timothy's left where the three men sat, "were pivotal in adding dimensions to my own study and reading. I hope you will be able to share some of your insights later."

Mark nodded in acknowledgment.

"In the years since then," David continued, "I believe the Lord has given the insight I have prayed for, though from what may seem a most unlikely source. That revelation has come upon me slowly, quietly, stealing into my heart by degrees over the years. Many have written me off as a kook . . . and," he added with a smile, "there are those who think so not even knowing my unconventional perspectives about prophecy!"

Light laughter circulated through the group.

"No one here thinks that, David!" said Mark. "You are held in the highest esteem."

Many affirmations followed Mark's comment. Gradually an even more serious expression settled over David's countenance. The room quieted as they waited.

"Thank you, Mark," said David at length. "With a humble heart, if I may say it, you are all most gracious in the honor you show me. And I do feel a sense of stewardship to faithfully follow in Stirling's footsteps, before such time as our Father takes me to join him, and articulate what I am sensing through the glass darkly of my human perceptions.

"Though I do not feel that we are in what has been called *the* Great Tribulation, we are in *a* tribulation, a season of change and probable persecution in which a remnant of true Christians will be called out of the church of man and out of a world fast being overwhelmed by the deception of Islam—called out for the purpose of preserving the true faith during what may be dark and perilous times.

"We are of that remnant. The St. Louis bombing, the election of a president committed to Sharia law, the signs are all around us that the United States as we have known it, is dying. We are in a post-Christian world. However, as Jesus said, I believe the end is not yet. The persecutions to come do not, in my opinion, herald the so-called *end times.*

"I may be wrong. Worldwide nuclear holocaust is a very real possibility. It could come at any moment. But if humanity is not wiped out, God's people must be faithful to preserve truth for the following generations, just as St. Benedict and those of his order did in the fifth century, as countless monks did through the Dark Ages in preserving the Scriptures, as Stirling Marshall did in writing his prophetic Benedict Brief, and as you will all do by passing God's eternal truths into the lives you influence—all of us together sending truth into the future on the wings of our prayerful obedience."

David paused. He closed his eyes briefly. They all knew that they were participating in an historic crossroads moment none of them would ever forget.

"God is building an invisible eternal Church of individual living stones," David went on after fifteen or twenty seconds. "That Church and that process transcends the temporal ups and downs of this world. He was building it before, during, and after the destruction of Israel by Assyria in 722 BC. If ever God's people must have thought it was the end of the world it was then, or when Jerusalem was razed in 586 BC by Nebuchadnezzar and Judah's people carried to captivity in Babylon or in AD 70 when the city was destroyed by the Romans.

"These were times of terrible persecution. But the end was not yet. It was but the beginning of birth pangs. Through these and many times of tribulation that followed, God continued to build his invisible eternal church, which, in the fulness of time, became *Christ's* Church.

"Such it remains in our own times. That building of God's eternal temple continues. We are on an eternal continuum. The prophecy fever paralleling my life has created the unseemly arrogance of assuming that we of *this* time in history are somehow more set apart than any other generation of believers throughout history because Jesus will return in *our* lifetimes. I call this assumption arrogance because I believe that is exactly what fuels end-times fever.

"We mustn't forget that people of many times in history have succumbed to this same self-righteousness, seeing the signs and wonders of *their* times as specially endowed precursors to the Lord's coming that no other people in history were privileged to witness.

"But the end was not yet.

"Nor do I believe, in spite of the persecutions that may await the people of God in the near future, that the end is even now at hand.

"Yes, we are a remnant. But that does not make us a unique and special remnant. Let us take heed unto ourselves that we do not invest the word *remnant* with the hubris of self-righteousness.

"We may not be an *end-times remnant.* Rather I believe we represent a remnant that God is raising up to preserve his Church through one more era of tribulation. He has had a remnant people in *all* times. Now is our season to join our brethren from the past and step into the holy calling to be his faithful remnant people for *our* times.

"We must look to Jesus for what to expect in the days ahead, not to the false prognosticators of every age. Jesus said, 'They will persecute you, even kill you and think they are offering service to God. They will do so because they have not known the Father or me.' Let us carefully heed what the Lord also says: *But the end is not yet.*

"Therefore, I exhort us not to appropriate unto ourselves too much approbation because we live in the end times. We may not live in the end times at all. Nonetheless are we called to live as his obedient and humble people, faithfully preserving God's truth for those of what will perhaps be *many* generations yet to be born and live and die on the earth before the end comes.

"The call of faithful obedience is upon us, not because we live in the end times but because God's people must continue to enter and possess and inhabit the land of promise so that his remnant will endure for a thousand generations."

Again a thoughtful silence followed.

106

A Thousand Generations

DAVID WAS in no hurry.

"I rarely say such a thing," he resumed after a lengthy pause, speaking slowly and weighing his words carefully. "I rarely even *think* it. Actually—I'm not sure I have ever *said* it aloud in my life. However, I will say it now. I believe the Spirit has revealed a truth to me about the times ahead. It came to me from an unexpected source. It came as I was reading through Deuteronomy and reflecting on the farewell message of Moses, that dear man, to the Israelite people.

"I suddenly saw in Moses's words to the Israelites as they were about to enter the promised land almost a roadmap, a blueprint for us today more than three thousand years later as we face uncertain, probably perilous, times—*tribulation*, if we want to use that word. I saw in Moses's words why, in the following centuries, a remnant survived through all the ups and downs that befell Israel and Judah. I saw why the Jews have survived those three thousand years, yet also why many were lost to the world. Whole tribes of Israel were lost—yet from among them a remnant survived, and kept their faith strong.

"The history of Israel is one of ups and downs, of triumphs and persecutions. From rising to be one of the greatest nations on earth under David and Solomon, Israel was overrun first by Assyria and then by Babylon and taken into captivity. Those were times of *great* tribulation. But remnants survived.

"I believe we have been given a window into their survival from Moses's words. Moses foresaw and predicted that captivity and its remnant long before David and Solomon rose to prominence on the world stage.

"Moses's words are chillingly prophetic, then and now. 'The Lord will scatter you among the peoples. . . . But from there you will seek the Lord your God, and you will find him if you search after him with all your heart and with all your soul. When you are in tribulation, and all these things come upon you in the latter days, you will return to the Lord your God and obey his voice.' *

"The same charge, and the same warning he issued to the Israelites in his farewell address, stretches forward to us today. His words light our way in a season of darkness that may descend upon Christendom as Islam and hedonism and ungodliness sweep across the nations of the earth.

"I believe it is Moses and the remnant peoples of the Old Testament that illuminate the path God appoints his people to walk through this spreading darkness coming upon us. The rapture will not give the light we need. Moses's words light our way.

"Some of you may be shocked for me to say that I do not believe we are living in the end times. My reason goes back to Moses's farewell charge in which he made this astonishing statement. *Acknowledge and take to heart this day that the Lord is God of heaven above and on the earth below. Know, therefore, that the Lord your God is God. He is a faithful God, keeping his covenant of love to a thousand generations of those who love him and keep his commandments.* **

"Was Moses using hyperbole to make a point? Or might more truth be embodied in that statement than we have assumed? Might God have many more generations of people to raise up to follow and love him and keep his commandments?

"Stop and think a moment—how many generations have passed since Moses's time? Depending how one computes it, I calculate it between 100 and 120 generations. We sitting here today are approximately the hundredth or maybe the hundred-twentieth generation since

* Deuteronomy 4:27, 29–30 RSV.

** A loose paraphrase of Deuteronomy 7:9

Moses. Yet Moses declares God will keep his covenant to a *thousand* generations!

"Those who might say that he was speaking metaphorically to mean *a long time* miss the import of the rest of the book. Of course Moses could be poetic at times, but normally he spoke actual realities. A land flowing with milk and honey—there *really* were bees and cattle in the land they were going in to possess. Was he speaking metaphorically when he predicted that Israel would be scattered among the nations? Those words have been precisely and literally fulfilled many times throughout history. I do not believe we can so easily ignore the potential import of his thousand generations statement.

"Moses is talking about earth-generations, not eternity. There will be no generations in eternity, for life will go on forever. Thus, it may be that God has yet only *begun* his thousand-generation work upon the earth!

"With Moses's words echoing out of the past, we then come to Jesus, trying desperately to make himself heard in a church easily deluded into gullibly chasing every false prophecy that comes along:

"But the end is not yet.

"However, few are listening. They prefer to trust in the words of pseudo-prophets more than in the words of the Lord. Jesus says:

"And when you hear, 'Lo here, lo there,' do not believe it . . . take heed that no one leads you astray, for many will come in my name, but see that you are not alarmed, for the end is not yet.

"Because of this gullible blindness energized by the hubris of self-righteousness, in every generation God requires a remnant people to probe the deeper and eternal purposes of his heart who will quietly and humbly carry forward the charge of Moses.

"All around us for years we have watched as the church of man has made itself the ally of the world. Yet through it all, God continues to raise up a remnant people. He continues to call them out of man's worldly church, lighting the path forward in the world's darkness for the future men, women, and children of his thousand generations.

"If I could," said David, turning to Timothy, "I would like for Timothy to share some of his perspectives. Most of you, I believe, have read the transcripts of his lectures on Islam from several years ago. They too,

I believe, like Moses's farewell address, were prophetic, as recent events in our country confirm.—Timothy, perhaps you could speak to what you see having changed in the ten years since your lectures."

Timothy nodded thoughtfully.

"Sure," he said. "Why don't we first take a break . . . walk around, stretch our legs.—Heather and Jaylene, would the two of you mind running up to the house and put on coffee and water for tea. The rest of you, as a reminder when you go upstairs, please stay inside. We remain concerned about surveillance of our activities. We still need to keep our presence together here off the radar."

107

The Prince of This World

HALF AN hour later, after much animated discussion, the group was seated again.

"What David alluded to before," Timothy began, "is certainly true. The ten years since my lectures have witnessed unbelievable changes on the world stage. As prophetic as was his Benedict Brief, my father could not have possibly envisioned all that was coming. The godlessness of progressivism and the normalization of its numerous sexual depravities is truly disgusting, not to mention the violence against Christians. Yet we find ourselves coming awake to the fact that an even greater enemy of truth than liberalism has all along been the deception of Islam.

"It is unimaginable to realize that progressives elected President Bahram, and then, after the mask hiding his true intentions began to come off, *reelected* him. Progressives were so deeply and pervasively deluded for so long that this present delusion is but one more step in a delusion that has been steadily losing touch with reality for a hundred years. In relinquishing common sense, progressives have fulfilled Paul's prophetic words from Romans 1. 'They became futile in their thinking and their senseless minds were darkened. Claiming to be wise they became fools . . . they exchanged the truth about God for a lie. . . . Their women exchanged natural relations for unnatural, and the men gave up natural relations with women . . . committing shameless acts with men. . . . And since they did not see fit to acknowledge

God, God gave them up to a base mind and . . . they were filled with all manner of wickedness, evil . . . strife, deceit . . . haters of God, insolent, haughty, boastful . . . disobedient to parents, foolish, faithless, heartless, ruthless.'

"Paul exquisitely described the liberal progressivism that has systematically undermined the values of Western civilization, and sterilized our culture of virtue and truth. Biding its time for centuries, Islam has been allowed to enter the bloodstream of the West by stealth, as have China and Russia. All three powers have used liberal blindness to infiltrate America. Progressivism laid the groundwork for its own suicide, and still has little idea what it has done in making a pact with the devil. At the moment Islam seems to be in the ascendency. But China and Russia are waiting in the wings. Whichever world power ends up on top, whether by war or by stealth tactics against their adversaries, I think it is clear that the United States, and truth itself, will not be the victor in that invisible war.

"The church is as much to blame for America's decline as progressivism. The world has not caused the disintegration of the family. The church of man and its worldly clergy is directly responsible for the collapse of family structure and order. When a lesbian woman pastor or a gay man performs a same-sex marriage between two lesbians in the supposed name of Christ, we witness nothing less than blasphemy against Jesus and his Father. Is this the *abomination of desolation* that characterizes the antichrist as Jesus says in Matthew 24? Other translations call it an *abhorring abomination*, a *loathing and nauseating desolation*—a *desolating sacrilege* standing in the holy place. What more holy place exists than the pulpit of God's church being turned into an altar to the world's sexual perversion by men and women pretending to be God's ministers and priests. Jesus says to those who observe these monstrous evils in the churches of man, 'let them flee to the mountains.' In other words—leave those antichrist churches of the world. Come out from them and be separate. The remnant must flee or be consumed by the evil.

"What a hell of retribution awaits those false prophets and priests and ministers who blaspheme the Father of Jesus Christ and tolerate and endorse the hedonistic sin of their gay and lesbian followers. They will together find themselves in a hell worse than what may be endured by murderers and prostitutes, adding to the horror of their sin the abominable lie that God is pleased with them. May God have mercy on their self-deluded souls! I admit I can find nothing in my heart but loathing for the wickedness they have allowed to poison the body of Christ, and for their God-mocking effrontery to say they have done so in the name of Jesus.

"If the end times are upon us, this may be the sign that antichrist has come. And the church of man has bowed in allegiance to him.

"What a day of reckoning awaits. Islam's holy war will ultimately sweep away those who opened the door to its takeover of America with their liberal hedonism, including the churches of man and the pastors and priests who tolerated the world's evil and even contributed to it.

"I am sorry to say but I believe the United States of America is lost as the nation we have known and loved. Christianity is not lost, but the Christian underpinnings of America are lost. We have the liberalism of recent generations to thank for the loss of what America means, for the loss of the freedom which has been the lifeblood of our historic exceptionalism.

"I'm sorry to get so worked up. But I weep for our nation. My quiet fury is not primarily against the Clintons and Obamas and Bidens and Mark's friend, our former president Jefferson Rhodes, but against the foolishness of the multitudes—Christians among them—who allowed the hypocrisies of such leaders to blind them to obvious truth.

"So where are we now? I fear that what we have witnessed since President Bahram's first inauguration is only the beginning of birth pangs. I fear that freedom and democracy will soon be swallowed up in the tidal wave of Islam's worldwide advance.

"Satan has not won. But he is the prince of this world, and at present the world, through Islam, is in his hands.

"We as Christians are a remnant of the faith living in a world controlled by the enemy. We are an exiled people. Christians have to change their ways of thinking, imagining the world will be won for Christ, imagining that America will return from its present darkness.

"A new dark age of godlessness is upon us. We are not merely a remnant, we are a remnant in exile, hated by the twin evils that have risen in this century to bury Christianity for the foreseeable future—progressivism and Islam.

"Yet the church of man will continue. For all I know it may even thrive as it finds a way to make an alliance with Islam just as it made an alliance with progressivism. Both alliances are pacts with the devil.

"Our situation is much like those Israelites and Jews during the Assyrian and Babylonian and Persian captivities of old. We are not called to armed revolt. We are not called to overthrow the world's systems. We are called to *life* . . . to live in the captivity of our exile as a remnant—preserving truth, living quietly as God's people, *in the world but not of the world.*

"The Jews of old integrated into the society of their captors without allowing the evils and religions of their captors to dilute the essential truth of their faith. Some of course did succumb to the world's evils, and they were swallowed into them. But those of the faithful remnant, men like Ezra and countless others, kept the faith alive.

"So how do *we* live as a faithful remnant, integrating into the society of our exile without allowing it to dilute our faith?

"That is the question of the ages. True believing Christians have been asking it for millennia. Every remnant disciple, every remnant man and woman, has to walk in the way God leads. As David said about specifics, neither will I suggest a blueprint.

"That said, I do know that it is *not* the duty of a remnant people to take up arms against its captors, nor to think that we can hide from persecution by escaping to utopian retreats. Neither Masada nor the desert communities of the Essenes are our models.

"The duty of a remnant is to preserve God's truth and pass that truth into the future. Such has been the duty of all remnants through history, preserving truth until such time as God brings a Josiah or an Ezra or a Benedict or a Martin Luther or, dare I also say, a Stirling Marshall, to speak a vision that ignites a new flame or until God orchestrates events and steps into history to alter events as in the fullness of time Jesus stepped onto the planet.

"When such a time may come again, who can say. When will the Lord return in his glory? Will a worldwide holocaust of nuclear destruction lead God again to step personally onto the planet?

"I cannot even speculate on such things. Perhaps it may be so. I am left, as David has so perceptively illuminated, with Moses's words about God's thousand generations and the Lord's words, *the end is not yet.*

"I therefore will only say that we must not look for the Lord's return simply because we have a Muslim president. Nor must we be anxious to proclaim our president the antichrist. Our duty is to recognize that we are a people in exile as were the Israelites of old. Like them, we have been overrun by Babylon. Thus we are called to live in Babylon but not of Babylon.

"Small-scale deceptions may be part of life for God's remnant in Babylon for the purpose of saving lives. We are at present hiding in a bunker that David was led to construct in secret. Who can tell but that this bunker may save more lives in the future.

"But this is no Masada. We represent no outlaw community in hiding, nor will we take on the forces of evil with armed revolt.

"When the worst comes, we will raise no weapons but will rather lift the empty hands of faith and say, *Be it unto us, Lord, according to your will, for we are in your hands.*"

108

Be Careful Not to Forget the Commands

A LONG SILENCE filled the room.

"Thank you, Timothy," said David at length. "Frightening, chilling, sad . . . yet your insights are profound. I believe you have spoken great truth. I am reminded of Moses's words, again from Deuteronomy, *If your heart turns away and you are not obedient, and if you are drawn away to worship other gods and bow down to them, then you will certainly not live long in the land.**

"What Timothy has just described as characterizing these times in which we are living is the story of man's church in *every* age. Men have been drawn away to bow down to other gods and worship the unique gods of worldliness of *their* age, joining the particular manifestation of the Ally of *their* times.

"Moses's words are as timely in explaining what is happening around us as they explain the lure of worldliness throughout the ages. What is the progressivism of this century but the wholesale bowing down of an entire culture to pay homage to false gods mocking the Father of Jesus Christ? What is Islam now but the bowing down to the evil god of Mohammed that mocks the Father of Jesus by pretending that his Allah-idol is the same God worshipped and obeyed by Abraham and the patriarchs?

"In our own lifetimes we have seen those of man's churches drawn away into worshipping the god of music, the god of conformity, the god

* A paraphrase of Deuteronomy 30:17–18.

of doctrinal correctness, the god of experientialism, the gods of rites and ceremonies, the cult of personality, the idols of blessing and prosperity. They have fashioned idols out of superficial forms of worship, even turning the sacred communion sacrament into a talismanic ritual that becomes an idol all its own in place of a living reality. They have been drawn away to worship myriad other false gods, exactly as Moses warned against in place of obedience to the commands. Thus the church of man has succumbed to the very path of death Moses spoke of.

"Moses's farewell message, which I believe is a word to God's people of all times resounds with a single message:

"Obey God's commands. Be careful never to forget them. There are two paths in life—obedience to God's commands and disobedience to God's commands. Therefore choose life.

"I challenge you to read through the book of Deuteronomy—perhaps skipping the lengthy historical reviews of the forty years in the desert—for this message I believe God gave Moses for his people in every age. Read particularly chapters 4, 6, 7, 8, 11, 30. You will be amazed at the repetition of these words and phrases:

"Be careful, watch yourselves closely, be very careful, take heed to yourselves, be careful not to forget the Lord your God, failing to obey his commands and decrees, and laws, keep the Lord's command, be careful to observe his decrees and laws, faithfully obey.

"These commands are repeated over and over and over, always with the underlying if-then equation of individual choice informing the whole book:

"If you are careful to obey the Lord's commands, it will go well with you and your children after you. The Lord your God will bless you and you will live long in the land. But if you are not obedient and are drawn away to worship other gods, you will not live long in the land. I command you to love the Lord your God, to walk in obedience to him, and to obey his commands, decrees, and laws. I set before you life and prosperity, death and destruction, a blessing and a curse. Therefore choose life so that you and your children may live, and that you may love the Lord your God, listen to his voice, and hold fast to him.

"This is the message of Deuteronomy and to God's people of all times and eras. It is an eternal message of a creator-Father to his children.

With all my heart I believe that this is the message for God's people—you and me—in preparing to live in Babylon but not of Babylon.

"This is the message of the gospel Jesus taught, taking them out of the Old Testament Law of Moses and raising them, glorifying the commands into a New Covenant of obedience, with the same underlying framework—*Obey my commands, be careful not to forget.*

"I call it the 'Deuteronomy Protocol,' though we might just as well call it the Moses Protocol or the Jesus Protocol. Jesus essentially summarized the book of Deuteronomy and the if-then equation of life, at the end of the Sermon on the Mount. Read Matthew 7:24–27 with Moses in mind. He said, *Do my words and your house will stand, do not do them and your house will fall.*

"We are disciples and followers of Jesus Christ. The four Gospels represent our freedom manifesto as a remnant people. The words and commands of Jesus lay out the lifestyle of *in but not of the world* integration into the society of our exile, just as the commands, decrees, and laws that Moses enjoined upon the Israelites laid out the lifestyle of integration into the Babylon of Israel's exile that preserved the faith for men like Josiah and Ezra and the other prophets so that it would be passed down to us.

"Those who followed the commands, even in their exile, thrived. Those who did not were swallowed into the world around them and were lost. Those so-called believers around us today who are embracing the world's values will also be lost. But God's remnant will survive in its exile by following and living as Jesus commanded, heeding Moses's words to be careful not to forget God's commands.

"How we will face every challenge, I cannot say. With the threat to families, it may be that for a season some husbands and wives will choose not to have families rather than run the risks to which children are exposed in our day. We may not merely be a people in exile, the remnant may be forced underground in some ways. Not only are the Israelites of ancient Babylon our example, so too may be the courageous Christians of Rome who hid in the catacombs, and our courageous brethren during the years of Soviet oppression who worshipped in hiding. All these perils will face us. There will be ebbs and flows. Situations will change. We cannot predict nor lay out specifics other than that the Deuteronomy Protocol and the commands of Jesus remain our manifesto of life.

"Some may be martyred. Charlie Kirk was assassinated for his outspoken faith. Some may be imprisoned. Children may be taken away. Some will be arrested. Some will be led to speak out. Some will be led to be silent. Some gatherings may be public. Some may meet in hiding. Integrating into the society of our captors does not mean being foolish. Wise as serpents and innocent as doves may mean underground meetings. That is prudence not deception. If discovered we will not fight but submit in Christlikeness.

"The commands will lead us. I truly that believe *every* dilemma we face in the days of tribulation ahead has a solution to be found in one of the Bible's commands. We may have to seek hard and pray diligently and listen carefully to determine that solution and to find that command. But it will be there.

"We may be evasive and cryptic to protect life, to protect our brothers and sisters, but we will not lie. Jesus said, *Do not resist an evil man.* This command may tell us a great deal about how God's people are to face the persecutions ahead. We may meet in hiding. We may be arrested, but we will betray no one. We will resist the machinations of the Ally and the world's evil, but we will not fight. Questions we cannot answer truthfully without endangering another, we will meet with silence. We will hate evil, but we will hate no man or woman of God's creation no matter how lost or deceived in evil they may be. We will face persecution, tribulation, and even death with courage.

"There is a rumor that the Rhodes Freedom Bill passed several years ago, though it dramatically curtailed individual freedoms, was based on a secret document called the Freedom Manifesto. It is the long-used strategy of the Left to call untruth truth. Nevertheless, whether that is the case or not, we have a true manifesto for life and it is called the Bible. The Bible is mankind's *Freedom Manifesto*—freedom from sin, freedom from alienation from our Father and alienation from our brothers and sisters of humanity. Its precepts for freedom are called commands. Those commands are our manual for life in the exile of the new Babylons taking over our world."

109

The Deuteronomy Protocol

DAVID PAUSED and drew in a long breath, then took from his pocket a small leather book.

"I have been studying the book of Deuteronomy assiduously for the past months, ever since the revelation that in Moses's farewell address we find our own way forward into the season of our exile. I have compiled, paraphrased, and occasionally in my own words and for my own use, the high points of the six chapters I mentioned. Let me read a summary of what I call the Deuteronomy Protocol," he said. "Keep in mind *we* are spiritual Israel, God has a land for *us* to inherit, which is his eternal kingdom. Listen as if the words are meant for today, for the year 2061—for surely they are."

He turned several pages in the small book, then began.

> *"Now, Israel, hear the decrees and laws I am about to teach you. Follow them so that you may live and may go in and take possession of the land the Lord, the God of your ancestors, is giving you. I have taught you decrees and laws as the Lord commanded me. Observe them carefully, for this will show your wisdom and understanding to the nations.*
>
> *"Only be careful, and watch yourselves closely so that you do not forget the things your eyes have seen or let them fade from your heart. Teach them to your children and to their children*

after them. Watch yourselves very carefully, so that you do not make for yourselves an idol, an image of any shape. Be careful not to forget the covenant of the Lord your God that he made with you.

"Acknowledge and take to heart this day that the Lord is God in heaven above and on the earth below. Keep his decrees and commands so that it may go well with you and your children after you, and that you may live long in the land the Lord your God gives you.

"These are the commands, decrees and laws the Lord your God directed me to teach you to observe, so that you, your children and their children after them may fear the Lord your God as long as you live by keeping all his decrees and commands. Hear, Israel, and be careful to obey so that it may go well with you and that you may increase greatly in a land flowing with milk and honey.

"Hear, O Israel: The Lord our God, the Lord is one. Love the Lord your God with all your heart and with all your soul and with all your strength. These commandments are to be on your hearts. Impress them on your children. Talk about them when you sit at home and when you walk along the road, when you lie down and when you get up.

"Do not follow other gods, the gods of the peoples around you. Be sure to keep the commands of the Lord your God. Do what is right and good in the sight of the Lord.

"Make no treaty with the nations around you. Do not intermarry with them. For you are a people holy to the Lord your God. Know therefore that the Lord your God is a faithful God, keeping his covenant of love to a thousand generations of those who love him and keep his commandments.

"Therefore, take care to follow the commands, decrees and laws I give you today. If you pay attention to these laws and are careful to follow them, then the Lord your God will bless you and increase your numbers.

"Be careful to follow every command I am giving you today, so that you may live and increase and may enter and possess the land the Lord promised to your ancestors.

"Observe the commands of the Lord your God, walking in obedience to him and revering him. When you have eaten and are satisfied, praise the Lord your God for the good land he has given you. Be careful that you do not forget the Lord your God, failing to observe his commands, his laws and his decrees.

"Be careful, or you will be enticed to turn away and worship other gods and bow down to them. Fix these words in your hearts and minds so that your days and the days of your children may be many in the land.

"If you carefully observe all these commands I am giving you to follow—to love the Lord your God, to walk in obedience to him and to hold fast to him—then every place where you set your foot will be yours.

"See, I am setting before you today a blessing and a curse—the blessing if you obey the commands of the Lord your God; the curse if you disobey the commands of the Lord your God and turn from the way that I command you today.

"Now what I am commanding you is not too difficult for you or beyond your reach. No, the word is very near you; it is in your mouth and in your heart so you may obey it.

"I command you today to love the Lord your God, to walk in obedience to him, and to keep his commands, decrees and laws. Then you will live and increase, and the Lord your God will bless you in the land.

"But if your heart turns away and you are not obedient, and if you are drawn away to bow down to other gods and worship them, I declare to you this day that you will certainly not live long in the land.

"This day I call the heavens and the earth as witnesses that I have set before you life and death, blessings and curses. Now choose life, so that you and your children may live and that you may love the Lord your God, listen to his voice, and hold fast to him."

David closed the small book and breathed in deeply.

"I love these simple but profound injunctions," he said, speaking softly. "They take my breath away with their application to literally *every* instance through history where God's people and Christ's church have gone astray, taken the wrong road, and deviated from God's purposes. What I have just read summarizes the entire history of humanity on the earth."

110

Looking Ahead Eternally

"THIS SUMMARIZES what I have to say," said David at length. "I probably said more than I needed to. I have nothing to add to Moses's words. However, if you have questions, I would be happy to do my best to respond to them."

"What about the prophecies, David," said Court Masters, "—the rapture, the tribulation, the end times of Matthew 24 and the second coming? It seems that the Bible teaches that eventually, at *some* future time, these things will take place. Do you personally have any sense when those times will be?"

"What I've said about the thousand generations," replied David, "clarifies that I do not believe those second-coming prophecies will be fulfilled anytime soon. I could be wrong. The Lord may return tomorrow. I don't know. If God did not reveal those specifics to Moses or Jesus, is it likely he would reveal them to me, or to any mortal? I feel strongly that those millions who are expecting God to rapture them away without them having submitted to his purifying *becoming* are deluding themselves with utopian visions of spiritual immaturity.

"But for more specifics on what we might call second-coming doctrine, I would urge you to read Mark's book, *Have Christians Misread the Bible's End-Times Scriptures?* It is the best book on prophecy you will ever read.—Mark," he said, turning to Mark sitting beside Timothy, "perhaps you could give a brief overview."

Mark thought a minute.

"I agree with David," he said at length. "I don't know what the future holds. I would be hesitant to add to his words, or to the words of Moses and Jesus. As David has said, their commands are the marching orders for God's people in exile.

"However, for those who might want to dig deeper into a study of prophecy in Scripture," Mark went on, "let me just give you the foundational outlook upon which my book is based. If you care to investigate further, we have a limited supply left.

"The basic premise is that through the history of man's church, most Christians have misunderstood the intricate, complex, multi-dimensional prophetic paradigm of the Bible. They have misunderstood much of the Old Testament's message and import, and they have likewise misunderstood almost entirely the prophecies concerning the second coming of Jesus.

"They misunderstand because they read prophecy externally and temporally rather than internally and eternally. This causes them to view prophecy as played out primarily through world events rather than in the eternal tapestry that God is weaving in the hearts of the people of his creation. Such interpretations will never reveal the deepest purposes which are in God's heart to accomplish.

"The import of the incarnation cannot be found in Daniel's seventy weeks of years or in a stable in Bethlehem. The import of the incarnation is that the Fatherhood of the universe came to live in the hearts of mankind to reveal the nature of Sonship. The incarnation is a living *spiritual* reality that can only be fully understood *internally* and *eternally*.

"Many Christians also read prophecy with an escapism that is contrary to the way God carries out and fulfills his purposes among men. Not apprehending the *spiritual* significance of prophecy, they read into the prophecies what they want to read into them.

"The rapture is a perfect example of escapist wishful thinking. But we're in for the long haul. The rapture happens continually. It is happening all around us as God's people come out from the world and as the Lord's *coming* is manifested as a reality in their hearts. Whether Paul knew he was speaking metaphorically or believed that the Lord's return would be physical and temporal, I cannot say. I suspect he knew he was speaking metaphorically.

"Then finally I would mention another of the major thematic principles I find in Scripture that undergirds my entire outlook. That is the truth, as Jaylene articulates so insightfully in her books, that God's pattern generally is to work through time and the normal flow of events to accomplish his ends. Most of God's work is carried out *slowly* and is accomplished through *natural law.*

"These few points are probably enough for you to decide whether or not you want to explore my study of biblical prophecy further.

"Everyone lives at a certain point of time on the continuum of history. They therefore seek specific, temporal interpretations to Scripture's prophecies. All too often that practice misses their larger, sweeping, eternal themes. Moses, of course, spoke specifically to his people at a temporal time. But more importantly, his words are imbued with the high themes of God's purposes that transcend his own era with the music of eternity.

"This is why I believe we can trust the words of Timothy's father Stirling and our friend David. I know Timothy will agree with me. These two remarkable men constantly point upward and beyond temporal specifics to the high symphony of eternity.

"These men have been given for such a time as this to turn us toward God's high truths. Our progeny will make up the remnant of the future to expand these truths forward unto the generations. Our *brains* may want to know times and seasons. But our *hearts* do not need to know them. By hearkening back to Moses, David has left us a prophetic word that transcends the transitory temporal times in which we find ourselves, and points the way to the future for Christ's remnant Church."

111

Unto the Generations

AS THE gathering broke up with many animated conversations, Heather took her mother aside.

"Mom, would you mind watching Davie for a while after you're through here?" she said.

"Of course not, honey," replied Jaylene. "But I think Laura is fine with him."

"I know. But there's something I need to do. I may not be back for a while."

Heather went in search of Todd. He had drifted toward the front of the group where many were clamoring to speak with David, Mark, and her father.

Heather smiled at the sight. She was now accustomed to Todd's coming in for his own share of attention as Timothy Marshall's son-in-law. The talk, discussion, and hubbub on this day was especially spirited. Though all those present hoped for a gathering of some kind every year or two, no one could be sure what lay ahead. There were good reasons why this coming together of select individuals had been held in secret.

It was also on many minds that this might be one of the last times they saw David. Everyone hoped for a brief word with him. Timothy and Jaylene, too, with pure white hair and their contented visages reflecting their years, would not be with them forever. Of the older generation of unofficial leadership, Court Masters and Harvey Janson were mere youngsters at seventy-three and seventy, with Mark and Charles Reyburn following behind at sixty-one and sixty.

Todd saw Heather approach, turned and bent down as she whispered briefly in his ear. Heather then went to find the other three who had been impressed upon her heart.

After brief farewells throughout the room, she disappeared up the narrow stairs into the bunkhouse apartment at the back of the barn which had served as a temporary home for Todd and David, and where she and Todd still kept extra work clothes and boots on hand.

She changed quickly and walked outside and to the nearest pasture. She soon had five horses inside the barn and began saddling and tacking them in readiness for what she had in mind.

☆ ☆ ☆

Half an hour later, while the group in the bunker gradually made its way up the opposite stairway into the back of the ranch house—where Jaylene, Grace and Laura Forster, Stella Masters, Regina Reyburn, and Harriet Jansen were busily setting out a buffet—five riders left the Bar JG barn on horseback. They set out along the well-worn trail toward the wooded hills surrounding the ranch. After disappearing into the trees, the path veered and branched off in innumerable directions. The main trail, winding circuitously through woods, across several streams, and up and down through the foothills, eventually descended again into the precincts of the Circle F ranch where Mark Forster had been raised and which Ginger, riding beside her fiancé Bradon Rhodes and her brother Craig, bringing up the rear, now called home.

Leading the way, Heather's objective on this day was not the Circle F. When she turned at the next fork, they all knew her destination. Before long their way steepened.

Todd let her go ahead and fell back alongside Bradon.

"So how goes the apprenticeship with Mark and Grace?" he asked.

"If you survived Christopher's Plan, I guess I have to man up too!" laughed Bradon.

"It can't be that bad!" laughed Todd.

"I'm just kidding," said Bradon.

"You'd better be!" added Ginger at his side.

"Really it's great," said Bradon, growing serious. "I don't know what I expected. I mean, it's intimidating at first spending so much time with your future in-laws. But Mark and Grace are like no man and woman I've ever met. It's an amazing family to be part of."

"I would agree," said Todd. "You're a lucky guy."

"What I didn't expect is how, I don't know, it's made me feel, not exactly closer to my dad, but maybe able to love him in a new way."

"I'm happy to hear that."

"It's a remarkable thing to realize that my dad was here—maybe *right here*. He and Mark were best friends. The two of them rode these same trails. He met David Gordon too. He was exposed to such amazing spiritual influences. Gosh, can you imagine—my dad could be one of us now. He could have been at today's gathering. How could two such different men like Mark and my dad have once been so close?"

He paused and laughed lightly, though a little sadly.

"Actually, being with Ginger's parents, getting ready to join their family, it's made me *understand* my dad even less. I don't know that I've ever felt close to him. It's sad, really. Mark is more of a father to me than my dad was. I love my dad, but there's no deep bond, no *spiritual* friendship. Weird as it is to say, I almost feel sorry for him. He could have had so much more in life."

"More than the presidency?" said Craig, listening from behind them.

"You know what I mean, Craig," replied Bradon, glancing back. "He could have been part of all this. He could have been God's man."

"He made choices, Bradon," said Ginger. "Just like David said."

"What if he was *supposed* to be part of it? What if that's why he met Mark at that camp? What if God planned for my dad to follow the same path in life that Mark did, even be at Mark's side today—two men of God, brothers in the Lord?"

"We all make choices," said Todd. "It's the *if-then* equation David spoke about. Your father *could* have been there with Mark. But when life's crossroads came, one after the other, he and Mark chose different paths."

"I know you're right. But it's still a mystery *why* people make different choices."

"I don't know if it's scriptural—we'll have to ask David!" Todd added laughing. "But I wonder if God always has a Plan B. Maybe you are his

Plan B. That didn't sound right—I don't mean second best! But if your dad *had* made the life-choices to be God's man, then you would have been raised with your roots of personhood going down into the good soil of God's truth. Hopefully you would be right where you are today, walking with God as you are. But since your dad didn't make those life-choices, God wasn't about to forget about *you*. So in the fullness of time, he brought you and Ginger together, and brought you into Mark's life and mine, and raised you up just as he intended all along."

"That's amazing to get my head around!"

"God wanted your father to be part of it all too. But when he took that possibility out of his hands by his choices, God used different means to reveal himself to *you*. And you *did* respond when he put life choices in front of you. You made the choices your dad never did. That's what I mean by God's Plan B."

"That's a pretty remarkable thing the way you explain it."

Bradon let out a long sigh. "Even though part of me feels sorry for my dad," he said, "at the same time, looking at it over a lifetime, the path he took seems so foolish. How could he have been so blind not to see Mark and David for who they were? He could have still gone into politics, maybe still have become president—but as God's man. Though I suppose he would never have gotten anywhere in politics if he hadn't been such a liberal. Yet still, how could he not see all this for how wonderful it is? He *still* doesn't see it."

"Is he pleased for you to be marrying Mark's daughter?" asked Todd.

"I honestly don't know," replied Bradon. "My mom is overjoyed, and my grandmother."

He smiled morosely. "But my dad . . . he's an enigma."

"There have been big changes for you and me both," nodded Todd, "coming into a fellowship of Christians not having spiritual upbringings. I went through my own growing pains, I guess you'd say, though not about my father."

Todd paused thoughtfully.

"I realize many children don't have Godly parents, but even those who do often don't have the humility to trust them. That's one of the reasons I admire you, Craig," he said, glancing behind him, "and you, Ginger. You are a son and daughter to make your parents proud. You exemplify what I meant by the humility to trust your parents. As does my dear wife!" he added.

Heather turned around and flashed a beautiful smile.

Todd leaned forward in the saddle and glanced over at Ginger. "Have you two set a date yet?" he asked.

"Spring is always nice for a wedding," replied Ginger. "We're thinking next March or April . . . possibly May. Bradon and I are talking about it with my parents. You and Heather will be the first to know!"

"And at the ranch?"

"Where else!" said Bradon.

"That should be interesting for your father! Returning to the Circle F after so many years."

"And, like you said—after a lifetime of choices. It will be a much different reunion between him and Mark as the two fathers of bride and groom than their reunion in Washington when my dad was president."

☆ ☆ ☆

Climbing the last mile in single file, twenty-five minutes later they crested the summit of Rustler's Butte. Not only were the horses breathing heavily, so were the five riders on their backs. They dismounted, tied off their horses, and walked quietly about the familiar plateau.

Heather wandered toward the overlook and sat down. One by one the others joined her. They sat for some time in silence gazing out in different directions over portions of the two ranches below.

"You're probably wondering why I called this meeting," said Heather at length. The four laughed. They were wondering exactly that.

"I was listening to what you were talking about earlier, Bradon," she said, "about your father and why he wasn't among us today, and how his life choices diverged from Mark's. I've wondered exactly the same thing. My dad has two brothers and two sisters. None of them were here today. They were raised in the home of Stirling and Larke Marshall just as he was. They were taught and trained in the same spiritual principles. Why did my grandparents' legacy fall to my dad to carry on? Why aren't his brothers and sisters part of it in the way my father and mother are? Of course they love and revere their parents. Yet they don't fully apprehend the eternal impact of their lives, though I think my Uncle Woody is beginning to. But the others haven't made their parents' spiritual vision their own. I think what it boils down to is that they don't see who Stirling and Larke Marshall were. If they did, they would want to immerse themselves in that legacy, live by it, and pass it on."

She drew in a deep breath.

"It's like Bradon said about his father—it's a mystery. I have eleven cousins. Why am I the only one devoted to our grandparents' legacy? None of them are here today either. Why am I the one answering the mail? They all heard the same things from our grandparents I did. I'm no more special than any of them. Sometimes I think I'm the *least* qualified to be doing what I do. They know of my grandfather's writings and my mom's and dad's books. But none of them are interested. Maybe I'm God's Plan B too!" she laughed, glancing toward Bradon.

"You're my Plan A!" said Todd. "Both you and Bradon are A's in God's book!"

"If you say so!" laughed Bradon.

"It's not only a mystery, it's sad," said Heather, growing serious again. "Though in my weaker moments I admit it makes me angry that my cousins are so oblivious to the magnitude of what God has done and is doing through the Marshall family. I want to shake them and say, *How can you be so blind? Can't you see what's right in front of you!* But they *don't* see. They have the same Marshall blood in their veins. But they don't care. They don't have eyes to *see.*

"I guess in a way it's not a mystery at all. As David said, Moses laid all this out more than three thousand years ago. The *if-then* equation faces every human being every moment of every day. There are always two life paths. The forks in the road come continually and daily. We are always choosing, *constantly* choosing one or the other. Mark made choices, your dad made choices, Bradon. I make choices. I believe we *choose* whether or not to see. My cousins don't care about embracing our grandparents' spiritual vision because they *choose* not to see. They choose to see through the eyes of self, rather than through God's eyes.

"Todd, you made the choice to give your heart and your future to the Lord instead of chasing fame and fortune in the world. We all admire you for that. I'm sure it was hard. But most of the choices we face every day *aren't* hard choices. Moses said that exact thing—*Now what I am commanding you is not too difficult for you or beyond your reach.* The choices aren't difficult. But they have to be *chosen* and *made* and God's path followed.

"It sounds funny, but in a way it sums up everything in life . . . *we have to choose to choose* . . . we have to choose to make right choices."

Heather paused. It was quiet a long time.

"As I listened to David and heard him reading those words from Deuteronomy," she resumed after a minute, "and as he spoke about the generations who continued the legacy of Moses's commission through the years of the Old Testament, the realization filled my heart that we five are the future generation David was speaking about. *We* are the next generation of my grandfather's legacy, and of David's, and of my mom's and dad's, and eventually the next generation of the legacy of your parents, Ginger and Craig, and all the others. Their legacy will one day rest on *our* shoulders to pass on to our children and those who follow us.

"*We* represent the generations to come! What a privilege is ours. God has given us such Godly mentors, such a wonderful heritage—how can we not want to do everything we can to live by it and continue and pass on that heritage?"

She paused again and took a deep breath.

"That's what I felt I needed to say to the rest of you. I want us to commit to each other as a spiritual pact, a commitment, a lifetime pledge, that we *will* obey the Deuteronomy Protocol, that we *will* be careful, that we *will* watch ourselves closely, that we *will* take heed to ourselves, that we *will* help each other to pay attention to obey the Bible's commands.

"I want us here and now to consecrate ourselves to God, to be used to fulfill the wonderful legacy of these men and women of faith we have been given—to fulfill in our generation what Moses set down three thousand years ago. I want us to consecrate ourselves in the mutual promise that *we will be careful not to forget the things our eyes have seen.*

"We are the inheritors of an eternal legacy of God as he leads his people, generation after generation, into the land of his kingdom. *We five will be faithful to that legacy.* We will be faithful to pass it into the future as God leads and as he gives us wisdom to do so.

"So that's what I had to say," Heather concluded, drawing in a breath and exhaling a long sigh. "That's why I called this meeting."

"You're beginning to sound like David," said Todd. His words were spoken with deep reverence for the woman at his side. "That legacy is already passing to you."

Heather again exhaled slowly. It had obviously been an emotional outpouring. After a moment, she spoke again.

"Therefore," she added, "I commit myself to each of you, to help you be careful to remember the commands of the Lord. And I ask you to help me, and to turn *me* around if you see me faltering and forgetting and not choosing to do what is right and good in the sight of the Lord. I commit myself to *you,* and I ask you to commit yourselves to *me.* Together we will be God's faithful remnant people unto the following generations, and we will teach our children and their children in such a way that they will hopefully choose to follow our example."

It was quiet a long minute or two.

"Speaking not as your husband," said Todd, reaching over and taking Heather's hand, "but as your brother in Christ, I solemnly make that pledge and commitment to you. I receive the commitment you have just expressed and likewise give you permission and ask you to watch and help *me* to be careful and take heed to myself."

The five joined hands. One by one the other three voiced their commitments similarly.

"To you, Lord Jesus," said Todd softly after all five had spoken, "we give ourselves. We consecrate ourselves to sow, water, nurture, and spread the mustard seeds of your Father's kingdom. As your Spirit leads, we ask that you give us wisdom to heed and obey that leading by the individual paths you appoint for us to follow."

Epilogue

2064

TODD NEVER ran for president. He did, however, put his media experience to use, though not in front of the camera.

He and Bradon Rhodes began an audio program and podcast, alternating broadcasts and occasionally discussing pertinent issues together on air.

Because of governmental control of the media, and that no Christian content was allowed on radio or television, their episodes were aired by computer and phone subscription, sent remotely through different links around the world. Their identities and locations were concealed and, though sounding like normal, their voices were altered enough to keep them from being recognized. Because of their steadily expanding worldwide audience, attempts were ongoing to shut down the program and arrest its founders. But with technologically savvy loyal followers helping them, they had thus far avoided detection.

No one knew who "Titus and Silas" actually were. But the Christian world—many of its resources taken away, churches closed, books banned, and Bibles hard to come by—loved them. Growing by word of mouth, the program became a lifeline to millions. It was recorded and replayed among thousands of underground Bible study and prayer groups large and small.

Its most significant audience, however, were the individual men and women of faith who had few contacts with other Christians, and who often felt isolated and discouraged. For these it provided a tangible connection to the larger body of Christ. Without it, many knew they would sink in their private Slough of Despond. Listening to the familiar voices, hearing about Christians in other parts of the world, knowing people were praying for them, gave hope and encouragement to likewise pray for their brethren.

☆ ☆ ☆

When today's transmission began, the wife of the speaker knew her husband's voice immediately, though it did not sound like him.

"Hello, I am Titus speaking to God's remnant and underground Church . . . and I am Silas," added a second voice, she knew equally well. "We are coming to you from an undisclosed location somewhere on planet earth. This is the Titus Silas Report."

As Heather listened, she could not help the undefined angst that seized her heart briefly at the beginning of every new recorded transmission. Her thoughts filled with images of numerous hackers and computer nerds armed with the latest devices, methods and skills, using every available government source to trace the transmissions and identify who was behind them.

On this day, she knew that Todd was safe in his study. Yet she lived in constant dread of hearing cars roaring up the Bar JG drive, as they had that day when Mark was arrested and the Statler children taken away.

Todd had been greatly moved by reading Charlie Kirk's biography. The mission God had given Todd was not to address politics and the culture as Kirk had but to encourage the body of Christ. His hope was to remind the millions of God's remnant Church who were increasingly isolated in a world sliding into darkness, that, though the times were perilous, they were connected to the rest of that body.

Todd was aware of the danger. They talked about it many times. They prayed with Bradon, Ginger, and Craig to be given wisdom for the way they were individually to sow the seeds of God's kingdom. Almost within days of the gathering in David's bunker and their ride to Rustler's Butte, Todd and Bradon had both felt a desire growing within them to spread the same spirit of unity within Christ's body that was evident during the BCL gatherings. They hoped to spread unity among those who were isolated and alone who could *not* regularly experience such fellowship with other Christians.

How much longer Christians would be able to meet together was also uncertain. Among those not linked to a church or group, the bonds of spiritual connection needed to be nurtured and kept strong. Thus had originated the vision for their covert podcast.

As Heather listened to each new installment on her phone or computer, Todd was often in his study pre-recording a new episode, or adding to or editing a prior interview with Christians in other states or countries.

Occasionally he and Bradon recorded together. Broadcasting weekly and subject to the constraints and logistics of travel, they also made every effort to conduct monthly or bi-weekly interviews with individuals and groups whose experiences they felt would offer encouragement to the remnant Church worldwide. Alternating those interviews amongst themselves and between domestic and international travel, they each made four or five yearly trips away from their respective California homes.

Heather had long since discontinued work at the care home in Dorado Hills, and was now kept busy with her son and horses at the ranch. The ownership of the Bar JG had been officially transferred into the Stewart name, though David remained with them as the *Rancher Emeritus* of the Grass Valley community. Most of the Marshall and BCL correspondence work she now conducted at the ranch.

Stirling and Larke's house in Dorado Wood was now known as the *Marshall Center and Library*, used for occasional special events, a writing retreat for friends and family, or when Todd or Heather or one of their group needed a quiet uninterrupted day away from their normal routine. It housed the complete collection of correspondence and the writings of the Marshall trio of authors—her own grandfather and parents—and a collection of Bibles and increasingly difficult to find titles by Christian authors on similar deeper life themes. It had thus far avoided detection by the publication compliance authorities, whose mandate remained mostly unchanged under the successor to Bradon's father. The Dorado Wood home was one of numerous secret locations throughout the country resulting from the Alexandrian Project which many cells of the wider BCL fellowship had begun several years earlier.

In their later years, Heather's parents Timothy and Jaylene sold their Roseville home and moved into the Bar JG ranch house. All three of the aging elder statespersons of the BCL fellowship declared them to be the happiest years of their lives, given continual zest by the energetic growing grandson Jaylene and Timothy never expected to have.

Mark and Bradon, with Bob Forster watching and kibitzing from the sidelines, built a new four-bedroom ranch-style house on the Circle F property, nestled at the far end of the valley about a half mile from the main ranch house at the foot of wooded hills rising behind it. There Bradon and Ginger were kept busy with their two youngsters, toddler and newborn, who saw their grandparents, Mark and Grace, and their great-grandparents, Bob and Laura, every day.

Through the years, for unknown reasons, Court Masters had been drawn in a special way to Craig Forster, like the son he and Stella never had. After his graduation from Sac State, Craig spent much time in the Masters home, assisting with the newsletter and with many of the "helps" projects undertaken as a result of it. As Court's protégé, Craig gradually took over responsibility for the newsletter, and, under Court's guidance, learned the details of printing and book making.

Taking a page from David's playbook, the three generations of Forster men, with Todd's help and under cover of darkness, had excavated what became an underground basement beneath Bradon's and Ginger's new house which went up above it. Not shown in any of the blueprints, this secret underground location became the headquarters of their publishing operation. From it Craig published pamphlets, brochures, the *Master's Helps Newsletter*, and reprints of the Marshall writings, circulated by cleverly circuitous and oblique means through the clandestine network of the worldwide BCL fellowship.

After receiving his law degree, in addition to the podcasts, Bradon set up a private practice out of their home for the purpose of aiding Christians facing various legal challenges resulting from the policies of his father's presidency and the subsequent Bahram administration. He and Ginger and the children made at least one visit to Bainbridge Island every year.

During one visit, his father took Bradon aside.

"For better or worse, Bradon," he said, "you're part of Mark's group now. So you can tell me . . . who *is* the Prophet? Is it Mark or that old fellow Gordon?"

"Honestly, Dad," replied Bradon. "I've never heard the word used in connection with anyone. No one in the group, as you call it, is fond of those kinds of labels. We're just people trying to live faithful, virtuous, and obedient lives as Christians. I don't know where you got the idea there was some leader called the Prophet."

Marcia and Sandra Rhodes were regular visitors to the Circle F, doting on their son, daughter-in-law, grandchildren, and great-grandchildren. The friendship between Marsha and Grace Forster lasted for the rest of their lives.

After his son's wedding to the daughter of the best friend of his youth, however, the former president never set foot in California again.

☆ ☆ ☆

Heather's attention returned from her reflections to Todd's voice, setting the stage for Bradon to tell of his trip to eastern Europe two weeks earlier.

"We are two young men," he was saying in the voice known to his listeners as Titus, "who take our names from the companions of Paul who, with him, were instrumental in spreading the good news of the gospel of Jesus Christ throughout the first-century Mediterranean world. We hope you will subscribe to receive these reports regularly, and will circulate them among those who need encouragement in their walks with God. The attempts to silence our broadcasts are persistent. As we pray for you, we hope you will pray for us as well.

"All of us together, you and we and millions of our brothers and sisters, are seeking in the corners of the globe where God has placed us to live in but not of a world increasingly hostile to Jesus. Our hope in speaking to you is to increase the connections of unity and fellowship between the brothers and sisters of Christ's body trying to live by his commands in their daily lives.

"We know many of you feel isolated in a world intent on destroying our faith. Our message to you is a simple one—*You are not alone.* Do not give in to discouragement from what may appear to be your isolation as God's people. There are millions of your brethren praying for you and others like you. They likewise need *your* prayers. You will hear from some of those today. Pray for them as you listen, and as you receive their prayers, and ours, wherever you are. I repeat—You are not alone. God is with you.

"Now I will give you over to Silas from two weeks ago."

Bradon now continued as Silas.

"As you know," he began, "we try to visit a different gathering of followers of God's Son every month—some large, others only two or three, as the Lord said, gathered together in his name. From them we bring others of Christ's body greetings, stories, prayer requests, and encouragements.

"Today I am in Hungary, in a village whose name I obviously cannot divulge. With me is a daughter of God I will call Lujza, though that is not her real name, and her friend, Juliska, who will be our translator today. So, Lujza," he added, speaking to the two women, "what is your word for your brothers and sisters in other parts of the world? What do you have to say to them from Hungary?"

Ten or twenty seconds of rapid Hungarian came over the air. Then Juliska's voice, heavily accented but in tolerably understandable English, followed.

"Lujza wants me to tell you that in Hungary, she and her fellow believers pray for Christians around the world."

Another volley of Hungarian sounded, longer this time.

"She says that in Hungary, we are blessed with freedoms not known elsewhere. We know our brethren in China and the Middle East are suffering terribly . . ."

Another pause for Juliska's translation.

"We get news reports, we know that hundreds of thousands of Christians have been massacred for their faith.

"If you are listening from China or Iran or Syria or Egypt, know that we are praying for you, and especially for the growing underground church in Iraq. You are not forgotten . . .

"Our leaders years ago kept Hungary safe from many perversions, kept us safe from Islam and other evils. But we still need your prayers. We have our own struggles. Persecutions come to us here too. Christians are looked down on. Churches close all around. We pray for you, please pray for us."

"Tell me, Lujza," now said Bradon, "How many are in your prayer group, and what do you study when you meet?"

After Juliska's translation of Bradon's question, again Lujza's response came, first in Hungarian then in Juliska's English.

"We are sometimes six, sometimes twelve or fourteen. Our village is small but we meet every two weeks. Christians can meet here without fear, though there are not many of us.

"We read and talk about the book you send on Jesus's commands, but only Juliska can read English. She translates, then we talk about how to do the commands."

The somewhat awkward but fascinating three-way conversation between Bradon and the two Hungarian women went on for another six or eight minutes. At length Bradon resumed on his own, replaying what he had recorded after the interview.

"It was a remarkable visit," he said. "It was fascinating to see the long-term impact in Hungary from policies decades before to keep traditional freedoms vibrant and protecting their border from Islamic immigration. It was also encouraging to know that they are keenly aware of the sufferings of their brothers and sisters elsewhere. What a reminder to all of us to be diligent in prayer, especially for the Church in China and in the African nations and in the Middle East and other countries where Christianity is even punishable by death.

"Let me share an insight on the potential power of prayer that came to me as I was reflecting on the interview on my plane flight home. I hope it will encourage us all to follow the example of our Hungarian brethren to pray and not grow discouraged in our praying.

"I believe that God revealed to me that in miraculous ways he is able to transcend time and answer prayer in the lives of individuals beyond our reach. I am bound in the time of my humanity. But God dwells in eternity. Therefore, the person I am praying for is alive with God. In that world, my prayers can have miraculous power, whether I can see it or not, because God is at work in that realm.

"There are no limits to what God can do in eternity's time frame. He can transcend time altogether—he can take my earthly prayers and raise them into the realm of eternity, and accomplish with them *there* what may not be able to be done *here*.

"This kind of prayer will always be a mystery. We are praying into the realm of eternity though we cannot see into it. In a book Titus shared with me, Thomas Kelly wrote, 'All we can say is, Prayer is taking place, and I am given to be in the orbit . . . we bow in Eternity, and know the Divine Concern tenderly enwrapping us and all things.'*

"God is not bound by the smallness of our beliefs. Not even the smallness of our faith. He is not even bound by the lack of faith or belief in those we pray for. Whether or not those we pray for believe in him doesn't matter. Nothing can prevent God taking our prayers into his heart, and then launching them as arrows of light into theirs.

"When we pray into God's heart, from out of his heart he sends truth-beams and wakefulness-beams and healing-beams into those we pray for. One of old Thomas Kempis's prayers goes like this, 'O Everlasting Light, dart the beams of your brightness from above, which may penetrate all the most inward parts of my heart.'

"I believe we can pray this prayer for ourselves and for others. We can ask him to bring wholeness, forgiveness, wisdom, and reconciliation even when we are unaware of every situation where they are needed. We can ask him to raise our prayers into the timelessness of eternity, in his eternal present, in his timeless Now.

"We can pray like this—Eternal Father, by the miracle of your timelessness, accomplish your perfect work in me and in those I pray for. Endow my prayer with the timelessness of eternity. Loose repentance, forgiveness, growth, healing, and wholeness to transcend time. You hold in your heart every human exchange as an eternal present. Set flowing by my prayers a flowering of eternal healing in the hearts of those I pray for.

"Transcend time, heavenly Father. Make the prayer of St. Francis an eternally living reality. Give continually renewing birth to making your people everywhere instruments of your peace. May your people be made one in your eternal heart beyond what is possible in our humanity.

---

* *A Testament of Devotion* by Thomas Kelly.

Accomplish the finished work of reconciliation that is in your heart to glorify within your human family."

☆ ☆ ☆

Todd's voice now returned into Heather's hearing.

"This is Titus speaking again," he said. "When brother Silas shared with me this remarkable insight after his return from overseas about how our prayers transcend time, I was stunned by its potential power as we pray for our brothers and sisters around this world. The more I reflect on it, the more I believe this revelation holds a wonderful key to our understanding of prayer, and offers great encouragement to us, as well as an exhortation to be diligent in praying for our brethren.

"As Silas said, God is bound by neither time, location, nor our knowing. He exists in an eternal *Now* that is *Everywhere* at once. We cannot penetrate that Now and that Everywhere. The command upon us, in Kelly's phrase, is to enter God's orbit of timelessness, and to pray as we are led though we may not even understand the reasons for what we pray.

"Our prayers into God's *Now* and *Everywhere* may be lost to our sight. We cannot lament that we do not see past that veil. We are not given to see into the Holy of Holies of God's heart. But our prayers are not forgotten. In the *Now* and *Everywhere* of that holy Chamber, they are energized and glorified and raised into the eternal realms of God's purposes. In his time and his way, he sends them out into the children of his creation to accomplish their appointed destiny.

"Those answering arrows may be launched tomorrow, or in a thousand years or into the past life of one long dead in the earthly realm but alive in the *Now* of God's eternal presence, to achieve some work of ongoing transformation that was waiting for your future prayer to reach its desired fulfillment as you and that man or woman are brought into a unity of heart in the eternal orbit of God's heart.

"Our prayers reach into that realm and his answers flow out in myriad ways, in the times and seasons of his appointed eternal purposes. We many never see those results. But that must not keep us from praying for the brethren, and praying that God will perfect the unity among us inherent in our faith as Paul speaks of in Ephesians 4:13.

"There may be one listening at this moment, whom you do not know, whose prayer arrow will enter the Father's heart and an answer be launched from that Father-heart into your life. In the same way, *your* prayer today may be sent on the wings of angels into the life of one of your brothers or sisters whose need coincides exactly with what the Spirit of God led you to pray.

"We are interconnected in ways none of us will ever know. But God knows. And our faithfulness will have its result. As was revealed to a man dear to my heart, we are encompassed about not only by a great cloud of witnesses of those who have gone before but in a countless brotherhood of men and women who are upholding us in prayer.

"It may be that every whispered entreaty in this unbroken cycle of prayer originates in the heart of God, flowing out among his people, spreading through all mankind, where in his time those prayers are lifted back into the great Heart from whence they came. God's intercessions continually flow out into his world and into the hearts of those who are tuned to his Spirit, where they are sent back to him as their own prayers for those the Spirit leads them to pray for—universal prayers to and from God into the hearts of his humanity.

"You can know this—your brothers and sisters may not know your name, but they are praying for *you* because our heavenly Father knows all our names and he is continually interceding for us. He holds all our prayers in his heart and uses them to accomplish his eternal purposes."

He paused and allowed a few seconds of silence to pass.

"In closing," Todd resumed, "I remind you as we do every week—to pray for the brethren, and to live in obedience to the commands by which God instructs us to live. The Bible is our Freedom Manifesto, as I once heard another who is dear to my heart call it. Foremost among its commands are those of Jesus which he taught and exampled by his life in the four Gospels.

"Over three thousand years ago, Moses said, *He is a faithful God, keeping his covenant of love to a thousand generations of those who love him and obey his commandments.* We are among the generations of people he spoke of, with the truth still giving focus to our lives—to love him and keep his commandments.

"For the present, we can be contacted through what for now remains an untraceable contact point *TheTitusSilasReport@globalaccess.earth*, or on the media platform Q. Though Christian literature and Bibles are increasingly difficult to distribute, we are managing to keep limited resources available. We encourage you, if possible, to obtain the landmark end-of-life treatise on God's Church, *The Benedict Brief*, as well as the smaller related pamphlet *The Deuteronomy Protocol.*

"We close for now, exhorting you always to be of good cheer in persevering in prayer and in passing on the truth of God's infinite and eternal Fatherhood into the lives of the generations that will follow. Our call is to live as his faithful sons and daughters in the Eternal Now of the next five minutes, until he calls each one of us home to his Father's heart."

☆ ☆ ☆

Todd had only moments before turned off his microphone from recording portions of a future podcast when an eight-year-old boy ran into the room and jumped up and squeezed into the chair next to him.

"Hey there, David my boy," he said. "What have you been up to?"

"Mommy and I were listening to you. She cried when you were talking. I don't know why it made her sad, but when I asked her she said they were happy tears, not sad ones. But I didn't understand what you were talking about."

Todd laughed. "You will one day, Davie. You will understand it all. Have I ever told you about your two names, and the two men you are named after?"

"Yes, Daddy—you've told me many times."

"Then I will tell you again. Moses says, *Be careful that you do not forget.* He also tells fathers to teach their children all the things they must be careful not to forget. So I will tell you about them again. Your Godfather David, and your great-grandfather Stirling Marshall, were two great men of God. One day you will step into their shoes and follow their legacy into what God has for you to accomplish for his kingdom."

☆ ☆ ☆

Twenty minutes later, young David Marshall Stewart went in search of his namesake in the barn. Neither old nor young David would miss their time together every morning feeding the horses, an occasion the older of the two always used to obey Moses's injunction to impress the commands of God upon your children and their children after them, which he took to include his Godson. Young David's father now turned his attention to the podcast he was preparing.

Talking to his son about the legacy of the man he was now in the barn with reminded Todd of David's affection for the book of Deuteronomy, and the many conversations they had about the deeper meaning of the *land* during his apprenticeship as a young Christian during his first months in California.

He sat quietly reflective for several minutes, then again turned on his microphone.

"The land of Deuteronomy," he began, "does not merely refer to the physical land of Palestine the Israelites entered probably sometime between 1300 and 1200 BC. That land was a 'type,' a symbol of the eternal inheritance God is preparing and has promised for all his people throughout time.

"God's types, shadows, and symbols are continually unfolding themselves in deeper and more expansive ways. When Jesus said, *I go to prepare a place for you*, and when he told the parable of the prodigal son, these were illuminations of the truth of the *land*—the *inheritance* God has and is preparing us to inherit and inhabit. Everything Moses told the Israelites points to the spiritual truths embodied in the eternal inheritance the Father is growing his sons and daughters to be capable of receiving.

"The revelation of the land has been a continually deepening revelation through history for those with eyes to see it. Because most of those who consider themselves Christians, however, are like the Israelites who only believed superficially when God gave them manna but never truly *knew* him as the Father he was, nor knew that his true purpose was to raise them into sonship and daughterhood, at all times through history God has found it necessary to call out a remnant people to preserve the promise of the inheritance.

"Without the remnant, God's people would be scattered, swallowed by the world, and the inheritance lost. Most of ancient Israel was lost and scattered because its people did not heed Moses's words to remember and obey God's commands. They were not careful. They did not take heed unto themselves. They grew lax and forgot to obey the commands. But there was always a remnant to preserve the inheritance and inhabit God's spiritual land.

"Thus God's commands and promises have come down to us through time, all the way from Moses—not because we are an end times people but because we are called out of the world and called out of man's worldly church to be a *remnant people*. Like many who have come before us, we are commissioned to preserve the promised inheritance for those of God's generations who will follow.

"You and I are called to inherit, inhabit, and enter and possess the land of that inheritance in *our* time, so that future generations may inhabit it in *their* time. We stand on the shoulders of those faithful men and women who came before, just as those who follow us will stand on our shoulders for the tribulations that will come to them in their times, until at some point God chooses to close this present chapter of mankind's sojourn on this planet earth."

Character List

THE MARSHALLS

Stirling and Larke	1941–2032, 1942–2031
Timothy and Jaylene	1980, 1983
Heather [m. (2053) Todd Stewart]	2014, 2013
David Marshall Stewart	2056

THE FORSTERS

Robert and Laura	1973, 1976
Mark and Grace	2000, 2001
Ginger [m. (2062) Bradon Rhodes]	2028
Craig	2030

THE RHODES

Harrison and Sandra	1975, 1977
Jefferson and Marcia	2000
Bradon [m. Ginger Forster]	2027
Melissa	2029

David Gordon	1971
Court and Stella Masters	1988, 1990
Harvey and Harriet Jansen	1991, 1992
Elizabeth Wickes Hardy	1996–2052
Linda (Hutchins) and Cameron Trent	2000
Mike Bardolf	2001–2061
Charles and Regina Reyburn	2001
Hamad Bahram	2001

AFTERWORD

THIS FINAL book of *Tribulation Cult* sat three-quarters finished yet incomplete for eighteen months as I sought God for an answer to a simple prayer: "How should this series end?"

My thoughts and questions tumbled over one another from a lifetime of study and prayer about the future God's people would one day face. I was asking God about it as Judy and I prepared for marriage when Hal Lindsey's book was all the rage. I am still asking God an even wider range of questions fifty-five years later.

When will Jesus return . . . what will be the signs of his coming . . . will we be raptured away . . . will the end-times church go underground . . . will the Great Tribulation sweep over us in a flood . . . how should God's people respond to those times . . . how do we fulfill the Lord's prayer of John 17 when we are commanded to come apart from worldly believers and be separate . . . how do we maintain unity when we are called out of the church of man?

What will God have us do when persecutions hit us where we live, when the police appear at *our* doors, when churches are forced to close, when Bibles and Christian books are banned, when Christian home schooling is outlawed, when we could be arrested for meeting with other Christians, when I could be arrested for even writing a book like this?

What then?

What do we do when the lies of modernism are spoken in our hearing—speak up or remain silent? Do we argue with our adversaries in the cultural war or pray for them—or both? Do we remain in fellowship with worldly Christians, though the New Testament says to distance ourselves from them? Will unity in the body of Christ still be the hallmark of the end times Church when those in man's church are bowing to the idols of modernism?

The questions are hard. They're going to get harder.

For months, then a year, then a year and a half, no clarity came in the midst of such conundrums. I wrote four other books in the meantime. *This* book had to be completed. But I could not rush it. I had to await some sense of what God might want to say as I brought it to a conclusion.

Then slowly a still, small voice began to whisper into my mind and heart reminders and intimations about the ancient book of Deuteronomy.

My first reaction was, "What could Moses's farewell address possibly have to do with the end times?"

The answer to that question did not take eighteen months. It came almost immediately. The message was crystal clear.

Deuteronomy is a timeless book. It is God's revealed roadmap for his people of all eras. Moses's words reveal God's appointed way into the future not only for the end times. They give the blueprint, the manifesto for how God intended, and still intends, for his people to live throughout history.

How should we then live? How should we prepare for the end times? By living according to God's manifesto for *all* times.

Thus emerged what I have fictionalized as the Deuteronomy Protocol.

☆ ☆ ☆

Thirty years ago, when we still had our Christian bookstore and were selling the books of the *Left Behind* series by the dozens, people were talking about them excitedly, imbuing the fanciful stories with the authenticity of scriptural fact. They thought the scenarios portrayed in the books were *really* going to happen. They seemed to consider the books on a par with Scripture itself.

Occasionally Judy would say, "You *do* realize that they're fiction?"

Most of the readers of my books are unlikely to make that mistake. But for the record I must make clear that the *Tribulation Cult* series is indeed fiction. At the same time, I believe it contains *truth* about the directions our country and God's church have been moving during the last two or three generations.

As I look ahead, which I have done fictionally in this series, I focus on trends, possibilities, and probabilities. I would never attempt to predict actual events. The trends I have observed and portrayed in this series are alarming to contemplate. But I have no crystal ball. Nor can I claim to have been given divine insight into what the future holds. This is a novel based on *trends*, not specifics—a fictionalized trajectory of where I see things moving *if* those trends continue. Perhaps I might call this a worst-case scenario. Though for all I know, things could get even worse than I envision them. Throughout the writing of these four books, I have had to remove or rewrite several entire plot threads which I fictionalized taking place in mid-century . . . because suddenly I read in the news they had just happened! The trends I envision may be miles off in either direction. They may all transpire before 2030—or they may never happen at all.

As dire as some of these trends appear, change for the better is always possible. If a person or nation repents, trends do not have to continue along the same track. Individuals can change, churches can change. At any point history can take a different path.

Courageous men and women have changed the course of history many times in the past. Repentance has changed the course of whole nations. God's promise in 2 Chronicles 7:14 is timeless. It may have as much import for twenty-first-century America as it had for the ancient Israelites:

> *"If my people who are called by my name will humble themselves, and pray and seek my face and turn from their wicked ways, then will I hear from heaven and forgive their sin and heal their land."*

☆ ☆ ☆

If Supreme Court Justices Blackmun, Brennan, Stewart, White, Marshall, Powell, and Burger had had the courage in 1973 to side with Wade and stand up and say, "Abortion is murder . . . the United States of America, one nation under God, will *never* condone the murder of God's unborn innocents," instead of giving in to Roe's lie of liberal feminism . . .

History could have been changed and millions of lives saved.

☆ ☆ ☆

If elementary school teachers in America's public schools in the early 2000s, when required to put up posters labeled "What Is a Family?" illustrating two women with a child, two men with a child, and a man and a woman with a child, had had the courage to stand as one and proclaim, "No, this is a bold-faced untruth—the family of God's order is a man and women, married for life, with their own single-marriage children; we will *not* teach our impressionable young students such lies," and thus had they not given in to the depravity of same-sex partnerships . . .

History could have been changed.

☆ ☆ ☆

If the NEA and AFT had had the courage to stand against pressures of the LGBTQ agenda and refused to normalize homosexuality, rewrite American history, endorse and teach social justice, transgenderism, white guilt, American non-exceptionalism, and gender choice . . .

History could have been changed.

☆ ☆ ☆

If President Obama had had the courage to stand tall in the dignity of his office and say, "Members of Antifa and BLM are criminals and thugs and will get no support from the black community and will go to prison". . .

Racism might have been dealt a lethal blow, cities saved, and history changed.

☆ ☆ ☆

If doctors worldwide had displayed the courage to refuse to perform abortions and transgender surgeries . . .

History could have been changed.

☆ ☆ ☆

If pastors and priests had displayed the courage to stand against the pressures of liberalism and kept its perspectives out of their churches . . .

History could have been changed.

☆ ☆ ☆

If millions of Americans had not sacrificed right, wrong, reason, absolutes, logic, virtue, and common sense on the altar of progressivism . . .

History could have been changed.

☆ ☆ ☆

If millions of churchgoers had not placidly gone along with the unseen infiltration of worldliness poisoning the gospel fabric of their churches and had refused to allow worldliness to be subtly preached from their pulpits . . .

The church of Christ might have been preserved so that a remnant would not have been required to come out of it and be separate.

☆ ☆ ☆

I hope these trends do not continue. It is never too late for the trajectory of history to change. I hope events such as I have portrayed do not take place.

I hope that twenty years from now the books of this series are so outdated and their scenarios proved so off the mark that, should someone find dusty old copies in a used bookstore (if such iconic and beloved places still exist!), their reaction will be, "Boy, he sure got it wrong!"

With all my heart I hope and pray that the beacon of light from the City on a Hill that our country has been is still shining bright for God's truth in the world of 2060.

Seeing the trends around as I write in 2025, I cannot say I am optimistic. Yet I am hopeful that today's trends do not continue to extinguish that light.

So though this is fiction, I hope it may be more than mere fiction. I hope it can be a wakeup call to America.

"If my people who are called by my name
will humble themselves . . . and turn from
their wicked ways, then will I hear . . .
and heal their land."

EXPLORE THE WORLD OF MICHAEL PHILLIPS

- Historical and contemporary fiction set around the world
- Ideas and characters that inspire growth
- The Eyewitness Bible and Commands series
- Challenging devotional and theological titles
- George MacDonald publications, biographies, studies, devotionals, and new editions

Michael's fiction series and devotional writings take you on adventures around the world and invite you to grow.

His more than a hundred published books of both fiction and nonfiction evidence his gifts as a storyteller and communicator of God's truths.

THE FICTION COLLECTION

STONEWYCKE (with Judith Pella, 1985–88)
Scotland—Multi-generational family saga spanning 1860s to present

The Heather Hills of Stonewycke
Flight from Stonewycke
The Lady of Stonewycke
A Stranger at Stonewycke
Shadows over Stonewycke
Treasure of Stonewycke

THE RUSSIANS (with Judith Pella, 1992–92)
Russia—Late 19th early 20th century family saga

The Crown and the Crucible
A House Divided
Travail and Triumph

JOURNALS OF CORRIE BELLE HOLLISTER (1990–97)
California Gold Rush & Civil War series written as young woman's journal from teen years to her 30s

My Father's World, with Judith Pella
Daughter of Grace, with Judith Pella
On the Trail of the Truth
A Place in the Sun
Sea to Shining Sea
Into the Long Dark Night
Land of the Brave and the Free
A Home for the Heart
The Braxtons of Miracle Springs
A New Beginning
Grayfox

SECRET OF THE ROSE (1993–95)
Germany—WWII and Cold War drama

The Eleventh Hour
A Rose Remembered
Escape to Freedom
Dawn of Liberty

MERCY AND EAGLEFLIGHT (1996–97)
American West with "Western" motif, late 1800s

Mercy and Eagleflight
A Dangerous Love

THE MAXWELL CHRONICLES (1991–1992)
Contemporary drama of evangelicalism

Pinnacles of Power
Depths of Destiny

THE LIVINGSTONE CHRONICLES (1997–2000)
Contemporary archaeological thriller

Rift in Time
Hidden in Time

THE SECRETS OF HEATHERSLEIGH HALL (1998–2001)
England—World War I prodigal-themed family series

Wild Grows the Heather in Devon
Wayward Winds
Heathersleigh Homecoming
A New Dawn over Devon

CALEDONIA (1999–2000)
Michener-style epic of Scotland's history

Legend of the Celtic Stone
An Ancient Strife

THE DESTINY SERIES (2002)
U.S.—Contemporary with evangelistic theme

Destiny Junction
King's Crossroads

SHENANDOAH SISTERS (2002–04)
Civil war series featuring two girls orphaned by war

Angels Watching over Me
A Day to Pick Your Own Cotton
The Color of Your Skin Ain't the Color of Your Heart
Together Is All We Need

CAROLINA COUSINS (2005–07)
Sequel series to Shenandoah Sisters

A Perilous Proposal
A Soldier's Lady
Never Too Late
Miss Katie's Rosewood

AMERICAN DREAMS (2005–08)
U.S. Civil War era—Historical family saga

Dream of Freedom
Dream of Life
Dream of Love

A SCOTTISH DOUBLET (2011)
Scotland—Contemporary love story drama

Angel Harp (2011)
Heather Song (2011)

THE GREEN HILLS OF SNOWDONIA (2012)
Wales—Late 1800s family drama

From Across the Ancient Waters
The Treasure of the Celtic Triangle

THE BEYOND TRILOGY (1998–2015)
Afterlife fantasy

The Garden at the Edge of Beyond
Hell and Beyond
Heaven and Beyond

SECRETS OF THE SHETLANDS (2016–17)
Shetland Islands—Contemporary family drama and love story

The Inheritance
The Cottage
The Legacy

TRIBULATION CULT (2024–26)
U.S.—Futuristic political/prophetic drama spanning 1970s to 2060s

The Invisible War (2024)
Birth of a Remnant (2024
Hidden Jihad (2025)
Freedom Manifesto (2026)

SINGLE TITLES

The Peacemaker—contemporary (Phillips/Pella, 1985)
Murder by Quill—Scottish castle mystery (2013)
The Cappuccino Club—theological novel (2013)
The Eyewitness Gospel—a biblical novel (2017)
The Sword, the Garden, and the King—fantasy (2013)
Angel Dreams, with Chris Schneider (2014)

NON-FICTION

DEVOTIONAL

God a Good Father, 2001

Jesus an Obedient Son, 2002

Make Me Like Jesus, 2003

A Sacrifice of Obedience, 2017

Walking with God, 2024

A Book of Daily Memory Reminders, 2023

Principles of a Centered Life, 2017, 2024

Walking with God, 2024

TOPICAL

Best Friends for Life (with Judy Phillips), 1997

Universal Reconciliation: A Brief Selection of Pertinent Quotations, 1998

Is Jesus Coming Back as Soon as We Think?, 2004

Bold Thinking Christianity, 2013

Practical Essential Christianity, 2013

Out of the Wardrobe, 2018

Endangered Virtues & the Coming Ideological War, 2023

THE COMMANDS AND EYEWITNESS BIBLE

The Commands of the Prophets (Regular and Giant Print Editions)

The Commands of Jesus (Regular and Giant Print Editions)

The Commands of the Apostles

The Eyewitness Old Testament, Volume 1

The Eyewitness Old Testament, Volume 2

The Eyewitness New Testament, Volume 1

The Eyewitness New Testament, Volume 2

The Eyewitness New Testament, Volume 3

The Commands of Jesus Journal Edition

The Prayers of the Commands

The 360 Commands Tiny Edition

The Commands of Jesus Pocket Edition

The Commands of the Apostles Pocket Edition

BY AND ABOUT GEORGE MACDONALD

FICTION

The Cullen Collection (The complete 37 volumes of MacDonald's full-length fiction)

The Parallel Editions (5 diversely published titles in parallel format)

Mini-Signature Editions (8 of MacDonald's original novels in a matching mini format set)

STUDIES, COMPILATIONS, AND BIOGRAPHIES

George MacDonald, Scotland's Beloved Storyteller (1987)

Discovering the Character of God (1989)

Knowing the Heart of God (1990)

Your Life in Christ (2005)

The Truth in Jesus (2006)

George MacDonald and the Late Great Hell Debate (2013)

George MacDonald and the Atonement (2013)

George MacDonald's Spiritual Vision: An Overview (2016)

George MacDonald's Transformational Theology of the Christian Faith (2017)

George MacDonald: A Writer's Life (2018)

The Cullen Collection Reader's Guide (2019)

George MacDonald, Cullen, & Malcolm (2019)

The Gospel According to George MacDonald (2019)

The Pocket George MacDonald (2020)

George MacDonald's Theology: Introductions to His Sermons

☆ ☆ ☆

For availability, ordering information, news, articles, notices on other recent titles, and to contact Michael and Judy Phillips, see:

WWW.MICHAELPHILLIPSBOOKS.COM